Pahokee

Ann O'Connell Rust

The Floridians Series Volume V

Amaro Books

Published by
Amaro Books
5673 Pine Ave
Orange Park, Florida 32073

Copyright © 1992 Ann O'Connell Rust

All rights reserved. No part of this book may be reproduced in any form or by any electronic or mechanical means including information storage and retrieval systems without permission in writing from the publisher except by a reviewer, who may quote brief passages in a review.

First printing 1992
ISBN No. 0-9620556-9-7 (Volume V) Soft Cover
ISBN No. 0-9620556-8-9 (Volume V) Hard Cover
ISBN No. 0-9620556-4-6 (Seven Volume Set)
Library of Congress Catalog No. 92-97012

Printed in USA
Cover Artist: Linda Taheri

Books by Ann O'Connell Rust:
Punta Rassa
Palatka
Kissimmee
Monticello
Pahokee

ACKNOWLEDGEMENTS

The author wishes to thank Allen F. Rust, Editor/Copy Editor, and Jim Brown of Empulse, Gt. Barrington, Mass. And a special thanks to the helpful people in Tarpon Springs.

AUTHOR'S NOTE

The setting of this story is Florida, 1899-1928. The history is as accurate as is needed for the story line, and all the characters are fictional.

DEDICATED TO: The pioneers who through their vision and adventurous spirit settled this land for those of us who have come to love and cherish its uniqueness.

CONTENTS

BOOK I	*THE OFFSPRING*	
CHAPTER I	THE NECCESSARY JAR	3
CHAPTER II	SETH ROBERTS	13
CHAPTER III	UNCLE J. J.	32
CHAPTER IV	THE RUNAWAYS	41

BOOK II	*THE ADVENTURERS*	
CHAPTER I	CEDAR KEY	65
CHAPTER II	ALTHEA MANOR	76
CHAPTER III	THE ENCOUNTERS	92
CHAPTER IV	CHRISTMAS DAY 1899	109

BOOK III	*YEARS GO BY*	
CHAPTER I	SECRETS UNFOLDED	129
CHAPTER II	HEARTACHES	152
CHAPTER III	TARPON SPRINGS	175
CHAPTER IV	TITANIC	203

BOOK IV	*NEW BEGINNINGS*	
CHAPTER I	THE BIG LAKE	213
CHAPTER II	BIRTH OF A TOWN	233
CHAPTER IV	SURVIVAL	254

BOOK ONE:

THE OFFSPRING

CHAPTER I THE NECESSARY JAR

Christmas, Santa Fe River, 1898

His given name was George Wilburn, but he went by Poke. He didn't even remember who started calling him Poke nor why, but that's the name he answered to. He was twelve years old but passed himself off as fourteen. It was all on account of Catherine. Catherine was his six-year-old sister, and he was in charge of her and felt that if he said he was fourteen, then no one would question his authority. After all, fourteen was near 'bout a man grown.

It was hard for Poke to remember when everything started going bad for him. Probably when his ma died when he was eight. But maybe it all began even before then. He had tried to forget for so long that he had almost succeeded.

His pa worked as a mechanic in the railroad work yard for Mr. Henry B. Plant, the railroad man, in High Springs, the nearest town of any size to their cabin. His real name was George, too, but everyone called him Mac. He was slight of build, wiry, talked a lot, laughed a lot and drank a lot and knew everyone in the whole state of Florida, or so it seemed to Poke.

Poke's ma had been a quiet woman, some older than his pa, and she too had been thin. About the only time she'd smiled was when his pa was gone or when she'd take down the Necessary Jar to count the money. She'd make a big to-do about that. She'd say at least two or three times a day, "Think I'll take down the Necessary Jar to see how much we got." That had always excited Poke. Catherine was too young to understand the significance of the statement, but Poke would hang around the cabin all day long waiting - just waiting for her to take it down.

The jar sat on the high shelf above the small square table in the kitchen, right behind his ma's Bible. The Bible had belonged to her ma, and it had the most prominent place in the entire cabin, for Inez Milligan thought as much of that Bible as she did her two living children, and next to them came the Necessary Jar and its contents. "Their future", she'd say every time she'd take it down.

Poke wondered why his ma never took it down when his pa was around but somehow knew that he shouldn't ask. It seemed to be his and his ma's secret, and since his pa never read the Bible, he had no reason to go to the high shelf. He kept his shine under their bed, so that's where his hands ventured most often.

Sometimes his ma would wait until dark. That was Poke's most favorite time. She'd light the oil lamp and place it on the table next to the wall. Then she'd call, "Poke," in that whispery voice of hers, "how'd you like for me to take down the Necessary Jar? How'd you like that, huh?" He'd feel his heart beat faster and could even see it thump clean through his flour sack shirt his ma had made. Once in a while he'd even let a smile escape, he'd be so excited.

She'd pull up the straight-back chair, stand on its rush seat and reach for the jar. It was a pretty jar, dark green in color but with the lamp light playing on it it would go from gold to almost black. Then she'd slowly sit, and that was Poke's sign to also sit. He'd put his chin on his hands that rested on the table and stare as his ma took out coin after coin until practically the entire table was covered. She'd count each one as the lamp light bounced off the copper pennies and nickles and silver dimes. Then she'd say with a grand smile, "Your turn, Poke. It's your turn."

Slowly he'd count and stack them, pennies on top of pennies - then nickles - then dimes. Tower after tower he'd form. There wasn't anything in the whole world that pleasured him as much, not fishing or trapping or even riding the train with his pa. His primary teacher said that he could out count any pupil she'd ever had.

But it all stopped when his ma died. There didn't seem to be that same pleasure when he'd force himself to take down the jar to see if it was still full or if he would need to sell more fish or eggs or chickens in order to replace the coins he'd had to use when his pa wouldn't come home for a long time. Their milk cow had died the year before, so there was no money coming in from the rich, creamy milk and butter his ma had sold to the river fishermen. His pa had assured him that he'd get them another cow, but he never did.

He'd wait 'til Catherine was abed and his pa was gone before he'd take it down. It was his alone time - his visit with his memories - and when it was pitch black and the lamp was lit he'd feel his ma close beside him, and sometimes if he tried real hard he thought he could hear her voice as he sat quietly counting the coins.

Everything changed when he had to drop out of school to take care of Catherine. His pa never let him ride the train anymore. Sometimes he'd be gone for three or four days, and when he returned all he'd do was fish and drink his shine and yell at Poke. He'd complain about Poke's cooking, but Poke knew it tasted 'bout as good as his ma's. He could do a hoecake and cornbread real good now, and he even let Catherine help in the garden. She was good at hoeing, and you'd never find a grain of sand on the greens. She 'bout washed them to death, Poke often said. They never lacked for fish and the hens laid real good most all year. But it seemed to Poke that his pa couldn't find kind words in his mouth and that he and Catherine got along better when he wasn't around.

Mr. Bunnell, who ran the trading post on the Santa Fe River close to town, would always ask Poke how they were doing whenever Poke and Catherine went to shop every two weeks, second and fourth Fridays just like their ma had done. Poke would smile a little smile and say, "We're doing fine, Mr. Bunnell, just fine."

"How's Mac a doing? Haven't seen him in a month of Sundays."

"Oh, he's doing fine, too, thank ya."

"Well, the Widow and me will be right here if'n you need us, Poke. Now, you know that, son." Mr. Bunnell married the Widow James and even after their marriage everyone still called her Widow, just dropped the James. She was nice enough, but Poke didn't like the to-do she always made over Catherine Inez. Just couldn't seem to keep her hands off her. Maybe it was because she didn't have any girl children, he reckoned, but it did annoy him.

The trading post was just about the only place Poke and Catherine went anymore. He missed going to church with his ma. Not that they went every Sabbath, 'cause sometimes she'd be ailing. She seemed to need to take to her bed often those last few years.

It was Christmas Eve, and Poke and Catherine had sold his morning catch to the fishermen, and three fat hens, too, for their Christmas dinner. He needed to row to the post for their supplies and he hoped to find a special gift for Catherine. He knew he'd not have enough money, without going to the Necessary Jar, to get her that china head doll he'd been eyeing for the past month. Every little girl oughta have a doll, he reasoned. Maybe next year. But he hoped he'd see something at the store that she'd like and that he could afford. He hadn't had time to whittle her any more farm animals like he'd done for the past few years. His ma had always said that he was real good with his hands, and whittling did give him pleasure.

Mr. Bunnell met them on the worn steps and opened the store door. He had been a blacksmith and had the roughest and biggest hands Poke had ever seen. But he was a gentle man. Widow was standing behind the counter doing her paper work and smiled as she looked up. She always had a freshly sharpened pencil and tablet paper handy whenever anyone entered the store. She took great pleasure in her ability to write and do her figuring rapidly and always correctly.

"You and Catherine going to the church Christmas play, Poke?" She ought to have known better than to ask 'cause they hadn't been since their ma had died. But she was just passing the time of day and he knew it.

"No ma'am, won't be able to. Got too much work that needs tending to."

"They gonna have a tree with candles and a taffy pull and oh my... little girls need to go to..."

"Cain't, Widow! Not this year," he answered sternly.

She glanced at the mister, slowly shaking her head, thinking but not saying, poor little things, no ma and a no-good pa who's always full of shine.

"Cain't we, Poke, cain't we?" Catherine begged excitedly, pulling his shirt sleeve.

"Catherine Inez Milligan, you rightly know we cain't!"

"You're welcome to stay over with us, Poke," Widow said. "We got plenty room what with Jeremy and Sloan gone. Got us a empty house, we do - just a empty house."

"Please, Poke. Cain't we? Cain't we?" Catherine said, not willing to give up on it.

He grabbed his purchases off the counter, and Widow rounded the counter at the same time. Poke knew just what she was about, and sure enough he saw her slip two lemon drops into Catherine's hand. He pulled Catherine out the door calling over his shoulder, "Thank ya for your offer, and we'll be seeing ya in two weeks just like always." Now why can't that woman leave her be? he questioned silently.

"I oughta tan yore hide, Catherine Inez. Making a to-do about a old Christmas play..."

"But I ain't evah seen one, Poke. Not evah..."

"I got something more important for ya to see."

"What? What ya got...?"

"Well, if ya don't tip the skiff over, I'll row on home and tell ya about it."

"I'll be real still. I won't move even a little bit - not a bit." She sucked on the lemon drop allowing the tart, sweet juice to dribble out the corner of her mouth while looking up at him as he rowed, the oars lifting the lazy amber river water while barely making a ripple. Her face fidgeted with anticipation, but she knew better than to give in to her feelings.

Poke had been thinking and thinking about what he could get Catherine. He'd always whittled her the farm animals - horses and cows and pigs, and the chickens he'd given her last Christmas had turned out real good, he thought. It gave him something to do of a night when Catherine was asleep and his pa was gone, but he sure wished he could give her something better. But wasn't until he was in the store and Widow said, "we got a empty house" that he knew exactly what he was gonna give his sister.

Poke could go a long time on his memories of their ma, but Catherine couldn't remember a thing about her, except when she was real little and her ma had let her sit on the edge of the big wash tub splashing her tiny feet in the pine scented wash water while her ma scrubbed the wash. She'd get real excited when they'd walk through the piney woods after a rain, and she'd smell that clean pine scent and remember. She'd say, "I smell Ma, Poke, just like she's walking beside me. I smell her real good. Poke, did you hear me? I smell Ma." Poke would sadly bite his lip and lower his head.

Catherine was getting impatient. "Poke, when ya gonna tell me? When?" She trudged after him trying to keep up as he avoided the tree roots that led up to their cabin. He didn't answer. Why's he so mean to me, Catherine wondered. Bet it's because Widow slipped me the lemon drops. I bet that's it, and he's not gonna have any old surprise waiting for me like he said. I just bet!

She was helping him put the meal and coffee into their ma's tight lid cans when he finally answered.

"Soon's we finish supper and it's dark, that's when. Now don't go gettin' antsy on me. Go on, check the chickens' water and scatter some corn, then I'll tell ya." He didn't add, if Pa's not back. He'd been gone near 'bout a week, so he guessed he'd been given the Tampa run after all.

Catherine ran back from the chicken coop. Her bare feet, hardened against the sand spurs that grew thick in the side yard, were covered with sand, and Poke had the left-over greens with a slice of side meat and a pone already on their tin plates. Catherine ate rapidly. "Don't gobble your food. Now, you know Ma would fuss at you. You rightly know that!"

"How'd I know? I don't even remember Ma."

He lowered his eyes. Yes, how'd you know? You were too little. But I'm gonna give you your ma for Christmas, Catherine Inez. I'm rightly gonna do it. That's the best Christmas present I can think of 'cause we don't have a empty house like the Widow. Not by a long shot, we don't!

She could stand the waiting no longer. Her thin legs began to twitch and she wiggled her toes underneath the table. He saw that she was about to give in to her fidgets, so with great pomp he stood erect, his straight, brown hair fell damp on his forehead, and with grown up authority said, "Catherine Inez, this is your Christmas present. Now, I know Jesus's birthday isn't 'til tomorrow, but I want to give you your present now."

She watched as he lit the lamp and its soft, glowing light filled the small square room casting shadows off the coat rack beside the door and the cupboard that held their ma's pretty flowered bowl and pitcher. Then the shadows eased and darkened the big bed in the corner.

Her pale eyes were big with wonder. If he carved me another old animal, I'm gonna pop, she thought. But then he pulled out the chair, stood on it and reached behind the Bible pulling out the green jar, holding it gently like he would a handful of eggs and said, "This is the Necessary Jar our Ma left us." He was slightly smiling and for the life of her she couldn't understand what was so all fired important about an old jar. It was pretty though, she could see that, but she'd just as soon have had an old oak animal for her present.

Poke sat down and began taking the coins out one by one so slowly that she thought she'd burst. They did look pretty in the lamp light, she'd have to admit, but since she had never had any money she couldn't figure out what was so important about it. She'd seen Poke give Mr. Bunnell and Widow some when he'd make their purchases, but it hadn't meant anything to her 'cause she was too busy waiting for the candy she was sure Widow would slip her.

But then he started counting and stacking the coins and talking - slowly at first - and telling her about the day she was born and how Mrs. Driggers had taken the buggy from High Springs to the river then rowed all the way to their cabin to help with the birthing. And then he told her about when their ma won the prettiest quilt contest in the whole entire county and about the wonderful church picnics and about all the food he'd helped her take to them. He said that once the bottom of their skiff was so loaded with pans of fried chicken and corn pudding and jars of pickles and peach pies they were taking to a picnic that when the Reverend and Mrs. Smythe rowed by the waves from their boat almost tipped him and ma and the food into the river.

"Was Ma upset? I bet she 'bout cried," Catherine said excitedly.

"No. We thought it was funny." He thought, but didn't say, we were happy then. Those were the good times.

He explained what ice cream tasted like and how they'd have to pull the hot taffy with buttered hands to keep from blistering them and how it tasted, sweet and gooey. And on and on he talked about their life when their ma was alive, while stacking the coins - copper pennies on copper pennies, shiny nickles on nickles - and she'd excitedly ask, "What then, Poke, what happened next? What'd you and Ma do next?"

Soon the entire table was covered, and they both sat and stared at the sight. Finally Poke broke the silence and said just like his ma used to say, "Our future. This is our future, Catherine Inez. Happy Christmas."

"That's nice, Poke, and a happy Christmas to you." She suddenly yawned and sleepily said, "See you in the morning, Poke." As she crawled onto her corn husk pallet and pulled the wash-tired sheet over herself she thought she heard her ma's laughter. It was just like Poke told her it sounded, sort of low and raspy. When she heard the chair scrape on the wooden floor she knew he was putting up the jar, and as she closed her eyes she heard him say softly, "Happy Christmas, Ma."

Catherine drowsily added, "Happy Christmas, Ma," and in her half sleep thought she heard her ma respond, "Happy Christmas, Catherine Inez. Happy Christmas, Poke." She was sure as shooting that she heard her, but sighed, turned over and faced the bare wall and was soon asleep.

Poke glanced down at the sleeping Catherine. He realized that he was the happiest he'd been since his ma had died. He gently closed the front door behind him and sat on the steps looking at the moonbeams playfully tease the river. He said aloud, "Ma, I gave you to Catherine Inez for Jesus's birthday. Oh, Ma, I sure hope you saw how happy she was when I told her about you and the good times. I surely do." He smiled as big a smile as he could muster and leaning against the wooden post added, "You're our future, Ma, not the money. Now, Catherine Inez will have some memories too." Suddenly his pa's face appeared. Hopping up he looked around and realized that he'd just imagined it.

"I'll not let him spoil this night! I'll not, Ma! This is our Christmas! Yours and mine and Catherine Inez's."

Christmas dawned just like every other day, and Poke awakened but decided to lie in bed a little longer than usual. Catherine was on her pallet curled up almost in a knot. He could tell that she was cold, so he spread the quilt over her. Should do something special for Jesus's birthday, he thought, letting his mind wander. If Pa doesn't show up, Catherine and me could go into town and just mosey around after we get our chores done, that is. His thoughts were interrupted when he suddenly imagined his pa's angry face. What if he comes while we're gone? Oh boy, he'd be mad. Probably take the strap to us both.

Maybe I'll just row up and down the river and stop in to see Billy Rawls and let Catherine play with Maudie. She doesn't ever get to play with girls her own age. I bet Maudie got a doll for Christmas. I bet Miss Memphis got her a doll. I just betcha. He didn't hear the front door creak or he'd have jumped up like a shot. But he did hear the bellow when the door burst open. Catherine jumped straight up, the quilt tumbled in a heap finding the pallet in a hurry.

Poke shouted, "Pa! That you, Pa?"

"And who the hell you think it is, boy? Course it's yore pa!"

It was obvious to them both that he'd been drinking. The strong smell of shine permeated the small room, and from the looks of him he'd been at it a long time. His dirty overalls were rumpled and barely fastened.

"What you doin' still in the bed? Don' you sass me, boy!"

"I wasn't gonna sass..."

"Best not or I'll tie yore tail in a knot, I will." He looked at the two of them shivering before him and steading himself against the table said, "Ain't ya got any grits and biscuits cooked? What good are ya, anyway? Yore pa comes home and least he should expect is dinner..."

Poke could tell that he wasn't gonna beat them cause he was already reaching for the bed. His head was bobbing, eyes half shut. Sure enough, he pushed past him and aimed for the mattress, not even removing his muddy boots. Didn't take him a minute to start snoring, and Poke and Catherine looked wide-eyed at each other.

Poke whispered, "He'll be out 'til nightfall from the looks of it. Get yourself dressed and we'll tend the outside chores so's not to make any noise."

He reached inside the covered iron skillet and took out the corn pones, stuffing them inside his shirt then hurriedly buttoning it. Slowly he opened the door and he and Catherine crept outside on to the kitchen stoop and into the morning mist. The chickens started their cackling soon as they saw them. Poke handed Catherine a pone and told her to sit on the stoop to eat it while he scattered the corn for the chickens.

I wonder if Pa'd have a fit if I killed one of 'em for our Christmas dinner? Sure would be nice to eat some stewed chicken, and I could chop up some wild onions in the broth like Ma used to and cook up some rice. That'd most likely please him, and maybe he'd be feeling good enough to tell us about his new route and what all he saw, like he used to long,

long ago. Oh, he could really spin a yarn - good as Mr. Ernest Maxon - good as Kuyper Groff - good as the county's best story tellers, folks used to say.

Poke scattered the corn in the sand and called, "Chick - chick. Here, chick." Wonder if I cooked one of you Pa'd sit with us on the porch near sunset and talk like he used to. He shook his head, sighed, took out his pone and began eating. Got this a might too crumbly. Probably put too much drippings in it. The chicks pecked at the crumbs he dropped and followed him as he walked to the stoop to join Catherine Inez.

I'm gonna do it! If he beats me, then that's all right. It's Jesus's birthday and I want to do something special.

"What you grinning about, Poke? What's funny?"

"Oh, nothing's funny, Catherine Inez. I was just trying to remember how stewed chicken with wild onions would taste for Jesus's birthday, that's all."

"Best not do it, Poke. Pa won't like it..."

"It don't matter what Pa likes or doesn't like. I'm head of the house most all the time now. If he wants to beat on me, my cooking the chicken won't cause it. He'll beat on me 'cause he's mean, that's what! Just 'cause he's mean..."

"Now, you stop that sniffling, you hear! It's Jesus's birthday, and we need to do something special. I was gonna row over to Billy and Maudie's for a visit, but since Pa showed up we cain't. So, next best thing I can think of is cooking up one of Ma's fat hens. You gonna help me catch one, or you gonna sit there sniffling like a big baby - huh?"

She saw his determination and knew Poke well enough to know not to argue with him. When his mind was made up it was made up.

"I'm gonna catch that fat Plymouth Rock 'cause she ain't been laying too good of late. You want that I should do it, Poke?"

He grinned a conspiratorial grin with his head cocked. "We gonna have us a chicken dinner fit for all the kings in Persia, we are." He wanted to shout but knew better.

"Where's Persia, Poke? Can we row to Persia instead of over to Maudie's house? How far is it? Can we go all the way on the river past the trading post to it?"

Poke shook his head. "We gotta get you to school, Catherine Inez."

He almost said, I'll ask Pa about it, then changed his mind. I'll just up and do it. She's coming along on her numbers real good, but she cain't do her letters good yet. Think I'll just go back, too. He ain't home long enough to know the difference. And if'n he don't like it then I'll just take the Necessary Jar, and me and Catherine Inez will move along. HELL! - he enjoyed saying Hell when he was determined. HELL, I'm near 'bout a man grown. 'bout time I did what Ma'd want for me and Catherine Inez. 'bout time!

The smile he was wearing would be the last one he'd be wearing that day and for a long time to come.....

CHAPTER II SETH ROBERTS

Monticello, December, 1899

Seth stood inside the lobby of the St. Elmo Hotel. He was seething. Didn't know how much longer he'd be able to hold his temper, of which it was reputed he had plenty. He was twenty years old, hovered around six feet, was slender with a shock of brown hair and warm brown eyes, a ready smile, and he was madly in love. But what good did it do him when Delia Rose O'Farrell didn't know he existed? He could hear her laughter, then the bass of Tucker Williams as they dined in the hotel dining room.

Seth knew that he couldn't compete with Tucker, who was well educated and the son of the prominent state senator Layke Williams. He had wanted to further his education after he was graduated from the Jefferson Academy but knew that his Aunt Rose couldn't afford it. So he had busied himself at her and Delia's mother's dress shop, Cherie's House Of Fashion, making deliveries, cleaning up and doing odd jobs. He had lazed around the summer after he was graduated, taking time out to play baseball, and was active on the Monticello Rifle Team. But he knew that he was just whiling away his time until he really made up his mind about what path to follow. And that path always seemed to lead straight toward Delia.

It was Harrison who had suggested that he apply for a position with the newspaper, the *Tribune*. Harrison was the colored man who had been with the O'Farrell family for many years and who had accompanied them to Monticello from Kissimmee down in the center of the state. He had been with Conner O'Farrell since they were young men in New Orleans and worked with, not for them, for he was as good a friend as a person could have - he was family and also a good friend to Seth.

If Seth needed advice, he went to Harrison. Since he had no folks of his own and didn't want to turn to his Aunt Rose with his personal problems, he listened to Harrison's advice. He was the smartest and best educated man Seth had ever known except for Delia's father Conner, who was as polished a gentlemen as you'd find anywhere. Harrison often said that Conner could have put royalty to shame with his airs, when he wasn't drinking, that is. But for the last ten years of his life he had kept his drinking under control and was one of the most respected men in Jefferson County. It was a tremendous loss when he died suddenly of a heart attack.

The *Tribune's* owner, Bonaparte Arnett, called Bonehead behind his back by his employees, had hired Seth as a printer's apprentice, but, wanting to get the most out of his employees, had him act as a correspondent as well. Juanita O'Farrell, known as Cherie by most, and his Aunt Rose were incensed. "The old skinflint could have given Seth a decent wage," they complained. But one thing that could be said about Arnett, he was a stern taskmaster, and Seth was learning the newspaper business from the ground up.

"He's found his trade," Rose proudly proclaimed to Juanita.

"And a fine one it is," Juanita replied. "You should be very proud of him, Rose." She hesitated but, being Juanita, continued. "Have you ever thought of what your life would have been like had you run away with Joe Bob? Now don't get upset with me, Rose Shorter. I know you don't like for me to bring it up, but..."

Rose looked down at her hands, that were busily attaching the lace edge to the neckline of Mrs. Fraser's ball gown, and decided that it would do no good to ignore Juanita's question.

"Well, yes, Juanita, I have." She spoke almost in a whisper. "But what good does it do? It's best that Seth think I'm his aunt and that his ma died in childbirth. It's best." She hesitated, then continued. "What good would it have done for me to run away with Joe Bob, anyway? He'd still have been hanged, and I'd have had to see it, and me carrying his child..."

The tears started.

"Rose, I'm sorry. I didn't realize after all this time that the wound was still raw. I didn't, honestly," Juanita lamented.

"I've never told a living soul, you know. Sometimes it hurts so much that I can hardly stand it, Seth not knowing he's mine," Rose murmured through her tears.

Juanita went to her - hugged her. "It'll be all right - it'll be fine, my friend." Juanita sat back down and resumed sketching Mrs. Starling's gown.

"Rose, we're alone. I just now realized it. We're all alone. I know that I can never love another man like I do Conner. Not ever. What're we going to do? Athea practically runs itself, what with Harrison and Easter there. I wish I could give it to them..."

"Don't be ridiculous! Now, how would that look? This town wouldn't stand for it, two colored people the owners of such a grand plantation. Now, you know that, for Heaven's sake, Juanita!"

"Of course you're right, but the life's gone out of Athea, Rose, now that Conner's gone, and I..."

"Don't you dare talk like that 'til after Delia's debut, Juanita Jane Graves! Don't you dare!"

For one who seldom showed her backbone Rose Shorter had recently found hers. When Conner died suddenly, she had been the take-charge person. Juanita, who had always been the dominant one, had actually allowed Rose to make all the business decisions for their dress shop. That had pleased Harrison, who, as Conner's and Juanita's best friend, had known that Juanita would need a long healing time.

And when sixteen-year-old Delia had informed her mother that she did indeed want to make her debut after all, even though her father had just died, Harrison knew that would give Cherie, the name he and Conner had known her by, something to hang on to - something to plan. But Juanita, being the consummate business woman, used her head and decided that they'd wait until spring. That should be long enough to keep the tongues from wagging. Perhaps May would be nice and not too warm, and Delia would have returned from St. Joseph's Academy in St. Augustine. The Monticello elite would certainly understand the necessity of Delia's early debut, even though a year had not passed, as was customary.

The Queen of May celebration would end Delia's school year, and Delia had been told by her school friends that she stood a wonderful chance of being selected the May Queen. That possibility and the very formal debut that Juanita was planning had buffered her loneliness somewhat. But Juanita still found her bed unbearably empty without Conner. She still found the excitement gone - there was no one to spar with - no one to get angry at. The patrons and their silly complaints couldn't evoke even a raised eyebrow from her when all Conner had had to do to get her dander up was hold his head just so with that superior look on his handsome face, and her mind would go lickety-split as she barraged him with her argument. Harrison had loved their verbal exchanges, knowing how they stimulated the two of them.

"Cherie's the only woman who held any fascination for Conner for any length of time," he told Easter.

"You right. Miss Conner shore got a tongue on her."

"But he finally bested her, Honey."

"How's dat?"

"He left her..."

When Harrison said that, Easter glanced at him and decided to not say anything. She just patted his shoulder. His hand soon covered hers. I've found the woman who understands all my needs, he thought. Even Conner could see that. It's true that she can't converse on many subjects, but she has more insight than most - more than Cherie or Rose. We need to get married. I've put it off too long. After Delia's debut, that's when we'll plan it. That'll give Cherie something else to look forward to. She needs to get her fire back. She's become almost docile.

But Harrison needn't have concerned himself about Juanita. Seth took care of that that blustery morning in December. Delia was home for the Christmas holidays and without her mother's knowledge had invited Tucker Williams to Athea Manor for a visit. Had Juanita known she would have had one of her grand fits, and Athea would have been infused with life once more.

Seth had been planning all the activities to which he wanted to escort Delia when she came home for the holidays. In the past she had been escorted by her father. Seth was nervous about the prospect. What if she declines? No, she'll have no one to escort her, and, knowing Delia, he knew she'd be bored to death at Athea. Juanita will probably insist that she accompany me, he decided.

There were already planned festivities at the Opera House, and grand balls were planned at the area plantations. Juanita would protest with just the right amount of theatrics, "It's so soon after dear Conner's death. I really shouldn't allow..." or, "Dear Delia knows that she shouldn't accept Mary Agnes's invitation, still in mourning, you know. But then she's so very young and shouldn't be expected to be cooped up in dull old Athea..."

Of course the townspeople would insist that she reconsider, stating "Now, you know Mr. O'Farrell wouldn't want you and Delia to be lonely during the holidays. Why, if there was ever a man who enjoyed a ball it was Mr. O'Farrell." They didn't have to prevail upon her for long. Juanita always managed to dismiss her own protestations and attend the event in question.

Seth had known from the beginning that Conner had disapproved of his attention to Delia, but he had not understood why. He could also sense Juanita's disapproval but felt that he could handle her. When Conner died, Seth honestly felt that he'd be rid of all obstacles. He knew Delia liked him. She was always asking for his help on one thing or another.

It was, "Seth, would you be a dear and drive me here, and Seth, would you please fetch me this or that." He was so in love that he had no idea that she was just using him.

After he'd been with the *Tribune* for a year he began making his plans. He knew that he was smart - learning came easily to him. He also knew that he had a penchant for writing. The story he had written on the decline of cotton production in Jefferson County had been carried in the leading newspapers from Atlanta to Palm Beach.

He was also very popular with the townspeople, and the lassies took a fancy to him. But Seth hadn't given any of them a tumble. He had eyes only for Delia Rose O'Farrell. But those eyes were now blood-red with hatred. Tucker Williams had arrived from Virginia on the noon train. He hadn't even gone home to Tallahassee first.

Juanita had Harrison meet the train, and when he saw Tucker Williams with Delia he knew that all hell was going to break out at Athea. If there was one thing that Juanita loved to do it was plan, and with Tucker just showing up unannounced she'd be deprived of her pleasure.

"Delia, your mama is going to have your head. You won't have a single strand of that black hair left when she's through with you! Why didn't you have the manners to wire her?"

"I didn't know, honestly. He just showed up in St. Augustine unannounced, and..."

"Delia, you're speaking to Harrison, not Easter. Unannounced? I think not."

"Well, he did! I don't care whether you believe me or not!"

"You'd better go by the shop and inform your mother, young lady. I'm not going to be the one to announce it."

"Please, Harrison. Won't you at least go in first - then I'll follow in a little while...promise," and she made a hurried sign of the cross.

Just like her da she is. Every time I look at her I see Conner. "All right, but you're to follow shortly." He let her squirm, then said, "I think I have a better idea. Why does she have to know right away? Why not put Mr. Williams up at the St. Elmo until we break the ice?"

"Oh, Harrison, you're an angel. I'll tell Tucker that it'll be a little while before we can drive out to Athea and that he'd be more comfortable at the hotel. Oh, Harrison, I don't know what I'd do without you."

Yes, she's just like her da. Always getting into trouble and giving me the privilege of bailing her out. He chuckled. I miss you, my friend, but your beautiful daughter does give me pleasure, or as Thackeray stated,

A good laugh is sunshine in a house. There will be sunshine at Athea this holiday season.

Delia nonchalantly informed her mother, "Oh, by the way, Mama, Tucker said that he could spend a few days with us over the holidays. Isn't that nice?" Juanita had been excited by the news. She had been dreading the prospect of the holidays without Conner. She replied, "That's nice, dear. When can we expect him? I need to have Easter and Melvia get the guest room aired.

She got a faraway look. Delia knew that she was remembering her da's funeral and the many guests who had stayed at Athea.

"Oh, Mama, don't make a fuss for Tucker. Men don't notice those things."

"You're probably right, Honey. But, I'd feel better about it and I'd like to get in some extra..."

"He'll be here on the evening train."

"What! When? Delia Rose O'Farrell, you've gotta be foolin' a person!" Juanita always reverted back to her childhood speech habits when she lost her composure. Conner had loved it when he got her so riled that the country girl came tumbling out, and every time it happened she'd vow vociferously that that was indeed the last time he'd do that to her. She'd usually end up in his arms, the outburst soon forgotten.

"But, Mama, that's the only time he can be here. His folks are going to Old Town to their ranch for the holidays. Tucker said that since his sister, you know Raine, his twin..."

"Yes, I know he has a twin sister, Delia. What does that have to do with his visit, anyway?"

"He wrote that his mother has been so upset since Raine ran away after they had that big fight and that they haven't heard a word about her whereabouts since last August - I told you about that, didn't I?"

"I could crown you, Delia..."

"Mama, Tucker said that his dad thinks that things will be better for his mother down at the ranch, so he has to go there and doesn't have much time..."

"Here I was thinking that we'd have a lonely, boring holiday and your..." she almost said boyfriend, but caught herself in time, "friend will be with us. Don't you understand, Delia? I would have enjoyed planning the menu and some small parties - we can't have anything elaborate since it's so close to your Da's death, but we could have had some of your friends in for..."

"Oh, Mama, don't! Tucker and I'll be fine. Why, he likes to ride and he can even help me with my paper. Can you believe that old Sister Theresa gave us an assignment over the holidays? I don't for the life of me know why they're called Sisters of Mercy. They don't even know what mercy is."

"Stop it, Honey. You know your da wanted you to finish your schooling there. It won't be much longer. Then we can seriously talk about Miss Baldwin's College at Staunton."

Juanita patted her hand. She knew that Delia wanted to be closer to Tucker's school in Williamsburg.

Harrison got Tucker situated at the St. Elmo and told him that he'd be back that evening to pick him up for the trip to Athea. If Juanita had calmed down when he got back to the shop, he planned to suggest that she and Delia remain in town and have supper with Tucker at the hotel. That would give him time to run the errands he was sure Juanita already had planned. He knew that she would want him to go back to the train station for ice and that he'd have to get a blanket from Rose to wrap it in.

"Wouldn't you think that some enterprising person would build an ice plant here? Has to come all the way from Jacksonville. Ridiculous!" he said to Tucker as he bid him good day.

Tucker agreed. "Father mentioned that very thing to Mother just recently. He said that the small towns of Florida will have the telephone before an ice plant."

"I believe you're right, Mr. Williams. I believe you are."

Juanita was none too pleased with the news of Tucker's early arrival but somehow managed to remain calm. Rose glanced at Amanda and they both smiled. They'd discussed only yesterday about how Juanita had settled down since being widowed. "She's not really lost her spunk, Amanda. It's more like she's resting. The old Juanita'll be back, I'm sure of it. By this time next year she'll be giving Delia what for if she pulls one of her tricks."

"I've no doubt that you're right, Rose. No doubt, but it's kinda peaceful for a change. Remember last year? My, my! She was giving us some kinda grief about everything - the ball gowns - Conner's carrying on at the St. Elmo instead of overseeing Athea! Remember?"

"Do I ever! Juanita's always loved excitement. If it's not around, well, she'll make sure that it soon arrives."

She smiled and said, "She'll be back - she'll be back. I know Juanita."

The excitement arrived, but not via Juanita. It arrived when Rose told Seth that Tucker Williams had accompanied Delia home to visit for two weeks - that his father and mother were so unsettled about his twin sister's running away and their inability to find her that they had both gone to their ranch while the detectives from the Pinkerton Detective Agency searched for her. Tucker said that they were searching from New York City to Key West and that his father said money was no object. He said that if he had to sell everything he owned, they'd find her.

It was the talk of all Florida, Raine's vanishing. No one had seen nor heard of her since last August, and because everyone would be gloomy at South Spring, Tucker didn't think he could stand being around them the entire vacation. He hadn't added, "Besides, I want to be with my love."

He made no attempt to hide his feelings. Juanita was delighted and Delia beside herself with love. It was all she could do to concentrate on her schooling, but she knew she had to in order to be accepted at Miss Baldwin's so she could be close to Tucker's school.

"I don't know why you're so upset, Seth," Rose exclaimed. "You know, you rightly know how Delia feels about the young man..."

"And how is that, Aunt Rose? How does she feel? A silly school girl crush, that's all it is. You know Delia. She'll be all over him even before he leaves for South Spring. All over him."

Rose knew better but also knew that she'd not be able to convince Seth. She wanted to say, "She's just like her mama. Once she sets her cap for a man, then he's the only one for her. Just like Juanita was about Conner." But she knew it would be useless to say anything.

She was upset with Seth. She was also tired. They'd had more orders for gowns then ever before. "Where are all these people coming from?" Amanda had asked back in November. They had been unable to get experienced help other than Granny Todd and her daughter Kansas, and they could work only part time. Kansas's husband Tiny had a large mule business, and he expected every member of his family to work in it. But Kansas could out-sew anyone they'd ever hired, and Granny had been her teacher.

Seth got up and stated, "I'm going back to the paper. Can't wait 'til I get enough money saved to leave this lousy town!" He slammed the door hard. Rose bit her lower lip and brushed away the emerging tears. He hadn't mentioned leaving in months. I don't know what I'll do if he leaves. I really don't. Why can't he love one of the local girls? He's so popular, they're always dropping by the paper to see him, and Reverend Stokes said just the other night at prayer meeting that he was undoubtedly the most popular young man in all of Jefferson County. Perhaps he said it because his Helen was sweet on Seth. Everyone knew how she felt, but he won't give her the time of day. Delia - it's always Delia Rose O'Farrell. She doesn't know he exists.

She put her sewing back in the basket. Her hands shook as she put her head down on the round oak table and sobbed, something she hadn't done since Joe Bob Skinner left Alva twenty-one years before. She hadn't known she was pregnant with Seth. If she had, she probably would have followed Joe Bob. But then she would've had to watch him be hanged, like Juanita had to... "I couldn't have stood that," she said aloud. "I'm as bad as Juanita and Seth. I can't seem to love but one person either."

Seth knew that he had to remain calm and pretend, but with Delia and that Tucker Williams laughing so loud that everyone in all of Monticello could hear them he was having trouble containing himself. When Harrison had ridden over to the paper that morning and asked him to see to Tucker, that he was staying at the St. Elmo Hotel while Delia prepared her mother for his sudden appearance, Seth wanted to say, well, if he's not wanted here why doesn't he just go away. But he knew that Harrison had been given a dozen errands to run and that he didn't have time to see to Mr. Williams's needs. Seth had reluctantly agreed to do it. He hadn't been happy about it, but agreed. After all, the O'Farrells were practically kin.

Rose had told him that Delia and Tucker had been corresponding, and he'd been upset at first, but then rationalized that Tucker was way up in Virginia and Delia all the way in Florida and that he'd be able to see her, whereas Tucker couldn't. But here he was in Monticello, and Seth hadn't seen her but once since she went back to school in October and then just for a few minutes.

What's he doing here, anyway? Doesn't he know that her daddy hasn't been in the ground but four months and she's got no business at all entertaining folks. Bet he's even planning on coming to her debut - I just bet. He was getting madder and madder and wondered why they hadn't asked him to join them for supper.

He had to admit that Tucker was good looking with those blond curls and dark blue eyes. Not one bit like Delia, whose hair was raven black like her daddy's, and she had his black fringed pale blue eyes that seemed to be able to see clean through a person. He was tall, though. A good half-a- head taller than Delia, who was almost six feet. People said that the senator was a very tall man and that he wanted his son to follow in his political footsteps.

Well, let him! I'm going to be editor of my very own newspaper one of these days. I'll just show that smart-ass would-be senator what I...

His thoughts were quickly dashed when out of the corner of his eye whom should he see enter but his boss Bonaparte Arnett. Seth whipped out his pad and began writing furiously. He walked - sauntered - over to Arnett and said, "Thought that you might be interested in a story on the young Mr. Tucker Williams, Sir. You know, the senator's son. He's visiting Athea Manor for a few days..."

"Good thinking, Roberts. That's very good."

Seth could tell that he was taken aback. He also knew that he was late returning to the paper, and Bonehead watched that clock like a hawk. He wouldn't allow for more than five minutes past the hour. Hell, old Bonehead will be early for his meeting with the Lord, he will. Never saw anyone look at his watch as often as he does. Probably times every one of his farts.

"I'm just about finished, Mr. Arnett. Have just a few more questions for Mr. Williams."

When Seth looked inside, Delia, Juanita and Tucker were having their dessert and coffee.

"No, don't get up, Mr. Williams. I don't want to interrupt, but Mr. Arnett, editor of the *Tribune*, has asked me to do a story about your visit and to inquire if the rumors we hear have any truth. You know, is the senator really grooming you for a similar position?"

Seth was filled with confidence. Boy, I bet Delia is impressed by me now. Look at how she's smiling. But his cocky grin was quickly erased when he saw that her attention was focused only on Tucker. When Juanita saw Seth's forlorn expression she knew that they were in for trouble. Conner was right, she thought. Seth's feelings for Delia are more than protective. He loves her. Dear Lord! He loves her.

Delia, completely unaware of Seth's presence, continued looking at Tucker, drinking in his every word. Seth pretended to write but knew he'd not be able to read a word of it later. Finally, he found his voice.

"I do hope that you enjoy your stay at Athea Plantation, Mr. Williams. Perhaps we can get together for a drink while I'm in Tallahassee. You see, I'm joining the *Tallahassee Democrat* early next year. Good evening to you, and, ladies..."

He left with a grin on his face. When he said that he'd be joining the *Democrat*, Delia's eyes got big and her mouth was open with amazement. So were Juanita's. Now how in the deuce am I gonna pull that off, he wondered, barely catching his breath and grateful that his back was toward them?

Juanita's brows were knitted together. She wanted to laugh - laugh out loud. Oh, Conner, are you watching this charade, my sweet? Oh, I do so hope you are. I truly believe life has just returned to Athea Manor once more. I truly do.

But then it hit her. Rose, dear Rose. She suddenly became furious at Seth. How dare he! What will Rose do without him? He's her life. Maybe he was making the whole thing up to impress Delia and Tucker. I do hope so for Rose's sake. The ungrateful young...

****

August, 1899

When the steamship *W. C. Bradley* had returned from Apalachicola to Blountstown with Conner's body on board, Juanita, Delia and Harrison had remained with the body until they departed from Blountstown. Tucker and Raine Williams had also been on board. They were returning to their home in Tallahassee without their parents, Berta and Layke, who had elected to remain in Apalachicola with their friend, a former senator. They would remain with him until their daughter SuSu and her children, who had been made homeless by the freak hurricane that had devastated the small town of Carrabelle, joined them.

It had been particularly tearful for Berta when they left Apalachicola and she found out that Conner O'Farrell, an acquaintance from her youth in Macon, Georgia, had suddenly died of a heart attack while on the *W. C. Bradley* as it steamed toward Apalachicola to assist the hurricane victims.

Juanita, Delia and Harrison had taken the train from Monticello to the Blountstown landing after the telegram arrived informing them of Conner's heart attack. Berta, Layke, Tucker and Raine had been on the same train and boarded the steamship for Apalachicola and they knew not what. All they knew was that a terrible hurricane had struck Carrabelle, and their daughter and her two children were there. Jay, SuSu's husband, was in Arcadia attending his father's funeral.

Berta was confused. Should I go to the O'Farrells and tell them how sorry I am? My nerves are so frazzled about the hurricane and now Conner. I'm not sure I can be calm enough to say the right words. And why did Raine insist on coming along, anyway? She doesn't care what happens to SuSu or to anyone else for that matter. She shook her head, breathed deeply, trying to calm herself. I truly should go back on board and offer my condolences to Juanita and her daughter.

I know Layke is wondering what has come over me, why I don't do the proper thing. He's been looking at me carefully - no, suspiciously - ever since Tucker told us about Conner's death, wondering how I'll handle the news, no doubt. I know he knows. I'm sure of it, but there are some people you meet in your lifetime who have a significant bearing or impact on who you become. I truly believe that. When I remember how shamefully Conner and his family were treated by my own father, shunned, made to feel inferior just because they were Irish and Catholic, I'm so ashamed. I wonder what would have happened if Father had accepted him into our home? Again, she looked off into the night.

Back to reality, she said to Layke, "Honey, I feel that we should offer our condolences to Juanita and her daughter, don't you?"

Layke studied her, then replied, "Yes, my sweet, we certainly should. Here, I'll give the boy our traps and will join you shortly."

Berta's attention was drawn toward the noise - a shrill noise. "Dear Lord, it's Raine! Now what's she up to?"

"Don't, Mama," Tucker said restraining her. "I'll tend to her. She's just letting loose some steam now that she knows that SuSu and the kids are all right."

"You know better than that, son. She's just having herself a good time and doesn't have the compassion for the O'Farrells during their loss or for the rest of us for that matter."

"Mama, I'll tend to Raine. Now don't fret so. You and Dad go on up to visit the O'Farrells - and, Mama, pay close attention to Miss Delia."

"Who, son? Who did you say?" Berta could hardly think much less speak what with Raine laughing and joking with the rowdies who had debarked from the lower deck.

"Miss Delia, Mama, the O'Farrells' daughter. She's the most beautiful girl I've ever seen. Her eyes - well, her eyes are like..."

Berta heard no more, but knew what he was going to say. Her eyes were just like Conner's - pale, pale blue, opaque, strange, but with wisdom and mischief shining through. Oh, dear Lord, will I ever be rid of him? Do I want to be rid of him? But she's Juanita's child, too - ambitious, willful. She almost thought *crude* but remembered the last time she had seen Juanita that she had been so refined, ladylike, not at all like the wild girl who had run away with the Skinner Gang and ended up at Berta's ranch, South Spring, after R.J. Skinner and his brother Joe Bob had been hanged. I'm sure Delia has her mama in her as well as Conner. I'll have to keep a watchful eye on Tucker.

When Layke returned from making their arrangements with the purser, he gave a questioning look at Berta, and she, without saying a word, took his arm. Tucker called back to them, "Don't worry about Raine. I'll straighten her out." She and Layke turned to each other but didn't respond. They could read each other's thoughts. Berta thought - no, Tucker, that's not likely. If there's any straightening out done it'll be at Raine's request. You've never bested her and you never will. You don't have the rebelliousness. It's just not in you. Layke thought - I wish you did have some of Raine's killer instincts, my son. You'll have need of them if you do go into a political life.

The fight that Delia had told Juanita about between Berta and Raine had indeed taken place. It occurred after Berta and Layke returned to their home in Tallahassee with SuSu and her children the week after the hurricane. All hell broke loose on that warm summer day.

Berta was in her flower garden off the colonnade. She could see Salome through the French doors. She was moving slowly, setting the long mahogany dining table for dinner. Berta had to keep busy. She simply could not let her mind dwell on the past few weeks. SuSu's and the children's presence helped, but in the dark of night when the house was quiet and only an occasional hoot from an owl broke the silence she thought of the past and Conner - so vital - so intelligent and she had to admit - unobtainable. Not that she had wanted to be with him. She had Layke, who should have been enough for any woman, and he was, except when Conner's tragic face would appear. She longed to stroke the unhappiness away. She didn't understand her obsession - she never had.

Is this the unrequited love I've read about? It must be. But why after all these years? Why? She knew Layke sensed her attachment and it bothered her, for she loved him dearly - passionately.

25

Her reverie was not for long. First the shrill scream that could have come only from Raine. Then J.P.'s boisterous laughter - then - well, Berta had had it.

"Can't even have peace in my own flower garden," she lamented. "Raine," she called loudly. "Raine Trudy Williams, do you hear me?"

Raine peeked around the heavy dining room drapes and sheepishly answered, "Yes, Mama dear."

" Mama dear, my eye! You know good and well that that cavorting all over the house yelling like a wounded panther is simply not ladylike. Not that that ever bothered you before."

Berta took off her gardening gloves, put down the clippers and basket of cut flowers and walked toward her. Raine stood with J.P. behind her full, blue twill skirt holding on to its folds as if to say, "See, Aunt Raine, I caught you!"

But Berta had decided that there would be peace at the dinner table, and that meant that Raine would not continue getting J.P. all riled up.

"Can't you find anything to do that doesn't require a lot of noise? Don't you have a book that you'd enjoy reading, or maybe you can take J.P. to the side yard to swing, or perhaps you could read him one of his story books or perhaps..."

"In other words, Mama dear, you want me to be mouse-quiet and bored. Is that what you're trying to say, Mama dear?"

If she says that one more time I think I'll cuff her, Berta thought. Raine could see how upset she was and delighted in it.

" Actually, I thought that after dinner you could ride over to Barbara Halsey's for a visit. You used to enjoy spending..."

"Enjoy, my eye! She's probably the dullest person I've ever known. The only reason I ever visited her, Mama dear, was so I could spend time with Andrew, or better yet, Senator Halsey. Now that's an exciting man..."

"Raine Williams, what're you saying? If Alice Halsey knew or even suspected that you were enjoying her husband's company, why your father and I would be disgraced. I don't believe you! You're just trying to upset me as usual and I'll..."

"Not so, Mama dear. Henning Halsey is the most exciting man I've ever met except for Father, that is."

She simply had to stick the barb into Berta. She knew just how to hurt her - she always had.

Berta decided that she'd not let her see how upset she was. Instead she faked a smile and replied, "Now what on earth do you think the distinguished senator could possibly see in you, Raine dear? Do you truly believe that he'd think your screaming at the top of your lungs enchanting, and you only twenty years of age? Do you honestly think that the distinguished senator would find your unconventional behavior fascinating? Do you?"

Raine whirled around sending J.P. tumbling to the floor. Berta grabbed him. Raine turned for one more thrust.

"Mama dear, if you think that Henning does not find me fascinating perhaps you'd like to read some of the - shall we say - notes that I've received from him. Would that interest you, Mama dear?"

Berta breathed in deeply. Is she lying? Is this another bluff? Aloud she replied, "No, my dear Raine, I'd not. It's obvious to me that you need that kind of attention. You always seem to need what is unobtainable, don't you? Afraid of a true relationship, Raine? Is that it?"

She knew she had scored when Raine hiked up her skirt and bounded up the stairway. But Berta knew she'd get one last barb from Raine - she always had to have the last word.

"Speaking of true relationships, Mama dear, how about your lusting after the Irish gambler Conner O'Farrell?" She let that sink in. "Didn't think I knew, did you? You really should keep your correspondence under lock and key, Mama dear."

Dear Lord, why have you sent this child to me? Is she my Hell on earth?"

Berta had gone to their room to change for dinner. Layke had sensed how upset she was when he joined her to remove his coat. "Is it Raine again, my sweet? Now, don't say that things will be all right. You always say that, and always there is the tension between you."

Berta turned toward him, walked over to their bed, smoothed the ecru coverlet and sat.

"I want you to insist that she go to South Spring until school resumes. Now, I mean it, Honey. She can't say a civil word to me, keeps me upset all the time, is driving SuSu to distraction and..."

"Don't, Honey. Don't cry. You've been upset enough lately, what with the hurricane and your friend's death." She looked quizzically at him when he said that.

"It's not just about Conner's sudden death, Layke. It just seems that our world is falling apart - breaking up - around us, what with Trudy so sick - I expect a telegram from Old Town any day - and then Parker Meade passing on. I don't know. It just seems that our world is crumbling, and she is taking extra delight in rubbing salt in my wounds..."

"Now, Honey, don't! I know she's an unthinking girl, and I think you're right - about sending her to South Spring, that is. Young Reuben would keep an eye on her. She's always got along with him. Would that suit you?"

She sighed and went to him, holding him close to her. "That would suit me fine. I just need to have her at a distance. When she's not here, I worry about her. I truly do, and I know down deep that I love her, but I do not like our child. I'm sorry, Honey, but I truly do not."

Raine was smiling broadly - actually grinning. She had removed her blouse and skirt and unhooked her petticoat. "I got her! I did!" All those letters from that dowdy Mary Garvin telling her about the Irishman and his harlot Juanita. I can't believe that Tucker doesn't care that his darling Delia Rose is the product of that twosome. The would-be senator should care more. Mary Garvin wouldn't have gone into such detail if Mama hadn't asked her about the two of them, and it's not Mama's nature to be interested in gossip.

She flipped over on her stomach, cupped her chin in the palms of her hands and raised herself up on her elbows so she could see out the window. She was enjoying reliving the incident on the *W.C. Bradley* when Tucker told her about their mama's reaction when he told her about Conner O'Farrell's death. He said, "I thought Mama was gonna faint, and Father had such a strange look on his face."

Raine grinned broadly. I knew it! Wonder what was between him and Mama in Macon? Bet Grandaddy Norwood had a hissy fit thinking that she was taken with an Irishman. I just bet he did. Aunt Lamorah said that he was very strict. I wonder if she loved him all those years and Father found out about it. I wonder how I can find out? Now that would truly fix her.

Raine's day dreaming was shattered by the dinner bell. She got up slowly. If I weren't so hungry I'd just stay up here. But Raine was always hungry, so she swiftly slipped into her blouse and skirt, smoothed her hair back, positioned the large bow that confined her straight brown hair and hummed as she ran down the stairs.

Her father was wearing a very stern expression and Berta was without a smile. SuSu was also subdued. Delilah had already fed J.P. and

Elizabeth and put them down for their afternoon nap, so there were just the four of them dining.

Layke was the first to speak. "SuSu, did Tucker tell you when he was returning from Wakulla Springs?"

"He thought he'd stay about a week, so I imagine he'll be home by week's end, about the same time Jay should arrive from Arcadia. I can't believe he's been gone three weeks."

Berta interjected, "He'd have been home sooner, Hon, if he could - now you know that."

"Oh, I know, Mama. He wanted to work with Meade on the sketches. I'm glad I insisted that Meade return to Tall Ten. I know I shouldn't fuss about it, but it's just not fair, losing all their illustrations in that hurricane, and now the book can't come out on time. I'm just glad that the publishers are understanding, but it's not fair at all."

Raine reached across the table for another biscuit. "Father, pass the gravy."

Berta ignored her poor manners. She was determined to have some peace at the table. She knew they were in for a tantrum after dinner when Layke told Raine of their plans for the remainder of her summer vacation. But he was hoping that she'd be agreeable. After all, he rationalized, Berta had more to deal with than she needed. She didn't need nor want any more of Raine's shenanigans. We'll all be better off.

Raine knew that something was in the wind, but what? Has Mama dear told Father about the notes she claimed his friend and colleague had sent her? Probably not. She knows that I'll retaliate with my knowledge of her unusual curiosity about one Conner O'Farrell. I'm just going to plan a trip to Monticello to visit that country bumpkin Tucker's so smitten with. Bet I can pry and find out just what did happen to her highness and the Irishman.

"Raine," Layke said again.

"Yes, Father," she said sweetly.

"I'd like to have a word with you - in the study." He smiled at Salome and told her that dinner had been delicious, as usual.

Berta kissed his cheek, squeezed his hand and said, "Think I'll take a little rest while the children are sleeping, Honey. Are you going back to the capitol?"

"For a short time only. Feel like I might be coming down with a summer cold. Head's all stopped up..."

"I noticed you clearing your throat often last night. I'll have Brevard fix you a hot toddy when you return." She squeezed his hand hard three times. It was her signal for *I love you.* He responded by squeezing her small hand four times for *I love you, too.* Raine was disgusted by the exchange.

God, she gushes all over him! I don't know how he stands it. Bet he's got a mistress in every town in his district. I'll bet! But she didn't really believe it. She just needed something to bolster her confidence, because she knew that he was unhappy by her actions and was going to give her a tongue lashing.

When she was younger he'd often side with her, but since she'd been away at Miss Baldwin's School it seemed that Mama dear had a strangle hold on him. He seldom hugged Raine anymore, and that bothered her. She needed his acceptance. She didn't give a fig about the rest of them. They could all jump in the St. Mark's River as far as she was concerned.

Layke got right to the subject even before Raine sat down. "Your mother and I have decided that you should spend the remainder of the summer at South Spring until you have to return to college in October. The decision has been made, so there is no use to argue."

He stopped, looked at her surprised expression and, not being able to read her thoughts, continued.

"I'll have Delilah help you pack and make the necessary arrangements with Brevard. You have put us in a distressing position by your total lack of consideration for the other members of the family and, I might add, the servants as well."

Raine thought, so the old biddy squealed, did she! Should have known that I couldn't trust that black wench! Should have known!

Layke had not told Berta what Delilah had told him when they returned from Apalachicola about Raine staying out to all hours, unchaperoned, and that Tucker had been so upset by her actions that that was the reason he went to Wakulla Springs. He didn't want any more responsibility for her behavior and had thrown up his hands in disgust.

Raine rose and said, "As you wish, Father," and left the room.

He knew that she'd retaliate - she was cornered. But he felt just as Berta. I need some peace, too, Raine my darling. He was weary. He sat quietly in the leather wingback chair and stared at the rows of books worn from years of use. Why can't she adjust to the world around her? She's living in the most exciting time in this nation's history. The state is opening up to tremendous progress. The telephone will be in full use in a few years bringing our world close around us. We can now get on a train and visit almost every city in the state in a matter of hours. The air is electric with excitement, the kind she should respond to.

Women will be a powerful force in their own right soon. Raine has every ingredient to become a candidate for the women's movement, and I'd be proud if she should. I'd be willing to write Carrie Catt and Miss Anthony for her and put her on a train for New York. But she'll never work for them. She's too consumed by this ridiculous jealousy of Berta. It's an unhealing sore, this jealousy. The problem is that she delights in it.

As usual the South's dragging its heels. Heavens, a majority of the western states have already given women the right to vote. They've come a long way from the meetings in Miss Anthony's house in Rochester. Even have their own headquarters in New York City now. Raine could be an integral part of their thrust, but when I mentioned it recently and said that she had evinced an interest only a few months ago about working with Miss Anthony, she just shrugged and said, "Oh, Father, now what on earth would I wanta do that for. We probably won't get the vote for another fifty years, and I'll be dead by then."

Berta's right. Raine does only what will serve Raine. Self-serving Raine. I'm weary. I'm weary of it all. I'll be glad when the session is over. Berta and I need to get away - a nice long vacation. When I finish this term we're going to take that trip to Europe like I promised. I'd love to stay an entire year, but she'll perhaps manage a few months and not even that if Trudy is still ailing. He was soon dozing, his brown hair flecked with gray rested against the chair's wing, his brown leather boots on the needlepoint covered footstool Berta had made for him the previous Christmas.

He awoke with a start, looked at his pocket watch and with his head in his hands thought, I have to get to work. He rose and reached for his coat from the hall tree. I've got to get my mind on things other than Raine, but I know if I told Berta what Henning told me - well, I can't, I simply can't. But I am grateful to him that he felt he should confide in me that he felt that Raine was being taught too many unladylike ideas at Miss Baldwin's and that I should look into the school. I agreed. Oh, if Berta only knew. Raine practically propositioned her friend's father - well, he didn't actually say proposition, but he might as well have. And when Delilah told me that she'd been out, unchaperoned by Tucker as was expected...

He sighed deeply, coughed, and said aloud, "Well, Raine, my headstrong child, I had to take a stand. I had no choice."

CHAPTER III   UNCLE J.J.

South Spring, August, 1899

"Now, you know that I don't mind Raine spending the rest of the summer, Reuben. It's just that..."
"It's just that she'll drive you up a tree - go on and say it, Nora. If she's gonna stay at South Spring she's gonna work just like the rest of us. Now, don't look at me like that. I mean it! She'll carry her load!"
"What're you going to have her do - go on the cow hunts with the rest of the cowmen and do the branding and ...?"
"If that's all she's willing to do, yes!"
"Well, you know she's not about to set foot in this kitchen. Oh, she'll eat like a cowman wolfing down everything in sight, but help?..not Princess Raine Williams."
"Now, Nora, she's not that bad..."
"Not that bad! Have you ever seen her turn a hand to help your mama when they're here between sessions? No, she's always off riding or down at the river swimming or ..."
"Oh, that reminds me," Reuben interrupted, "Layke wants me to worm Uncle J.J. so that by the time he and Mama arrive he'll have his strength back. Remind me to have the boys pull some ague weed. I'll grind it up and put it in his mash this very day. He loves that horse as much as he does Mama, I'm believing, and he'll want him to be strong enough for him to ride. He's more protective of J.J. than he is of his own children, I'll swear he is."

****

"Jonah," Raine gushed sweetly, "How nice of you to meet me!" Jonah, Raine's half brother, was very aware of Raine's affectations. She should know by now that her sugar-coated words are lost on me, he thought.
He replied, "If Reuben could've met you, Raine, I'd not have ridden all the way to Gainesville. I'm here because Layke requested it."
"Oh, my, so we'll have another dreary drive out to South Spring with you not saying a word. Really, Jonah, as the proprietor of the grand Stucky Hotel I'd think your manners would've improved."

"It'll never be a grand hotel in your eyes, but to Myra's and mine it's all we want or need. Too bad you can't find something as meaningful, Raine. Too bad that Layke and Mama had to send you packing to South Spring so that you won't continue to disgrace them in Tallahassee."

"Disgrace?! Disgrace?! What on earth are you babbling about?"

"You heard me. You're not talking to one of their servants, Missy, you're in Old Town now, so get off your blooming high horse. I'm thinking that this is your last chance, sister mine."

Raine turned her head from him and inhaled mightily - her chest heaved. Jonah was smiling. He had scored. They'd never got along. He simply couldn't stand her. Reuben was the only one who could control her, but he did it with humor and a firm hand. Besides, they had always got along. Guess Raine knew that he understood her. But since he'd married Leonora and had Sammy and Oliver, they weren't as close as before, that and the fact that she and Tucker lived in Tallahassee most of the year when they weren't in school in Virginia. The only time she was in South Spring was when the legislature wasn't in session and she was home on vacation.

Reuben had sent Pierre deMoya to meet and drive Raine out to South Spring five miles west of Old Town on the Suwannee. When the deMoya family had performed in Old Town with their medicine show in '78 Layke met them and had taken a liking to the family. He had told them that if they ever decided to retire from the show there would be a place for them at South Spring. After a year on the road they returned to South Spring and settled there. Pierre, the youngest son, and his wife Elysse had built a house about a mile from the main house. He was still handsome, in his early forties, and Raine had always liked him. When Jonah and Raine arrived in Old Town from the train station in Gainesville, she saw Pierre and anxiously hopped down from the buckboard.

Jonah saw him, too. What the hell! Why did Reuben send Pierre? God, she'll be all over him, Jonah thought as he watched her preen. And he was right. She could read Jonah's expression. Guess I'd better not disappoint dear Jonah. I'll just give him some hot gossip so he can fill his dear little Myra's shell-like ears.

Raine hated anyone with small ears. Hers were like an elephant's, she thought every time she studied them. They weren't overly large, but she took particular pleasure in dissecting her anatomy. Her hair was just dull brown, her eyes no particular color and as dull as her hair, she had decided by the time she was thirteen. She couldn't find anything terribly wrong about her skin, so she ignored it and immediately lambasted her straight up-and-down figure that she felt looked like a boy's.

Actually, she had a nice shape, but not curvy like her mother's or the ladies' in the magazines. And she was positive that if she ever got lost in an African jungle some ape tribe would adopt her, thinking she was one of them, what with her huge ears and long arms. She tried mightily but couldn't find any fault with her shapely legs, so she tackled her feet instead.

"I know I must have the ugliest feet in the entire universe!" she exclaimed every time she allowed herself to study them. "Tree frog toes. I've got tree frog toes! Grief! They're almost as long as my fingers and just about as ugly." She also hated her hands with their long boney fingers. If they weren't so almighty ugly, I'd not bite my nails, she rationalized. Oh, well, no man will ever look at me, anyway, so what difference does it make.

"Why, Pierre deMoya, how good it is to see you again after such a long time! It's so nice of you to meet me. I must remember to thank Reuben." She glanced at Jonah for his reaction, and sure enough his brows were knitted and he was gritting his teeth, trying to stem an outburst.

Myra opened the screen door of the hotel in time to witness the scene and knew that she'd have to listen to Jonah's tirade after Raine and Pierre left for South Spring. And listen she did. He got so out of control that Trudy Stucky, who had previously owned the hotel and remained in her old room upstairs, had banged her cane on the floor to shut him up.

"Now, see what you've done, Honey! You've awakened Trudy. No, don't, I'll go to her."

Trudy had been bedridden since breaking her hip back in '80, nine years before. She had become steadily weaker, her voice not carrying downstairs, so she banged her cane for assistance.

Myra was an even-tempered, sweet girl, never getting out of sorts. She called upstairs, "I'm coming, Miss Trudy. Be right there." She turned toward Jonah and said, "Why don't you have Dollie fix you a cup of tea? I bet Mr. and Mrs. Halling would enjoy some too."

Jonah kissed her cheek. "Why can't Raine have just a smidgen of your thoughtfulness, Miss Myra?"

He went to the kitchen and told Dollie that Myra had requested tea for him and the Hallings, who were guests at the hotel while they visited

Etienne deMoya, the town's school teacher. Etienne was assisting them in their research of the medicine shows, their origins, etc. Hazel and Hurley were a nice, elderly couple, who had taken such a liking to the Old Towners that they'd practically become permanent residents.

When Myra got to Trudy, she didn't like what she saw. Dear Lord, is she gone? Aloud, "Miss Trudy." Again, "Miss Trudy, it's Myra."

She took Trudy's thin wrist in her hands and felt the weakened pulse. To herself she thought, I doubt if she lasts the week - maybe not the night. Trudy's eyelids fluttered, and Myra pulled up the chair, leaned over and stroked her dry brow.

Trudy whispered, "Berta," so softly that Myra was unsure what she said.

"Did you say Berta, Miss Trudy?"

She managed to repeat it and Myra knew then that Trudy knew her time had come, for she and Berta were as close as mother and daughter.

"I'll be right back, dear."

Jonah saw her expression as she rushed down the stairs. "What's wrong? Is Trudy all right? Myra, what's wrong?"

"She's asking for your mother, Jonah. It's all she said. Berta - Berta."

"Do you think I should telegraph Mama and Layke? Do you think that this means that her time is near?"

She shook her head yes, and Jonah saw the tears begin. "I surely do. I'll have Dollie go to her to see what she thinks, though. She knows more about these things then we do."

"Ain't no need if'n she a callin' fer Miss Berta. No need a'tall," Dollie said, her eyes large with fear. But she went anyway, mumbling that someone best git Miss Trudy's dog out'n dat room 'fore she start wid de howlin'. Not able to restrain herself from saying it loudly, she called down to Jonah, "You know dat Beauty start a howlin' if'n Miss Trudy's soul go up to de Lawd. You rightly knows dat, Mistah Jonah."

Jonah followed behind her to get Beauty, not that he believed that old wives' tale about dogs' howling when someone died, but mainly to please Dollie. And he did need to see Trudy. She was like a second mother to him and everyone in Old Town, having delivered most of them around there.

When he looked at Trudy he glanced at Dollie for her reaction. She was standing over the bed humming softly and shaking her head up and down swaying from side to side with her eyes closed, her hands raised.

Jonah clicked his fingers at Beauty, and she jumped out of her bed and followed him downstairs.

"Myra, I'm going over to Stu and Rabel's to wire Mama. I think she needs to get here in a hurry." He hesitated and added, "But I don't think she'll get here in time from the way Dollie's carrying on."

He hadn't been gone fifteen minutes when he heard Beauty howling. When he ran past the vacant lot between the general store and the hotel and rushed back into the hotel parlor, there she was, head thrown back and howling mournfully. He looked up and Dollie was at the top of the stairs, tears streaming down her black face.

"I told you dat Beauty gonna start wid de howling, Mistah Jonah, when Miss Trudy go to de Lawd. Miss Trudy done gone to her maker, Mistah Jonah. She alookin' down on us dis very minute. Miss Myra, you wants me to fetch Little Leon and Daddy Leander? You wants me to?"

Myra knew that Dollie just wanted to escape the hotel. She didn't take kindly to dead folks, she'd said many a time in the past, and she'd always been afraid of being left in the hotel alone for fear Trudy would die. Little Leon, her son, or Franklin her husband, had been encouraged to stay with her whenever Myra and Jonah had to be away. Once in a while Luta Brewster, Trudy's closest friend, who lived across the street at the blacksmith shop, would stay with Trudy when Myra and Jonah went to Gainesville to visit Myra's parents for a few days.

"Dollie, go for Leander and tell him and Franklin to start on the coffin. We need to spread the word and make all the arrangements..."

"Yessam, I tell all de folks in colored town 'bout Miss Trudy. Dis gonna be a sad day fer sure...hmmm, a real sad day..."

****

Nora rose from the heavy oak dining chair. Raine and Reuben had gone down to the river. Normally, they would have had breakfast in the kitchen, but with Raine visiting Nora felt that she should serve in the dining room. The kitchen held four adequately, and that's where she, Reuben and their two sons ate except for Sundays. She liked having Sunday dinner in the more formal dining room. It gave her the opportunity to use her pretty things.

Often they'd invite Myra and Jonah or Pierre and Elysse and their children, Rosa and Paul, for dinner following church. Rosa and Paul were younger than her two boys, but other than the colored children on the place they were the closest children around. With Raine visiting, she decided that they'd have all the meals except breakfast in the dining room. Reuben thought it was foolish, she knew, but she'd made up her mind.

Berta and Layke still owned South Spring, and Young Reuben was the salaried manager. Berta had had the main house enlarged and redecorated after Reuben and Leonora were married and took up residence there. On either side of the main rooms, large double parlors, dining room and kitchen, was a hallway leading to bedrooms upstairs and down and baths on both levels. She had kept the cedar natural, and there was a balcony across the entire front of the house above the long porch. It was a comfortable house and not nearly as formal as their home in Tallahassee.

If Raine loved anything in the entire world, it had to be South Spring. That was her and Reuben's bond, for he loved it as much as he did Nora and the boys - well, almost. The old saying about the Scots certainly applied to him: "Take the land away from a Scot and you've stolen the song from his heart." Actually, he'd heard the saying attributed to the Irish as well. His father had felt the same about South Spring. He'd inherited it from his uncle, and when he left Georgia to claim it, he'd asked sixteen-year-old Berta to wed.

But Reuben McRae died young - just forty - and Berta with four children to raise had struggled to hold on to the ranch. Reuben was the oldest, and after his father's death he'd been hired on at the Oliver ranch outside of Perry. There he met and fell in love with Sam Oliver's daughter Leonora. Four years later Berta and Layke Williams were married. Layke built South Spring into a fine ranch once more and was elected to the state senate. Reuben and Leonora married and moved to South Spring, and he assumed the manager's position.

Jonah, the second son, eventually moved into Old Town, the closest town to the ranch, met and married Myra Judson from Gainesville, and since he had no particular fondness for South Spring, Layke and Berta bought his share of South Spring, enabling him and Myra to purchase the Stucky Hotel from Trudy.

Son Wes had followed in Layke's footsteps and attended the Citadel in South Carolina and had since become an instructor there. SuSu, the only daughter by Reuben, had married Jay Meade, an acclaimed artist from Arcadia and son of the prominent rancher, Parker Meade, owner of Tall Ten.

Twins, Tucker and Raine, had been born the first year of Berta's and Layke's marriage and spent their pre-school years at South Spring. Raine had never taken to the more sophisticated life style in Tallahassee, being rebellious by nature and preference. She gave in to her leaning at every opportunity.

She and Reuben sat on the landing that his father had built and that Young Reuben and Layke had rebuilt many times over the years. The golden water of the Suwannee seemed without life - quietly still - with an occasional fish surfacing, flipping its tail, then submerging. The air was heavy. Reuben was lying on his back talking.

"We could have a great summer, Raine. I say could have. You're going to have to do your...now don't interrupt me. You're going to have to carry your load. Now, I know you can't stand house chores. That's fine, but you do enjoy the boys and they like you, so you could take some of the burden from Nora's shoulders..."

"I wouldn't mind that, but I'd rather ride with you, really I would."

"I wouldn't mind one whit, Raine, but you enjoy causing the men to get riled up with your teasing. Now, I'm not finished...Just like this morning when Pierre drove you home. Hell, Raine, he's a married man with kids and...you were all over him..."

"All over him, my eye! He's the one who started it!" she exclaimed dramatically, her arms raised, gesturing.

"Hey, sister, you're talking to your oldest brother. I know better. Pierre deMoya and I've ridden together the whole length of this state, and when you ride with a man you get to know him. No, Raine! He did not start anything. He's devoted to Elysse."

"What difference does it make who started it, anyway?"

"It makes a difference, because that same thing could happen on a cow hunt, and I simply won't put up with problems that can be avoided. We have enough that the beeves and mother nature deal us without your brand, young lady."

She didn't respond.

He continued, "Why do you do it, Raine? I mean - hell - you're pretty..." That was the wrong word for him to use and he soon found that out.

"Pretty!" she shouted. "Pretty, my eye! Look at this face - look at these hands!" She unlaced the kid shoes frantically and shouted, "And these!"

"What're you yelling about? There's nothing wrong with your face or hands or feet - he hesitated when he looked at her feet - "Well, maybe not your feet. Lord, I never saw such long toes..."

"See!" she shouted triumphantly. "See, I told you. I've got the ugliest feet in all creation!"

"But, Raine," he said trying to stifle his laughter. "You can keep 'em covered up and no one will ever..."

"You stop laughing at me, Reuben McRae! You stop, you hear!"

By then they were both laughing uncontrollably and didn't see Leonora and the boys walking down the sand path toward them. When Sammy began running and yelling, Reuben jumped up, turned around, and somehow Raine was off balance and with arms waving in the air fell backwards into the river.

She came up yelling and Reuben shouted, "Come on, boys, we've got to save your Aunt Raine." He grabbed hold of their hands and called out, "I believe there is a damsel in distress. Do you think we should save her?"

"Yeh, Daddy, let's save her."

Before Nora could say, "Not in your good clothes, you won't," they had jumped in. Nora sat down on the rough boards, smoothed her long chambray skirt and thought, let them enjoy themselves. I hate to tell them about Trudy. I'll wait until we're at the house. He'll hate it so. She kept his family going when Mama Berta was so alone. Oh, how he'll hate it. A part of his life is gone forever. She wiped away the tears that slid down her cheeks and smiled at them cavorting in the river. She looked at Raine splashing and dunking Reuben, then Sammy. It's going to be a long two months - a long two months.

"Here, Raine, give me your things and I'll have Bernice wash out the river water." Nora hesitated before she continued. "Your folks will be arriving on the train in Gainesville tomorrow, Raine."

Raine shot a look at her, "What on earth for? Can't they at least let me have a few months' peace?"

"I'm sure they want you to have some peace, but Trudy died a few hours after you and Pierre left Old Town yesterday evening. Jonah wired them - they'll arrive tomorrow afternoon."

Not one word of remorse for her godmother did Raine utter. All she could think was, I'll have to think of something quickly. I'm going to get even with them!

She raised her eyes to an expression of expectancy on Nora's face and thought, I'd better show some sadness, or she'll think the worst.

"I know Mother and Father will be upset, but then they've been expecting it almost forever. She was my godmother, you know." She thought a while and continued, "Whatever do godmothers do, anyway? I mean, aren't they supposed to do something special for a person?"

"I'm sure I don't know, but anything Trudy Stucky ever did was special. She'll be mightily missed."

Raine shrugged her shoulders and thought as she walked into the kitchen, I wonder if she left me anything? If she did, I'll be out of here in a minute. She stood munching sugar cookies, one after the other, looking out the small-paned kitchen window toward the corral next to the barn. Uncle J.J. was standing, eyes closed, next to the fence. His only sign of life was an occasional flick of his tail to ward off the pesky flies.

I bet he hasn't been ridden in years. I don't understand Father's reasoning. You'd think the old thing was made of egg shells the way he treats him. Heck, if he's good enough to stud he can certainly be ridden. It hit her then. What would they do if I rode him? What could they do? Not a blasted thing - that's what. Not a blasted thing.

She left the kitchen hurriedly not bothering to brush the cookie crumbs off the table. When she got to her room in the south wing she searched the chest for Tucker's old pants that she'd cut off. I'll have to ride him before Reuben gets home. Throwing her blouse and skirt on the quilt-covered bed she slipped into the too-big pants and gathered them around her small waist with a belt. She didn't bother to tuck in the chambray shirt. Looking from side to side she darted out the parlor door undetected.

Raine knew just where the tack was and pulled Uncle J.J. into the barn and in no time had him saddled, being sure no one saw her. She knew that Nora was in the garden gathering greens for their noontime meal, and the boys were at Bernice's playing with her children. She could hear them in the distance. When I come back I've got to make sure that they see me so they can tell Father. God! He'll be upset!

He's so old that he's not one bit spirited like he once was. It used to be that Father was the only one he'd let ride him. She led J.J. out the gate and in a slow trot headed for the river road. When she got to the road she decided to see if he had any steam left in him. Taking her crop she flicked his dappled rump and dug in her heels.

"Well, old boy, I think you've got some life in you after all! She shouted excitedly as she raced him down the sand road. When she got to Pierre deMoya's spread she slowed down. There appeared to be no one in the yard but she hugged close to the riverside, anyway, and headed for North Prong, her favorite place on all of South Spring.

But Raine didn't get to North Prong...neither did Uncle J.J.

CHAPTER IV THE RUNAWAYS

The clearing of his Pa's throat alerted Poke. He got up from the table and told Catherine Inez to go outside to play. She didn't have to be told twice. Poke pretended to clear the table. There was no mistaking the aroma of chicken in the room, the only room. Mac managed to get to the edge of the rumpled bed and mumbled something unintelligible. Poke decided to not respond as he normally would. Again, Mac made a guttural sound and Poke thought, I sure hope he doesn't puke all over the place. Mac caught hold of the table's edge, steadying himself, and slowly rose. He managed to open the heavy wooden door, but before he got down the steps began relieving himself. Poke shook his head in disgust. Holding on to the door, Mac turned and slowly walked back into the room.

He was bleary-eyed and reeking of shine and urine, and Poke thought, bet he wet the bed again, but continued cleaning the pots. Finally Mac spoke. "Where - where's the coffee?" Poke reached to the rear of the black, wood-burning cook stove for the pot and poured the steaming liquid into a large tin cup.

"Here, Pa, best sit down. It's mighty hot. I been keepin' it hot fer you."

"Where's that girl? She best be doin' her chores."

"Oh, Catherine's outside doin' jes that, Pa. She's a hard worker."

"So you been tellin' me."

He blew on the coffee trying to cool it, then said, "Gimme a saucer. This goddamn stuff's too hot. Whatcha tryin' to do, scald me?"

Poke handed him a saucer from the shelf above the work table. Mac splashed some coffee into it, getting as much on the table as in the saucer. Poke had his back to him and heard him slurp the coffee. He decided that he'd let his pa do all the talking except when an answer was required, but knew he'd catch the very devil about the hen, and he did.

"What's that I'm a-smellin'?"

Poke breathed in deeply.

"Is that chicken I'm a-smellin', boy?"

Poke decided that he'd have to bite the bullet and answered, "Thought it'd be nice to have a special chicken dinner for you, Pa, seein' as how it's Christmas..."

"What did ya say? Did I hear you right? Did you up and kill one of my chickens?" he shouted.

Poke could see Catherine, her nose pressed against the small window that faced the river. He shook his head at her and she ducked down, but he knew she'd be beside the door listening.

"I wanted to cook you a nice dinner, Pa. Something besides fish. It's Christmas and Ma always cooked..."

"That old woman's dead, boy! Cain't you get that through that thick skull of yours? She's dead and gone and good riddance! If I'd a known she was in such a hurry, I'd a helped her along, that's what."

His head was lowered and Poke thought, good, he's gonna pass out at the table. Think I might just take Catherine Inez over to Rawles's after all. He was bolstering his nerve when all of a sudden he felt himself go down hard on the floor. His pa had lunged at him, catching him off guard. He was known as a fighter in the area, and Poke had seen him take on a man twice his size when Poke was little and his pa had taken him to High Springs to the railroad yard. But that was when things were good and Poke had been proud of his pa for besting that man.

Poke didn't have time to think - just react. He didn't even remember later picking up the piece of firewood from the bucket beside the stove. But he never forgot the sound of the crunch when the wood met his pa's head. He shuddered every time he thought of it. Catherine was yelling for him to stop but he couldn't seem to. When he finally did his pa was curled up on the floor and his head was covered with blood.

"Stop screaming! Stop it, Catherine Inez!"

"Is he...is he...dead? Is he?"

Poke didn't stop to examine him, just turned to Catherine and said, "Get yore things! GET YORE THINGS! Right now!"

He scurried around gathering everything he could, then climbed up on the chair for the Necessary Jar. When he reached it he said a little prayer. "I'm sorry, Ma. I didn't mean to kill him. Please don't be mad at me. Honest, I didn't mean to." Catherine stood beside him and made sure that she looked everywhere but at her pa's lifeless body curled up on the floor. Poke grabbed her arm and they headed for the skiff.

"Where we goin', Poke? Where?"

"We'll head to town to tell the Widow and Mr. Bunnell that we're goin' down state to be with Aunt Mums and Uncle Ray..."

"But they gonna find Pa and know you killed him."

He thought a minute and said, "You're right. You stay right here. Don't you go anywheres, you hear?"

He ran back to the cabin, grabbed the quilt off the big bed, rolled his pa up in it and dragged him down the steps and headed for the river landing.

"You ain't gonna take him with us, are you? Oh, Poke, please don't take him with us." She began to sob.

"Hell no, I ain't! I'm gonna throw this baggage to the gators!" He gasped when he said it. "Oh, Ma, I sounded as mean as Pa...oh, Ma..."

He brushed his runny nose with the back of his hand, pulled the rolled up body behind him to the water's edge and managed to lift it and place it among the roots between two cypress trees. He pulled the quilt from around it and tossed it into the river, thinking the gators were gonna have a feast this day if the cats didn't get at him first.

"What'd you do with him, Poke?"

"I gave him a fisherman's burial."

"What's that?"

"The kind all fishermen want, that's what. Live by the water, die by the water."

They headed toward the trading post with Poke rehearsing Catherine so their story would be the same - as how they hadn't seen their pa for going on three weeks and that they were going to High Springs to look for him. If'n they couldn't find him, then they were going on down the Santa Fe to the Suwannee and on to Fannin Springs to live with their ma's sister and her husband, and for the Bunnells to tell their pa, if and when he came back, where they'd gone.

Widow asked, "What you want done with yore spread? It's yours, you know."

"Me and Catherine Inez done made up our minds, Widow. We believe Pa done got hisself drowned or beat up or something. He's not been hisself since Ma was taken, you know."

"Yes, we know, Poke. Not hisself at all." She looked sideways at Mister, both thinking, yeh, he's drunk all the time. Don't know how on earth he holds down a job on the railroad.

Widow hugged them to her. "We want you to let us know how you're doing. We want you to write to us." Before he could say, "I don't write too good," Catherine spoke up, "I'll write to ya Widow. Poke done promised me I could go to school in Fannin Springs, when we get to our new home, that is."

"Don't worry about the spread, Widow. If Pa don't come back inside of a month or two you can tell Billy Rawles that him and Maudie can catch the chickens fer their own. Ain't much around there anyone would want. You might tell Billy that he can start gathering the eggs. Ma always said, 'waste not, want not' ". He could hear her just as plain as if she were right beside him.

He and Catherine waved to the Bunnells, who were standing on the store steps. "I'd gladly strangle that Mac Milligan if I could get hold of him. There goes two of the sweetest and best younguns I ever knew." She was crying loudly, and when Widow gave into her feelings, the whole settlement was alerted.

"Now, Honey, don't carry on so. You know Poke can take care of Catherine jes fine. He knows this old river as good as any fisherman I ever saw." But her sobbing could be heard all the way to Thompson's icehouse, and it wasn't long 'til people started arriving to find out what had happened.

When Poke saw them go inside and shut the door, instead of heading east to High Springs he headed the skiff west toward the Suwannee. "Might take us a few months to get to Fannin Springs. We'll fish along the way, sell our fish for meal, grits and coffee and take our time."

Catherine was humming, "Down On The Riverside", and Poke soon joined in, paddling slowly, in no particular hurry. He'd already forgotten his pa.

He shouldn't have!

****

Billy and Maudie Rawles lived about half a mile west of the Milligan spread on the Santa Fe and were Poke and Catherine's best friends. Their ma Memphis and pa Darius had sent them to the Milligans' to find out if Mac had returned for Christmas, and if he hadn't, then Memphis wanted the children to come for supper and to stay the night. She had made Catherine Inez a corn husk doll, and Billy had used some of his fish money and bought Poke a bright red pocket knife. Memphis and Inez had been best friends, and Memphis still missed her. Their chats on a Sunday afternoon when Mac wasn't home had meant a lot to both of them.

They had worked together on the church socials and done canning and jam making together when they first homesteaded their places. But when Mac started hitting the shine so heavily, even before Catherine Inez was born, the spirit seemed to go out of Inez. When she died, Memphis declared to Darius that she'd take those two little tykes in if Mac didn't straighten up. But when she mentioned it to Poke, he informed her that he'd promised his ma that he'd take care of Catherine Inez and that if anything happened to his pa, then they'd go to one of his ma's sisters.

His Aunt Vonne lived up in Lake City, and Aunt Mums, his ma's baby sister, in Fannin Springs, south on the Suwannee. Ester lived in a hamlet called Big Bend on the Kissimmee just before it went into Lake Okeechobee. His ma had encouraged him to go to Lake City because Vonne's husband had a good job on the railroad. His Aunt Mums's husband Raymond worked for a lumber mill, and Ester's husband Floyd was a fisherman. All the sisters knew of Mac's drinking and Inez's illness, and each had offered to take Poke and Catherine Inez and raise them as her own.

It was late afternoon when Billy and Maudie rowed up to the landing. Maudie saw the quilt that had hung up in the cypress knees at the water's edge. She commented on it, but Billy didn't pay much attention. He was busy calling Poke, and since Poke's skiff wasn't there but Mac's was, he knew that Poke was probably off fishing and that Catherine Inez was with him. He never left Catherine alone with his pa.

"Maybe you best not make so much noise, Billy. Mister Mac's probably sleepin'"

"Sleepin', my eye! More like passed out."

They tied the rowboat to the piling and walked up the path to the front stoop. When Billy knocked, the door opened. It hadn't been latched. He knew something was amiss. Poke would never have gone off without latching the door. He called softly, "Mr. Mac, it's me, Billy. You in there, Mr. Mac?"

He motioned to Maudie to get behind him. He didn't have to encourage her. She, too, knew that something wasn't right. Sure enough, the room was empty of Poke's and Catherine's things, and Mac was nowhere in sight. Billy told Maudie to head on back to the boat, that he was going to look in the yard, that maybe Mr. Mac was in the outhouse, but he was pretty sure he wasn't.

He was puzzled. *Where have they gone? I can't believe they'd just up and leave without coming by, and Mr. Mac never went anywhere with them, not even to the trading post.* As he thought, the outhouse was empty, the door pushed to but not latched. No one was in the chicken coop. He called and called. No answer.

When he got back to the boat Maudie was holding the quilt and crying. "Something's wrong. I just know it. This is the quilt Miss Inez made, and it never left her bed."

Normally Billy would have told her to stop her sniffling, but he felt that she was right. He untied the rope from the piling, and when he pushed the boat away from the landing with the oar, he saw Mac. Not saying a word to Maudie he poled the boat toward the lifeless form, eased himself down to the water's edge and carefully turned the body over.

"Gawd Almighty! It's Mr. Mac! Now don't you start with the crying, Maudie, ya hear? Don't you! You gotta help me get him into the boat. Gimme that quilt and I'll wrap him in it. Now, Maudie, don't you get girlie on me. You gotta help."

All she said was, "Is he dead, Billy? Is he?"

"Don't know but he sure hit his head bad when he fell. Messed it up bad."

By the time they got back home, Mac was twitching. In a way they were glad that he wasn't dead, but in another they had almost wished he were. Their folks had no use for him and neither did they. When Darius examined him he said, "Probably fell outa his skiff and hit his head on a cypress knee. Think maybe we'd better row in to the store and tell Widow and get Brother Blalock? Maybe they'll know where Poke and Catherine Inez are. You say all their things are gone? Sounds to me like maybe they went to the Post looking for Mac, and I just bet..."

Memphis finished his sentence for him as she often did. "That they are staying the night with Widow and Henry, that's what, and they don't even know that their pa come home for Christmas. Poor little tykes - poor things."

Billy spoke up, "I don't think so, Ma. Why'd all their things be gone if'n they was just gonna spend the night? And why didn't they tell us? Not like Poke to go off without tellin' me. Not like him at all."

Darius spoke up, "Come on, son. We're going to the Post to find out, and maybe Brother Blalock will come out for a look-see. Doubt that Mac'll last the night. He needs doctoring bad."

Memphis went to the kitchen and sliced up some of the baked chicken left over from their dinner. She placed it between two fried corn cakes, wrapped them in a tea towel and handed them to her men.

"Billy, get the lantern from the porch, and Memphis, you stay calm. If Mac comes to, you best should wrap him up in a sheet in case he gets wild. Me and Billy should be back by midnight with news about the children and, I hope, with Brother Blalock. He might not be a bonafide doctor, but he's the closest one we got outside of High Springs. It'd take too long for us to go all the way to High Springs." Memphis knew that he was just rambling, trying to ease her fear. She patted his back and cautioned them to be careful.

"What's he yellin' about, Maudie?" Memphis asked. "Can you make sense out of it?"

Maudie shook her head no.

"You don't hafta look at him, Honey. Here, just take these strips of sheet and tie his ankles together and I'll hold him down. He's raving some kinda crazy. I wish yore pa'd hurry up."

Memphis was sitting on the straight-back chair beside her and Darius's double bed. Mac had come to about an hour ago and it was almost midnight. The lamp light filled the large square room. She had wrapped his head with strips of clean cloth that she'd spread with prickly ash salve, the same salve she used for everything from croup to a burn. She mixed the inner bark with bear grease and declared that it was the best remedy she knew of for most everything. It made a wonderful tea for colic, and when you chewed the bark it sure took care of a toothache. It grew all over the low, swampy area near the river and was easy to harvest. Her ma and her grandma before her had sworn by prickly ash as had the Indians, whose land she and Darius now homesteaded. There wasn't a home on the river without it.

"Shhh - shhh, Maudie. Is that your daddy and Billy?"

Maudie hopped up, ran to the front door that faced the river. She could see two lanterns and hear talking. "Don't look like Brother Blalock come with them, Mama. Don't see but two lanterns."

Billy hung the lantern on the nail on the porch and even before she could ask about Poke and Catherine Inez he began telling her about their trip.

"Brother Blalock and the rest of 'em went up to Cletus's for Christmas, Ma, but Widow and Mistah Bunnell told us the whole story. Seems like Poke and Catherine Inez got tired of waiting for Mistah Mac to come home and headed for High Springs to see if they could find him. They said that if they couldn't, then they were going to move either up to Lake City or down to Fannin Springs or maybe even all the way down to the big lake to live with Miss Inez's kin and that they'd write them to tell them where they went." He caught his breath.

"How's Mac doing, Honey? I can see he's restless." Darius patted her back affectionately.

"Come to just a-screaming, but me and Maudie couldn't make out a thing he said."

"Well, I'm not surprised. Widow said that after Poke left for High Springs, Morris Lovell come by and told her the news. Seems that Mac up and got hisself laid off over two weeks ago, and Morris said that he'd been drunk ever since. Mr. Proctor got so put out with him that he said he didn't want to see his drunken face hanging around the roundhouse ever again, and Mac got so mad that he really caused a ruckus. Morris went on to say that Mr. Proctor had his hired men drive Mac to the river, and they put him in his skiff and towed him down river most all the way to the Post. Guess that's when he decided to come on home and fell outa his skiff."

Darius sat sipping the hot coffee Memphis handed him, then continued. "Cain't for the life of me figure out why the kids didn't see him in the river..."

Billy interrupted, "He probably went to Jimbo's for some shine, Pa. Probably slept out in the woods and passed out - probably."

"Well, that could be...could be."

"Maybe he fell in the river even before they left to look for him," Maudie interjected.

"No, they'd 've seen his skiff..."

"That's right, I forgot."

"We'll know soon enough when he comes to and can tell us, won't we?" Memphis said in a low voice. "You'd best make plans to take him to Mr. Plant's hospital in High Springs, Honey. Seems to me that he's gonna be needin' more than we can give him." She was getting weary.

She turned to Darius, "You can put him on Billy's pallet, and Billy, you can sleep in the barn, and..."

"I don't mind a bit, Ma. I don't much like Mistah Mac, but maybe this losin' his job and gettin' hurt will straighten him up. I sure hope so. I'm gonna sure miss Poke."

****

Catherine felt the rain splash on her face. It was just a drizzle but enough to awaken her. Snuggling into her blanket, she tried in vain to stay dry. She heard Poke call to her, "Catherine Inez, come on over by the fire." He had got up at first light, cut palmettos and stuck the fronds into the sandy soil. He found four forked oak limbs and stuck them in the ground for the frame alongside the fronds, placing a long oak limb on top. He thatched more palmettos along the oak beam, and if a strong wind didn't come along it should shelter them for a few days. He was in no hurry to get to Fannin Springs.

The sweetness of the damp grass filled the air. The frying corn cakes sizzled in the pork drippings, and the aroma of the food made them both hungry. "I'll catch us some fish for lunch, but we best come to a settlement soon or we'll be outta meal and side meat." He now wished that he'd taken the time to pack more supplies or at least have bought some from the men at the phosphate mine they'd recently passed before coming into the Ichetucknee.

It was the end of January. They'd been gone for over a month and hadn't even got to the Suwannee. They'd taken their time and ventured onto the Ichetucknee River, exploring it for a good five miles north before turning around and heading back to the Santa Fe. Never had they seen the likes of it, water crystal clear, spring fed and always cool. Poke couldn't get over being able to see the fish he'd hooked even before he pulled it up.

Catherine Inez asked him, "Poke, you reckon that this is what heaven looks like? Do ya, huh?"

He hesitated before answering, "Might be. I ain't evah seen the likes of this place. Might be."

"I wish we could stay here forever," she said lazily.

"But then you wouldn't be able to go to school, would you?"

"Oh, I was just dreaming. I know we can't. I bet Ma's in a place just like this. You think she might be?"

"Don't think so, Catherine Inez. Don't remember hearin' 'bout anythin' like this in the Bible. Seems to me she's floatin' in the clouds and..."

"That wouldn't be bad if God would let her visit a place as pretty as this from time to time. Seems to me that clouds would be, you know, sorta the same all the time, but here ya got fish a-jumpin' and birds a-singin' and frogs a-croakin' and water lilies and ..."

"I gotta get to my fishin'. Won't be gone for long. Don't you go near the river, you hear, or I might hafta tie you to a tree like I used to..."

"No you won't, Poke Milligan. I'm too old for such as that, now you rightly know it."

He laughed, then whistled as he climbed down the bank to the skiff.

"Ma, Poke's happy. Listen to him whistle, would you? Bet he ain't whistled since you went up to the clouds."

Catherine Inez soon joined in. She'd always been able to whistle Dixie real good.

****

"Thank ya, Widow. I'll tell Darius what ya said," Memphis called out to her as she was leaving the Post. She thought, Mac's crazy - crazy as a bedbug, stirring up trouble about those kids. Now, why can't he leave them be? Wants them back so's they can look after him, my eye, just so they can keep him in shine, that's what.

It was now July, and Mac Milligan had been back at his spread since March. He still had not regained his speech - mumbled mostly, but could make himself understood using sign language. The dark purple scar on the side of his face had faded somewhat, but the sight in that eye was blurred. The blow to his head had affected the use of his arm and leg, but he used a cane, just a gnarled cherry stick, and hopped around fine. Everyone said that he was lucky to be alive and that he should be beholden to Billy Rawles for saving his life.

But Mac wasn't beholden to anyone. The only thing that kept him going was his plans for revenge on Poke and Catherine Inez. Widow had been hesitant to tell him where the children were, but Henry prevailed on her, stating that Mac had changed since the accident, and now that he wasn't drinking as much perhaps they should write the Hawks to let them know his condition and that he wanted the children back.

The Bunnells received the letter from Inez's sister that the children were living with them and that Catherine Inez had been able to attend school for the last month it was in session. She also said that they had fit in nicely with her family, were hard workers and that she and her husband Raymond had decided that their place was with them. When she told Poke and Catherine Inez that their pa was alive and wanted them back, they had become frightened and said that they didn't want to return home, that he was drunk all the time and beat them.

Widow took it upon herself to write the Hawks and to tell them what Mac had said, that if those children weren't home by the end of July, he was going down river after them, and they'd be sorry that they'd put their pa to so much trouble.

The letter trembled in Mums Hawk's weathered hands. The years of hard work told on them as well as her furrowed brow knitted tightly on her too-thin face. One could see that she had once been a handsome woman. She was in her mid-forties, wore her still dark hair in a tight knot low on the nape and in repose had a dour expression. But when she smiled or laughed, which she did often, her face would light up a whole room, her husband of twenty-plus years always said.

Catherine Inez had taken a real liking to her aunt and she to Catherine. Mums's only daughter who had lived, Beth, was married and lived a few miles up river near Hart Springs. Her husband had a fine plantation and grew Sea Island cotton. Three of Mums's four boys had moved over to Trenton to work. She missed them. It bothered her that none of them had wanted to stay on the farm. Baby Ray, who was now called Babe, had remained at home with his parents and worked at the lumber mill with his daddy in Fannin Springs.

There were Williford, Hayes and Brooker. Williford, who was always called that, never Will, had taught school at the Trenton Academy until it was destroyed by the Big Blow in '96. Then he went to work at Hayes' and Brooker's turpentine still until another school was built on the other side of Trenton at the Cross Roads. The boys' still hadn't been flooded by the Big Blow like their neighbors' had at Yular on the Suwannee, so they were doing right well. Then the freeze hit later that fall freezing even the water in their wells and causing a number of families to move from that area. The boys just dug in their heels and declared that that was home and it'd take more than back-to-back disasters to send them packing for somewhere else. Hayes always said that trouble would find you if you were in the market for it. He had a good disposition like his ma.

Poke and Catherine Inez must have heard the stories about the Big Blow and Big Freeze a hundred times. But they didn't pay much attention to the grown-up tales, for their minds were on their pa. They knew that if they didn't go back he'd track them down, and Poke, though he never mentioned it to Catherine Inez, knew that his pa would have to get his revenge - he knew his pa.

He lay on the cotton-filled pallet. He'd never slept on one before. It was nice, a lot softer than the corn husk mattress back home. When he thought about the time he and Catherine Inez had spent on the rivers on their way to Fannin Springs and at the Hawks' home, he realized that he hadn't been this happy since his ma had died.

But it's all over now, he realized. We gotta move on. Don't want to cause any grief for Aunt Mums and Uncle Raymond. They've been too good to us. Oh, how he hated to tell Catherine Inez! She had so looked forward to going back to school in October. But they had no choice. We'll leave at first light, he decided.

He got up and walked over to the small pine table in his room - his room, he liked the sound of it - his own room. Well, it wasn't exactly all his, for he shared it with Babe. But since Babe was at the lumber mill all day long Poke thought of it as his own. But Catherine Inez did have her very own room with a dresser to hold her few items of clothing and even had a hand mirror with a bone handle that had belonged to Beth when she lived at home.

Poke wished that he could leave her there, he truly did, but his pa being his pa, well, he'd probably cause her a lotta grief like he'd done his ma. Poke knew that he couldn't stand for that and that it'd plague him for all his days if he left her.

His mind was made up. First light they'd leave. He began writing the note. Painstakingly he formed the letters.

Dear Aunt Mums and Uncle Raymond...

****

Raine could see North Prong in the distance. She was so excited that she didn't pay much attention to Uncle J.J. when he started shaking his head from side to side and snorting. She just dug in her heels. But instead of racing forward, he reared up and fell to his side. She felt consciousness leave her. That was the last thing she remembered.

But, Reuben, when I told her about Trudy she didn't seem that upset, honestly!" Nora explained.

"Raine's a little girl underneath that tough act she puts on, Nora. I'd think you'd know that by now!" He was shouting.

She lowered her head and slowly turned from him. She wasn't used to his anger. He had always been a gentle man, like his pa before him. She decided that she'd explain further.

"When I left for the garden, she was standing right here at the table, and from the looks of it she'd been in the cookie jar. She was standing right here, Honey, staring at Uncle J.J., and, Reuben, she was smiling. I'm sure she'll be back soon."

He left the kitchen mumbling about how he hoped so, that it was enough to lose Trudy without having to worry about his little sister.

Nora thought, that's how he thinks of her, as a little sister. He's always taken up for Raine. Guess he's the only one in the family who even likes her. She's rotten! She's spoiled rotten, but he can't see it. Nora realized that she might be a little jealous.

Reuben walked toward Uncle J.J.'s corral, that was apart from that of the other horses. He'd already checked them and none was missing, so he assumed that Raine had left by foot. That wasn't like Raine at all. He walked to the barn, and, not seeing Uncle J.J., thought, he's around back. He knew that he hadn't got his strength back since his bout with pneumonia last spring, but J.J. wasn't there either.

He went back in the barn and checked the tack. He then realized what Raine had done - the unthinkable!

"God!" he said aloud. "I just wormed him!" He knew that J.J. was still weak and that Layke would kill him for letting anyone ride him. "Hell, he'll have a fit!"

Nora saw him walking toward the house and by the way his shoulders were hunched knew something was up. Holding the dish towel she opened the door, but even before asking him he said, "That God-damned Raine's ridden J.J. off to God only knows where, and Layke'll ..."

"Reuben, watch your tongue! You know I don't like to hear you call the Lord's name in vain. The boys will hear you."

She could tell that he was more worried than angry with Raine. She began patting his shoulder and quietly said, "What could she hurt? What?"

"What? What? That horse is still weak from spring, and I just had Moses worm him. Hell, Layke wanted him rested for a good two weeks before he got here so's he can ride him. That's what!"

"Well, mister, you don't hafta shout! It's Raine you oughta be yelling at - not me," and with that she fled the kitchen sobbing.

"I'm sorry, Honey, I'm sorry," Reuben called after her. But she had slammed the door hard, and he could hear her muffled sobs through it. He eased the door open and went to her. Sitting on the edge of their bed he began speaking.

"Nora, I want you to listen, please. Now you know how I feel about Raine," he laughed. "Heck, you remember when I got to your pa's spread, and the first thing he had me do was select one of Lady's pups for my own, and how he got upset, plumb out of sorts with me 'cause I took so long."

She smiled up at him. "That's when I fell in love with you. You picked out the one Lady kept pushing aside, like she didn't want it. I remember - that was Lonesome, wasn't it?

"Yes, that was Lonesome. Just about the best puppy Lady ever had." He sighed and continued, "That's sort of how I feel about Raine, I guess."

Not that no one wanted her, for they did and still do. It's just that she can't seem to fit in, kinda like Lonesome."

Nora's sniffling stopped. "I understand, Honey. It's just that she's so exasperating. I don't mind her being different, honest. But it seems that she actually enjoys hurting people. Now, why did she have to ride J.J.? She knows that she's not supposed to..."

"That's what I mean, Honey. She doesn't seem to know how to get noticed except by doing things like that - just like Lonesome."

Nora wanted to say, but Lonesome minded you, Reuben, and Raine doesn't or won't mind a living soul. Raine does what suits her. But instead of saying hurtful things she pulled herself up and kissed his cheek. She could tell how distraught he was. First Trudy and now Raine.

"Don't just sit there, Honey! You've gotta go after her. She's probably headed for town so she can parade up and down main street so everyone can see her riding Uncle J.J. No doubt that's what she's done."

"You're probably right. I'll get Moses and Pierre to go with me, and we'll comb the woods in case you're wrong."

"For Heaven's sake, Reuben. Why'd you hafta go to all that trouble. Raine's fine, just like Lonesome always was. Heavens, she'll die of old age just like he did," and she laughed when she said it. To herself she said, she's in town prancing all around when she oughta be mourning her godmother's death. Like Lonesome, my foot...

****

Poke crept past Babe's bed and carefully closed the door. He had told Catherine Inez what his plan was the night before, and though she was visibly upset, she understood his reasoning. She was still asleep but he could tell she was fitful. When he shook her shoulder she sat straight up.

"Shhh - it's me, Poke. Get your things."

He'd left the note and some money for the grits, meal, coffee and smoked slab he'd taken. His ma would be proud of him, he thought. He'd already started another Necessary Jar. Well, not exactly. He'd had to take the money from the dark green jar and put it in a heavy leather pouch, buy another pouch for the money he'd made working at the lumber mill part time and from selling his daily catch of fish.

His Uncle Raymond had said many a time, "Poke can out fish anyone I know, boy or man. Yep, he's the best fisherman from Fannin Springs to Cedar Key, he is." That sure made Poke stand tall.

54

He paid his Aunt Mums room and board every week, not that she asked for it but because it was the right thing to do. If he'd had his wish, he'd have been at school with Catherine Inez instead of at the mill. But now that he was the man of the family, that wasn't possible. He didn't mind that much. He was just happy for his sister.

He and Catherine Inez got into the row boat his uncle had given him and that Poke had repaired. It was much larger than his old one. He'd decided to go all the way to the Gulf. He'd heard the men at the mill talk about Hog Island at the mouth of the Suwannee and Cedar Key, where they'd fish and take rich northerners out fishing. Good money in that. They said that if you had a good boat you could get as much as $4.00 or $5.00 a day, but you had to be a good sailing master, as the northerners called them. And besides, there was a school in Cedar Key for Catherine Inez, and there were cedar pencil factories, though not as many as before the big blow in '96.

He hadn't mentioned in his note where they were going, just that he and Catherine Inez couldn't go back with their pa. He knew that they'd understand and that he could take care of the both of them.

They'd been gone for almost three hours when Catherine Inez said she was hungry. He rowed to the bank, tied the boat to a low hanging oak limb and climbed the steep bank. Poke said, "Think I'll build us a fire and fry up a big batch of corn cakes, enough for dinner too. Would you like that?"

"They'd taste mighty good. Would you like me to get the water for the coffee?"

She hadn't got it out of her mouth when they heard a noise. Not wanting to be seen, they ducked back of the thick brush.

Poke whispered, "It's someone on a horse - don't make a sound."

When Uncle J.J. reared up they could see him above the bushes and saw him and the rider go down. All Poke could say was, "Lordie, Lordie, Catherine Inez. Lordie, Lordie!" It had been his ma's favorite expression.

When he got to Raine and Uncle J.J., he knew that the horse was dead. Raine was unconscious, and her foot was underneath J.J.. Poke was able to lift J.J. enough for Catherine to pull Raine's foot out, and he told Catherine Inez to go to the river for the water. Before she returned Raine was moaning and shaking her head from side to side. Her eyes fluttered, then opened wide.

"You're all right, Miss. You're gonna be fine." He hesitated, then said, "But, I'm afraid that your horse up and died on you."

She sat up when Catherine handed her the tin cup of water but didn't drink any. She just sat there staring at J.J. She knew that she was in for trouble, and when Poke said that he and his sister had been heading for Cedar Key when they decided to stop for breakfast, she blurted out, "Well, that's just where I was going, too. I was headed for the Fannin Spring landing to take a steamer to Cedar Key." She made up her mind that very minute. I'm going with them, that's what. Didn't want to go back to Virginia, anyway.

Poke and Catherine were washing up the pans at the river's edge when Raine asked, "Would it be too much trouble for you to give me a ride? I mean, I had planned to sell my horse for passage money, but now that's no longer possible."

Poke didn't even think on it, just answered, "We'd be happy to help you, Miss."

"Oh, call me Maggie. I'm recently widowed and heard that there was a teaching position open in Cedar Key, and since my husband died suddenly and we didn't have the funds saved for the trip..." and on and on she fabricated her tale.

Poke could tell that she was well educated but couldn't understand why she was dressed so poorly. When she saw him looking at her cut-off pants, she quickly said that she had given her trap of good clothes to a farm lady in exchange for food and lodging. Then he understood.

By the time they had rowed a few hours Poke said, "Think we'll just stop for the day, Miss Maggie. This looks like a good spot. How'd you ladies like some quail for supper? Huh?"

Raine, without thinking, said, "You need help shooting them?" When he appeared astonished, she added, "My husband always let me go hunting with him."

"Don't have but one gun." He could tell that she was disappointed. "Why don't you and Catherine Inez catch us some fish? They'd be good, too."

He didn't have to suggest it twice. Raine hated to cook except for out in the open. She, Tucker and Mose's boys used to camp out often, and she could fry up corn cakes and cook range coffee with the best of 'em.

For a school teacher, she sure knows her way around the woods and river, Poke thought. But, she'll come in handy, maybe even help Catherine Inez with her lessons along the way.

It took them a week to get to Hog Island. They had taken their time fishing and exchanging their catch for supplies at the fish houses along the way. Poke insisted on Raine's getting a big hat, 'cause ladies weren't supposed to get suntanned, and he wanted her to look nice when they got to Cedar Key, so at Clay Landing he encouraged her to buy a blouse and skirt. He had wanted her to get shoes as well, but they didn't have her size. He was surprised that she had shown no disappointment. Didn't seem to bother her a bit. She constantly amazed him, and he had decided that she was about the prettiest girl he'd ever seen - just kinda sparkled with life - and, boy, did she know a lot of things!

Every night around the fire she'd tell them tales about her home in Virginia. She was actually describing her home in Tallahassee. She said her parents hadn't wanted her to marry her husband, but when she insisted, they told her that they never wanted to see her again. She said that she had attended Miss Baldwin's School in Staunton, Virginia to become a teacher, so, since she knew she could take care of herself, she followed her intended all the way to Trenton, Florida, where he had a real good job with a turpentine still. They hadn't been married very long when he suddenly died. The doctor told her that it was his heart and that he must have had a bad heart from the time he was real little, 'cause he was only thirty years old.

She was so busy spinning her yarn that she was afraid that she would forget just what she'd told the two wide-eyed youngsters. But, oh, she was having a good time. When Poke or Catherine would ask her a question about her past life and she couldn't remember what she'd told them previously, she'd sniffle and say, "I would prefer to not discuss it further," and turn her head. Finally, they just quit asking.

It was a hot, muggy August night. Every insect that could bite a person seemed to have slipped beneath their mosquito netting and to be especially hungry. They tossed and turned. Poke was the first to give in to wakefulness.

"Bet we got four hours 'fore first light, I bet."

"What are we going to do until then?" Raine asked exasperated, swatting another insect that found its way to Heaven.

"We could sing!" Catherine Inez said. Oh, how she dearly loved to sing. Poke wasn't much for that.

"I know," Raine declared enthusiastically. "I know some poems. Not just sweeter-than-honey poems, but real good ones. Did you ever hear, "The Midnight Ride Of Paul Revere"?

They hadn't.

Up she jumped, "Get the fire going again, Poke, and put on some damp moss. That'll smoke the bugs away."

Now if they didn't present a sight. Here was twenty- year-old Raine Williams, daughter of the popular senator and his fine wife, on the banks of the Suwannee shouting for all the night critters and two wide-eyed youngsters, waving her arms, dramatically reciting every stanza of her favorite poem.

By the time they arrived in Cedar Key, Poke and Catherine could recite it almost as well as Raine, for every night after supper she'd give them their lesson.

The mouth of the Suwannee was rough. Wind blowing from the southwest. "Poke, we gonna be able to row all the way to Cedar Key?"

"Don't know, Catherine Inez." He sure hated to part with any more money for a ride on a steamer.

"Maybe we can get a tow from one of the lumber barges, Poke," Raine said. And that's what they did.

He and Catherine Inez had never been on the Gulf. Hadn't been anywhere but west on the Santa Fe to the Green's Store and east to High Springs. Catherine was particularly concerned. She couldn't conceive of not being able to see the other side, and Raine tried to ease her fears. She told her about when she had gone to the Atlantic Ocean for the first time and how high the waves were and how white the sand beaches were and if she could have seen the other side, then she would have been able to see Europe.

"What's that?" Catherine asked.

"What's what?"

"What's Europe?"

Raine couldn't believe she'd never heard of Europe. It was then that she decided that when they got to Cedar Key, she really would inquire about a teaching position. She'd also have to come up with a last name. She'd chosen the name Maggie because the only true friend she'd made while at Miss Baldwin's was Maggie Pope. She was certain Maggie wouldn't mind if she borrowed her name for a little while, just until she decided what to do. She was also certain that she was not going to return to South Spring or Tallahassee. I'll just put that part of my life behind me. She could hardly wait to continue. Now, this was a true adventure. Sure beat going to boring old Miss Baldwin's. If she did become a teacher she intended to make it exciting...she truly did.

Maggie would love the drama of the situation, she thought. She was smiling, her long, brown hair with sun glinted lights flowed from her tanned face. You know, she thought, I think I'm happy. Poke watched her as she hugged Catherine Inez to her, and they began singing the sea chantey Reuben had taught her. Poke decided, I think the best thing that ever happened to us was finding Miss Maggie. She's gonna teach us all about Europe and teach Catherine Inez how to read and help me with mine and - he hesitated - I wonder if Ma sent her to us. I just bet she did.

He joined in, and although he wasn't quite on pitch, sang louder than he usually did. He'd do anything for Miss Maggie.

Poke was singing, but he was also planning. He thought, if Pa does come looking for us, he won't be looking for three people, only two, and if Catherine Inez and me change our name to Pope, then we can pretend to be a family. We all got the same color hair and eyes and could pass for family easy.

Not having much time left before they arrived at Way Key, he decided that he'd have to confess to Miss Maggie the true story as to why he and Catherine Inez were on their way to Cedar Key.

When he told her, she began to laugh. To herself she thought, we've all been playing a game. They aren't who they said they were and I'm certainly not. She got into the excitement of the event.

"Poke, you've got to change your name all right. How about Jack and Nellie? I had friends in - she almost said Tallahassee but caught herself in time - in Virginia and they're common enough names, that is, if your pa gets to Cedar Key and..."

"He'll get there, Miss Maggie, you can count on it," he said loudly in order to be heard above the wind and waves splashing their boat.

"I know!" Raine shouted. "Let's say we're going to Tampa to live with our aunt, that we all moved from Virginia to Jacksonville, Florida, where our folks died of yellow fever. There was a bad epidemic there, you know. If we like Cedar Key, then we can stay for a while."

Catherine Inez spoke up. "I'd like to go back to school, Miss Maggie..."

"You've gotta stop calling me that. Just call me Maggie. Remember, I am your older sister. Now, we've gotta practice all the way there. Start calling me Maggie, and I'll call you Jack and Nellie. Come on - let's practice."

Raine thought, this is perfect. My folks won't be looking for a family of three orphans, either - this is perfect.

She resumed singing. When they docked at Cedar Key, they thanked the men who had given them a tow. "My brother Jack and sister Nellie and I want to thank you for helping us. We've decided to stay here for a while before going on to Tampa. Would you happen to know of any work here-abouts? Jack is very good with figures and..."

They left the dock and headed for Second Street, where the men said there was an available apartment above a grocery store. Holding hands, smiling and singing, the three were light hearted and excited about their adventure. But they wouldn't have been singing if they'd known where Mac was.

****

"Reuben," Nora called. She was on the front porch. "Now where's he gone off to? Reuben!" No answer. She went down the wooden steps past the red and white camellias that were in full bloom on either side of the steps. When she got to the side yard facing the barn, she saw him with Layke. She knew that if Layke was there Berta wouldn't be far away. He'd become so protective of her since Raine ran away.

Leonora, Reuben and the other children had discussed it at length, but none had found the courage to bring the matter up to him. Berta was a strong woman. She'd had to be. After all, she had South Spring to operate and four children to raise when her first husband suddenly died. No, Layke was overreacting, and they all felt that if he backed off and behaved normally time would be the ultimate healer.

Why Berta felt somehow responsible for Raine's running away they couldn't figure. If Layke would just talk some sense into her, she'd realize that Raine left because she was too ashamed to face them after what she did, especially at the very time Trudy died, her mother's best friend.

Reuben had tried in vain to explain to his mother, but Layke interrupted, stating that she had heard enough, that he wanted the matter dropped and not mentioned again. The Pinkerton detectives were the best on two continents, and he and Berta had put everything in their hands. Berta corrected him. "Not everything, Layke. We'll leave some room for the Lord's hand." They could all tell how worried Layke was. There had also been no more discussion of a trip to Europe. Layke knew Berta wouldn't even consider it.

Nora walked down to where they were standing. When she didn't see Berta, she wondered what was going on. "Reuben, I've been calling and calling you. I declare, I think you're losing your hearing." She squeezed his heavily muscled arm.

"Layke and I were discussing the news that Pierre just brought. It seems that the detectives believe they're on Raine's trail."

"But you're not to mention it to Berta, Nora," Layke interjected.

"Of course not. I wouldn't dream of it. Where is Mama Berta?"

"I suggested that she and the boys gather the holly and mistletoe. I think that's the first time she's said Raine's name in two months. She said, 'that was always Raine's job, wasn't it?' But at least she composed herself." Layke added.

Reuben spoke up, "When I said that I bet that was what Raine was doing right this very minute, she even smiled. Then she hugged me and said that we were going to have a wonderful Christmas like we've always had."

"Oh, Reuben, did Pierre say whether or not Rabel got in the boys' presents? I ordered them a good month ago. I'm so afraid they'll not arrive in time."

"They weren't on the *Louisa* or Pierre would've said. But don't worry, Honey. If Rabel said they'd be here in time, then they will. We've got over a week..."

"But the presents for the church Christmas party were ordered at the same time, and that's in four days..."

"Well, lady mine, then put on your thinking cap and come up with another idea."

"Wouldn't you know that they both would draw girls' names? What can I possibly make in such a short time?"

"Ask Berta for ideas, Nora. It'll give her something to do instead of..."

"Well, Senator, that's exactly what I'll do. Between the two of us, I'm sure we can make two straw dolls with dresses. I have lots of leftover dress pieces that would be perfect, and as clever as Mama Berta is with her hands she can embroider aprons and matching bonnets..." She mumbled all the way back to the kitchen stoop.

"You've married yourself a lovely girl, Young Reuben. We're lucky men, aren't we? Now, if those detectives are on the right track, who knows? Maybe Raine will be home for Christmas. That'd be the best Christmas present your mama could have. I'd like it too."

He laughed. "But I wouldn't know whether to spank her or to hug her."

"We both know which it would be, Layke," Reuben replied with a warm smile.

BOOK TWO:

THE ADVENTURERS

CHAPTER I CEDAR KEY

When the school bell rang, Raine Williams, now Maggie Pope, was the new school mistress. As luck would have it, Margie Schueler, the school teacher, was large with her first child and due to deliver the first of October. When Raine took her application to the city hall for consideration, the town clerk Deanna Lincoln was most solicitous of her. "Miss Pope, you're the answer to our prayers. We had no idea what we were going to do when Margie's time came. The pay is $25.00 a month," she said proudly, "and the school year is from October 'til May. Would that be satisfactory, Miss Pope?"

Raine was beside herself. She'd never earned a cent in all her twenty years. She rushed down Fourth St., and there Poke and Catherine Inez were waiting just as they had promised in front of the two-story, wooden school house. It was situated beside the Methodist Church, and though it was not an imposing building Raine thought it beautiful.

They had found rooms above the Schlemmer Grocery on Second St. The building was of brick and the apartment upstairs barely large enough for the three of them. Most of the buildings were made of tabby, crushed oyster shells mixed with oyster shell cement, and some of the walls were three feet thick. The streets were also of crushed oyster shell and sand, and there were wooden sidewalks in front of the buildings. It was a charming town, and the people were especially friendly.

The population of 1500 had diminished since the closing of most of the cedar factories. The final blow came with the devastating West India hurricane and tidal wave that almost wiped the town off the map in October of '96. Heavy damage was done to the Methodist Church, the Cedar Key High School and the Christian Church, plus three Negro churches. Over twenty of the sponge boats of a fleet of over a hundred were destroyed along with their passengers. Small houses were swept off their foundations and with their occupants buried in the mud.

The Eagle Pencil Factory and the Suwannee Ice Factory were also destroyed as well as all the lumber mills on Atsena-Otie and Way Key. The *Tampa Tribune* listed over 200 families destitute. But it was a miracle that anyone was left alive. All the bridges connecting the small islands were destroyed along with four miles of track of the Florida Railroad Company. When the fires broke out destroying the remaining wharves and six of the standing houses, that seemed to be too much for the residents. As soon as they were able, many left, never to return.

Raine could hardly wait to tell Poke and Catherine Inez about her new position as teacher. They had become a family, and they were getting used to their new names. "We have to always use our new names, you hear." Maggie reminded them. "Even when we're thinking, we have to use them." They had agreed, but it was still difficult.

Poke had assumed the dominant role because he was the breadwinner. The first few weeks he'd fished and sold his catch; then he got work at the remaining cedar factory and began replenishing the money he'd had to take from the Necessary Jar.

When a small house on "B" Street became available, they moved from their apartment above the grocery store. It had only two rooms, not fancy, but adequate, and it did have a few pieces of furniture, a small square table with four chairs and a large bed that Maggie and Catherine Inez shared. Poke broke down and ordered a cotton-filled mattress for himself. He made a wooden platform for it and a long work table for meal preparation. There was a wood burning stove for cooking and heating.

They went to the Mercantile Store on Fourth St. and picked out the necessary pots and pans and other utensils. When Mrs. Sears asked if Maggie wanted to select fabric for curtains, Maggie said that she couldn't sew. Poke couldn't believe that she couldn't sew. He'd never heard of a girl not knowing how to sew, but when she explained that her mother had engaged a lady to do the family sewing and that she didn't have the patience to teach her how to sew, Poke accepted her explanation.

Maggie had fallen in love with the townspeople, and they had taken a real liking to her. Mrs. Bascom, who had six children of school age, told her that she was by far the best teacher that the town had ever had. Maggie seldom thought of Tallahassee or South Spring or her folks. Her days were filled with teaching and in the evenings she worked with Poke on his reading. He was very bright, she discovered, but how he found time to practice she didn't know, because he was so busy at the mill.

His writing had improved tremendously. He wanted desperately for Maggie to praise his work. He knew he wasn't her equal, but he knew that he could be, so when the opportunity came for him to assist Mr. Buford Justice in the mill office, he took it.

Most of the mill workers could barely read or write, and, as Mr. Justice said, he needed someone who was dependable, hard working and who didn't waste his pay on shine. Plus he wanted to train Poke so he could keep the mill's books.

Was he excited! He could hardly wait for Maggie and Nellie to get home from school so he could tell them. He was going to be making $15.00 a month, and Mr. Justice assured him that if he did well and the cedar held out, he'd be getting a raise by year's end.

Catherine Inez thought that he shouldn't have lied about his age in order to get the job. He told them that he was sixteen, but Maggie said that it was all right. Of course she thought that he was fifteen when in fact he was only thirteen, but no one questioned him when he told them. He was tall, took after his ma's side of the family and was usually very sober. He saved his happy side for Maggie and Catherine Inez. They had some real happy times.

They attended oyster roasts at the shore, and Maggie and Catherine Inez sang in the Methodist church choir. Maggie had taught them how to ride a horse. Her friend Isabel Smith, whose father owned the newspaper and who lived only a few blocks from them, owned two beautiful stallions. Isabel had attended Rollins College in Winter Park and had planned on a music career but fell in love with Arnold Smith, a widower and one of the town's doctors, so instead of returning to Rollins she and Arnold were married, and she remained in Cedar Key. Isabel taught music at the school and played the piano and organ at the Methodist Church. She and Maggie hit it off right away. She loved the outdoors almost as much as her music, and any free time they could find was spent riding or fishing.

They had been in Cedar Key for three months, and though Poke thought of his pa less and less, he knew that he'd find them one of those days, so he had to remain on his guard. He'd thought of all the ways that he could defend himself and Catherine Inez, but now he had Maggie to think of, too. In his heart he knew that his pa didn't want them back, and he was sure that he would probably kill them if and when he got the chance.

Poke had written his Aunt Mums to let her know that they were all right and also to show off his improved handwriting. He also told her that he didn't want anyone else to know where they were. She had written him that indeed his pa had shown up in Fannin Springs not long after they left. She said that his Uncle Raymond had told Mac that Poke and Catherine Inez must've left by foot 'cause his skiff was still tied up at the dock, but she didn't know whether or not he believed him.

Raymond had also told Mac that Poke had made friends with a young man from the mill who was from the town of Arcadia down on the Peace River and that the lad had returned there, so maybe that's where Poke and

Catherine Inez had run off to. He was just trying to throw Mac off their trail.

Mac had hung around Fannin Springs about a week and asked a lot of questions, but they didn't know whether anyone had told him about Poke's rowboat. Aunt Mums said that she hoped that they hadn't and that she could see why they didn't want to return with him. She agreed with what they had told her, that he was indeed evil through and through.

Poke knew that if his pa was told about the other boat that it was just a matter of time before he showed up at Cedar Key. If he was headed this way then he must've been working along the way for it to take him this long. Since Poke was at work most every day he was afraid that his pa might show up while he wasn't at home and head straight for the school house for Catherine Inez.

It'd be just like him to snatch her and force her to go off with him. That would be one way of getting even with Poke, because he knew Poke would follow him in order to get Catherine Inez back. He rightly knew that. So every morning before he left for work he'd warn Maggie and Catherine Inez to be on their guard. It'd been almost a year since that fateful Christmas day, but it was still very vivid in his mind.

****

Detective Roy Kenton was hot and tired. He was also worried. He'd been with the Pinkerton Detective Agency since he was a young man of twenty, and twenty-five years later he could proudly say, "We never sleep" like the agency's motto boasted. He'd been assigned to the Williams girl's case when the agency was first contacted in August. First he went to Virginia to see if the girl had decided to return to her school - but she had not. Then he headed for Florida, going to South Spring to talk to the senator and his wife. The only picture that they could produce of Raine was taken when she was sixteen and she and her twin brother had sat for a photograph.

When Berta first saw the picture, she stated that it didn't look one bit like Raine and that it was the only time she'd ever seen her daughter with her mouth closed. But Roy took it anyway.

Roy left the ranch and headed for Old Town. There he talked to everyone around and seriously felt that he'd have the case solved in no time. He figured that she probably went to Fannin Springs and took a steamboat, but no one of her description had sailed from there. Besides, where would she have secured a buggy in order to get there, and if she had, where would she have got money for passage. She had to have left by foot, and everyone who knew Raine stated that was not likely.

So he headed south. Berta and Layke told him that Raine had no skills, had spent most of her life in school, that she wasn't even skilled in housework. Since she had no funds, he decided that she would have to find work in order to survive, so he asked in all the small towns and hamlets along the route about any newcomers fitting her description. There were no leads. He was stumped.

He was forced to re-think the situation. He knew that she was an expert horsewoman and loved the out-of-doors. Maybe he had been on the wrong track. She could easily have worked herself in with one of the backwoods cow camps and worked the range. So from October until mid December he combed the area from Old Town to Bartow. He had no idea of the immensity of the operation nor the hardships he'd endure. He soon replaced his suit with heavy cotton trousers, high boots and long-sleeved shirts to ward off insects, putting his suit on only when in a town - Pinkerton's required it.

In the middle of December he got his first good lead. He was told that there was a young woman of Raine's description riding for the Bullseye Ranch up in Crescent City. He left Bartow immediately for the St. John River and prayed that the girl was indeed the Williamses' daughter, for he wanted to be back home in New Jersey for the holidays. He wired Layke that he had a good lead and hoped his daughter would be reunited with them soon.

Since the Big Freeze the Garvins, Mary and Pierce, owners of the Bullseye Ranch, had been forced to sell off part of their vast holdings. Their ranch was located between Georgetown on Lake George to the west and Crescent City to the east. Their citrus groves had been killed, and although they replanted part of the groves, they had resumed raising cattle, rebuilding their large herds of previous years.

They were a close family and everyone worked - husbands and wives, in-laws and children. Bit Garvin, the youngest daughter, had married Harry Fremd from Palatka, and they owned the Blueberry Hill farm south of town. But when cow-hunt time arrived she joined her relatives for the hunt, and if she was needed for the annual drive to Punta Rassa, she went with Harry's blessing.

When Roy arrived in Crescent City and made his inquiries he was devastated by the news. The cowmen who had told him about the new girl had mistaken Bit Fremd for Raine. They were unaware that she was

Garvin's kin, because she had been treated like any other cowman, did the work of one and was given no special favors.

Roy didn't like to fail. It didn't sit well with him - never had. Now he'd have to return to New Jersey to Jean and the children and have to listen to his mother-in-law's tireless tirade about how wonderful her husband Luther had been, how he was always home every single night and didn't find it necessary to go traipsing all over the country looking for runaways and goodness knows what all. He loved his Jean but he had truly looked forward to his away time ever since Mother Lola had to move in with them.

He took the train to Fernandina but didn't have to decide whether to return to New Jersey or not, for while he was at the train station he struck up a conversation with a man who represented the Cedar Key Lumber Co. and was on his way back home for the holidays.

He began telling Roy about Cedar Key and what a delightful town it was. In their conversation Roy nonchalantly asked about schools and churches and said that he'd like to get away from the city, Newark being just too big for raising children. The man got real excited and proceeded to tell him how pleased he and his wife were with their church, and the new school teacher was the best one his children had ever had. When he spoke of her a light went on in Roy's head.

"I've found her!" he exclaimed aloud.

"What did you say, sir?"

"Oh, I mean that I think I've found the perfect place for me and my family to settle. I've been looking for one for a long time. Thank you so much. I think I'll just change my ticket and go have a look-see at Cedar Key before returning north.

****

Raine was standing beside the north window of the school house. She had written the assignment on the blackboard for the older students and was assisting the younger ones with their spelling. "That's very nice, Willy. Your writing has improved immensely."

She saw the man approach. He had on a brown suit and was wearing a brown derby. To herself she reacted but did not dare speak. She began shaking. He's here! I'm sure of it. I knew they'd send someone for me, but I'll not go back. I'll not!

When Roy Kenton departed the primitive train in Cedar Key he was sore from head to toe. The jerks and jolts left him bruised all over. Never had he had such a ride. After they had left Gainesville, they came into hilly limestone country with open forests and stands of cypress hammocks. Then the fragile looking trestle appeared and stretched across the islands from the mainland to the Gulf terminus in town. The coquina buildings and shell streets reminded him of an old Spanish seaport. But he had more on his mind than sight seeing.

He said his adieus to Lester Hatton and again thanked him for his assistance. He was glad to be rid of the man, who talked incessantly all the way from Fernandina. To himself he declared that had to have been the worst trip he'd ever taken. The small train was on its last legs and should have been confined to hauling lumber - wasn't fit for people. He was also hot and sore from sitting for so long but was positive the miserable trip would be well worth every bruise.

Roy went by his instincts as well as his training. They had never let him down. He took pride in both. He wanted to return to Newark with good news. He could hardly wait to see Mother Lola's surprise when he proudly told them that he had cracked the case and returned the senator's runaway daughter to her grateful family. That should shut her up for a while.

Charles and Lois Echols ran as good a store as could be found anywhere. They'd been in Cedar Key since before the War, could boast of having sold provisions to Senator David Levy Yulee, for whom the county was named, had five children and raised them right in Levy County. When the stranger walked in he removed his derby and asked right away about the new school teacher. They could tell that he wasn't a drummer, and he certainly wasn't a sportsman wanting provisions or inquiring about a sailing vessel and guide. He was bad news.

Charles looked at Lois and they both became suspicious. "You must mean Miss Maggie, mister."

"If that indeed is her name, sir," Roy said confidently. "I have reason to believe that is not her name..."

"Well, I guess that her brother and sister ain't got their right names either..."

"Brother and sister!" he shouted.

"Yes, Jack works at the mill - keeps books." Lois shook her head at him, indicating that he was saying too much.

"How do you know that they're her brother and sister?"

"Begging your pardon, mister, but anyone with eyes can tell they're kin." Lois shook her head to confirm it.

Roy was truly upset. All this way for nothing. Now I'll be late getting home and will have to turn right around and come back to this Godforsaken state. But he decided to check out the school teacher, anyway.

All the way along the shell road he berated himself for his stupidity. Why didn't I ask that Hatton man more questions? As much as he talked, not one word did he say about her having a brother and sister. Not a blasted word!

Lester was anxious to get home, but first he had to get to the office of the Cedar Key Lumber Co., usually referred to as the Mill. It was the remaining cedar mill on Way Key. He waved to the men in the tin shed and opened the office door. Poke looked up from the ledger he was working on, rose and shook Lester's hand, took the invoices from him and said, "I'm sure Christine will be glad to see you, Lester. Every one of your kids has got chicken pox, and she is worn out."

Mr. Justice came out of his office and was laughing at Lester's expression. "You're in for it. She's worn to a frazzle. I even had to send Laurie over to help out. All six of 'em. Not gonna be too good a Christmas, I'm a'thinkin'."

They chatted for a while, then Lester said, "We might just have us a new neighbor. Met him at the Fernandina station and had such high praise for Cedar Key that he wanted to come for a look-see. He got real excited when I mentioned..."

"What'd he look like?" Poke asked quickly, not thinking. "I mean was he a fancy dude or a fisherman or what?" To himself he prayed that he didn't have a scar.

"You know, he never did say what line of work he was in, but he sure was interested in the school teacher."

"What on earth for?"

"Guess it's because he has kids of his own and he's wanting to leave New Jersey. Said that he'd heard that Florida schools ain't fitten for anyone. But I set him straight, and you know, he changed his ticket right then and there and came with me..."

"Mr. Justice, sir," Poke interrupted, "I need to run over to the school for a minute. Need to tell Maggie and Nellie that I'm not gonna be able to get home for supper. Gotta finish these books now that I got Lester's invoices."

"Course, Jack, course. Go right along."

When Poke left, Buford turned to Lester, "Best bookkeeper I ever had, Lester, the best. I sure hope I can keep him from going down to Tampa to be with that aunt of his."

When Poke approached the school he could see Maggie talking to the man outside on the steps. He wore a full mustache and was a large man, so he knew that it wasn't his pa. He was relieved to see that Maggie was smiling, but curious, he continued down Fourth Street.

Maggie saw him and waved. When he got to the top of the stoop she introduced him. Catherine Inez came out then and Maggie, with her arm around her shoulders, hugging her close.

"Jack, this is Mr. Roy Kenton from New Jersey. I was telling him about how nice it is here and that I hoped he and his wife would decide to move down. That would give us four more children in the elementary school," she said proudly.

"Nice to meet you, Mr. Kenton," he said, shaking Roy's hand firmly like Maggie had taught him. "I just came over to tell you that I'll not be coming home for supper. Lester got back from the main office, and I need to finish up the books so's the men can get paid tomorrow."

Nellie said enthusiastically, "I'll take him his supper, Maggie."

"No you won't, young lady," she winked at Roy. "She's got a good friend who lives next to the mill, Mr. Kenton, and she'd rather play then do her take-home work."

He laughed. "Children are all alike." Looking at the three of them he sighed and thought, my instincts certainly played a trick on me this go, but something's still not right, I'd swear on Mother Marie's Bible. Don't know what, but I'm not going to give up on this. I'll be back. Something doesn't fit.

Before he left for the terminal he stopped at the Echolses' store and inquired about available houses. When they asked him if he'd found out whether or not the Popes were the people he'd been seeking, he shook his head and said that they didn't appear to be, but they didn't like how he responded nor his expression.

Charles said, "Don't believe there's an available house in the whole town, Mister. Now, on the mainland there might be a few houses for rent, but then your children will hafta go to the school in Otter Creek, I'm believing."

Roy looked suspiciously at the two of them and said, "Well, I do thank you for your help. Could you tell me when the next train leaves for Fernandina?"

"Won't be one going back 'til tomorrow morning.."

"Not til tomorrow?" he shouted. Underneath his breath he said, "Hick town! Nothing but a lousy hick town!"

Charles and Lois stood on the front porch of the store and smiled at the disgruntled man, who was mumbling all the way down the sidewalk. "Backward! Everyone in the whole town is backward!"

Roy went to the hotel across the street and inquired about a room. When he was told that it and every hotel on Way Key were filled up, he almost exploded. "Hafta get your rooms in advance this time of year. Always filled up with northern fishermen and hunters," Janet Backs informed the red-faced gentleman.

She had a difficult time keeping a straight face. Unknown to Roy, when he was visiting Maggie at the school house, Lois Echols went across the street to tell Janet that there was a stranger in town asking all about Miss Maggie, and she and Charlie didn't like the looks of the Yankee. So when he asked about a room Janet was ready for him.

"My husband has to go to the mainland, and if you'd like he could give you a lift in his boat. Has plenty of room, and you probably can get a room at the Boseman Hotel."

Roy knew he'd been had. One horse town with every room filled, indeed. I'll be back, old woman. You don't treat a Pinkerton Detective like this and get away with it.

He tried to engage Bill Backs in conversation all the way to the mainland but got only a few throat clearings and one-word replies. But when he tried to pay him for the trip, Bill spoke up very clearly and in a polished manner. "Was no bother at all, Mr. Kenton. Have a nice trip back to Newark. It's an interesting city. Good day to you, sir."

That did it! How did he know that I was from Newark? And now that I'm leaving they behave almost civilized. He had to admit that the school teacher didn't look a bit like the picture the Williamses had shown him. This girl was dark skinned like her brother and sister. There - they've even got me believing that they're kin. Well, I'll have to admit that the three of them do resemble each other, even have the same smile. But something doesn't hold true, and I'll not rest 'til I find out what. Think they can pull this on a Pinkerton...not today and not tomorrow, they can't.

Raine was sure he was a detective but hoped that they had convinced him they were who they said they were. But she was afraid that they hadn't. After all, her father wouldn't have hired just any detective - he would have hired the very best. Four more months of school. Can we take a chance on staying that long? All we'd need now is for Jack's pa to show up. But probably not for a while. The last letter from his aunt indicated that she thought he'd gone to Arcadia and was working the phosphate mines along the Peace River. Maybe he was the one who hired the detective and not Father.

She watched Nellie doing her school work. She was bright and loved to read and write and had been able to master second grade numbers. Raine was so proud of her. Nellie looked up and said, "Maggie, do you think Pa sent that man to fetch us? Do you?"

"I'm not sure, Honey, I'm just not sure. But he wasn't who he said he was. I'm positive and so are the Echols es." Raine decided to tell Nellie what they had told her. "They said that he seemed very suspicious to them, so they told Mrs. Backs at the hotel..." Raine started to laugh.

"What's so funny?"

"Mrs. Backs told him that they didn't have a room, that all the rooms in town were taken. Imagine! Mrs. Echols said that they couldn't afford to loose such a good school teacher and bookkeeper, so Mrs. Backs had her husband take him to the mainland to get rid of him." By now Raine was hysterical, bending over with laughter.

"I still don't see what's so funny, Maggie."

"Oh, Nellie, don't you see? They think that he was here to cause us harm, so they were protecting us. When in truth he was partially right about our or, at least, my identity, and they believe us and not that uppity Yankee. Oh what a farce! I don't know when I've had such a good laugh. It's like a Shakespearean play, or an operetta by Gilbert and Sullivan..."

"Well, I don't think it's funny one whit. I'm afraid Pa sent him, and he's gonna make Poke and me go back and..." She began to cry.

"Don't, Honey. Now don't cry." She pulled the sobbing child to her, brushed her long hair from her brow and thought, I wish I could tell you that it was my folks looking for me, but I can't.

"Nellie, I'm sure that your pa didn't send him. The people in Cedar Key are very suspicious about strangers. Remember how they acted when we first got here? Took them a little while to get used to us, remember?"

"I still bet Pa sent him! I bet he did!" She jumped up, hugged Raine around her knees and continued to sob uncontrollably.

When they heard the footsteps on the front stoop, they thought that it was Poke coming home for his supper. Probably finished up early, Raine thought. When she opened the door she was staring right at a stooped man with a dark red scar down his face

CHAPTER II ATHEA MANOR

Athea Manor was ablaze with lights. Juanita had managed to plan a party for Tucker Williams after all, and although it was less than five months since Conner's death, the townspeople had not faulted her for it. Tucker had assured his parents that he'd be in South Spring for Christmas and New Years and that he'd leave the day following the party.

Juanita checked the last-minute details. The tall fir tree in the corner of the parlor was glowing with tiny candles, and Rose had helped her make and attach hundreds of gold and royal blue velvet rosettes. Granny Todd had made an angel for the top of the tree, and everyone said how it looked like Juanita with its long, white-blond curls and lace and blue velvet gown.

The highlight of the evening would be when Delia Rose placed the angel on top, and Young Nolan was having his usual younger brother fit about how she was always the one who got to do it. Why couldn't he have a turn? Finally, Juanita just gave up and turned him over to Harrison to deal with. They ended up in the kitchen with Easter's stuffing him with leftover batter from the sugar cookies and allowing him to eat the tree and star shaped cookies that had got too brown or had crumbled.

"Now dat's 'nuff, Young Nolan. Ya gonna be sick. Harrison bes' take ya to de side yard fer more wood. We gonna have us a cold snap sure as shootin'. Get me some fat wood, Honey. Gonna be needin' dis ol' stove goin' all de night long - Unhuh, all de night long."

"Come on, Nolan," Harrison said. "Easter's right as usual. You see those clouds and that grey sky? A sure sign that the wind is coming down from Canada, and we'll have ourselves a true nor'easter. I just hope it'll hold off until after your mama's party."

"You suppose that's my Da telling us not to have that old party, Harrison? You suppose?"

"What ever gave you such an idea as that, Nolan? Have you been hanging around those quarters again? Have you?"

Harrison knew even as he asked that Young Nolan had been listening to Brewster and his young son Dusk. He was named that because his mama Light had been taught that you named your baby after the first thing you saw when it was born.

Juanita had specifically asked Harrison and Easter to keep Nolan away from their quarters, because they filled his head with all their crazy superstitions. But Nolan being Nolan sneaked over every chance he got and would sit, mesmerized, listening to them tell their tales about how the dead paid visits to earth. Sometimes the dead would visit during small storms, but mostly they liked to come when there was lots of lightning and thunder, but the most favorite time of all to come calling on the living was during nor'easters.

The day would begin sunny and clear, just to throw you off, then quickly, before the living folks could send up any prayers, that old cold wind came a howling, and before they could say *Moses in de rushes* the crops would be blacker than smut. They cited incident after incident, and Nolan believed every word they said. He did have trouble figuring out how Dusk could have witnessed all this death and destruction when Dusk was a whole year younger than he was.

Seemed to Nolan that his da wasn't trying very hard to talk to him 'cause whenever there was a storm he'd pay real close attention. He listened intently to every single rumble of thunder. But he never heard him, not even a whisper. One night he thought he did, but it turned out to be his mama closing his window and saying," Shhhh, son, shhh". He'd just about given up on his da paying him a visit.

While he and Harrison were gathering wood for the six fireplaces in the main house, he looked at the storm clouds gathering over the barn, and his heart seemed to tighten in his slight chest. He knew that tonight would be the night his da talked to him. He just knew.

The buggies began arriving with the guests. Brewster and Dusk and Melvia's husband Willem unhitched the rigs and got the horses in the stable. Harrison had told Juanita that if they had had a telephone like Mr. Lloyd she could have canceled the party, but then Easter reminded him that Mr. Lloyd's telephone went only from his store to his sawmill two miles away, and unless Miss Conner had invited Mr. Lloyd's kin or help it wouldn't have done her one speck of good to telephone 'em. Besides, Easter didn't hold with that new contraption, stating that she thought it was sure 'nuff the work of the Devil himself.

Harrison replied, "Well, sweet Easter, you might as well get used to the idea because they're already talking about putting in a line in Monticello, and I know Cherie will be one of the first to sign up for one, if not the first."

"Dat don' mean Ah gotta talk on it. Miss Conner can jes teach Melvia how. Ah ain't a goin' to, Harrison. Ah ain't!"

He thought, I just bet your curiosity will win you over sweet Easter, but he was wise enough to not say it.

By the time Rose and Seth arrived it was already chilly. Harrison met them, and Rose spoke up, "We'll be spending another night at Athea Manor, Harrison. Just look at that sky! Pewter gray it is."

"That won't be so bad, Aunt Rose. We can all bundle up like we did last year, remember?" Seth was remembering Juanita's and Conner's party last Christmas. Instead of a nor'easter putting a damper on it, Juanita and Conner turned it into the most talked-about party that Monticello had ever witnessed.

It got so cold that Conner put all the young men in Nolan's room and had Brewster and Dusk tell their ghost stories in front of the fire. Then in Delia's room he had Juanita tell the girls and ladies about their life on the steamship *Savannah*. About all the famous people she had met, presidents and their wives, Henry Flagler and Henry Plant and Hamilton Disston and famous actresses and actors. She described their dress and went into minute detail about the ladies' gowns. She gave samples of the famous menus and how festive it was in Savannah on St. Patrick's Day.

Conner and the older men gathered in Conner's study. He told tales of his life on the Mississippi and in New Orleans, and about his and Harrison's harrowing experiences in the War. It was in the wee hours of the morning before anyone fell asleep.

Easter and Harrison were still awake. "You bes keep dose fires a-goin', Honey, an' bank 'em when dey finally doze off. Now, if dat ain't a sight - all de highfaluttin' folks of Jefferson County all wrapped up on de flo' bundled up like dey is babies listenin' to de tales. Miss and Mistah Conner gonna be de laughin' stock of all de county..."

"Now, Honey, you know those people haven't had this much fun since they were wee ones."

They tiredly walked out the kitchen door and were pelted by the freezing rain. "Der goes de garden!" Easter lamented. "You have enough canned and pickled food to feed Napoleon's army, my sweet. Don't worry so. We'll replant."

He hugged her close to him, "Besides, this might be the last real cold spell we'll have for years - the very last."

The guests awakened to the smell of bacon and ham and rich coffee and to a sight every man, woman and child said they'd never seen, the sun coming up over the horizon painted its rosy glow on the ice edged pecan trees that lined the long driveway and two inches of snow spread like divinity icing on the swells of Athea's rolling grounds. The young men were up first. Yelling and laughing and even before eating breakfast they were outside in their party clothes making snow balls and frolicking like young children. Their breath puffed white smoke whenever they shouted at each other.

Delia and the girls soon joined them. Juanita said later that Delia's wardrobe was emptied in no time as the girls layered garment on top of garment. All the grown ups stood shivering on the balcony holding steaming cups of coffee, some laced with brandy, as they watched.

It was Conner who decided that they were having too much fun, so pulling Wylie after him he shouted to the others, "Come on! Let's not let them have all the fun. I haven't seen snow since I was in New York years ago and have never made a snowball. Come on! A man shouldn't go to his grave without making at least one snowball, huh, Wylie!"

"Conner O'Farrell!" Juanita exclaimed. "Why, act your age, for heaven's sake!" But when she could see what fun they were having, she and most of the ladies joined them. Only Leona Smart and her prissy daughter Charlotte remained inside simply because they had rather eat than play.

Easter stood just inside the large pantry between the kitchen and dining room watching them and thinking, I bes put on another ration o' bacon de way dose two ladies is shoveling it in. Now where's Melvia? She done been tol' to hep me. Dose white folks gonna be hongry as field hands after a day in de cotton. Humphhh! She bes git her fat self in here an' hep me!

Seth knew that this party wouldn't be anything like last year's, what with Conner gone and that Tucker Williams here. Even so, he was in a festive mood. Rose couldn't figure her son out. She knew how crazy he was about Delia, but she also knew that Delia couldn't think of him as a suitor. Wouldn't you think that he could sense it? But no, he just keeps on wishing and hanging around. I wish I could sit him down and talk some sense into him, but I just can't. She had even asked Harrison to talk to him, but he assured her that it would do no good, that Seth wouldn't listen to him any more than he would her. So they both watched and worried.

Nolan's room had been set aside for the young men as it had the year before. Nolan would spend the night with Harrison and Easter, something that he always looked forward to. When Seth entered Nolan's room he could see Tucker's trunk and small trap already there. John and Francis Taylor had arrived just before Seth and Rose, and since they came by horseback they were changing into their good suits for the party in Nolan's room.

"Looks like we're going to get to spend the night again this year, boys," Seth said with a laugh, playfully slapping Francis on the back.

"Guess these trunks belong to Delia's boyfriend, huh Seth?" John said stroking the rich brown leather of Tucker's trunk.

Seth quickly replied, "He's not really Delia's boyfriend, you know. He's just a friend of the family."

"Not by the way she looks at him, he isn't. She acts like he's syrup candy and she could eat him with a spoon. You're not jealous are you, Seth?" John teased him. Everyone in Monticello knew Seth Roberts was smitten by Delia O'Farrell.

Seth's face reddened. "What would it matter to me, anyway? I'm leaving this one horse town soon's the new century hits. Got only two more lousy weeks here, then I'm off to Tallahassee to work for a real newspaper. Got more girls there than you can count, John Taylor, more than you can count..." he mumbled as he left the room.

John said loud enough for Seth to hear, "Maybe you can't count 'em all because you're sweet on Delia."

Tucker laughed as he burst in the room. "You can say that again, for indeed I am sweet on her. I'm Tucker Williams, gentlemen." They shook hands formally and introduced themselves.

"Delia was just telling me about last year's shindig. What a delightful time they must have had! We had three inches of snow in Tallahassee and Raine even made a snowman. Imagine! A snowman in sunny Florida!"

He continued in such a self assured manner that John and Francis looked at each other as if to say, he's taken over. Poor Seth. "If Conner were here I'm sure he'd invite us into his study for a whiskey, gentlemen, but Harrison said that we can help ourselves. Want to join me? From the looks of that sky we'll have need of all the fuel we can handle, but not too much. Don't want to spoil my beloved's party, do we?"

"We certainly don't, Tucker. Miss Delia and her family are highly thought of in this part of the state."

"But of course they are. Now, why wouldn't they be? I've been told by a number of residents about how cultured and likeable a man Mr. O'Farrell was. Why, I was on the train coming from Virginia and sat next to a gentleman from Savannah who had known Mr. O'Farrell very well, and he said that he was undoubtedly the most polished man he'd ever met. Now, how's that for an endorsement of the father of the girl I hope to marry?"

John and Francis restrained themselves. Then John answered, "I think that's a fine endorsement, Tucker, but I'm sure that with Mr. O'Farrell barely in the grave you plan to postpone your declaration so's to protect Miss Delia's reputation. I mean..."

"But of course, John. I may call you John?"

"I am not offended, Tucker. We're not very formal in Jefferson County, just friendly country folks."

If Tucker had been more astute he would have known that they found him ostentatious and were having sport with him. Both boys were graduated with honors from Emory University in Georgia, and their father was one of the wealthiest and most influential men in the entire state. Tucker's overconfidence amused them.

"Then let us adjourn to the study, gentlemen."

They followed him down the stairway that Melvia and the quarters girls had spent the better part of the afternoon decorating. They'd made cedar, pine and magnolia leaf garlands, winding them around the pale magnolia banisters and hanging them above the wide double doors that led into the parlor and entry way.

Harrison had changed into his dark blue pants and starched white coat and was pouring the whiskey into the small gold rimmed glasses when they arrived. Seth, Morris Slocum and Gentry Oberhelman were standing in front of the marble fireplace. It was a handsome room. On the long, highly polished walnut desk inlaid with white oak, that Conner had designed and had made in Thomasville, there stood a tall ornate vase holding three palm fronds. It seemed out of place in such a handsome room.

Harrison saw Tucker glance at it and decided to let Delia's future husband in on her da's humor. "Mr. Conner always said that one should not forget his beginnings, that the lowly cabbage palm had been the best friend the Southern settlers had," he explained. Tucker raised his brow.

"I'm sorry that you did not have the opportunity to know Miss Delia's da. He was a unique human being. He often explained the palm as... forgive me, Mr. Williams, sir, as a good wench." Harrison laughed and continued, "She gives you shelter and warmth, a nice lap to sit on and food to satisfy your hunger..."

Tucker was obviously perplexed. Harrison explained further that the palm trunk and fronds were used for shelter, that it was a good source for firewood and thatch for a chair seat, and as you know, sir, heart of palm is enjoyed by the most discriminating connoisseurs. It's also called swamp cabbage, and when cooked with smoked meat and spices is quite delicious. It was also one of Mr. Conner's favorites and a dish that he introduced to many of his northern friends. This vase has sat on his desk ever since he had it made as a reminder." He laughed, "He named it Sophie."

"I had never thought of the palmetto in that vein, Harrison. May I use your analogy in future conversation? Interesting - very interesting," but he saw nothing humorous in what Harrison said.

Harrison thought, he's no match for Delia. Tall, yes, and handsome too, but no match. I just wish that Cherie could see it. I'm going to have to give this some serious thought. What would Conner do? How would he play this hand? Yes, I'll have to study this but must play the hand close, very close. Cherie musn't know. I no longer have Conner to aid me. I miss him so. So much of my life was attached to his, so much.

"Oh, I'm sorry, Seth. May I pour you another?" Harrison could tell that he'd have to dilute it. Seth was looking none too sober.

Pet Flannagan was seated at the Chickering baby grand piano in the front parlor, and her brother Timothy had brought his fiddle. Sarge Phillips had arrived late but in time to join them in playing for the dancing. His banjo was always appreciated. Harrison had supervised the moving of the furniture in the double parlors, placing the love seats and chairs along the damask covered walls. The double parlors were softly lit - Conner had refused to have the chandeliers electrified, saying that he preferred the soft glow of gas light.

Everyone enjoyed visiting Athea Manor. It was by far the handsomest plantation house in the area, they said. Conner had actually allowed Juanita to assist in the decorating. They had selected a soft jade damask for the walls, rich, royal blue velvet for the drapes and matching love seats. The oriental rugs were jade, deep blue and a soft rose on ecru. They selected rosewood and cherry tables, and Conner had sailed to New York City and conferred with Mr. Louis Tiffany himself, who designed the lamps and chandeliers for the parlors. Comfortable soft rose and deep blue floral wing-back chairs were placed beside the rose marble fireplaces with needlepoint covered footstools in front of them.

Easter, Melvia and two of the quarters girls were clearing the long dining table. The gold encrusted epergne with its crystal dishes filled with dates and toasted, salted pecans and matching candelabra had been placed in the center of the lace-covered table beneath the Waterford chandelier.

Louis Ferraud had driven out from town to supervise the cooking. He was the chef at the St. Elmo Hotel and had been a good friend of Conner's.

Easter and Melvia hadn't minded. Actually they were relieved, for neither had mastered the French pastries that Conner had appreciated.

Louis wrapped the asparagus spears that Melvia had canned with paper thin ham and a pungent mustard sauce in flaky pastries. They had surrounded the roast duck with orange sauce that Conner had taught Louis to make, stating that only Valencia oranges would do and to always add a dollop of Scotch whiskey. Sweet potato souffle with bits of citron, pineapple and raisins accompanied it.

Juanita had always insisted on having some basic dishes to satisfy the less educated palates. She had Easter roast a haunch of venison with browned new potatoes and scalloped onions, glazed carrots and, as always, a large pan of Easter's biscuits. Rum and pound cakes, pecan and sweet potato pies, mincemeat pastries with lemon sauce and ambrosia were for dessert. The O'Farrells set a good table.

The main meal had been served at 1:00 o'clock. Then the young ladies had retired to Delia's room. Melvia had the quarters girls place the pallets on the floor. Their brightly colored gowns for the festive holidays hung in profusion from the canopy above Delia's bed. Blankets and feather pillows had been taken from the linen chiffonier in the large closet off the pantry.

The giggles had long ago ceased. Everyone was napping peacefully, everyone except Delia. She couldn't relax enough to join them. She couldn't stop thinking about Tucker. He was so handsome and attentive, so cultured and mannered. Even the Taylor boys couldn't compare. She was trying to figure out how she and Tucker could be alone.

This miserably cold weather truly foiled her plans. Normally they would have gone horseback riding. Juanita had no reason to have Harrison accompany them. She had told Tucker when Delia was not present on his last visit that she knew that he was a gentleman and would respect Delia's youth and inexperience and the fact that her father was so recently deceased. Tucker said that he understood completely and that she was not to concern herself about Delia's welfare.

Juanita trusted him implicitly. It was Delia she didn't trust. She had good reason to suspect her daughter, for she was almost as headstrong as Juanita had been at the same age.

Delia twisted and turned but ever so slightly. She didn't want to awaken Adele. It'll be too blasted cold to even go on the terrace during the dancing, when everyone is so busy that they'll not miss us, she thought. If he doesn't kiss me on this visit I think I'll die. I'll just die! But where can we go to be alone? That brat Nolan will probably spy on us. I don't know why Mama lets him join in, he's such a baby. He needs to know how to act at a party, my eye! And if he's not watching us, Seth will be. I don't know why he thinks he has to protect me. He's worse than an older brother would ever be, honest he is. She flipped over and sighed mightily.

Her hands swiftly found her mouth to stave off the outburst. After everyone is asleep tonight...that's when. Maybe I can meet him in Da's study? No one would even think to go in there. That's it! That's exactly what I'll do, she yawned, stretched her long, slender arms and curled up on her side. But how can I suggest it without appearing brazen?

Her eyes fluttered, and as she drifted off she smiled and thought, I'll get my kiss tonight. Tonight's the night....

Seth joined in the dancing, even getting several dances with Delia. Her full, green moire taffeta skirt swirled around her. While Juanita and Rose were designing her dress Juanita had said , "She'll not be wearing black, Rose. She's too young to have to wear black. There's not a thinking woman in all of Jefferson County who would insist on her daughter wearing black, and you know it. It's a stupid custom...out of respect, my eye!"

"Juanita, calm down! Everyone in this town respects you and certainly did Conner, and they understand that our young ladies shouldn't be punished just because they've lost dear ones. Heavens, with the typhoid and yellow fever taking so many lives our ladies would be wearing nothing but black like they do in Europe. Now, you know that!"

"I hadn't thought of it that way, but you're absolutely correct. What would I do without you, my dear friend?"

Seth wasn't drunk, but even he knew that he'd had a wee bit too much, enough to become upset when Tucker whirled Delia around and around the room. They were a handsome couple when they danced, even he admitted and all the older ladies remarked. They were remembering their youth and their special dances with their special young men. Memories flowed and their comments got under Seth's skin. "They're such a lovely couple, Mrs. O'Farrell, both so tall, he so fair and Delia just like dear Mr. O'Farrell" ...or, "Why, Mrs. O'Farrell, I know that it's so near Mr. O'Farrell's passing, but do you believe that Monticello might be having a special occasion, perhaps a wedding, that we could look forward to, say, before the year's end?" and they giggled nervously.

All this whispering about Delia and Tucker behind their lace fans irritated Seth. But Juanita smiled sweetly and answered, "Delia's da had insisted that she have a good education, and I for one think that he was wise in his reasoning. She'll be going to Miss Baldwin's in Virginia next fall, you know. But I believe you're correct in your observation, dear Gladys. The bloom of young love is certainly evident at Athea Manor, isn't it?"

Seth opened the door to Conner's study. Harrison was clearing the room of cigar butts and preparing the tray of glasses to take to the kitchen. "You need hep, Harr..i.. here, let me hep ya.."

"Don't think so, Seth," he laughed. "Think Miss Cherie would have both our heads if you dropped this tray of Conner's Waterford glasses. You're none too steady on your feet, you know."

"Hell, Harri..'m fine," he slurred.

"Fine, perhaps, but certainly not sober, my friend. A few minutes out in this freezing weather will help clear your head, or I could bring you some strong coffee. What do you...?"

Seth left for the back hall even as he spoke. "Think I'll just go for a little walk, Harri..think I will..." He circled the house, pounding his hands together to warm them, then blowing on them. "Won't be anything left in this whole county if it gets any colder...not a... a goddam thing."

He could hear the music and began humming, dancing round and round. God, he was cold. He put his arms out to pretend that Delia was in them. He stumbled, laughed, then around and around he went hanging on to the pillars as he whirled, the brick piazza hard under his boots. He found himself outside the parlor doors. The heavy drapes had been drawn, and although he couldn't see inside, he knew that Delia, his Delia, was there dancing with that Tucker Williams.

Suddenly he was freezing, teeth chattering, having trouble getting his breath. He rushed around behind the house into the hall and burst into the study - it was empty - only silence, the crackling fire and Conner's bar. His hand trembled as he poured a large whiskey. Not wanting to leave the fire and wishing to be alone he turned out the lamp on Conner's desk and stood in partial darkness.

I've got to get my life together. I'll lose her if I'm not worthy. How can I win her when I don't have his..his polish, his wealth? He eased into the wing-back chair he had pulled up close to the fire, and his boots soon found the leather footstool. His arm holding the whiskey soon relaxed and the empty glass rolled onto the carpet as he eased into a sound sleep.

"Shhhh, Delia, you'll awaken your mother. Now, we wouldn't want that would we?" Tucker whispered pulling her into the study.

"Indeed, we wouldn't." The house was dead still. Only the hissing of the fire invaded the quiet. Delia and Tucker had made arrangements for their rendezvous before their last dance. It had been so simple she couldn't believe how it had happened. Taylor had walked her to the punch table after their waltz. They were good friends and had been ever since Delia had begun school at the Jefferson Academy in Monticello. Tucker was engaged in light conversation with Margaret Powell, but his eyes never left Delia. When Delia and Taylor approached, Tucker extended his arm and Delia was quickly beside him.

"May I offer you some punch, Miss Delia?"

"Why, Mr. Williams, that would be lovely, thank you."

She laughed as she continued, "I'm going to sit out the next waltz. I'm delightfully exhausted," and she was. She hadn't missed a dance since the music began.

"If I may, I'd be pleased to accompany you," Tucker quickly added. He offered her his arm and they went to the other parlor and sought the most isolated corner. They began speaking at the same time, and that evoked nervous laughter.

"You were mentioning the weather, Delia," Tucker said. They spoke informally when they were alone.

"Yes, Harrison said that the fires would have to be kept going all night long. My, we'll barely be retired when the servants will tiptoe into our rooms to add more logs."

He looked longingly down at her, "Will that give us any alone time, Delia? I must leave tomorrow for South Spring." There was passion in his question.

"Da's study should be unoccupied, Tucker...Oh, I do hope that you didn't find that remark too bold..."

"Delia, you could never be anything but genteel, my sweet. Oh, Delia, I do long to hold you and tell you of my feelings..."

"No more than I..."

"When everyone is asleep, would it be too much to expect you to venture into your da's study?"

"Oh, Tucker...Oh...I'll be there."

He had taken her hand, raised it to his full, moist lips.

Delia knew that she'd never forget that moment, not if she lived to be as old as Methuselah...not if...

When she heard Margaret and Taylor laughing, she took her hand from Tucker's and smiled conspiratorily, her young breasts swelling with anticipation, shuddering in the dark green taffeta gown. He had never seen anyone as beautiful, not in all his twenty-one years. Funny, but he had known immediately that she was the one for him and didn't understand his parents' reluctance to accept his feelings as genuine. He rationalized that they thought it a passing fancy and that he needed to mature and to seriously embark on his political career. But he knew that his feelings for Delia were deeply entrenched. He knew that he would never again feel this way.

Conner's study was still cozy. Apparently Harrison had recently added a log, Delia thought. Neither one saw Seth asleep in the shadow of the chair in front of the fire. They sought the darkest corner. Delia was in his arms even before he pulled her down to the settee. Her pale wool wrapper was tight around her, she released the sash and his arms found her small waist, the flannel-lined, satin night dress was warm against her pale skin.

Tucker had removed his formal waist coat in Nolan's room and had only his ruffled shirt on over his trousers. He hoped that he hadn't awakened the Taylor brothers when he left and doubted that he had, because they both were breathing steadily. No one knew where Seth had gone, but John said that he'd been acting so strangely lately that he had probably driven the buggy back to town, even as cold as it was. He was so unpredictable.

When Tucker released Delia they both had trouble catching their breath. Delia broke the silence. "It's going to be forever before we see each other again..."

"I don't know if I can stand it, my sweet. I don't think I can..."

"Oh, Tucker, do you think that you could come to St. Joseph's for the May Day festivities? Do you?"

She sneezed. They laughed. He pulled her to him.

"Don't want you to catch your death, my pretty one. Let me warm you."

Her long slender hands soon found the warmth of his skin. She could feel his smooth back underneath her hands as she stroked him. He kissed her passionately - this time she kissed him back. She was burning all over. When he released her she clung to him, her raven hair was loosened and swirled around her. When she sneezed again and they laughed, they heard Seth stir and clear his throat.

Delia quickly tied her wrapper. They remained quiet, blending into the shadows. Seth rose, stoked the fire, then turned up the desk lamp. He turned and saw them. He said not a word, turned back to the door leading to the hall, and closed the door soundly. Grabbing his coat off the hall rack he walked slowly outside into the freezing, black night, thinking, I'm just not worthy of her. I'll never be worthy of Delia Rose - never - I've lost her.

****

It was as cold a morning as Seth had ever seen. He knew that Harrison would drive his Aunt Rose back into town to the shop, and he wanted to be gone by the time they arrived. He was sure that they'd be late. After all, who in his right mind would be out early on a day like this even if it was Monday and a short time before Christmas. He was already packed and had written a note telling Rose that he'd decided to leave for Tallahassee earlier than expected and that he'd let her hear from him when he got settled.

He went to the bank and withdrew his savings, explaining to Mr. Tewksbury that he had a good job offer with the *Tallahassee Democrat*. Then he went to the *Tribune*'s office. He wasn't looking forward to his encounter with Mr. Arnett but had decided to tell him that he'd not expect his last week's pay since he was leaving on such short notice. That should placate old Bonehead, and Seth hoped it would secure a good reference out of him as well.

Mr. Arnett had been visibly and vocally upset, but as Seth had suspected when he said that he'd not expect pay due him, Mr. Arnett calmed down and wrote Seth the needed letter of reference. Next, he went to the train depot and bought his ticket for Tallahassee. It wasn't until he was almost to Tallahassee that he changed his mind. I'll be too near Tucker Williams in Tallahassee. I want to get as far away as I can.

When the train arrived in Tallahassee, Seth went to the ticket counter, looked at the map posted on the wall and decided on the spot to head for unknown territory. He knew he'd have to go to a sizable town, one that had a newspaper. He didn't want to go to Jacksonville or even Tampa, but to a small town where he would have a future. Since Henry Plant had opened the western part of the state with his railroad line, he decided that the town of Bartow looked like a good prospect. And if he couldn't find work there he could go on to Arcadia in De Soto county or farther on the line to Punta Gorda or Charlotte. He liked the idea of being near the Gulf. He'd heard about it so often from Juanita and his Aunt Rose.

He sat on the wooden bench and gazed out the window. The pine forests were thick, mile after mile - sameness. I wonder if Delia will be upset when she finds out I've left. Heck, she'll probably not miss me even one little bit.

"I'm sure he saw us, Tucker," Delia lamented.

"My darling, if he saw us, I'm just as sure that he'd have acknowledged it."

"You know Seth. Why, he's just like a big brother to me, protecting me from as far back as I can remember. No, he saw us all right, but I'm not sure that he'll tell on us. He's become so peculiar lately. Why, I've caught him looking at me in the strangest way..."

"How do you mean?"

"I don't know how to describe it exactly. He's just different, that's all. I'd better slip up to my room. Oh, Tucker, these next few months will be an eternity."

He pulled her to him, his lips finding her welcome ones instantly. She shivered.

"I'll try to stop by on my way back to school, my darling. It'll be only a few weeks..."

"But then we'll be apart until May. I don't think I can bear it - I don't..."

She didn't have a chance to finish. She heard Drucie and Marva coming downstairs to add another log. Quickly she pulled Tucker into the shadow of the study and pushed the door to. Her ear was pressed against the door. She heard the girls talking as they went toward the back parlor. She kissed his cheek and tiptoed up the stairs. He soon followed.

Delia slipped underneath the down comforter and curled up. As she lay quietly, Seth's expression kept interfering with her reverie. His face was the last thing she saw, then Drucie shook her saying, "Miss Delia, yore guests is all done had breffus an' is gittin' ready to leave. Yore mama done sen' me fer ta fetch ya."

Delia thought of Seth. "Has Mister Seth got up yet, Drucie?"

"Up! Why he done lef 'fore fust light. Harrison said he take Miss Rose's buggy and dat Willem gonna hafta drive Miss Rose to de shop."

Delia smiled. He didn't tell on me. Thanks, Seth. When Drucie got to the linen closet, she told Marva, "Miss Delia's sho up to somethin'. She up in her big bed grinnin' jes lak a chessie cat, she is. You bes go tell Easter. She up to somethin'.

Rose's hand shook as she read the note from Seth. As Seth had suspected, she was late in arriving back to town. Harrison had not accompanied her, because Juanita wanted him to drive Tucker to the train station early in the afternoon and bring back some supplies from town. She couldn't believe that eighteen people could have consumed so much food.

It was too cold for Melvia to supervise the washing, but Juanita had her, Drucie and Marva strip the beds, anyway. It would appear that the Willingham girls and their mother would remain at Athea Manor for another day. What on earth will I do with those three for an entire day, Juanita wondered. When the Lord doled out dull, they must have got in line twice, I declare they did. She laughed when she thought it. That was a favorite saying of Easter's. Everyone else has gone home, thank goodness. She was tired and she missed Conner so. He would have enjoyed the party so much..I musn't cry...I musn't...

Rose sat down on the channel-back chair in their upstairs living quarters. Why am I so upset? I knew he'd be leaving. He simply can't stand to see Delia with Tucker. He's been threatening to leave for so long, but it's still not easy on me. I can't for the life of me understand why he won't try to make a life for himself right here. Running away won't help one bit - not a bit.

She rose when the tinkling bell rang downstairs announcing a customer. It was that nosy Charlotte Reynolds. Bet she already knows that Seth's gone, and she's here to ask a million questions. "Why, Charlotte, out on such a raw day? My, my. What would you be needing, dear?" Rose and Charlotte had worked on the church raffles and had become well acquainted. She was a tireless worker, but Rose still didn't like or trust her.

"Wanted to get an early start, Rose, and had no idea that you would've already returned from Athea Manor this early, but when I went to the bank for Sydney, Mr. Tewksbury said that Seth had been there, took out all his savings and was headed for Tallahassee to join the *Democrat*. Well, I knew how pleased you'd be and..."

"No, Charlotte, I am not pleased. I'm surprised that you of all people would think that I'd be pleased. He had a perfectly good job right here with..."

"But, my dear, the *Democrat*!" Rose could see her drooling with excitement. She decided to give her some more gossip to spread, and was sure that it'd be all over Jefferson County by afternoon.

"Now, Charlotte, you know that Seth is like a son to me - you know that - and yes, I'm excited and pleased that he'll have more opportunity with the *Democrat*. But," she brushed away her tears, "I'll miss him so, and Delia, well my dear, Delia will be beside herself. Surely you know how much they care for..."

"You don't mean that Delia O'Farrell and Seth are ...well, you know what I mean...that they're..."

"Well, I thought that all of Monticello knew. Oh, she'll be beside herself. He didn't even say when he'd return. The young are so unpredictable these days, aren't they? Seeking his fortune, indeed!"

"I never even suspected..." Charlotte said while pulling her gloves on and hurriedly wrapping her heavy wool shawl securely around her. Out the door she went mumbling all the way down Jefferson St. Rose watched her. Aloud she said, "That's my parting gift to you, my son. The entire town will think that your Delia will be beside herself, that she'll be devastated because you are off seeking your fortune. Oh, Seth..." she rushed upstairs, threw herself on her bed and sobbed.

CHAPTER III ENCOUNTERS

It's their pa! Raine almost said aloud. She found that she couldn't take her eyes off the pathetic looking man before her. She had shoved Catherine Inez behind her and said, "What can I do for you, sir?"

Mac mumbled unintelligible sounds and knew by her perplexed expression that she didn't understand him. Then he began using his hands pointing to his mouth, then his head and took out a broken pencil and torn piece of paper.

Raine interrupted, "I'm very sorry, sir, but I believe that you have the wrong house. You must need to see someone else."

But Mac insisted on writing his message. He placed the paper against the rough boards on the side of the house, Catherine Inez pushed around Raine's skirt and almost died on the spot. She gulped, wiped her tears and her runny nose using her apron hem and dug deeper into Raine's full checked gingham skirt. When Raine took the piece of paper she could barely make out the scribble. She read, *boy and girl - runaway.*

"I really cannot help you, I'm so sorry. I know of no runaways in Cedar Key. I'm sure that the Echolses at the general store over on "G" Street will probably tell you the very same thing. They've lived here for a very long time. I and my sister and brother have been here for only a few months, and we're on our way to Tampa to live with our aunt because we lost our parents to yellow fever. I'm sorry I cannot be of more help.

She closed the door and secured the latch. She shoved Catherine away from her as she ran to the window to see if he was leaving. She saw him walk slowly, turn around and look at the house, then reluctantly head toward the docks. At least she hoped that was where he was going.

"Don't say a word, Nellie, not a word. We've got to get word to Jack. Right now! But how? Don't you dare start crying. I've got to think." She sat down hard on the bed.

It came to her like a flash. She jumped up. "I know! I'm going to walk over to Isabel's the back way and tell her that I'm sure that you and Jack are coming down with the pox, and that I think it best that you be quarantined, keeping my eye out for your pa just in case he tries to follow me. On my way back I'll go to the mill to tell Jack. But instead of returning to work he can stay here with you. I'll tell Mr. Justice that I'm sure you'll be all right but that you'll have to stay in the cabin until you're well. I'm sure he'll understand."

"But who's gonna take your place at school?"

"Stop your sniffling, Nellie. Margie Schueler can take my place for a few days. It'll work out, I'm sure. Now, do just as I say. Do not open the door to anyone - I mean anyone - I'll not be long. Nellie, stop I say! You must be brave. Remember Paul Revere and how brave he was. I'll be back in a wink," and out the door she ran, looking right and left as she rounded the corner.

Nellie latched the door, but afraid that it was not secure enough, she managed to push the heaviest table in front of it. There were only two windows in the room but hot as it was she removed the wooden prop and closed and latched the one facing the front of the house. Then she walked the few feet to the other window over the kitchen table. She could see Maggie's skirt in the distance but she also saw her pa crouched down in back of the salt barrels behind Meases' house.

"Ohhhh," she moaned. "I've gotta warn Poke, but how? Pa'll see me sure as shootin'! Maybe if I climb out of the other window and run around behind Caruthers' I can get to Poke to warn him. Ohhhh!"

She took one more look and her pa was gone. She knew that he'd be following Maggie to Isabel's, at least she hoped so and that she could get to Poke before they did.

Maggie was out of breath by the time she arrived at Isabel's. As she had hoped, Isabel was home. "You're not to worry about a thing. I'll talk to Margie about taking your classes, and if need be I'll take care of little Hiram for her. I understand your concern, Maggie, especially since you lost both your parents not long ago. It's all right to feel this protective of Jack and Nellie, really it is."

"You're a dear friend, Isabel Smith. The best I've ever had." She hugged her and turned to leave.

"Don't worry about cooking, Maggie. I'll see to it that you have plenty." She laughed. "But I'll have Lottie do the cooking. I don't want you to worry about a thing." Isabel hated to cook almost as much as Maggie.

When Maggie got to the mill she was surprised that Jack had already left, then when James Arthur told her that Nellie had come running around to the back of the shed and had him fetch Jack and that Jack had told Mr. Justice that there was an emergency at home and he and Nellie left near 'bout running...

First Maggie was shocked, then worried. She thanked James Arthur and left in a hurry. He stood inside the shed and watched her, shaking his head curiously, then he saw the crippled man with the long scar follow her. He turned to Roscoe and asked, "Who in the world's that? You ever see him before? Don't like the looks of this, Roscoe. Here, you finish this. I'm just gonna see what he's up to."

Maggie couldn't believe that Nellie would disobey her. Just wait 'til I get hold of her. Just you wait, Nellie Pope! She had truly begun to think of them as her real brother and sister.

Mac hobbled along the sand and shell path hanging close to the weeds that bordered it. If that Miss thinks she's foolin' Mac she's got another think comin', he thought. She's hidin' something for sure. I can spot a liar ten mile off. Her pretendin' she don't understand me - not so! He didn't see James Arthur, who was no more than thirty feet behind him.

When Maggie got to the cabin she knocked and called, "Nellie, you let me in, you hear - this minute, I said."

Catherine with Poke right behind her lifted the latch, shoved Maggie away from the door and quickly latched the door behind her.

"What the...!"

"He followed you, Maggie! I saw him!"

"You're sure"

"Yes, I'm sure! I watched him out the kitchen window, then I climbed out the front window and ran to the mill to warn Poke. He knows we're here...I know it..."

"Nellie, come here, Honey," Maggie said stroking the tears from her face, soothing her with, "He's not going to get anywhere near you."

She was interrupted by Jack. "Here he comes, oh Lordie, Maggie. Who's that following him? It's James Arthur. Now, why's he doing that?" Poke was peaking through the knothole beside the kitchen window. Maggie shoved him away so she could have a look but couldn't see anyone.

"I don't see..."

Just then Mac got up from the clump of weeds and on his hands and knees scooted to the other side. She saw James Arthur do the same.

"Jack, James Arthur knows we're in trouble. I'm going to go down the path and drop him a note..."

"No, Maggie, don't! There's no tellin' what Pa'll do!"

"But he doesn't know that you're here. There's no way that he can..."

"But he must or why's he crouched down there looking at us!"

"He might suspect that I wasn't telling him all I know and wants to have a look at my brother and sister so he can satisfy himself. Maybe that's all..."

"I'm not thinking that it's a good idea for you to go out there, I'm really not! You don't know Pa!"

Maggie ignored his protestations and got a piece of paper and wrote the note to James Arthur. *This old man is bothering us. Please get help. Maggie*

She folded it and put it in her skirt pocket, pulled on her bonnet and said, "I'm going to pretend to not see your pa, walk on past him and then drop James Arthur the note. He'll know to get the law. What can your pa do to harm me? Surely he's not stupid enough to attack me..."

"Take this just in case," Poke begged. "It's got a good sharp edge on it," he said handing her his pocket knife.

"Jack, for Heaven's sake! Now what on earth would I do with it?"

She would soon find out.

Mac saw Maggie come out onto the stoop. What's she coming back out fer? Maybe I'd jes best be asking her. When Maggie got to where Mac was crouched he suddenly stood up. She knew where he was hiding but he startled her nonetheless.

"Oh, you startled me, sir!" she yelped. Poke was watching through the knothole.

"What's happening, Poke? Is he still there?"

"Shush, Catherine Inez! Shush!"

Maggie tried to compose herself, but Mac could see that she was afraid. He liked that. He wanted to see the young miss sweat. Did she think he was stupid? Did she?

Maggie knew James Arthur was just a short distance away but even so, she had to admit that she was frightened.

"As I told you before, I don't know anything about..."

He began walking the few steps toward her. He was smirking. Her hand soon reached for the comfort of the knife in her pocket.

"What do you want of me?" she shouted, backing up. When she tripped on the tree root and stumbled, Mac grinned, and she saw his arm reach for her.

"I said..." she started fumbling with the knife, trying to open it, then heard a grunt. Mac went sprawling in front of her. James Arthur, who was not a large man and certainly no match for the wily Mac Milligan, crippled though he was, was soon on his back, spitting shell and sand.

Maggie yelled, "You let him up this minute, for if you don't, you're going to feel this steel between your shoulder blades, mister. I said let him up!"

Mac rolled off him. He could see the fire and anger in her eyes. He sat there grinning and making signs in the air pretending to not understand her.

"James Arthur, I think it's time to get the law. This man has been harassing me, claiming that I know something about some runaway children. I want the sheriff to make sure that he's out of Cedar Key before nightfall and to give him strict orders that he is not to return. Do you hear, James Arthur?"

He nodded that he did. By then Mr. Justice and two of the mill workers came running toward them inquiring about her health and muttering that they'd see to it that the low scum was on the mainland and out of the county. He wasn't going to be the cause of their losing their school teacher, not today and not tomorrow.

Maggie, was obviously shaken by the incident. Mr. Justice wanted Roscoe to escort her home, but she thanked them and said that she just needed to rest. She turned back toward the cabin. When she got inside she sat down on the edge of the bed and stared straight ahead. Catherine and Poke sat beside her, each holding one of her hands and patting it.

"We've got to leave," Maggie said sadly. "First, the detective, for I'm sure he was, and now your pa. We've got to leave Cedar Key first thing in the morning. I'll go see Isabel to tell her that you didn't have the pox after all, but that I heard from our aunt in Tampa and that she insists that we go immediately, because she's not well and needs us. That's what I'll tell her."

"But, Pa'll follow us! I know it. Everyone in town thinks we got an aunt in Tampa..."

"But, where can we go if not Tampa? Where?"

Poke thought a minute then answered, "We can go to Arcadia. Pa's already been there and stayed a few months working the Bone Valley Phosphate Works, where my friend works - you know, on the Peace. Aunt Mums wrote me and said so. He'll not be returning there, I'm sure."

"Then that's that! Maggie said jubilantly, her recent fright already a memory.

The entire time Maggie packed she was trying to get everything straight in her mind. She knew that Jay's folks' ranch was near Arcadia. He was her half sister SuSu's husband. But his parents had only seen her once, and that was at Susu's and Jay's wedding. Come to think of it, they're both dead, and SuSu and Jay rarely visit the ranch. I just hope that

Jay's nephew Meade will still be in school, for he'd be sure to recognize me. After all, he visited us in Tallahassee just last summer. Oh well, I'll just cross that bridge when I come to it, she declared silently.

"Jack, I've decided our course. Now, you two listen. I'll go back over to Isabel's and tell her that you do not have the pox as I suspected, and that we've had the letter from our aunt, and that I plan to go to the city hall and ask for a reference first thing in the morning. Isabel has already got Margie to teach school, so I don't feel like I'm letting them down." She caught her breath. "If there's no teaching position open in Arcadia, perhaps there will be one in another town close by," she continued.

"He'll not stop looking for us until he finds us...not Pa." he said quietly, not really listening to her.

Catherine looked up at Maggie, "Would you have stuck Pa with the knife? Would you?"

Maggie thought a minute, sighed heavily, and said with conviction, "Yes. Yes, I would have stuck him just like I threatened. And if I need to in the future..." she gulped, "I'll do it."

She looked from one to the other, "You see, he needs killing. He's evil through and through, just like you said..."

"But the Bible says that it's a sin to kill, Maggie.." Poke protested.

"I know that, Jack, but it would be him against me and I simply can't allow him to harm either of you. Maybe I'll have to be the Lord's instrument. Isn't there something in the Bible about that?"

They looked at each other. Finally Poke said, "If Ma was here she'd be able to tell us, but I don't remember anything about it. Maybe we'd best ask the preacher before you go and get yourself in trouble with the Lord, Maggie. Maybe we'd best. I don't want Pa to be the cause of you getting in trouble. I don't think I could stand that."

She hugged them both to her and realized that she was the happiest she'd ever been. She smiled in amazement. Here I am just having been scared out of my wits, traipsing across the state with a crazy man chasing me, no job and no place to stay and having in my care two unfortunate children, and I'm happy. There must be something terribly wrong with you, Raine Williams..oops..Maggie Pope...terribly wrong.

****

It was Christmas eve when Seth pulled into the depot in Arcadia. He had first stopped in Bartow, a town of three thousand, thirty or so miles east of Tampa and a good fifty miles north of Arcadia. He visited the

Courier-Informant's newspaper office, and although Mr. Dixon was very nice, even having him out to his house for dinner, he had no opening at the paper.

He had recently purchased the paper from Mr. B.B. Tatum, who, like a lot of locals, had sold out and moved to Miami, purportedly the up and coming town on the Atlantic. Mr. Dixon suggested that Seth go on down to Arcadia to speak to Mr. John Jones, who owned the DeSoto Abstract Co. and also published the *DeSoto County News*. Seth was pleased by his interest, which he showed by writing a nice letter to Mr. Jones on Seth's behalf.

Before Seth left Bartow he found out why Mr. Dixon was so accommodating. He had three unwed daughters, very attractive and personable girls, and had Seth not been so in love with Delia, he probably would have considered keeping company with Betsy, who attended the Summerlin Institute right there in Bartow.

Mr. Dixon had suggested that he seek employment at the cigar factory part time and even invited him to stay with his family during the holidays, but Seth wanted to get on with his life. It would have been nice, for he wasn't happy to leave Bartow right at Christmas time.

He had been able to find a room at Mrs. Harkness's Boarding House for $3.00 a week including table fare for the week that he was in Bartow. It was a progressive town and in the '95 census was the thirteenth largest city in all of Florida with electric lights, some paved streets and an active social life. It even had the wonderful Biograph or, as some called it, a moving picture.

It was so different from Monticello! While he was there Mrs. Dixon, Flora, had an in-fair that consisted of a soiree with a music program and dramatization. And the girls had begged him to stay for their annual New Year's observance, when on New Year's Day the local gentlemen would don their most formal attire, including top hats, to pay their respects to the ladies of each household on their lists. Refreshments were served at each home, usually pound cake, eggnog and syllabub. When Seth advised them that he was so new in Bartow that he'd indeed have no one's name on his list, they quickly said that they could remedy that.

Horace, the oldest son, who was nineteen and attended the local South Florida Military and Educational Institute, founded by General E.M. Law, took Seth aside and said that he could accompany him. He had been very kind to Seth, taking him to the ice cream parlor on Main St. and Broadway, a favorite gathering place for the young people. Seth was surely tempted to stay.

When Mr. Dixon told Seth that Arcadia wasn't nearly as progressive as Bartow, not even having electric lights, but being the county seat it was bound to grow, he decided that he couldn't afford to not move on.

Seth walked the wooden sidewalk to the Young Hotel and wondered if he had made the right choice. Oh well, he declared to himself, while opening the heavy oak door that led into a large sitting room, I can always catch a train back to Bartow if things don't work out here. There was no one about. He noticed that the furnishings were in need of repair, but it appeared to be clean and was a comfortable looking room.

He could hear sounds coming from behind the door back of the wooden counter. He rang the bell again, and finally from behind the door someone shouted.

"I'm comin'! Be just a minute!" A large, elderly woman probably in her late sixties opened the door. She was frowning, but when she looked up at Seth a warm smile transformed her plump face.

"Good evening, young man, and how're you doing on this Christmas Eve?"

"I'm doing right well, Ma'am. I'd like a room if you have one. Just got off the train from Bartow."

"You're in luck. We have plenty of rooms. Now, the Arcadia House over on Magnolia is all filled up. Maybe you've heard of it. It's a grand hotel and can brag about having Henry Ford, Thomas Edison and Harvey Firestone as winter visitors. You here to spend Christmas with relatives?"

"No ma'am. Actually, I'm here to see about work and would've been here earlier, but Mr. Dixon, publisher of the *Courier-Informant* newspaper in Bartow, insisted that I stay there for a few days. Next thing I knew a week had gone by."

Beulah could see that he was a gentleman and a nice looking one at that. "Well, you're the second boarder I've had this very week come down by train lookin' for work. Yessir, just day before yesterday a young lady and her younger brother and sister arrived. She's a school teacher. What line of work are you lookin' for?"

"Well, by trade I'm a printer and reporter. Worked on the *Tribune* up in Monticello. Mr. Dixon gave me a letter of introduction to a Mr. John Jones of the *DeSoto County News*. Said as how he had a good newspaper and that he heard he might be able to use me, that is..."

"Heard the very same thing only last week," Beulah interrupted. "Seems like John's having trouble gettin' qualified people to help at the abstract company and the paper, too, since Minor Green moved down to Punta Gorda to work on the *Punta Gorda Herald*. My young boarder Jack Pope applied at the abstract company, and I do believe that John will give him a try, and his sister Maggie should know next week when Professor Wilson comes back from Lakeland whether or not he'll have an opening at the high school. Got over 160 pupils...imagine!"

She caught her breath and handed him the register. "So it's Seth Roberts of Monticello, is it? Have a cousin who lives in Capps just south of Monticello. Don't hear from her often though. Do you happen to know a Jane Turner? Married to Theo. Been there for 'bout thirty-some years."

"No ma'am. Don't believe I do, though I recognize the name."

"Well, Mr. Roberts, I'm Aunt Beulah to everyone in these parts, but my last name is Young. My husband George and I run this hotel and have, it seems, forever. Room and table fare by the day or week. How'd you want it?"

"By the week'd be fine, Aunt Beulah, and call me Seth, ma'am."

She smiled and thought it's good to have young people movin' in. Such a nice young man - so polite. I'll have to introduce him to Maggie. They should hit it off real fine, both so educated and being new in town and all. Near about the same age, I'd say. Seth stooped down and lifted his small trap and told Beulah that he'd left his trunk at the depot, and since tomorrow was Christmas Day maybe he'd better have it brought over before dusk.

"I'd have George help you, but he's ailin', but I'll see if Jack can give you a hand when he and his sisters get back. They insisted on havin' a Christmas tree and talked Sap and Toad into takin' them out in his wagon to cut one."

She laughed, "George and I don't have a tree anymore. Our daughters live in town and one or the other has us over for Christmas. No need in foolin' with one, I told Maggie, but that young lady insisted. Even went over to Gus and Ione's for candles and holders and said they would string some corn and make some colored chains and I don't know what all."

Seth started to respond but got a lump in his throat. He hadn't allowed himself to think of his Aunt Rose or Christmas in Monticello. Beulah could see his sad expression and suddenly said, "We're gonna have us a big dinner right here in the hotel. I told Maggie that George and I usually ate with the girls but that somehow I'd see to it that they had a nice dinner.

"Maggie said that she wasn't much of a cook, but that if the girls and their families could each bring a few dishes of food she'd help me with the chicken or whatever I decided on. When I told Marta and Maida about it they thought it was a grand idea, so they and Maggie planned the whole thing. My..." she got a faraway look, "it's like old times when we'd have as many as twenty-some people for chicken dinner." She wiped a tear away and continued. "The girls said that it'd be just like it used to be when Kate and Parker would come in for church, and everyone would gather around the piano, and we'd sing and open presents and..." She couldn't go on.

"Aunt Beulah, here," Seth patted her bent shoulders. "Here, sit down and tell me. I never had any folks, just my Aunt Rose. I'd like to hear about how it used to be, honest."

Maggie burst inside calling, "Aunt Beulah, we found the most beautiful tree in all DeSoto County, didn't we, Nellie?"

When she saw Beulah and Seth sitting immersed in conversation, she stopped. He stood and extended his hand. "You must be Maggie. I'm Seth - Seth Roberts."

He has a nice smile, she thought, accepting his hand and squeezing it as firmly as any handshake he'd ever had from a man. Beulah couldn't help but chuckle at his expression. *She reminds me of Callie at the same age. Got a lot of tomboy in her.*

Beulah broke up their exchange. "Jack, how about helping Seth with his trunk? You can take the buckboard, and I'll get George to help you..."

"No need, Aunt Beulah, I can do it."

Maggie watched them go out the door to the kitchen. *He must be about twenty-something,* she thought. Beulah interrupted, "Seth came by train from Bartow. Used to be with a newspaper up in Monticello. Hopes to get on with the *DeSoto County News*." She sighed tiredly then continued. "Be nice to have another eligible young man in town..."

"He seems real nice," Maggie said. Nellie interrupted, "Maggie, I'm going up to my room." She wore a secretive smile. Maggie winked at Beulah, and when Nellie anxiously ran upstairs she whispered, "She's going to wrap her presents she got at Jeeters' yesterday. Been saving her fish money."

She stopped, plopped down on the parlor sofa, sighed and said, "This has got to be the best Christmas in the whole world, Aunt Beulah. The best!"

Beulah sat beside her, smoothed out her flowered apron, patted Maggie's hand and said, "We'll make it the best, Maggie. I can tell that

Seth is homesick. You know, I'm gonna have Gus open up the store. We've gotta get that young man a present for under the tree. Doesn't have to be much, just something..."

"I know! How about a nice pen and ink well? Mr. Jeeters got in some real fancy ones, brass and crystal, you know, to sit on a desk."

"Well, I wasn't thinking of anything quite that fancy. Just some little thing, maybe some handkerchiefs or..."

"I guess you're right. But that was certainly a pretty set. I'd thought of it for Jack, but he needs new clothes more than..."

"Gus got in some pretty shaving mugs with gold initials on 'em. Maybe one of those..."

They heard the back door close and Marta yelled, "Mama, brought over the cornbread and leftover biscuits for the dressing..."

"We're in the parlor, Honey. Be right there."

Jack and Seth passed the old Presbyterian church and continued down West Hickory St. talking non stop all the way to the depot and back. Jack inquired about why Seth had come to Arcadia and volunteering why he and his sisters were there. "Maggie thinks I oughta go back to school, but if Mr. Jones'll hire me on full time, I'll take it."

"You might be wise to listen to Maggie. I mean, you'll go a lot farther if you have a good education." He stopped talking, looked soberly at Jack and continued, "I wish I could've gone on to college, but didn't want to burden my Aunt Rose, who raised me. She's always worked so hard..." His voice trailed off. He thought of Delia.

"I've been thinking on it, Seth, honest I have. You might be right. Besides, I don't have that job with the abstract company yet. Rube said I might be able to get on at the DeSoto Fruit Company, you know, the one beside the depot on West Hickory - we just passed it. Shoot, I could walk there in no time from Oak Street." He thought a minute, "If we stay at the hotel, that is. Maggie'll want to be getting us a place of our own, I know."

Maggie heard the buckboard. She was sitting on the high stool chopping onions on the heavy maple board on the kitchen table. Marta and Beulah were in the parlor. Sniffling, Maggie used her apron hem to wipe her nose. She thought, I look a mess, gracious, eyes all red and runny nose. What'll he think? She heard them laughing and when they came inside carrying the heavy trunk asked, "What's so funny, you two?"

Jack responded quickly, "Not for your ears, sister dear."

"You're up to something, Jack Pope!" She jumped down and rubbed her onion smelling hands all over his face yelling teasingly, "Tell me! I said tell me! What're you two laughing at?"

"I give up! Stop that, Maggie - stop!"

He ran around the table. Maggie dodged the table, reversed, and ran smack dab into Seth who had entered into the rumpus.

"Oh, I'm sorry," she said laughing so hard she was bent over. He held her by the shoulders.

"It's all right. Jack and I were exchanging jokes, you know, men's jokes."

"Men's jokes, indeed!" When she straightened up and looked at him she stopped talking, bit her upper lip, pushed back the brown strand of loosened hair, fidgeted with her hair bow.

Jack could tell that she was uneasy. Maggie had always been so sure of herself that he was taken by surprise. He interrupted, "We were just funnin', Maggie, that's all. Where'd you put the tree?"

Seth was quick to speak. "I'll help you, Jack, soon's I get this trunk upstairs. That is unless Maggie wants me to assist her in some way."

She was suspicious. Why's he being so polite? Acts like a blooming preacher. She turned from him and shook her head no. Don't suppose he's a detective? I wonder. I'll just keep my eye on him for sure.

Jack helped Seth with the trunk and said, "She's not your usual girl, Seth. I mean, she's not upset about us joking or anything, it's just that Maggie is, well, she's just not all girly and silly like some. She likes to horse around with me and my friends, even if she is a school teacher."

"I don't see anything wrong with that. When Delia was little she acted the same."

"She your sister?'

"Who, Delia? Oh, no..." he stopped, then said, "She's just a friend."

Jack knew better. More than a friend, I bet. Beulah called after them. "Jack, tell Nellie that when she's through with her doings in her room we could surely use a helping hand. I think you three got the biggest tree in the woods, I declare I do." She turned to Marta, "Go get Rube and ask him to go to the back shed for that deep tub, you know, the one he uses to dip the hunting dogs in."

"I don't think it'll be deep enough, Mama. Maybe the wooden keg would be better. Don't know why they had to get such a big one. But it is pretty, isn't it? Nice and full, and the pine scent is smelling up the whole place. Be back in a minute. Don't you dare try to lift it by yourself, now, you hear?"

"What do you take me for, Marta? I declare, you girls don't give a soul credit for a thing."

Nellie came tiptoeing down the stairs. When Beulah looked up Nellie raised her finger to her mouth. Running to Beulah, she whispered, "I got all my presents wrapped, Aunt Beulah. Oh, I can hardly wait! Do you suppose my Ma can look down and see 'em? You suppose?"

Beulah got a catch in her throat. "Course she can, Honey, if you pray real hard she can."

"She'll be so excited when she sees Poke's" - she gasped, stopped, "I mean Jack's face." She thought a minute. "He was called Poke when he was real little, but he doesn't like it now that he's near 'bout grown."

"I understand, Honey. I won't let on." Nellie seemed relieved.

Maggie couldn't stand it any longer. Stuck in this old kitchen. Wonder what they're doing out there? She said aloud, "To heck with it!" She burst through the door to the parlor saying, "So there you are! Thought maybe you'd died or something." She'd hoped that Seth would be there. Nellie ran toward her. "I got Jack's present wrapped, Maggie. Got the bow tied real pretty. Oh, he'll be so excited!"

Maggie thought, so will you, little Nellie, so will you. She and Poke had pooled their money and bought Nellie her very first china head doll. Poke knew what he wanted to get her but wasn't sure how Maggie would feel about it. It sure cost a lot. He'd never spent that much on any present in his entire fourteen years, but when he pointed it out to Maggie, she didn't even hesitate, just told Mr. Jeeters that they'd take the one with the pink rosettes on it's cap. It was near about the prettiest doll Poke'd ever seen. Never saw one that looked so real. It wore a long white batiste dress with lace and ribbons and goodness knows what all. He knew that Catherine Inez would have a fit when she saw it. This'll be the best Christmas we've ever had.

Suddenly he thought of his pa. I'll not let him upset this day. I'll not let him ever upset us again. If he comes for us, I'll kill him - I swear it! He thought a minute, I'm sorry Ma. He couldn't go on with his thinking.

Seth and Jack spoke animatedly as they rushed downstairs. "Here, Aunt Beulah, Jack and I'll set that tree up for you."

Marta called from the back porch and Beulah answered that she'd send the boys for the keg. "You'll need some sand to put around it to anchor it, boys," Beulah reminded them.

"I'll help," Nellie called after them.

"So will I," Maggie yelled.

Seth took charge. He told Jack that they could partially fill the keg out in the back yard, then after they got the tree positioned in the keg, they could put some broken bricks or rocks around the trunk, then pour on more sand and wet it down. "We don't want the tree to get dried up and perhaps cause a fire, now, do we?"

Maggie stood aside and listened. She would usually have argued but since everything he said made sense, she got busy and began shoveling sand into smaller buckets to take inside.

"Nellie, you get the water from the pump, but don't fill it real full. Don't want to spill it on Aunt Beulah's floors."

She could feel Seth looking at her. She felt flushed and ducked her head. He had thought earlier, she's no where as pretty as Delia but seems nice enough. At least she's not giving me the moon eyes like the girls in Bartow did and putting on fancy airs. They seem like a real nice family.

When they returned to the house, Beulah's other daughter Maida had arrived with her three children, a sack of fresh corn and a bucket of snap beans. She sent the children to the back porch to shuck the corn and she and Beulah were in the kitchen snapping the beans and talking. Seth thought, this isn't home, nor is it Monticello, and it isn't Athea Manor. I wonder if they have any help around here? But, I like it. It's like one big happy family all sharing - all working.

George came into the living room from next door. Rube was helping him, holding on to his arm. They had been out on Jeeterses' porch. "Gonna get pretty cold tonight. Gus said near 'bout freezing, Beulah, honey. Best get out the quilts."

Seth didn't know that he was senile and almost said something about how warm it was for December, but Maggie interrupted. "I'll go tell her, Uncle George. She's in the kitchen. Yes, gonna get mighty cold," she winked at Seth as she passed him.

Rube spoke up, "Mistah George, suh, don't hafta worry 'bout Miss Beulah and her quilts. She 'doubtedly got more covers dan de law 'lows, she do," he chuckled.

George sat in the parlor chair and stared at the tree. "Gotta put the angel on the top, Marta, or is it Maida's turn? Rube, whose turn is it, you remember?"

"No suh, Ah sho don'. Maybe Miss Beulah members. She got a good memory."

When Maggie came back in she went to Rube. Taking his arm she pulled him aside and whispered. He shook his head that he understood and followed her. Seth, Jack and Nellie continued filling the keg with sand, rubble and water. When Maggie returned she stood back from the banister and exclaimed, "Now that's a Christmas tree! Prettiest I've ever seen!"

Seth went and stood beside her and said, "I believe you're correct in your observation, Miss Maggie. It's indeed a beauty," and laughed heartily. Jack saw her bite her lip again. Now what's she acting like that for? he wondered. Don't suppose she's going and getting sweet on Seth, do ya? Well, I wouldn't care a bit. He's a nice one, all right.

"Mistah George, suh, Miss Beulah said she want Miss Jenny Sue to have a turn at puttin' de angel on de top. Said as how Miss Lori done it las' year." They were Maida's and Marta's young daughters, who were the same age as Nellie.

"Why can't Maida or Marta do it...?" He started to cry, his chin finding his chest and bumping up and down unable to control himself.

"Here, Mistah George. Ah be takin' ya to ya room. Don' ya fret. Ah'm sure Miss Beulah let Marta and Maida do de angel. Don' ya fret, don' ya."

Rube nodded to Maggie, and she rushed into the kitchen to alert Beulah that George was upset and that Rube was taking him to his room.

Seth whispered to Jack, "What's wrong with Uncle George? Is he sick?"

"Aunt Beulah says that he's in his second childhood, you know, like some folks get when they get old."

"I've never seen that before. Poor man."

Beulah wiped her hands on her apron, rushed into the parlor and called after George, "Don't you worry yourself, Honey. Don't ya. Think maybe you'd better take a little nap before we have the singing." George didn't even look up. Beulah followed them into his room. They had long ago divided the second parlor with curtains and put his bed and chiffonier there so they wouldn't have to carry him upstairs. It had worked out just fine. When Beulah couldn't be with him or when he had an especially bad day, she got Rube or one of the grandchildren to help out.

"All this excitement has got to him," she said to the questioning faces. "He'll be fine by the time you finish the tree, just fine."

"We'll be all done in no time, Aunt Beulah," Maggie assured her.

Seth spoke up, "Won't take us long to clip on these candle holders and drape the chains."

"Don't forget the lace bows and red rosettes, Maggie. Kate made those for me the year before she died."

When Maggie raised her brow Beulah realized that she didn't know who Kate was. "Kate Meade, my best friend. She and Parker owned the Tall Ten ranch about three miles from town. Biggest ranch around Tater Hill. I want you three, no four of you now, to meet Callie, Kate's daughter, who runs Tall Ten. She and her husband Clay Willett got a girl 'bout Nellie's age named Annie. Her son by her first husband, who was my nephew, is a little older than Jack, I think."

She turned toward Marta and Maida, "How old's Meade now? About seventeen or eighteen?

Marta answered, "More like seventeen. He's a year older than Josh."

Maggie could feel her heart race. Well, if the jig's up, then it's up.

Beulah continued, "Guess Meade's home for the holidays."

"Yes, he got home from Summerlin over two weeks ago," Marta said.

"Is that Summerlin Institute in Bartow?" Seth inquired.

"Yes. He's been going there this past year. They have an excellent art program there, and his Uncle Jay thought he should attend. Don't know why. Miss Fraser is a wonderful teacher, and she's right here in the new high school. But since Callie married Clay Willett and inherited the ranch, she's got mighty uppity..."

"Now, Marta, that's just not so. Shame on you," Beulah chastised her.

"Shame on me, my foot! All of Arcadia knows how uppity Callie's gotten..."

Beulah interrupted one more time. "That's enough, young lady. She's not uppity one bit. It's just that she has so much on her mind, running the ranch almost by herself. That's a man's job - not fittin' for a woman." She stopped suddenly. "Enough of that."

She directed her next remark to Maggie and Seth. "You'll get to meet all of them soon. Comin' for dinner after services tomorrow."

Maggie gulped. Well it was nice while it lasted, she thought. But I hope I can warn Meade and ask him to not give me away at least until after Christmas Day.

"Mama, you want me to ask Rube to bring Daddy in now? You know how he likes to look at the tree when it's all lit up. Then we can have the singing."

"That'd be nice, Honey," Beulah answered. "And, Maggie, how'd you and Seth like to get the boiled peanuts out of the kitchen? Just use the big strainer and dip then right out into the big bowl on the kitchen table. Best bring in some napkins and hot sauce from the sideboard, Jenny Sue."

Beulah dearly loved giving orders, always had, but no one seemed to mind. Jenny Sue, Lori and Nellie finished draping the popcorn on the tree and Josh and Jack were sitting on the stairs watching them. Josh was telling Jack about the baseball team he played for and asking him if he liked to fish or hunt. Jack listened and thought this is where I want to live. For the rest of my life this is where, and if Pa shows, then I'll just deal with him. But Arcadia is going to be home for me and Catherine Inez.

Maggie scooped the boiled peanuts out of the big pot while Seth held the bowl. She was having trouble not looking at him. What's wrong with me? she questioned. He's just like every boy I've met before. Not one thing different about him. Maybe a little shyer than the boys in Tallahassee and Tucker's friends, but why can't I talk to him? Never in my entire life have I had trouble talking to boys.

They heard the piano, then Beulah's high soprano. "We'd better hurry, Miss Maggie, they're starting the singing," Seth commented.

"Almost finished - there - that's the last dipper." She reached for the towel, wiped her hands and replaced it on the table. Why am I so blasted nervous? Don't suppose I'm coming down with something do you?

Seth thought, she's prettier than I thought. Sure has got pretty all-color eyes. Bet if she wore dresses like Aunt Rose makes she'd really look nice. But why am I thinking like this? Doesn't make any difference if she's pretty or not. I'm here to make as much money as I can and get back to Monticello to claim Delia. Can't afford to get side tracked.

"Ready, Seth?" Maggie asked again. His mind's surely not on this party. Bet he has a girl back in Monticello, I just bet. I don't care one whit if he does. But Maggie had trouble appearing nonchalant as she opened the door to the parlor for him.

Jack jumped up and Josh followed. "Here they are. Boiled goobers. My favorite!" Jack shouted. Nellie was remembering how he had loved them when they were home. They'd sit on the banks of the Santa Fe, and he'd eat himself almost sick. She looked around her, her large hazel eyes filled with the wonder surrounding her. The fragrant scent from the tall pine filled her nostrils, the singing. Imagine having a piano right in your very own home, even if it was a hotel. I've never seen the likes of this day, she thought. I bet tomorrow will be even better. Poke will be so excited when he sees my present, and Maggie - oh my, my own money to spend. I just hope we can stay here. I hope Pa can't ever find us. I'm not going to think of him. I don't want to ever think of him again.

CHAPTER IV   CHRISTMAS DAY 1899

SOUTH SPRING

Layke was determined that Berta have a nice Christmas and had so informed Tucker. "You'll not upset your mother, young man. I do not want you to mention a word about a betrothal, do you understand?"

"Yes, I understand Father, but just because Raine ran away, her actions should not interfere with my feelings for Delia, should they? She has always kept this family in an upheaval of some sort, and here it is the most important event in my entire life and her very absence has precedence over everything else. It's not fair!"

Layke placed his arm around Tucker's shoulders. "It does seem that way, doesn't it? But we have to be especially considerate of your mother during this time."

"I'll do my best, but I'll only be here a few more days before returning to school, and I do so want to go to Monticello to speak to Mrs. O'Farrell about..."

"This simply is not the time, son. Bad timing altogether. Your mother and I will stay here at South Spring, maybe take a trip up to Carrabelle to see SuSu and Jay and children and check on the house in Tallahassee later. But your mother has made up her mind that this is where she wants to be until we've found out about Raine, and you need to be here for as long as you can. Surely you can understand that..."

"But I won't be returning to Florida until May - that's five long months. I've already accepted the invitation to the May Festival at Delia's school in St. Augustine. I do so want to..."

"That's enough, Tucker! Delia is only sixteen, and if she cares for you I'm sure a few months won't make a difference..."

Tucker whirled around and called over his shoulder as he left the study. "That's easy for you to say, Father. You're not the one who loves her."

Layke, his head in his hands, elbows resting on the leather topped desk thought, you're absolutely right. The young always think that they're the only ones who are capable of loving with such intensity. I could not love Berta more. He'll learn to live with his longing. It won't be easy, but his entire future is at stake with two more years at William and Mary, then law school. I'll not bring up the four years of waiting for him to claim

Delia. If she is as impatient as her mother was, she'll not wait that long. She'll find someone else.

He had moved to the leather sofa and was resting. The noise from the kitchen was barely audible, but he knew that Berta, Nora and Bernice were busily preparing their feast. Best thing for her - keeping busy. She'd be at her wits' end if we were in Tallahassee. She's right. She needs to be here doing chores with Nora and helping with the boys. He dozed off thinking, where are you Raine? If you cared for anyone other than yourself you'd let us hear from you...

****

ATHEA MANOR PLANTATION

Juanita was dressing her hair, and Delia, propped up on a profusion of pillows, was watching her in the dressing table mirror. "Rose has not heard a word from Seth - not a word. I cannot believe anyone could be that inconsiderate of..."

"Not so, Mama," Delia informed Juanita. "He wrote her that he was going somewhere to earn his fortune. At least Rose knows he's not in Tallahassee."

"That's just what I mean. It's a despicable act on Seth's part. Don't you ever do that to me, young lady. I mean it! It's hard enough bringing you children into the world and raising you..."

"You don't have to worry about me. I'll be right where Tucker is, that's where."

"Don't be so sure of yourself, Honey." Juanita twisted the long strand of blond hair around the heavy chignon. "He's not even out of school yet, and..."

"Oh, poo! There's not a law saying that we can't get married while he's in that dumb old school..."

"No law, perhaps, but his folks are determined that he'll follow in the senator's footsteps, and you know that for a fact. I'd not be surprised if they opposed a marriage between you, Delia. Not surprised at all."

"Why'd you say a thing like that?" Delia jumped off the satin comforter.

"You'd better prepare yourself for that very event, young lady. I'm not trying to be unkind. I just don't want you to be hurt. The O'Farrells don't have the political connections..."

"Political connections, my eye! What does that have to do with us getting married?"

Juanita studied her beautiful daughter and thought, I don't think I was ever that naive. You'd think that with all her advantages and schooling that she'd be wiser. She shook her head in disbelief and walked over to Delia. Looking up at her she said, "I'm sure Tucker loves you, Honey, and I'm sure that if he followed his heart you'd be married very soon. But his future is already planned for him, and you both will have to be practical and no doubt wait a long period of time before you can wed..."

"How long? How long do you think?"

"I'm sure that they'll not approve a union until after he's out of school..."

"But that'll be four years or more! Mama, I can't wait four long years..."

"It'll go quickly, Honey. You'll be at Miss Baldwin's next year and meeting lots of new people..."

"I don't care about meeting new people! I don't!" Delia thought, they'll not make us wait any four years. I'll think of something to change their minds.

They both heard the carriage and knew that Rose had arrived from town. "Delia, lets put on a happy smile for Rose. Her spirits are going to be so down this year.

"I'm gonna miss Seth, too. This will be the first Christmas that I can remember when he wasn't here. How many years?"

Juanita answered, "At least ten, I think. Yes, it was ten years ago that we moved from Kissimmee and he and Rose accompanied us to Monticello. It's hard to believe, isn't it? He was always so fond of you." She didn't dare say that he'd always loved her, and that's why he left - couldn't stand to see her with Tucker Williams.

"Rose, we're upstairs. Be down in a minute. Go on to the parlor and I'll have Harrison pour us a nice glass of sherry."

She turned to Delia, "Let's see that smile, young lady."

****

HIGH SPRINGS

"Now, what's he doing back here, do ya suppose?" Widow asked the mister. They had been sitting in the rockers on the front porch overlooking the Santa Fe when Mac rowed up and got out of the skiff.

"Might be going to work the phosphate again like he did after they kicked him off the railroad. Might be."

"Howdy, Mac, sure been a long time. Where ya been?"

Mac hobbled up the worn path, stopped, leaned on the cane and, using signs and mumbling, made them understand that he had been looking for those children. Widow shook her head and said, "Thought they were with their aunt and uncle over on the Suwannee."

He let out a growl. She knitted her brows together, got up, smoothed her skirt, and the mister knew that she was upset. She'd never taken kindly to Mac. He could understand why. He heard her grumbling about how he wasn't gonna spoil their Christmas party at the church and how she wasn't gonna have him at her table, not even on Jesus's birthday.

Mister turned around to face Mac. "We're gettin' ready to closin' up Mac. Goin' to the church party. You best get what you be needin' now 'cause we gonna be closed for Christmas day...all day."

Widow thought, he'll not be wantin' anything but shine, and he'll not be findin' any here. Mac pulled out the broken pencil and wrote, *grits, coffee, bacon.*

"You gonna be stayin' at the house? Billy Rawles and Maudie been keepin' a eye on it fer ya."

Mac indicated that he'd be staying there and dug deep in his overalls pocket for the coins. "Well, you have a nice Christmas, Mac," Widow made herself say. Mac knew that they were just words and grinned derisively at her. She understood his look, and as he hobbled back down the steps she turned to the mister and said, "I hate it that he's back here. Him being here is gonna spoil my whole Christmas, it is."

"Now, Honey, don't you go gettin' yoreself all upset, not by the likes of him. He'll be in his shine and we probably won't see him the whole time he's here."

They were wrong!

****

ARCADIA, TALL TEN RANCH

"Why do we always have to wait on Annie, Mama?" Jimmy inquired impatiently. Callie turned around to the back of the buggy and admonished her young son. "Maybe it's because she's a slow starter, son. She plays hard and sleeps so hard that she has trouble getting an early start."

"My beautiful philosopher," Clay said patting his wife's hand.

"Well, it's true and you know it, sir."

"Yes, I know she's just like her mama was at age eight..."

Meade interrupted their tete-a-tete from the buckboard that he'd pulled alongside of theirs. "We'll be late for services again. Annie! Shake a leg!" he called. They heard her as she slammed the porch door and yelled, "I'm comin'. What's the hurry? Same old thing every Christmas..." and on she grumbled.

"That's enough, young lady," Clay said sternly, and Callie chimed in, "Not this year, not the same old thing at all. Aunt Beulah has a surprise for us.

"Probably something dumb..."

"Annie," Callie continued, "you're going to be pleasant whether you like it or not. Do - You - Hear? And I mean all day long."

Jimmy quickly stifled his outburst, because he could tell that Annie was getting riled up. If he let on how much he was enjoying her being fussed at, she'd probably have his leg pinched black and blue by the time they arrived in town. But he did dearly love it when she got what for.

Cora Anders Willett, called Annie from birth, was the first child of Callie and Clay. Meade was Callie's son from her marriage to Thom Garvin, who was Beulah's nephew and who had been killed by a panther when Meade was six. Jimmy was three years younger than Annie and a constant thorn in her side. She was, as her father said, very much like her tomboy mother had been at that age except for one definite characteristic. She was not just undaunted but totally unimpressed by everything around her. Or as her father had once said, "Annie was born old."

She was an unusual child. When she was younger she had been frightened by the ferocious thunder storms that plagued that part of the state. But once she understood that they would arrive without her invitation and that she would be unable to control them when they did, she just naturally went about her business and ignored their very presence.

Callie called to Meade, "Slow down, Meade. Don't want you to jostle the food." She and Lily had carefully packed the pots of collards, creamed cut corn and pumpkin and mincemeat pies along with the jars of pickled watermelon rinds and beets. Beulah always had more food than they'd ever eat, but Callie wanted to make sure there'd be plenty this year.

She was excited about Beulah's surprise. It was good to feel this way. Clay sensed it and so did Meade. Annie could feel it, too, but, not wanting to be disappointed, she wasn't about to give in to it. Let dumb old Jimmy act like a clown on a string - not her. She had actually allowed her curiosity to surface when her mama had said a few days earlier, "Your Aunt Beulah has got a surprise you won't believe, young lady." At first she wondered what it could be but, being Annie, refused to dwell on it for long.

She got herself busy organizing a new game that she had invented. Usually she'd talk Sap's and Lily's four children into playing it, and sometimes the three children of Callie's overseer, Sweet Harrington. If she couldn't talk them into participating she'd allow Jimmy to play, but only as the last resort. Annie dearly loved to organize. Her father said that she was a natural leader.

She had spent the week before Christmas making up clues and maps for her new treasure-hunt game and could hardly wait for Christmas to be over so she could get started on it. All this fuss about Christmas was a real bore. Same old thing every year. She had to get presents for everyone, and then they'd have to go to the old church party, and then Santa Claus was supposed to arrive and come down the chimney carrying a huge bag of presents. How could anyone in his right mind believe that?

When she questioned her mama and daddy, and they said it was a fairy tale, she said it would have to be. Anyone who'd believe it had to have had their wits dulled by shine. Callie told Clay that child was to stay away from the bunk house from now on. Where on earth would she get such ideas if not from those rowdy cowmen.

Callie reminded Annie that the real meaning of Christmas was commemorating Jesus's birthday and how the wise men brought gifts to Mary, Joseph and baby Jesus, and that was why they exchanged gifts. Annie replied, "Don't you think Jesus must get tired of the same old thing every year? I mean, if I feel like giving a present to Lily, I give her one. Doesn't hafta be her birthday or anything. I give it to her because she's my friend."

"That's very nice of you, Annie, I'm sure. But Jesus is God's son, the one the Bible is all about. If we follow his teachings, then we'll be assured of a seat in heaven." Annie looked at her, decided to not say anything, turned away and left the room shaking her head in disbelief. Callie could hear her mumbling but couldn't understand what she was saying. She decided that she'd speak to Clay about Annie, but she never did. She got busy running the ranch, and Annie continued to think that Christmas was dumb.

Jimmy jumped down from the back of the buggy and ran inside the hotel calling Aunt Beulah. Annie let out a long bored sigh. Callie, with a conspiratorial glance at Clay, turned around and said, "Annie, help Meade with the food while I get the presents."

Annie shrugged and got out of the buggy slowly - definitely not her nature - and took the pot of greens that Meade handed down to her with a reminder, "they're hot. Don't burn yourself." She thought but decided to not say, "How dumb do you think I am? Course I'm not going to touch a hot pot. Grief, Meade!."

It was heavy and it took both her hands to carry it up the steps. She didn't change her bored expression until she heard his voice and felt his hands take the pot from her. "Here, I'll help you," he said, and she looked up into dark hazel eyes deeply set.

"Who are you?" she quickly asked.

"And who's asking?"

"I asked first," she countered.

"Well, you're a feisty one, aren't you?"

"Just who're you talking to, because if it's Annie Willett you'd best be watching your tongue." She stopped dead still and glared up at him.

"Oh, I'm sorry if I got you all riled up, Miss Annie. I'm Jack Pope."

"Well, I'm not Miss Annie to you. I'm just plain Annie to everyone in these parts, and that includes Mama's hired hands and everyone else including you, Jack Pope."

He looked down at the young girl, not much taller than Catherine Inez, and for the life of him couldn't understand why she was so out of sorts. Annie saw the door open, and a slight girl about her own age, she figured, came out wearing a smile. Are these kin of mine or something? Is this the surprise Mama was talking about? What's going on here, anyway?

The girl rushed over to her and gushed, "I'm Nellie, and I'm new to Arcadia, and I'm gonna go to school and..."

Jack interrupted. "That's all right, Nellie, this is just a little girl called Annie something-or-other, who must have got up on the wrong side of the bed, 'cause she's sure a grump."

Meade was enjoying every minute of the scene before him but, knowing Annie's short fuse, decided that he needed to interfere. "Annie's my sister, and I'm Meade Garvin, her half-brother." He held out his hand to Jack, who shook it firmly, and they smiled at each other. "Happy Christmas and welcome to Arcadia."

Annie glared at all of them and erectly walked into the Young Hotel. Nellie was chagrined. "What'd you say to her, Jack? I can't believe you'd say anything mean, especially on Christmas Day."

"He didn't say anything wrong, Nellie. It's just Annie. She doesn't like anything where she isn't the leader. All the school kids call her General behind her back."

"But I don't understand. Why's she upset?"

Meade continued, "Well, it's like this. Annie didn't come up with the idea of Christmas first. Someone else beat her to it many, many years ago, and Annie likes to be first. She likes to think the idea up, run the entire operation and have everyone do her bidding, and she's angry at God for thinking up Jesus and the wise men and all..."

"I still don't understand," Nellie said, shaking her head. "I want her to be my friend."

Meade laughed as he said, "I wish you luck, Nellie." He turned back to Jack, "So, how long you been in town, Jack?"

"Maggie, my older sister, and Nellie and me've been here about a week." They walked into the parlor, and Meade's mouth flew open. He was staring right at Raine Williams, the missing daughter of Senator and Mrs. Williams. She smiled, put out her hand and, before he could say anything, said, "I see you've met my brother and sister. I'm Maggie, and I'm hoping to find a teaching position here in Arcadia so we can all stay here. This is a lovely town, isn't it, Jack?"

"It sure is. I hope I never have to leave."

Meade knew that he was expected to go along with the ruse and decided that it was the thing to do, but he also knew that when he got Raine alone he planned to give her a good talking to. Her folks deserved to know that she was alive and well, and, by gum, he was going to make sure that the spoiled brat did what was right. But where did she acquire a brother and sister? That was a puzzle.

Beulah rushed in, pulling her apron off, pushing her hair back from her beaded brow. "'bout time you arrived. Now, let's get over for services. Preacher Barlow's probably having to wait services for us."

"Here, Aunt Beulah, let me help you into the buckboard. I'll even drive you."

"Drive me, my eye, Meade Garvin! Only a few blocks. Listen! The bell's already pealing. Bet Rube's already got George into our pew. Come on, Jack. Call Maggie and Nellie. Where's Seth? Gotta make tracks." No one ever stopped to argue with Beulah, not even Annie, who sighed and took her own sweet time following the entourage down Oak St. to the First Baptist Church. The steeple towered above the wide double doors, and Annie could see the shadow of the bell moving in the bell tower.

Looking at Jack's back she thought, just who does he think he is, anyway? Same old Christmas - same old thing...

MONTICELLO

Delia had insisted on going into Monticello with Harrison to meet Tucker, who had only an overnight in which to visit her. "You're being too bold, Honey," Juanita had said.

"But he'll be here and gone in no time, Mama. I don't know why he couldn't have left South Spring sooner. Everyone in the whole world thinks they're our bosses."

Juanita smiled knowingly at Rose, who was painstakingly attaching the bugle beads on Elda Shifrar's gown. It was the week after Christmas. It had been a lonely one for all of them. Juanita had been very depressed, particularly since Young Nolan seemed so forlorn. He missed his da so. Harrison had taken up a lot of time with him, but it wasn't the same. A ten-year-old boy needed his da, and Juanita needed Conner, her man. But at least I have the children, she rationalized. Poor Rose doesn't even have that. I know in my heart that Seth is all right - I know it - but try to convince her! She isn't about to be convinced. Rose is determined that he is dead and gone.

Juanita's energy was spent throughout the holidays putting on a happy face and keeping everyone busy. Easter and Harrison had been amazed by her resilience. It wasn't like Juanita to be so concerned for others, even ones she loved.

"Miss Conner's ridin' fer a fall, Harrison, honey. Ah jes knows it."

"Why're you thinking that, Easter?"

Easter handed him the tray of cookies to put in the earthen jar. "Ah can jes tell. Not lak her to be happy fer others. Not lak her at all."

"She's not been the same since Conner's death. Nothing she does would surprise me anymore. There was a time that I could predict her every move. Now, Delia, well, she's just like her mama was when I first met her - headstrong and predictable. But Cherie tried harder than any woman I've ever known to one-up her man. She couldn't stand for Conner to outsmart her. Delia's not as clever as her mama, and I'm afraid she's the one who's riding for the fall, not Cherie."

"How dat?"

"Because Tucker Williams will abide by his parents' wishes. Doesn't have the backbone to oppose them, and Delia, being Conner's and Cherie's daughter, will certainly oppose their decision."

"Ah don' understand, Honey. Why wouldn't dey lak Miss Delia? Ain't evah been a more beautiful young lady anywheres den Miss Delia."

"They're not interested in her beauty, Hon." He couldn't bring himself to confide in Easter that he was sure that the senator and Berta knew that Delia was illegitimate and also knew that when their son ran for political office that his opponents would find it out. No, they'd protect Tucker.

Harrison figured that the only reason they'd allowed him to even see Delia was that they thought her harmless. You'd think that they'd remember how very clever her mother and father were. Harrison was concerned and had said a few things to Cherie concerning it, but she brushed his remarks off. The old Cherie would've had a well worked out plan. But seemed to him that Conner's death had taken the grit out of Cherie. Maybe he'd have to intervene.

"Harrison, what ya got dat furrow on yore brow fer? Now don' ya go an git yoreself 'volved in Miss Conner's 'fairs. She do fine widout ya interferin'."

He pulled her to him, kissed the top of her turban and said, "Now, why would I do a thing like that, my lady? Why?"

"Cause ya miss Mistah Conner much as dey do, an' ya always gotta be doin' what right by dem, dat's why."

Dignity forgotten, Tucker Williams virtually leapt off the top step of the train as he raced toward Delia. Harrison had to curtail his laughter when Delia jumped into his anxious arms. A good thing that his parents didn't witness this scene, or they'd insist on sending him to school in Timbuktu, he thought. Juanita had stayed in the shop with Rose. Kansas and Granny Todd had both been down with the grippe, and Rose was at her wits' end trying to complete the many gowns for the New Year's party at the Opera House.

"1900 - I can't believe it, can you Rose? Oh, what a to-do Conner would have made of it. I'm sure we would have attended a dozen balls here and in Tallahassee. You know, I've been thinking that if he had lived he'd have been talked into running for office. I'm sure of it."

Rose didn't bother to answer Juanita's remarks, and Juanita knew she was thinking of Seth and probably hadn't heard a word she said. Juanita saw Richard Lamar rounding the corner of Jefferson St. "Here comes Richard with the mail. I wonder if..." She didn't finish.

Rose hopped up and met Richard at the door. The bell tinkled as she opened it. Richard was smiling broadly as he handed her the letters. Placed on top was a letter with Seth's name and an Arcadia return address. Richard and Seth had been classmates at the Jefferson Academy, played baseball on the same team and were active in the Jefferson Rifle Club. He knew how anxious Seth's Aunt Rose was to hear from him. Actually, everyone who knew them was anxious.

Rose's hands trembled. Richard spoke up, "He's in Arcadia, Mrs. O'Farrell. I've got kin there." He stood waiting for Rose to open it. She held it to her breast, the tears started. Running to the workroom behind the curtains she sniffled loudly. Juanita and Richard stood waiting. It seemed like forever before she returned.

Juanita began to speak, "I told you he was fine, Rose, and..."

Rose handed her the letter. Juanita read aloud.

Dear Aunt Rose,

I'm sorry that I didn't tell you good-bye before I left. After I went to Tallahassee I decided that I wanted a real change of scenery, so I took the train to Bartow. It's on the Peace River and a nice town. I met some nice people there who told me that they thought there would be a position on the DeSoto County News in Arcadia, so I came here, arriving Christmas Eve.

I found a nice room at the Young Hotel run by an elderly couple, Beulah and George Young. They are real nice, but he's not well. There are some other young boarders staying here, too, and we had a wonderful Christmas yesterday. At church I was introduced to Mr. Jones and his son, who own the newspaper and title company. Mr. Jones asked me to go see him tomorrow because he was sure that he could use my services.

So, you see, my decision to come to Arcadia was right. The people are very friendly, and Miss Beulah has given me a good weekly rate. I'm to help her with the repairs around the hotel, so my board will be free.

I have to go now. Jack Pope, who boards here with his sisters Nellie and Maggie (she's a school teacher), is calling me. He wants to go next door to shoot some billiards.

You may write me in care of the Young Hotel. If for some reason I move on, Aunt Beulah will have my forwarding address. Please tell everyone hello for me, especially the O'Farrells and Harrison.

Love, your nephew, Seth.

Juanita lowered the letter, and Rose reached for it, folded it neatly and replaced it inside the env elope. She was smiling broadly. Finally she spoke, "When he gets more settled, Juanita, I want to go down for a visit.

Think I'd like to go on to Alva, too. It's been so very long." She turned and slowly went upstairs to her and Seth's quarters.

Aloud Juanita said, "Well that's the last bit of sewing I'll get from her today," but she understood.

"'bye, Mrs. O'Farrell. I'm sure glad Miss Rose heard from Seth and that he's doing so well. I'll tell everyone on my route." He didn't have to say that. Juanita knew Richard was a bit of a gossip but she felt he was harmless.

When Delia and Tucker burst into Cherie's House Of Fashion, Juanita was grumbling to herself but managed to put on a smile for them. "But why do we have to stay in town, Mama? Can't Harrison ride back in for us?"

"Delia, that's thoughtless of you, dear."

Delia sighed loudly and looked longingly at Tucker. Juanita understood. They wanted to be alone. Delia continued, "There's not a thing to do around here - nothing at all. Tucker will die of boredom. He has to leave day after tomorrow. Oh, please, Mama. Just this once."

Tucker was shuffling his feet but, not wanting to interfere, said nothing.

"That's enough, young lady. These gowns must be completed by this afternoon. Mrs. Dinkins is sending her man for hers and Emily's, not to mention Yvonne's and Esmeralde's. Now your protestations are to no avail."

Delia knew from past experience that when her mama began speaking in an authoritative manner, she might as well give up. Pursing her lips and stamping her feet for one last defiant act, she grabbed Tucker's arm and shouted, "Well, we'll just go to the old ball park and watch some dumb old baseball game. Come on, Tucker. Some vacation! You'll probably die of boredom."

He hugged her to him as soon as they were outside. Juanita could see them as he nuzzled her neck, and she heard Delia giggle girlishly.

I'll have Harrison watch those two carefully. I'm afraid the flame might get out of hand. I don't feel like finishing these gowns. I feel like cuddling up in our bed with a mountain of covers over me and reminiscing about my Conner. I truly do. But she continued attaching the beads, and that's how Rose found her an hour later deep in her reverie.

"What's so amusing, Juanita?"

"I was remembering the day I showed up in Conner's cabin on the *Savannah*, and when he opened the door and found me there, the expression on his face was one of complete surprise. You know how controlled he was. Oh, that was a day, Rose - that was a day."

She proceeded to give a highly embroidered account of the event, and Rose thought Juanita was getting to be as good a story teller as Conner. She had even begun using her hands and arms dramatically like he did.

"That's enough, Harrison," Juanita said. "I want you to keep an eye on the lovebirds - not to spy on them." He put down her empty sherry glass.

"Is there a difference?"

"Yes, there is a difference. I don't want Delia to do anything foolish. She's so young and so in love and..."

Young Nolan, hand over his mouth, could barely control his laughter. He was behind the folding doors to the front parlor. He hadn't planned on eavesdropping, but when he heard his mum's voice grow louder and he knew that Harrison was with her, well, he just had to listen closely.

I'll help Harrison, I will. But I best not let him know. Nolan knew Delia's habits very well, and spying and telling on his sister had always been one of his favorite pastimes. They'll be riding down by the stream where it's shady, sure as shootin', right after breakfast tomorrow. He thought a while and realized that maybe he'd better plan to stay awake this very night. About time something exciting happened around here.

"No more cookies, Young Nolan," Easter chastised. "Ya gonna be sick all over creation, and wid yore sister havin' company an' celebratin' de new century...ummm, now ain't dat somethin'. Ah lived ta see 1900. Harrison, honey, ya be sure ta git Melvia an' dose quarters gals up here early. Miss Conner want everythin' special, and de crystal bes' not have one lil ol' spot."

Harrison took Nolan by the elbow and escorted him out the kitchen door. "You know when Easter's got a lot on her mind that you shouldn't be under foot, Young Nolan. When Eli is cooking a brace of ducks, that should tell you that there's extra work for us. Smell them - permeating the whole countryside."

"That's the suckling he's roasting that smells so good, Harrison." He got a faraway look. Harrison knew he was remembering his da. Oh, how

Conner loved to supervise the roasting of the meat and fowl. But Eli had learned well. That suckling would be glazed to perfection with a candied pomegranate in its mouth, resting on a bed of shiny holly leaves and wearing a holly leaf collar. He'd have to give Cherie credit. She had tried to keep Conner's traditions alive, not just for the children but for them all.

The fog was rolling in over the fields as he walked the brick path to Melvia's quarters. It was one of his favorite times of the year at Athea Manor. The river and laurel oaks were bare allowing him to see for miles, hill to rolling hill from atop the highest hill where the manor house stood. He heard the screech owl calling to its mate, and the mate soon responded. I hope Cherie will continue to stay here, but I have a feeling that by the time Nolan is out of school she'll be anxious to move on, maybe even before then.

He'd been thinking about that a lot lately. I'm sure Easter won't want to leave the area. After all, this is her home, and I'll never leave her. "Fate has been kind to me, my friend," he said aloud. He often talked aloud to Conner. When he confided the habit to Easter, she patted him like a mother and said that she understood, and that if the Lord chose to take him first she was sure she'd be talking to him the very same.

"Why can't he behave, Mama?" Delia had asked Juanita after she had sent Nolan to bed.

"He's not doing a single thing that any ten-year-old boy wouldn't do, Honey."

"Oh, yes he is! I can tell by the way he's acting..."

Tucker intervened, "I was the youngest so I never had to..."

"Well, you're fortunate. I've had him spying on me almost forever."

Juanita smiled at Rose, who had not removed her satisfied, complacent expression since receiving the letter from Seth. "If Seth were here, Delia, he'd keep Young Nolan busy playing ball or something. He always knew how to handle him, didn't he?" Rose said.

"I miss Seth." When Delia made the remark Tucker removed his hand from hers and rose. Delia was the only one who paid the gesture no attention. Juanita and Rose looked at each other - their expressions were the same. He's jealous of Seth, Juanita thought. I'm glad he can react to something. Jealousy is a healthful emotion if used wisely, Conner always said. But I still don't think he's strong willed enough for Delia. I'll have to admit that she's calmed since Conner's passing, and maybe with the schooling in Virginia she'll not be so headstrong. If she's to become Mrs. Tucker Williams she'll need that reserve. She could feel Harrison watching them while he cleared the champagne glasses. He'll be watching Delia this night.

Juanita rose, "I think I'll turn in."

"I'll join you, Juanita," Rose responded. "This has been a big day, hasn't it? I bet the goings on at the Opera House will last into the wee hours, don't you?"

"And if Conner..." Juanita's emotions got the better of her. She cleared her throat and decided not to continue. She turned to Rose, put her arm around Rose's waist, and they tiredly walked up the stairs. Juanita turned around and called to Delia, "Delia, I don't want you and Tucker to stay up late."

"We won't, Mama," Delia answered, winking at Tucker conspiratorially. Harrison pretended to not see them. Delia whispered to Tucker, "I'll meet you in half an hour right here." He squeezed her hand.

"Good night, Harrison. Why don't you leave those things 'til tomorrow?"

"Easter would have my head on this platter, just like Sampson, Miss Delia. You know how she likes things just so. Good night, Mr. Williams." Tucker acknowledged the gesture with a bow of his head.

Delia flung herself on her bed. She wore a Cheshire cat smile. I'm going to make sure that we don't have to wait four long years - this very night I'll make sure. It's ridiculous to think that we must wait that long. She hopped up, unfastened the bodice of her garnet taffeta gown, unlaced her bustier, stepped out of the petticoats and her pantaloons and pulled on her new wrapper.

It was a warm night for this time of year. The soft silk clung to her damp slender body. She shivered. I feel so devilish! I wonder if Tucker will think me too forward. I mean being totally naked underneath. I wonder if he's ever been with a woman? Of course he must have. He's almost twenty-one. I wonder what it's like? She remembered what Helen Mansfield, one of her roommates at St. Josephs, had told her, about how her oldest sister said it felt. But what if he doesn't want me? I might be too bold for him and he'll stop loving me.

She curled up on her side hugging the pillows to her. "I am not going to wait, Tucker Williams! I'm not!" she declared aloud. I wonder if the time's gone by? I'm going on down, anyway. I'll be there when he arrives. Won't he be surprised !

She slipped outside her room pulling the door to softly. Tiptoing down the stairs, digging her bare feet into the soft carpet, she listened. As she suspected Melvia had drawn the drapes and there was no sound from the parlor. She turned up the gas wall lamp above her da's desk just a little, so Tucker could find his way, and opened the double doors into the parlor a crack. A small shaft of light found its way into the darkened parlor.

Delia curled up on the leather couch and waited impatiently. Over and over again she said to herself, I must not get too excited - I must allow him to make the first gesture - I must appear ladylike. But how can I when I'm so excited. She heard him; at least she hoped it was Tucker. She tried to compose herself. If it's Mama I'll tell her I couldn't sleep and came down for a book, that's what.

Hopping up she grabbed the first book off the shelf. When she saw the title she laughed, *The Cabinet Of Irish Literature*. Grief! She'll know that this is much too advanced for me. She put it back hurriedly. Startled, she swung around. Tucker stood looking at her in the soft glow of the lamp. Her long black hair was loosened, flowing, covering her shoulders. He'd never seen anyone so beautiful.

Delia held her arms out to him. He came to her. Pressing against her he realized that she was naked underneath the silk dressing gown. Oh, Lord, is all he could think. Sighing deeply he whispered, "Delia, I love you so. Do you know how much?"

Nolan was in his room trying very hard to stay awake. As was the custom at Athea he had been allowed to stay up past midnight to see the new year arrive and also allowed to have a small glass of champagne with the grown-ups. His mum and da had usually had a large gathering of friends for the celebration, but this year there was only Aunt Rose and Tucker Williams. He missed Seth. At least he'd have played catch with him, whereas Tucker just wanted to hang all over Delia and didn't give him the time of day. He was nice enough, he supposed, but he sure wasn't Seth.

Stretching his slender arms and yawning, he pulled on his slippers. He was sure that Delia would have slipped out of the room by now and met Tucker either in one of the parlors or in his da's study. Listening intently as he crept down the stairs he heard nothing. I wonder if Harrison is spying on them, too. I bet he's in his house sound asleep while Delia and that Tucker are together.

He listened outside the front parlor and heard nothing. Melvia had drawn the heavy curtains and it was pitch black, keeping the harvest moon from lighting his way. He felt for the door to the adjoining parlor, and it was slightly ajar. The aroma of the suckling still permeated the air. He could hear something that sounded almost like snoring - it was heavy breathing. The next thing he knew a hand was over his mouth and he was being carried through the front parlor. He couldn't even scream.

Delia heard the noise. She quickly turned the lamp off. "Shhh," she cautioned. Aloud she said, "I bet it's that brat Nolan. I just bet it is!" She pulled Tucker with her, avoiding the wing-back chair. They could hear muffled noises, and then the front door opened and closed.

"Who's there?" she questioned. Again, "Who's there?" Again, nothing. Tucker hugged her to him. "Honey, we'd better go to our rooms."

"No!" She rushed to the front door, opened it, and saw somebody moving in the moonlight. Aloud she said, "She's having him spy on us, I know it!"

"Who?"

"Mum, that's who. She's gone and spoiled everything. I'll never speak to her again - not ever!"

Tucker held her out from him. "Honey, she's just thinking of you, you know, your reputation..." She wanted to say that she didn't give a fig about some old lily white reputation when he stopped speaking. They heard the noise at the top of the stairs and melded into the shadow of the hall curtains.

"Delia?" Juanita called softly. "Are you down there?" They both held their breath, then - it seemed like forever - heard her door close.

"I'll give her a few minutes then return to my room," Tucker said in a whisper.

"Why? Why are you going to let her win?"

"Honey," he said holding her shoulders tenderly, "I think it's best. She might forbid me from seeing you if she suspects anything." He hesitated then continued, "I couldn't stand not seeing you, Delia," and kissed her longingly. She clung to him never wanting him to stop. When he pulled away he whispered, "See, that's what I mean, Honey. I want you so that I'm afraid that I might not be able to stop with just kissing."

She wanted to say that she didn't want him to stop with kissing. But Delia knew that he'd find the remark too bold. She's won! She broke the spell when she sent Harrison in to spy on me. I'll never forgive her!

"Where'd ya find him? Ah declare to ya, Young Nolan, yore mama's gonna tan yore hide. Spyin' on yore sister and Mistah Tucker. Dat's no way fer ya ta act."

"Harrison was spying on them, too."

Harrison looked at Easter and said, "Not exactly, young man. Your Mum asked me to do the clearing up of the parlors, and then I heard Miss Delia come down the stairs. I was just leaving when you came sneaking down, planning some devilment, no doubt. You're going to spend the rest of the night right here with me and Easter - what's left of it. Must be almost 2:00 o'clock..."

"You think it's that late, Harrison? Really? I never stayed up that late before."

Nolan lay on the narrow cot in the front room of the small cabin. He thought of his da. *I wonder if he can see me and if he knows how late I'm up? I bet if he can, that he's mad at Delia. I don't think he'd like that Tucker.* He relaxed, turned on his side and was soon asleep.

Harrison came out from his and Easter's room, pulled the quilt from the bottom of the bed and covered him. He smiled down at the handsome boy. *You and Cherie did yourselves proud, my friend.* He wiped the tear away. He whispered, "I miss you, Conner. I guess I always will." Slowly he went to his room.

"Is he 'sleep, Honey?" Easter whispered.

"With the angels." He removed his trousers and eased onto their bed. She turned on her side and, holding his face with both hands, kissed him.

"I miss Mistah Conner too, Honey." She hugged him to her. "We gotta git some rest. Dose roosters gonna be crowing 'fore very long. Don' matter ta 'dem dat it's a new year. My, my, it's already 1900. 'magine dat!"

BOOK THREE:

YEARS GO BY

CHAPTER I SECRETS UNFOLDED

Delia had been selected to be the May Queen at St. Joseph's Academy, and excitement prevailed at Cherie's House Of Fashion, Athea Manor and all of Monticello. There had been a long, detailed article in the *Tribune* and the *Constitution*. Juanita was beside herself with pride.

"You know how proud her da would have been, Rose. Oh, I wish he were here to give us suggestions on her gown. You know what excellent taste he had..."

"Would you stop stewing, Juanita. You're going to make yourself sick and not be able to go to the festivities. I've never seen you like this. Your taste is just as good as Conner's ever was - it's just that you don't think so." Rose bit the end of the thread, held the dress out from her and said proudly, "Now, that is indeed a dress fit for a queen. They won't have ever seen anything this beautiful - not ever."

Juanita's hand soon found her mouth, restraining her outburst. "Why am I so antsy? It is beautiful, isn't it? The white crepe de Chine was a perfect choice. I know she'll look like an angel in it."

"Maybe not an angel, Juanita," Rose said with a chuckle, "but probably as close as Delia Rose will ever get to being one, I'm sure."

"I hope Nolan and I have time to do the sight-seeing he has planned. I wonder if it wasn't a mistake to send for the booklet that the railway puts out. He has poured over it and asked so many questions until Harrison and I are ready to cuff him one."

"Oh, he bent my ear for over an hour the other afternoon after school. I thought you wanted to stay in Flagler's Ponce De Leon Hotel?"

"I had planned on it, but when he read about the Alcazar's huge swimming pool, well I didn't have the heart to disappoint him. But it's just across the street from the Ponce De Leon so we'll dine there and tour it and the grounds. I've never read of anything so elegant. But the one I really want to visit is Flagler's Hotel Royal Poinciana in Palm Beach. It's right on the ocean. We'll plan to take a trip down there, maybe just the two of us. Wouldn't that be fun?"

"We'll talk about that later. Are you really going to let that child ride on one of those ostriches? I'd be scared silly to even get near one."

"He has his heart set on it, and I'm sure they're harmless, or why would they allow someone to ride them? They actually race them, you know, like a horse with a saddle, and bet money just like a horse race. I think it'll be fun. We need to have some fun, Rose. It's been a long time since any of us relaxed around here. Seems like all we do is work, doesn't it?"

"Juanita, I do want to take a few weeks off after ya'll get back. June isn't very busy, and I'm sure you and the Todds can handle anything that..."

"I've already told you that I want you to go to Arcadia to spend some time with Seth and on to Alva and any place else you decide. Take a month, if you want. I bet you won't recognize any of it since the trains got there. Bet it's grown beyond recognition. Honestly, Rose, you do fret about most everything."

Unbeknownst to Rose, Juanita's nerves were not caused by Delia's crowning, but by something much more serious. She had been thinking and planning for this event ever since Delia started keeping company with Tucker. She knew that she had to tell her before she and Tucker got any more serious so that Delia could have a voice in the decision.

Juanita's and Delia's relationship had been strained ever since New Year's, and try as Juanita did to repair the damage she had inadvertently caused, it had only been eased. Delia had her da's temperament, and forgiveness didn't seem to be one of their good qualities.

Mavis Thompkins burst into the shop. Juanita and Rose looked at each other, restraining their amusement at her appearance. Mavis was one of the town's matriarchs and felt that she should be consulted about every important event that went on in town as well as in the private lives of everyone she had endorsed. Conner and Juanita had fallen into Mavis's special people's category, and whether they liked it or not were subject to her opinions and plans for their future and that of their children.

"Where is it? Now don't you tell me that it's not finished, because Tasmania saw it and told Pretty and..."

"Mavis, sit right down here in this comfortable chair, and we'll show the gown to you. Now, surely you don't think that Delia would dare wear this without your..."

"Don't you patronize me, Cherie. I'm very aware what everyone in this town thinks of my opinions, and..."

"Now, you stop that, Mavis. Conner held your opinions in the highest regard, especially those of a political nature, and I know for a fact that your taste is impeccable, or why do you order your gowns from Cherie's?"

She relaxed as much as she was able, but sit she wouldn't. Rose came out from the back work room holding the gown. Mavis, with mouth open, declared, "It is, as Tasmania told Pretty, about the most beautiful gown I've ever seen. You two have done yourselves proud. If Conner is in a position to witness this, and I doubt that he is, Purgatory or no, he'd approve."

Juanita was going to tell her how pleased she was that she had indeed approved their month's efforts, when Mavis whirled around, her red straw hat festooned with huge cabbage roses almost taking flight, and out the door she dashed with the tinkling bell announcing her departure.

"I'll have to give Mavis credit, Rose. That woman has undoubtedly got the strongest opinions of anyone I've ever known, well, except Conner, that is. I guess that's why they loved each other so. Did you know that at least once every blessed week since he arrived in Monticello those two held court in the back room of the St. Elmo, downed a bottle of Scotch, and solved the world's problems? I doubt that many knew that. And when she shows her concerns for my family, I shouldn't find it amusing. I guess I should feel as honored as Conner did by her interest. They had a wonderful relationship."

"That's enough, Juanita! You can forget those tears right now. Why don't you go on home and I'll finish up here? Do you want me to press and wrap the gown in tissue paper before you leave? Won't take but a minute."

"No, I want to wait 'til the last minute so it won't get mussed. I'll stop by for it on the way to the depot tomorrow, dear. But, I'll take your suggestion and go home early. I could use a glass of sherry. I don't know when I've been this weary. Must be the excitement." But she knew better. She knew that she'd be rehearsing her proposed talk with Delia all the way to Athea as well as on the train to St. Augustine.

****

ST. AUGUSTINE

Juanita sat beside the rambunctious Nolan, whose nose had seldom left the train's window since they departed Monticello. She had wished that they could find time to visit Jacksonville, but she was determined to arrive in St. Augustine the day before Tucker Williams was due. Delia had confided in her that she and Tucker had been corresponding, so Juanita knew that their relationship was as before.

She and Nolan had changed trains in Jacksonville but did not tarry. She was relieved that the train's connections had been uneventful and that they were on their way. They rode through the elegant Riverside suburb. Juanita decided that she would not allow herself to think about her first ride through Jacksonville when she had been the star of the deMoya's medicine show and felt that nothing could have been more wonderful than that. Oh, how inexperienced she had been and how glorious everything seemed! Will I be able to convey the excitement of that time to Delia? Will she understand how a country girl, who had never been anywhere and who was determined to make something of herself, felt? I doubt it, but I mustn't dwell on it.

"Mum, look, we're on the drawbridge!"

Juanita moved closer to Nolan and gazed at the St. John. She could see the city stretched along its banks, the harbor, then the east shore of the river with its stretches of pine forests, orange groves and bits of hammocks. As she sat remembering, time swept by, and before they were expecting it, the quaint old Spanish city was in sight.

Why aren't you with me, Conner? Why did you have to be taken when we were becoming so relaxed with each other enjoying our lives? I'll never understand this master plan you always referred to. I wonder if you did? I wonder if you are as perplexed as I am at the turn of events? One of these days I'm going to get up the nerve to sit with Mavis in that back room at the St. Elmo, and we're going to split a bottle of Scotch, too, and maybe she can unravel the mystery of Conner O'Farrell. I miss you so!

"Mum, look! What's that? Is that the hotel? Mum, did you hear me?"

"How could I help but hear you, Nolan? Gracious, half the passengers on board can hear you. You aren't at Athea, you know. Now, what are you shouting about?"

She looked more closely. "Well, I don't know, but I'd say that it's the dome of a church."

The man on the bench ahead of them spoke up, "That's the Memorial Church, Ma'am, you know, the one Mr. Flagler built."

"Thank you. This is my son's first visit to the city, and as you can tell, he is excited."

"I'm gonna ride an ostrich, huh, Mum?"

"Yes." She smiled at the stranger, "I promised you that you could, and we'll visit the Atlantic and Fort Marion, too. There's so much to see that I just hope we have time to take it all in."

"My wife and I come down every year but usually in the winter. This is our first time in the spring. We're hoping that it won't be too warm. She doesn't like the heat."

"John, I can speak for myself." The woman turned around and glared at Juanita, her plump face grimacing. "We won't be here long, I can tell you. Already too hot!"

Juanita decided to not answer. The man tipped his hat to Juanita and asked his wife if she had her packages. She grumbled that she did, but for him to not expect her to stand around in the heat for their trunks. All Juanita could think was, if I had behaved in that manner, Conner would have told me to take care of my own trunks in no uncertain terms. Why does that woman not realize that he could die without warning, and then where would she be? Who would want her? Why am I letting this incident upset me? I know why. I'm afraid of Delia's reaction when I tell her. I'm afraid!

"Yes, Young Nolan, I'm hurrying. Don't get too far ahead of me! Nolan! Here, give me your hand, and don't you dare let go. This is a busy city and ... "

****

For many nights Juanita had lain awake and wondered how she was going to confess to Delia about her past. She knew that Berta and Layke had been so consumed by Raine's disappearance that Tucker's involvement with Delia had escaped their attention. But since Raine contacted them and told them that she was well but that she didn't want to disclose her whereabouts just yet, Juanita was sure that they'd turn their attention to Tucker and Delia.

Juanita was as concerned about Delia's happiness as her reputation. She wondered if Tucker was the right man for headstrong Delia. She didn't think so, and Harrison agreed with her. She needed a strong man like her da had been, not one who would necessarily control her, but one she could admire, allowing their love to grow.

Juanita had had a lot of time to reflect on her own life with Conner these past months and realized that their passion was almost as turbulent that last year as it had been when they first met. Delia needs a vital man who is instinctive and sensitive enough to force her to grow. Oh, she'll fight him just like I did Conner, but the results will be worth it. She's had too easy a life, Juanita realized.

Am I too late in dealing with Delia? She's not hungry enough! Where is her curiosity? My, at her age I was curious about everything. She doesn't seem to even care what's around the next bend like I did. I could hardly wait to experience it. Oh, Delia, I pray I'm not too late...

"But why do I have to get all dressed up? We're not going to church, are we?" Nolan asked, fidgeting some more, until Juanita could no longer hold her temper.

"Now you listen to me, Nolan. I've told you twice already. We're going to the school to visit Delia, take her her dress, and then we're going to the Ponce de Leon Hotel to view the grounds, have dinner and then, and only then, are you going to go back to the pool. This is not just your trip, young man. This is also my vacation. There now, turn around so I can comb your hair."

"I bet if Harrison was here..."

"That's quite enough! Harrison is not here, and I am in charge of you. If you continue to grumble you'll not go to the ocean, the fort or even ride the ostrich!"

"But you promised!"

"I can break my promise just like you can, Nolan. You told me that you wanted to accompany me here, and you promised to behave yourself. I could just as easily have left you at Athea."

He hugged her around her waist, buried his head in her pale yellow chiffon gown and muttered that he'd be good.

"That's better, son. Now get my parasol and I'll get Delia's gown and we'll be off to see the enchanting St. Augustine."

"May Ah git ya a carriage, ma'am?" the colored doorman asked. Juanita smiled, squinted in the bright sunlight, held tightly on to Nolan, who would gladly have broken free to pursue the children who were working their large hoops on the sidewalk, and said that would be lovely. "Is dis yore fust time heah?" Juanita shook her head yes. "May Ah suggest dat ya visit de shops on St. George St. All de ladies laks de shops..."

"We're going to the ocean tomorrow, aren't we, Mum?"

"Nolan, don't interrupt when someone is speaking."

"Dat's all right, ma'am, Ah got one 'bout his age and dey do lak to talk, don't dey?"

"Yes, this one most certainly does." Juanita thanked him and wondered if she had tipped him enough. By his big smile she figured that she had. All this is so new to me. Conner always took care of these things. But I mustn't let these small incidentals upset me - I musn't. Like everything it'll take its own time, or as Harrison constantly reminds me,

It is wrong to sorrow without ceasing. Is that by Homer or an American? I can never remember.

The school was as austere as Juanita had been told. She placed her parasol beneath her arm and walked Nolan over to one of the straight chairs along the wall. "Nolan, you sit right here until I finish fitting Delia's gown. Now, it won't take very long, and I'll speak to one of the sisters, who will perhaps take you outside so you can run around for a while, but don't you dare get dirty. Remember, that when we're finished here we're all going to the Ponce for dinner." She decided to not continue, because his face was already the picture of boredom.

She went to the front desk and spoke to the young sister, who smiled and said that she understood, because she had six younger brothers herself, and that Juanita was not to be concerned about Nolan. Juanita followed another sister, who led her to Delia's room. Juanita prayed that Delia's roommate would be absent, because she had no idea how she was going to begin her story - no, begin her confession.

"Mum, you brought it! Meriam is in town visiting her parents. They're staying at the Alcazar, too. I can hardly wait. Do you realize that I haven't seen him since..."

"I thought your enthusiasm might be about your gown, Delia. Do you realize that Rose and I worked on it for over a month? Don't you even want to see it?" *Why am I out of sorts with her? I know nothing else matters to her but seeing Tucker, so why am I acting this way?*

"Of course I want to see it, Mum, but I know it'll be beautiful."

Why is it she calls me mum when Tucker isn't around, and when he is, it's always mama? I must stop this. "Well, is it beautiful, or not? Better yet, does it fit? Here, slip it on so that if I need to take a tuck here or there I can do it tonight after we have dinner. You do plan to join us, don't you?" *Why am I so formal with her? I need to calm down or I'll never get through this. She'll shut me out, and I wouldn't blame her a bit if she did.*

Delia whirled around, the soft, creamy white crepe de Chine skimmed her firm body and flowed around her. "I love it, Mum. It's very beautiful, and every girl here will die with envy, I just know it."

"Do you like the double ruffled bertha? That was Rose's idea, that and the silk roses along the neckline. At first I thought we'd got the neckline too low, but when we added the flowers that just made it. Should we remove some of them from the hemline? Do you think they're too much?" I can't seem to stop jabbering. Oh, Conner come to my rescue. I must tell her before tomorrow and Tucker's arrival, I must.

"I like it just the way it is, honest I do. I know Tucker will love it. He'll be in on the morning train. Oh, Mum, I can hardly wait!"

"You must control yourself, Delia, or else Tucker'll think you very forward. Sister Mary Agnes told me that..."

"What did that old busybody tell you? What?"

"She was not being a busybody. One of the reasons you're at St. Josephs is for them to instill a sense of decorum in you, young lady. That's the very reason your da wanted you to be here, and Sister Mary Agnes said that..."

"I don't care one whit what she said! I've not done a single thing to cause her to tell on me. I wish I had, though. Serve all of them right!"

"Delia, sit down dear. Now - right now. I need to talk to you. I should have before now, but somehow - well, somehow I just couldn't. I had planned to wait until the summer, but I can see that I can't put it off any longer."

Delia's opaque blue eyes looked quizzically up at Juanita. She thought, what's she up to now? Hasn't she done enough interfering already? But I'd better go along with her, or she'll do something else to keep us apart.

"I know that you think I'm interfering unnecessarily with your relationship with Tucker. But, I am not. I have my reasons, and you're about to hear them." She took Delia's hands in hers, then sat beside her on the hard, single bed.

"One of the reasons that I'm being so cautious about your involvement is Tucker's decision to go into public life. Up until now you have been spared the gossip, the painful gossip that might be revealed if you and Tucker do become betrothed."

For once Delia was silent - questioning.

"Honey," Juanita bit her lip, clasped her trembling hands together and continued, "Honey, your da and I weren't actually married - that is, we weren't married until the night he died..."

"What do you mean you weren't married?"

"I mean that, for whatever reason, your da had not legally married me, and I mean," she hesitated and then continued, "you and Nolan for all intents were considered illegitimate. Now, don't Delia! Don't think less of your da because of it. He never seemed to like playing by others' rules. It was not his way..."

"But, Mum, Tucker won't mind, I'm sure. You did get married - I was there - I was a witness..."

"Delia, that's very important to me, but Honey, it won't mean anything to the person Tucker will be opposing when he runs for office. Don't you see? It'll hurt his chances of ever being elected if he marries you..."

"But, how would anyone know? How could they find out?"

Juanita took her in her arms and through streaming tears said, "My naive little girl, they have their ways, they and Tucker's parents as well. They probably already know."

Juanita wasn't being totally honest with Delia. She had purposely decided to omit her past involvement with the R.J. Skinner Gang and the fact that she had actually lived with Tucker's parents at South Spring when she was about Delia's age. And she certainly didn't tell her of her miscarriage of R.J.'s child. She was positive that Berta and Layke knew of that. What amazed Juanita was that they had allowed Tucker to even get involved with Delia.

Delia sat silently with Juanita beside her. Finally she spoke. "I'm going to tell him, Mum. He should know, and he should hear it from me."

"Oh, Honey," Juanita cried, "I'm so sorry that it's come to this. I was hoping you and Nolan would never have to know."

Delia did a very un-Delia-like thing. She hugged Juanita, patting her, back and said, "It's all right. If he truly loves me it'll make no difference, no difference at all."

Juanita knew better but didn't have the heart to tell her. Besides, she wanted her to have her day. Being crowned Queen Of May was quite an honor, for she wasn't selected for just her beauty but her high marks and popularity as well. Conner would have been so proud.

"Honey, do me a favor, please. Wait until after the ceremony. There is no need to tell him before. I want you to have the most perfect day of your life."

"I'll tell him the night before he leaves for South Spring. That'll give him until the July Fourth holiday in Monticello to think about it." She rose and pulled Juanita up beside her and continued. "But, Mum, I know, I'm absolutely certain that he'll be at Athea come July."

Her confidence didn't surprise Juanita. The young are always certain things will go their way. "Come on, Mum, no sad faces on my big day. Look at me, I'm Queen of May - Delia Rose O'Farrell." She twirled around, stopped, and the tears started.

"Oh, Honey, your Da's here - don't you fret - he's right beside us glorying in the occasion, as he would say..."

****

ARCADIA

Raine had managed to talk Meade Garvin into keeping her identity quiet that Christmas day but had promised him that she would let her parents know that she was well, but not where she was, and she had. She did it with the understanding that she would not have to reveal her identity to anyone else and was surprised when Meade agreed to go along with her. She knew that it was only a matter of time before the truth came out, but for now she was happy.

Meade seemed to understand her need to secure the teaching position and agreed with her that if it were known that she was the senator's missing daughter, it might adversely affect her chances. He could not get over how changed she was, affectionate, kind, helpful. He had also grown very fond of Seth and Jack, and they spent a great deal of time together over the holidays, because there was little to do around Tall Ten in late December.

Beulah had grown to love all four of them and prevailed upon Maggie to remain at the hotel. She knew that when school resumed she'd have every room filled with children from the outlying areas who boarded with her during the week, and she could certainly use her help. Many of the local families took them in as well, but with over 160 students enrolled the town's small hotels and boarding houses had to accommodate them.

Maggie had been promised a teaching position but would not begin until the following October, when school resumed. Her salary was to be $52.70 per month, and she was absolutely beside herself with excitement. Jack landed the job with the DeSoto Abstract Company, and Maggie spent her days tutoring the town's children in Beulah's parlor. They were doing fine financially, and Jack hadn't had to tap into the Necessary Jar. All three had let down their guard, and Nellie and Jack seldom thought of their pa.

There was always a lot of activity at the hotel. An occasional drummer would board and talk of his travels, or visitors from other states, who were seeking a new life, would rent rooms. There were much larger hotels in Arcadia now. The Southern and the Arcadia House Hotel were well established with winter guests from as far away as Canada, but none had the warmth of the Young Hotel.

It had been a very mild winter all over the state. An early spring followed, and the area baseball teams were active in the afternoons. When Seth finished work at the newspaper and Jack at the abstract company, they'd join the other young men at practice. Invariably Maggie and Nellie would be there to watch. Maggie was an avid fan, boisterous and enthusiastic, and the townspeople loved her outgoing nature - especially the young men. She had become very popular and was asked to all the functions. She wondered why Seth hadn't asked her out. Jack had told her that he was sure that Seth already had a girl up in Monticello. Maggie couldn't figure out why that would matter. She rationalized with the usual Maggie candor, she's not here and I am.

She and the children decided to join the First Baptist Church where the Youngs attended. They joined the choir, even Jack, who with Maggie's tutelage had become quite a good singer. At least he was loud and on pitch. She was especially excited when Seth started attending with them. The church activities were numerous. Every week there was some sort of function for the young people, a cakewalk, box supper, picnic, fish fry or barbecue. And at the end of the month there'd usually be a visiting preacher holding a revival with lots of singing.

It was obvious to Beulah that Maggie was sweet on Seth and felt that with a little urging he'd take notice. She'd seen him look at Maggie in that special way when she wasn't noticing and had even talked to her girls about it. But they prevailed upon her to not interfere.

"Now, Mama, remember when you tried to get Johnny Spears to notice Aunt Bit when she came to spend the summer with us? Remember? Why, the Spears have hardly spoken civilly to you since then, and Aunt Bit ran off and married Harry Fremd not a month after she got back to Crescent City. Aunt Mary said that you got her libido all stirred up, and there was no stopping her from trying her hand at being a girl after that. Remember? Why, she'd been practically all boy 'til then."

"Well, she's happy, isn't she? And so's Harry. Never saw a happier couple in my life. Don't see the harm in giving Maggie and Seth a little nudge in the right direction, just a little nudge."

And so she did, but she was wise enough to not let on to the girls. It was at the box supper at the church on the Saturday night before the annual cattle drive to Punta Rassa. Most of the young men from DeSoto County would participate in the drive, because most were from ranching families. This would be their last night to kick up their heels before the three-weeks drive, and kick up their heels they did.

Meade was home from Summerlin as were a number of the other Arcadian youths. He'd not be going with the other Tall Ten cowmen, because Callie had enough help without him. But a lot of the area families banded together and went on the drive, girls as well as boys, children as well as grannies. Everyone was needed.

Beulah had been working on Maggie's dress ever since the date for the box supper had been announced. She had asked Maggie if she intended to go, knowing full well that she did, and volunteered to help her make her dress. When Maggie said that she didn't know how to sew but that she did indeed want a new dress and was willing to hire whoever Beulah suggested to make it, Beulah anxiously jumped at the chance. She knew exactly what color, fabric and style Maggie would need to attract Seth. At least she thought she knew. She hadn't counted on Maggie's set opinions.

Maggie had wormed all the information she could get out of Jack concerning Seth's girl in Monticello. All he seemed to know was that she was the most beautiful girl in the world. Oh, she was very tall and had coal black hair and went to some school in, oh, he couldn't remember where. But he did say that she was the daughter of his aunt's partner.

Maggie was delighted. So she's in school somewhere and is tall and has black hair. That doesn't sound too difficult to overcome. She set her plan the very night Preacher Padgett announced the date for the box supper. Seth Roberts, you don't stand a chance. I'm going to see to it! She lay on the big bed she shared with Nellie. Looking at the high ceiling she reflected on the past year and had trouble absorbing all the details. Her parents' faces were even blurred. All she could see was now, now and tomorrow and all the tomorrows and Seth Roberts. Seth was in all of the images. She rose, went to the window, eased back the heavy lace curtains Beulah had insisted on hanging, and gazing down Oak Street at the rows of businesses along the dusty street, she said to herself, I'll never return to South Spring or Tallahassee. Maybe I'll visit, but I'll never return. I don't know why, but I can only be Raine...or Maggie ...when I'm away from them and rely on myself. Am I in love? Do I stand a chance at being Mrs. Roberts? Mrs. Seth Roberts? And why is he so different? Maybe I'm the one who is different...

It was the third Saturday in May. Beulah had conceded that lavender was not Maggie's color as she had previously thought, that is, after Maggie informed her. Ione Jeeters, after consulting every drummer on the Peace River and the railroad to boot, finally found the Chinese poppy color that Maggie had asked for. Maggie had walked into Jeeters' store and after not more than five minutes selected the pattern. When Ione told Tully and Narsa, the Marcos girls, that Maggie had selected her pattern inside of five minutes they could not believe it. Beulah could.

The next thing to set Beulah's plans askew was Maggie's declaration the very night of the party. "You're going to do what? Cut your hair? Maggie, that's ridiculous!" Everyone in the Young Hotel parlor shouted at once. All except Seth. He could feel Maggie looking at him, so he felt obliged to say something. He liked her hair, but if she wanted to cut it, then why not? After all, she was Maggie. It wasn't as if she were one of the young matrons, Marta or Maida, or even Callie Willett. She was Maggie, not Sue Ellen or Martha or any of the other young ladies he'd squired to the various parties...she was Maggie.

"Maggie, it's your hair, so if you want to cut it, then cut it. A lot of young ladies are cutting their hair. I don't mean to cut it a lot...but you know, well, here," and he pointed to below his shoulder.

"Whoa, Seth. Don't bring your radical ideas down here. They might be all right up north, but down here we like our girls' hair long," Josh Beavers shouted.

Seth knew Maggie was waiting for his retort. "Josh," he said calmly, "I don't have any radical ideas, and I'm not speaking for the newspaper. But if a young lady decides to cut her hair I cannot see why it should be the topic of conversation in Aunt Beulah's parlor or any place else. It seems to me that it should be up to the young lady and no one else."

Josh yelled, "Next thing I expect to hear out of your Yankee mouth is that women should have the vote. Is that not right, boys?"

Meade and Jack looked at each other, then at Seth. They shouldn't have concerned themselves, because Beulah had been tending to rowdies since the mid fifties, and if there was one thing Beulah knew, it was men's temperaments. She alerted Rube, and before any of them knew what was happening to them Rube and Daniel had escorted them out onto the porch and told them that Miss Beulah highly suggested that they make tracks. They didn't argue. Miss Beulah's word was law in Arcadia - they'd grown up on it.

Maggie was elated. Seth had stood up for her. They looked at each other over their punch cups, and their gaze was not lost on either Jack or Meade, and certainly not on Beulah. What do those girls know, anyway, she thought. Maggie was right, down the line she was right. Chinese poppy, my eye, just old Florida orange, that's what color that is. Maybe a tad darker, but it sure does complement her sun-tanned skin and dark brown hair. That young lady has some smarts. No lilac nor rose for her...

Meade was the first to speak. "Hey, Seth, we'd better head on over to the church. I wanta be the first to get a gander at the boxes. Hope the one I buy will have fried chicken in it, and maybe pound cake."

"I'll be there later, Meade. Need to tend to some things around here." He walked wearily upstairs. Maggie was at the landing. She wanted to follow him but knew better. The old Maggie would have. Beulah was at the door to the kitchen and was watching her. She knows enough to not follow him. Maybe the girls are right. Maybe I don't need to interfere like I used to. Maybe she knows what she's doing. She opened the kitchen door and thought, I guess they don't need me. No one needs me anymore, not even George. He's got Rube, and the girls have their husbands and... She put her head down on the kitchen table and sobbed. That's how Maggie found her.

"You're not wanted? What kind of talk is that, Aunt Beulah? I've never heard of such! Why, you're more mama than I've ever had, honestly. The kids and I were just talking of that the other night after supper, about how you were...Aunt Beulah, please try to get hold of yourself...I'll be right back."

Maggie, with her full skirt pulled up to her knees, ran upstairs. Seth, wearing that questioning expression he often wore, opened the door as soon as she knocked.

"I think you need to come downstairs, Seth. Aunt Beulah's not herself, and I think she needs us. The others are gone." She said no more. He ran past her and was beside Beulah even before she got there.

"Now, why'd you bother Seth, Maggie?" Beulah mumbled. "I'm fine. It's just that..." she couldn't finish.

Seth sat beside her, took her weathered hands in his, and began to talk. Maggie sat beside him. "Maggie tells me that you seem to think that you're not needed around here. Well, if that's so, then all those people that I talk to all day long on my rounds for the paper don't know what they're talking about. Why, I talk to the people at the DeSoto Fruit Company and the First National Bank and Eaton's Department Store and Mr. Seward's Merchandise Store, and I could go on and on, and when I tell them that I'm staying at the Young Hotel, they all, Aunt Beulah, they all say that I couldn't be in better hands 'cause there're not better people in the whole world than you and Uncle George."

Beulah sniffled, wiped her nose on her lace handkerchief, the one she always took to the church functions, put it back in her draw-string brocade purse and got up. "I'm an old fool. You children deserve better than this." She sniffled some more. "I promised Rosetta that I'd help her at the supper, and help her I shall. You two are as much like my own children as Maida and Marta ever were, and I've made you late for the party, and no one will buy Maggie's pretty box and..."

"And nothing!" Seth interjected. "You're on your way, young lady. Do you want me to escort you?"

"No, I don't, my kind sir, because here come Rube and Samuel, and they'll have some tales to tell me about those rowdies, I imagine." She looked up at him and whispered, "Why don't you take Maggie, Seth? Her box won't stand a chance by now..."

He bent down to her and replied, "Don't you worry about Maggie, Aunt Beulah. I'll take care of her." She smiled up at him and answered, "I thought that you would. You two are right for each other, you know," and having said that she quickly covered her mouth, and they smiled knowingly at each other. She thought, what do those girls know, anyway? I've not lost my touch!

"What'd she say, Seth? Is she all right?" Maggie questioned, her concern obvious.

"I believe she'll do just fine. Don't you have your box and things to get, Maggie? I mean that if we don't hurry all the boxes will have been bought, won't they?"

Maggie thought a while and realized that he was absolutely correct. She pursed her lips, placed her hands on her hips soundly and exclaimed, "And after all this bother!" She looked up at him and saw the glint in his eyes. "What're you amused at, sir?" Not wanting to be presumptuous she was hesitant to continue.

"I find the entire evening amusing. All except the part about Aunt Beulah feeling that she was not needed. That I found sad. Didn't you find that sad, Maggie?"

She felt his warmth when he put his arm around her and they walked back into the parlor. She knew that she had to answer so she decided to be direct. It was difficult for Maggie to be otherwise. "Yes, I did, Seth. We all need to be needed, don't we?"

His kiss was warm on the back of her neck and gentle and wonderful. She floated - she soared - and when she turned to respond to his hunger she knew that she surely had died and gone to heaven...

SOUTH SPRING

"How many times have you read Raine's letter, Berta?" Layke asked teasingly.

"And what difference does it make to you, sir? But I don't mind answering - about a hundred, I imagine. And I'll probably read it another hundred times before I'm through." She folded it, tucked it inside her apron pocket, rose from the rocking chair on the front porch and bent down to kiss Layke's forehead.

"I didn't tell you, not because I was avoiding it, but because until I had an answer from the Pinkerton's there was no need..."

"Tell me what? You said that you wanted them to drop the case..."

"Yes, that's exactly what I said to them as well. But I had a wire this morning waiting for me at the hotel when I went into town, and the man assigned to it had already come back to Florida. Now, don't worry yourself sick over this. I wired back and told them to get hold of that man and to pull him off the case right now. Jonah said that when he got an answer he'd send someone out with it."

"Layke, if that man upsets Raine, we might never hear from her again. She was so implicit about her desire to be left alone for a time. If he fouls this up I don't know what I'll do, and..."

"Stop it right now, Berta!" Layke had never raised his voice to her, and she found it upsetting.

He saw the tears form and her abrupt change of expression and got up to apologize. Berta turned from him, slammed the porch door and said not a word.

Why'd I do that? he thought. We're both upset, but I had no right to take out my frustration on her. I'm going to put an end to this this moment. He followed Berta, but she wasn't in the kitchen. Must have gone to the garden, he thought. Looking out the window over the work table he saw her pale grey dress in the garden behind the barn.

She heard him coming, but she decided to not turn around. He had no reason to yell at me, no reason at all. She felt his hand on her elbow, and when he pulled her around toward him she couldn't stay angry and was soon in his arms.

"Now, that's better, my love. Here, let me kiss those tears away." He lifted her chin and pretended to kiss away the tears.

"Stop it, Layke Williams. You know that tickles me." More soberly she said, "Don't get in the habit of yelling at me, sir..."

"I didn't yell! Raise my voice, perhaps..."

"It sounded like yelling to me. I didn't like it. I don't want you to ever do that again."

"We're both on edge, and you're absolutely correct, young lady. I had no reason to raise my voice. Let's go back to the porch and start all over again. What do you say?"

She didn't answer but linked her arm in his, and they returned to the porch. It was a glorious Florida day with few clouds and a cool breeze floating in from the river. A red shouldered hawk screeched overhead. Berta had not sat for more than a minute when she pulled Raine's letter out again.

"I know that you tried to explain how Raine feels about her new life, but I simply can't understand this, I simply can't. I go to sleep at night pondering it and wake up every morning doing the same. But I guess more than anything I wonder if we'll ever see her again."

Layke looked at the boys playing in the side yard. Reuben had made them a target, and they were throwing their knives at it over and over again. Let Berta ramble. She needs to unburden, he thought. "Why do I love this place so? You know I've never felt like this about a place. When I think of all the heartache that's visited me here, you would think that I'd hate it, wouldn't you?"

"Not necessarily," Layke answered. "Raine loves it, too. I was thinking just this morning as I rode into town that perhaps if we'd not moved to Tallahassee, she'd have been a happier child."

"But then we would have had to be separated during the sessions. No, we did the right thing. At least Tucker had no problem making the adjustment, and look at the advantages they both had. They would never have had as good an education in Old Town."

"I'm not so sure, Honey. Raine was never a good student, fought it all the way. I truly believe that if we had left her here and she had grown up here at South Spring like SuSu and the others did, she'd have not had so many problems."

"Raine brought her problems on herself, Layke. Now, you know that..."

"She just wanted to grow up in her own way, Honey, not the way that we thought best. Take Miss Baldwin's school. She hated it from the minute we mentioned it and wouldn't..."

"You're absolutely right, sir. *Wouldn't* is the right word!"

"I was just saying that I wonder how she would have turned out if we had not insisted on moving, that's all."

"Well, we'll never know. But for Tucker's sake I'm glad we did. Look at all the opportunities he'll have because of the schools he's attended."

"Let's hope that he doesn't throw it all away by getting more deeply involved with the O'Farrell girl."

"I believe the talk you had with him has already taken effect. He said this morning that he was racing in the bicycle race with the club in Tallahassee over the Fourth, so it looks like he'll not be going to Monticello after all."

"In a way I feel bad about all this, Berta. Juanita has made something of her life, and I know that you're as proud of her as I am. But they'll crucify her and her whole family if they do marry. I thought I'd get more of a fight from him, though. He certainly seemed smitten."

"Oh, Honey, he'll be in love a dozen times before he settles down. But, you're right about Juanita. I'm glad that Delia thought enough of Tucker to tell him about her parents. That was commendable of her, but then I guess they knew that we knew ..."

"We didn't actually know, Honey. We thought that they had never married, but we didn't know for a fact..."

"But had we needed to, we could have found out, couldn't we?"

"Just as easily as his political enemies will be able to, I'm sure."

"Let's hope for his sake that he'll find a girl who will be an asset to his career and, of course, one who loves him and will be a good wife."

"Like the prize I won, huh, missy?" He hopped up, yelled to Oliver that he wanted to play, too, and bounded down the front steps like a young man. Berta watched him and thought, he's just as full of energy as the first time I met him, and he hasn't changed that much. A few pounds and some gray at the temples but I declare he's no where near most other sixty-year-old men. I'm a lucky woman. I hope Raine can find someone who'll love her and take care of her and... She pulled the letter out again and began to read.

I wonder if Layke is right about Raine. She certainly loved it here. Just like a wild Indian, she was. But he is right about Susu. She had a good education right here in Old Town, and so did the boys. Wes had no trouble getting in the Citadel, and Etienne deMoya is a marvelous teacher. But wouldn't a body think that having the opportunity to attend as prestigious a school as Miss Baldwin's would give her a better chance in life. Well, it didn't work with poor Raine...there I go again calling her poor Raine. I've got to stop that.

****

I can't imagine what people see in this Godforsaken state, Detective Roy Kenton mumbled. His case was finished in Tampa, and he was on his way to Bartow to help on the recent robbery of the Polk County Bank. Stupid people said that they marched right down Main Street shooting everything in sight. Strangers, they said. Would be my luck if one of them was the senator's daughter. But, I'll find her yet.

He pulled his valise down from the rack above him and called for a porter. Another one-horse town to work. I'll be glad when I get back to civilization. At least Tampa had some decent restaurants. Could get used to that Cuban food in a hurry.

The girl in the bank informed him that Detective Donald Whitby was staying at Miss Payne's Boarding House over on Broadway. Just like Don, too cheap to stay at a decent hotel. Bet they even have greens for breakfast, and we'll pay a whopping $3.00 a week with all the wonderful country cooking we can down. Give me a good plate of corned beef hash topped with a couple eggs and some cabbage that's not swimming in their wonderful pork drippings.

God, it's hot! Must be a hundred degrees in the shade. He looked down Broadway and sighed. So this is the City of Oaks, is it? Well, for my money they can keep it. Give me a wide paved street and linden trees and people whose language I can understand. God, I have to ask them to repeat everything they say.

"I'm looking for Detective Donald Whitby. I'm Detective Roy Kenton." He still got a thrill every time he said that. Probably didn't mean a thing to these bumpkins, but it sure did to him.

"I believe the detective is still in the dining room, sir. Would you like me to get him for you?"

He shook his head no and said, "I'll stick my head in and tell him that I'm here. You do have a room for me, don't you?" She was a pretty little thing, and he understood every word she said. Must be from up north, he thought.

"Yes, Detective Kenton, we put you right next to Detective Whitby, if that's all right."

"That'll be fine. We should have this case solved in no time, but I'll go ahead and engage the room for a week. Have you finished serving dinner already?"

"Oh, no sir. We'll be serving until 1:00 o'clock. I'll have Jacob assist you with your luggage and then show you to the dining room."

"Thank you. You're not from around here, are you?"

"Actually, I was born in Arcadia about fifty miles south of here, but I lived in Chicago for many years until my husband was taken. Here is Jacob."

Roy tipped his derby, smiled his most ingratiating smile and thanked her. "Thank you, Miss..."

"I'm Mrs. Payne, and it's a pleasure to have you as our guest, Detective Kenton."

He whistled as he went upstairs behind Jacob. *A good thing that Jean isn't here or she'd recognize that tune. It was the tune, their signal, that he was hungry for her. It always evoked a smile in the Kenton household. That old battle ax Mother Lola probably has figured out our signal and presses her ear to our wall. I wouldn't put it past her. You'd think that having four children was a sin the way she carries on.*

The room was light and cheery. He could see that Mrs. Payne took pride in her place. *Dainty little thing, she is. He had always had a penchant for petite women. Jean had been at one time but with the children had put on a lot of weight, but she still could get him aroused. Bet that little Mrs. Payne is a hot one. There I go again with the whistling. Well, why not. Hell, it's been over two weeks since...*

The knock came again and Roy opened the door to a smiling Mrs. Payne. "Mr., I mean, Detective, I neglected to give you your fresh towels. I'm sorry if I disturbed you. And, Mrs. Stuart will be here the rest of the week, for I'm due in Arcadia for my sister's graduation."

"I'm disappointed, Mrs. Payne. I was looking forward to getting to know you better. You see I have the Florida territory even though I live in New Jersey. A man away from home sometimes needs a lady to converse with. Keeps us civil, I'm told."

She smiled up at him, and he knew that she was enjoying their exchange. *Think I've got me a hot one here. Might just have to hang around this town a little longer than I expected.*

"I can't imagine that you could be anything other than civil, detective. Perhaps you won't solve your case so soon, and we'll have the opportunity to get to know each other better, after all."

God, she means it. Well, little lady, I'll just see to it that this case drags on for an eternity. He took the towels and thanked her. "If you'd wait, I'll join you and you can show me the dining room."

"I'd be delighted."

"Don, old pal," he slapped Donald Whitby solidly on the back, "I was hoping it'd be you on the case." He turned around and smiled at Mrs.

Payne and said, "Those robbers don't stand a chance with the two of us on their trail. If they think they can rob a Federal bank and get by with it, well, they're mighty wrong, huh, Don?"

When Mrs. Payne left, Don turned to Roy and asked, "What the hell's happened to you? Why the last time I saw you, you were bitching about this Godforsaken hell hole of a state and..."

"Well, partner, I hadn't set eyes on that pretty little trick out there, had I?"

"Never knew you to be a cheating man, Roy. Always thought you put all your energy into the business and went home like a good little boy."

"That was the old Roy, my friend. Ever since that mother-in-law moved in with us things have got mighty boring around the homestead."

"Any leads? I was sorta hoping that they might head south, say to Arcadia, 'cause that's where Mrs. Payne is heading tomorrow."

"Funny that you would say that, 'cause that's just where they're headed. Just bet you might not mind going on the train with her, huh?"

"Not mind at all, detective. Pass those creamed potatoes and I'll finish up here and pay a visit to our landlady, I will."

"This is very pleasant, detective. I do detest this long trip all by myself."

"Please call me Roy. And what should I call you?"

"My name's Elizabeth, but my friends all call me Betty."

He raised her gloved hand to his lips and said, "Betty. That suits you. And I do hope we can become good friends, Betty." He squeezed her hand slightly and she almost purred.

I always was attracted to big men. I'm sure he's married and probably has a house full of kids. But I don't care anymore. I simply don't. And who's to know, anyway? I'm past child bearing, and he's about my age. I can't stand many more lonely nights. He seems nice enough, and his family is all the way in Jersey. Who's to know?

Maggie had left the hotel and was on her way to the church to attend the ladies' guild meeting. She had been feeling guilty about not writing her folks again and had decided that they must have believed her when she said that she didn't want them to know where she was just yet. *If I thought that they wouldn't be on the next train down here, I'd tell them where I* am. But knowing Mother, she'd hop the very next train and spoil everything. I've got to get that position, and maybe when Seth gets a raise we can talk about getting married. She'd spoil everything, wanting to plan the wedding and, well, she'd just play the senator's wife, and I'd have no say-so in anything, that's what.

"Hello, Maida. Did you and Marta get the baskets for the poor done? Aunt Beulah asked me to find out. Hello, Joyce. My, isn't that a pretty hat. I've always loved daisies on hats." Actually she hated hats of any and every description. I swear I sound just like Mother. I can't believe how silly I've gotten. If I'm not careful Seth will stop loving me. He said that one of the things he loves about me is my honesty. I'm sure glad he didn't hear that last remark about the hat. Whew!

"Maggie, come sit by me," Ava said. "Here, right here. Now tell me all about it."

"All about what?"

"About you and Seth Roberts, that's what. All of us are dying to know. Has he popped the question yet?"

"Well, Ava Spencer, how'd everyone in this entire town know about me and Seth? Heavens, we just started courting, and y'all have us practically married."

Maida spoke up, "Maggie, this is your typical small town, where everyone knows everyone else's business. Isn't that so, Ava?"

"Right as rain, Maida. I hope you don't have any secrets, Maggie, 'cause they won't be secret for long. Not in Arcadia."

Maggie bit her upper lip and smiled.

With both arms loaded with the food baskets the church women had made up, Maggie rounded the corner of West Hickory. As soon as I get these put away, I'm going to get to that letter. They've been very patient with me, and I do need to tell them how much I appreciate them doing what I asked. I thought for sure that they'd have that detective after me again, and that'd spoil everything. I wish school had already started and I had the position - then maybe I'd not mind so much.

"Nellie, come help me with these baskets. Where is everybody? Aunt Beulah! Well, I'll just tend to them myself. Never here when you need them..."

Jack burst in the door. "Maggie, he's here! He's here. I saw him go into the post office!"

"Who's here? Who are you talking about?"

"That man from Cedar key! That detective!"

"You're sure? Maybe it just looks like him..."

"No, it's him. I'd know him anywhere. What's he doing here?"

"I knew it! I knew they couldn't stop interfering in my life! I knew it! I'll never speak to them again - not ever again!"

"Maggie, what're you talking about? Who're you not gonna speak to again?"

"Well, Jack, if he finds me, then that's that. I just don't care anymore. Where's Nellie? I need to talk to you two. It's time. Actually, it's past time. I'll be in my room."

She removed her hair bow, shook her shoulder-length, straight hair loose, looked in the mirror and swore, "I'll never let you run my life again. I'm going to marry Seth, and I hope I never see you again. You should have done what I asked. It wasn't too much to ask."

Jack and Nellie eased the door open and sat on the edge of the double bed. They were scared. They'd never seen Maggie like this. She pulled the chair up to the bed, sat erectly and began her story. Only once did either of them interrupt. It was Nellie. "Maybe they didn't send him, Maggie. Maybe."

"They sent him all right. Why else is he here? Next thing we know he'll be asking questions, and I won't stand a chance at getting the teaching position. That's the only thing I ever really wanted..that and Seth, and they've spoiled it, they've spoiled it all with their meddling."

"As soon as Seth gets off work, I'm going to tell him, too." She began to cry then, and they were all huddled together when Beulah knocked on the door. "Shhh! Not a word. This has got to be our secret. Not even Aunt Beulah needs to know. Just us and, of course, Seth. I just pray he'll still love me. I pray..."

CHAPTER II HEARTACHES

HIGH SPRINGS

"Where's Maudie, Billy? If she's over at Mac Milligan's again I'm gonna tan her hide!"

"She's down by the river getting minnows for him. He pays her good, Ma."

"I don't trust that man far as I can throw him and neither does Widow. We were talking about him just this week about how he's spreadin' his good nature up and down this whole river."

Billy sat on the kitchen stoop of their small cabin tying the knots of his trot line. He could understand his ma's concern and so could everyone else who had ever known Mac for any length of time. Seems like this past year he'd got almost human, and the river people were suspicious.

Maudie came running up the sandy river bank with her pale sloshing. She stopped to retrieve a minnow that had fallen out, then resumed her climb. "Mama, Mama, look at how many I got. Bet Mister Mac will pay me good for all these!"

"Mr. Mac ain't gonna pay you a cent for those, Maudie, 'cause you ain't gonna go over there anymore, that is unless Billy or yore pa is with you, do you hear?"

"But, Mama..."

"But, mama nothing. If Poke wouldn't allow Catherine Inez to be around her own pa by herself, then you sure as shootin' ain't a gonna. Now, I don't want to hear another word. Sit right down beside Billy and help him with that trot line. That's where the money's gonna come from, not Mac's minnows."

Billy looked sideways at Maudie, then patted her hand. He whispered, "I'll go with you soon's I've finished mending this, Maudie. Ma said it was all right if you're with me or Pa. Don't ya fret."

She changed her expression in a wink, and Memphis, who was watching them through the window, realized that Billy had told Maudie that he'd go with her. Those two wouldn't know what to do without each other, especially now that Poke and Catherine Inez ain't around. Sure wish we'd hear about them. But if we did then that Mac would know where they are, too, and he'd go after them for sure. Best that we don't know.

"Best put those minnows in the shade, Maudie," Billy said loudly. "After I'm finished here, if'n Ma don't need me, I'll row over to Mistah Mac's with you so's you can sell them." He turned toward the window and smiled at his ma. He knew that she knew what he planned. His ma didn't miss a trick. He started whistling and Maudie joined in. Soon Memphis began singing along with them, *the little brown church in the dale - oh, come...come...*

Widow was giving James Jernigan her opinions on one Mac Milligan. "You know what Memphis said just the other day 'bout how he's play acting 'round her children. He's even buying up Maudie's minnows and acting real nice around Memphis. She even said she ain't smelled any shine on him for almost forever. Something's goin' on in that pea brain of his, and I'm here to tell you that it's so!" Widow handed James his supplies with him nodding in the affirmative at everything she said.

"And what's more...here James, best let Mister help you with all this...and what's more, if I ever hear from those children he ain't a goin' to ever hear about it. Nosiree, he won't! Not fitten to live, and why the Lord didn't take him when he had a chance I'm not knowing! I asked Brother Chipley about it at the last revival, and you know, even he couldn't give a good answer. Just stood there swaying back and forth like he was thinking on it, and you know what he said?"

"What, Widow?"

"He said, and I'm saying it just like he said it, 'the Lord knows what's best'. Well, I up and told him that I never doubted the Lord's wisdom but I thought for sure that him, being a preacher and all, could at least interpret some scripture so's we river people could understand why he decided to leave a no-good snake like Mac Milligan around to worry us with his devilment. And you know, James, he had the nerve to say that he'd pray for us. I about popped him one. Good thing for him that Mister was there to grab my arm...a good thing."

"I'd a thought Brother Chipley'd had some advice for us. You know, he's highly thought of all over the circuit." Having said that, James patted Widow's back and told her to not worry, that everyone up and down the river was keeping their eyes open for when Mac started up with the shine again, and that he'd be sure to tell Subee about all the commotion Mac was causing so she could spread the word to the men at the phosphate mine when she took them their meals.

"We appreciate that, James," Mister added. "Mac sure has got Widow riled up. He sure has. You know how she loved those children of his. She'd a taken them in if'n Poke hadn't already had his orders from Inez. She was determined that they would live with her kin, and now we don't even know where abouts they are. It's a true worry for Widow."

"Subee said that none of the men like him. Says as how he's always bragging to them about all the money he made when he worked the phosphate down on the Peace. Telling them that he piloted the tugboat that barged the pebble ore all the way to Boca Grande on Gasparilla Island and then put it in the holds of those great big ocean ships. Rupert Mock asked him why he bothered to come back to the Santa Fe, and he said ' 'cause this is home'. All the men laughed at that. Heck, they knew he'd probably been fired."

"He was telling us that very same tale when he got back. Widow asked him why he didn't get on one of those big ocean going steamers he was always talking about, and he said the same thing about this bein' home. What they got him doing at the mine?"

"Not a blessed thing but looking after the drying bins. Rupert told him that he read in the Gainesville paper as how the mining's 'bout played out from Arcadia south to Nocatee and Hull and that it was going to move up north to Polk County. And big mouth Mac said he knew that was gonna happen when he was down there. Now, how'd he know when the big boys didn't even know it? He's sure full of hisself. You'd think that with his bum arm and that gimp and scar he'd have been brought down a notch or two, wouldn't you?"

"Well, some men just got a high opinion of themselves, and guess he still thinks of hisself as a hot shot fighter like he used to be."

"Good day to you, Bunnell. See you next week. Subee's gonna be needin' 'bout the same amount of supplies. Don't think that mine'll be closing up any time soon, and those men sure got appetites."

"Good day to ya, James. Give a howdy to Subee, heah?"

Widow was on the porch waiting for him. "What you two been talking about?"

"Oh, he was a saying as how none of the men at the mine liked Mac and that he was always bragging 'bout how important he was down on the Peace."

"I for one wish he'd move back down there. We sure don't need him around here."

"Now, Honey, stop your fretting 'bout the likes of him. He'll get his."

"But, it sure seems to me that whoever's in charge is gonna make us wait for a long time. I wish I could hurry it up."

"You do keep a fellow on his toes, Honey. Maybe Mac wouldn't have been so mean if Inez had had some of your starch."

"I've thought of that a hundred times, I have. She was too easy on him." And with that she tugged on Mister's ear, then pecked him on his cheek. "But, I sure do like to love on you, sweetheart. Maybe she didn't do enough of that either." They walked into the store chuckling.

"Maudie, you ready to go over to Mister Mac's?"

"Be there soon's I get the bucket of minnows, Billy. Hey, Mama, we're going over to Mister Mac's. Won't be gone long. Bet I got two hundred minnows for him!"

"I want you two home 'fore your Pa gets back from town, you hear? Bet he won't remember to go by the store for that flour. Wait 'til I tell Widow 'bout those weevils. Never saw so many. Had to be old flour."

She sighed a big one and sat on the boat's thwart, swinging her legs.

"Stop that, Maudie. Ya gonna tip us over with your carrying on. Never saw anyone so anxious to get their hands on money as you are. What ya wanta be, a millionaire?"

She hummed the half mile to the Milligan landing, and could hardly wait for him to tie up the boat.

"Maudie, you hold still now, you hear? Grief! This'll be the last time I ever take you anywhere the way you're acting!"

"Howdy, Mister Mac. Brought you a whole bucket of minnows. Must be two hundred of em." Mac hobbled down the bank to meet them, and gave Maudie his hand helping her out of the boat.

"Well, that's real nice of you, Maudie. Real nice," he mumbled. He'd got so he could speak near about as good as he used to before the accident. Folks around there said that they wished that he'd go back to his hand signs, so they wouldn't have to listen to him so much. But Maudie felt sorry for him, and she was glad that he could speak better. After all, he was her best friend's pa.

Mac took the bucket from her, patted her on the head and said, "Billy, I been thinkin' about maybe leavin' this place. How'd you like to catch that big Rhode Island Red rooster to take on home to Memphis? I got no use for it what with the Plymouth Rock doing his roostering job so good." He laughed, and so did Billy.

"That's mighty nice of you, Mister Mac. Maybe I should ask Ma first."

"No need to 'cause it's a gift. Y'all been mighty good to me. Now you go and catch the critter while I settle up with Maudie here. Go on, now, might take you a while."

"Come on, Maudie, and let's count all these minnows. Oughta be 'nuff here to catch all the fish in the Santa Fe and the Suwannee to boot, huh?"

"Sure oughta, Mister Mac." She was hoping that he'd give her a piece of candy like he usually did. Last time it was a lemon drop and peppermint round, too. Oh, they were good. He told her to not tell her mama, so she didn't, not that she'd care. She always let her have a piece when they went to the Post.

Mac could see Billy chasing after the rooster, so he knew he had plenty of time. Hell, that rooster probably couldn't be caught inside a hour. He put down his cane and sat on the edge of the big bed. He held out his good arm and called to Maudie.

"Come on over here, Maudie, to your Uncle Mac. I got something special for you. Now don't be afraid, cause I know you're gonna like it. Oh, how you're gonna like it."

Maudie's eyes got big with wonder. I bet it's a whole sack of candy. I bet it is. She sat beside him and when he unbuttoned his overalls she was sure that he'd pull out a sack of candy. But when she saw what he'd pulled out, she got up off the bed. "Don't be afraid, Honey, I'm not going to hurt you. You ever see one of these before?" She shook her head no. "I gotta be going, Mister Mac, I gotta..."

"Don't you want to touch it? Here give me your hand and I'll help you..."

"I gotta be going, Mister Mac, honest..."

"Oh, it's soft just like velvet when it gets big like this. See, all the wrinkles are gone. Here, give me your hand and I'll help you."

By then he'd got off the bed and Maudie was backing up. She turned around quickly and sprung for the door calling over her shoulder, "I'm coming, Billy, I'll help you!"

"Bout time you got here. Here, hold this croaker sack so I can get him in it. Watch out! You wanta get yourself spurred! Grief! Maudie, what's wrong with you? You know better than that!" He turned back toward the house and waved to Mac, who was standing on the porch grinning.

Hell, she won't tell. Never saw a youngun who loved candy more than that little Maudie. She'll be back, and next time I'll do her. Oh, how I'll do her! He continued grinning and waving.

"Whatcha so quiet about? Didn't Mister Mac give you as much money as you thought?"

She mumbled that she'd forgotten to get it.

"Forgot! You want me to turn around and go back?"

"NO I DON'T, BILLY RAWLES!"

"Whatcha yellin' at me about? Here I row you all the way over there, and you proceed to yell at me. A fine howdy do that is, missy!"

She began to cry then and sniffle .

"I'm sorry I yelled at you, Maudie, honest I am. What's wrong with you, anyway? You sick or something?"

"No, I'm not sick and ain't nothin' wrong with me. Just leave me alone, that's all."

He turned to yell at her one more time before pulling the boat up on the bank. "I ain't ever going to take you any place ever again, Maudie Rawles."

"What're you two fussin' about? Here I was just thinkin' about how good you two got along, and here you are yellin' at each other. Well, I never! Billy, whatcha got there?"

"Where you runnin' off to, Maudie?" She turned to Billy and said, "What's got into her?"

"I don't know, but I ain't ever gonna..."

"What's in that sack? "

"Oh, Mister Mac said it was a gift..."

"A gift from the likes of Mac Milligan? I'm not believing that." She thought a while and slowly continued. "Billy, where was Maudie when he had you chasing after that rooster?"

"She was inside counting the minnows and like a fool forgot to even get the money for them."

"Maudie forgot to get her money? How long was she in there alone with him?"

"Ma, what's wrong? You don't think that he did..."

She left him standing in the side yard and ran to the cabin, burst inside and found Maudie on the bed crying.

She went to her and pulled her onto her lap. Stroking her hair back from her face she began to question her as to what happened. All she could get out of Maudie was that she didn't touch IT.

"Honey, I am your ma and I know that you didn't do anything wrong. That's not what I want to know. What I want to know is what Mac did, that's all."

"I thought he had a bag of candy in his overalls, Mama, and that he was gonna give it to me, but instead he pulled out his..."

"That's all right, Honey, I think I know what he did..."

"But, Mama, I didn't touch it, I didn't!"

"Honey, I believe you. Now I want you to lie down right here and rest. I'm gonna call to Billy and have him go to the Post and give a note to Widow and Mister Bunnell. Mister Mac is sick out of his head and needs to be put away. I think that knock on his head must've made him crazy or somethin'. Now, you rest. He needs to be put away..."

"Where will they put him? In the crazy house, Mama?"

"If that's what the law decides, then that's right where he'll go."

"Billy, now listen to what I'm saying. I want you to go to the Post and give a note to Widow. They've got to get the law over to Mac's before your Pa gets home. Oh, Lordie, if he gets to him first, then there's no tellin' what will happen.!"

"Ma, what did he do to Maudie? He didn't ..."

"No, son, he didn't, but he could have. Now, you've got to hurry. Your Pa will be home inside two hours. Don't look like that, son. You didn't do anything wrong. How'd you know..."

"But, I should've..."

"No! He's a snake, and can't many figure a snake."

Memphis rushed down the bank and handed Billy the note with orders to wait for an answer from Widow, then to make tracks back home.

"Ma, you think Pa'll kill him?"

"Not if you hurry, he won't."

Widow Bunnell was in her glory. A crisis! Wasn't anyone anywhere who took to a crisis like Widow. Billy was barely in his skiff and on his way home when she had Mister ride over to James Jernigan's to have him get word to the men at the mine, so they could head off Darius. They needed to get word to the law to get over to Mac's before Darius got home, or he'd kill Mac for sure.

Skeets Boe hightailed it to High Springs even before Darius got off work and got the deputy to wire Gainesville and get word to the sheriff. He deputized Skeets on the spot and didn't wait for the wire from the sheriff's office.

"Gonna have us a lynching on our hands, sure as shootin', Skeets. Not that he doesn't deserve it, for he does."

"That's a fact, Bruce, that's a fact. But we don't want Darius to get in any trouble because of it, now do we?"

"Nope." Bruce Lindrose was a man of few words, but every one he uttered carried weight. He was a big man, carrying well over two hundred pounds and standing a good two inches over six feet. If he ever let his temper take over, it was feared he'd be able to break a man in two. His biceps were the size of most men's legs. He'd been a blacksmith for most of his forty years before being made deputy, but he had a gentle nature. Few men had ever tested him.

The two boats skimmed up to the Milligan landing, and Mac was sitting on the porch just like nothing had happened.

"Evening, Bruce, boys. What you doin' out in this neck of the woods?"

Bruce answered. "We're here to try to stop Darius Rawles from killing you, Mac."

"What for? I ain't done nothin'."

"Well, then we don't have a problem, do we? But, in case Darius sees it otherwise, you'd better come with us."

Mac didn't argue. Wouldn't have done him any good and he knew it. Dumb ass kid. Couldn't keep her mouth shut. But it's her word against mine. I ain't worried. "Best have someone take care of my place 'til I come back, Bruce. Got some mighty fine chickens here."

Skeets spoke up, "You ain't gonna be coming back, Mac, lessen it's in a big old box."

"That's enough, Skeets. The law'll take care of his likes." Bruce said.

"Well, if it don't, I can guarantee you that we will. Don't nobody do what he did to a little girl and get by with it in these parts, Bruce. Now, you rightly know that."

"I said it once, Skeets. I ain't saying it again."

There was no more conversation all the way to High Springs.

There was an answer to the telegram waiting for Bruce. *Bring him down on the next train - stop - will take care of him - stop - Sheriff.*

When Bruce and Mac arrived in Gainesville the sheriff was waiting. "What's it like up there? The men getting anxious for a rope to stretch his skinny neck?" he asked Bruce.

"Yep!"

"Thought so. Talked it over with the judge, and we think it's best to get him out of here. Had Buck get him a crate and we'll ship him down state like the freight he is..."

"You mean we ain't gonna give him a trial?."

"It'd be his word against that little girl's, and you know as well as I do he wouldn't last a night. I've seen it before. You just don't mess with a man's little girl. Not in this state you don't. Saw it in the War. God, did I ever see it. Poor little things!" He got misty eyed.

Bruce saw them wheeling the big wooden crate out of the freight yard. The sheriff started laughing and said, "The last occupant in that was Bill Radebaugh's prize Brahma bull. Shipped him all the way to Texas and back and made over two thousand dollars in service fees. Doubt that Bill would approve of this baggage riding in his bull's box, though." He and the men around him laughed.

Mac was shaking his head at the crowd and yelling that he was a citizen and deserved a trial, and he wasn't gonna stand for this treatment, and on and on until Bruce had had enough. He grabbed hold of Mac's good arm, his hand went all the way around it, and with his face not three inches from Mac's very quietly said, "Get in!"

They stood along the track, and when the train pulled out Bruce turned to the sheriff and asked where they were sending him. "Got enough money out of petty cash to get him as far as Bartow. Wired the sheriff there - he's a friend of mine - to accept the baggage and do what he wants to with him." He began laughing.

"What's so funny, Sheriff?"

"Oh, I just wish I could be a witness to the expression on that bull's face if he could see what a puny looking specimen moved into his crate. I just wish I could. Come to think of it, his name was Mac too."

ARCADIA

"But, Seth, I'm sure he's a detective here on account of my parents. I'm sure," Maggie said.

"You don't know that for a fact. All I'm asking of you, Honey, is to approve my going over to the hotel where he's staying and finding out. That's all. I'd hate to be accused of something I've not done, wouldn't you?"

Jack spoke up, "Maggie, what's it gonna hurt? I mean, if he's not here on account of you, then you won't have any reason to be mad at your folks."

Seth pulled her up from the parlor chair, kissed her cheek, and left the hotel for the Southern Hotel and his hoped-for interview with the detective. He could understand Maggie's anger if her parents did go against her wishes, but what if the detective was here on another matter.

Secretly, he wanted Maggie to make up with her folks. Folks were important. How ironic it was, the whole thing. When Maggie had told him who she was, he sat on the sofa and laughed. He had just received a letter from his Aunt Rose telling him that it appeared that Delia's and Tucker's romance was not as before. When she came back from St. Augustine, Tucker had not accompanied her as planned. And, here I am in love with his sister and am here all because of him and Delia. It's hard to believe that I ever thought I was in love with Delia. I guess she was the sister I never had. The world's full of surprises.

He went up to the hotel desk and inquired about Roy. He was in the dining room having his breakfast, he was told. Seth had decided to treat the matter lightly and to use his position on the paper for an entry.

He walked up to the steward and was directed to the long table in the back of the room. The detective was not alone, but Seth proceeded to his table anyway.

"Excuse me, Detective Kenton, but I'm Seth Roberts with the *DeSoto County News*. I'm doing a special article on the reasons visitors come to Arcadia, you know, if it's for our wonderful climate or business reasons, and so forth. I'd like very much to interview you when you've finished your breakfast."

Roy looked upset by the intrusion, but his lady companion thought the idea of a newspaper interview delightful and said so. So Roy told Seth, "It'll have to be a short one, young man, because I have work to do. I'll meet you in the lobby as soon as Mrs. Payne and I've had our breakfast."

Seth had pulled out his pad and pencil and was standing at the desk talking to Blanche Stevens when Roy came in. They went to the two overstuffed chairs in the corner, but before Seth could get started asking questions, Roy explained about the robbery and that he didn't want news of his mission printed in any newspaper.

"You're quite right, detective. Had I any idea of the nature of your visit, I'd not have inquired. You can be assured that not a word will appear in the *News*, not a word."

Seth rose, shook his hand and said quietly, "I hope you solve the case soon, and I just hope that the robbers aren't here in Arcadia."

"I have every reason to believe that they've gone on south, and so does my partner. He's on his way to Punta Gorda right now. I'm to follow on the next train." Unsaid was that he had wanted to spend more time with the attractive Betty Payne; otherwise, he'd have accompanied Whitby.

Seth rushed back to the Young Hotel with the good news for Maggie and the kids. "You see, Honey, he doesn't have a clue that you're here."

In a way Maggie was relieved but on the other hand she wasn't totally convinced. "Maybe he said that just to throw you off, Seth."

"Maggie, you've read about the Bartow robbery in the paper, and you know that they haven't caught the robbers, and you know that it is a national bank, so the sheriff will be only assisting the feds. Now you know that. What more proof do you want? If you want, I'll go over to the court house and make some inquiries. Is that what you want?"

"No, it's just that he was the one that they sent before, and it's hard to believe he showed up here on something else, that's all. It's not like Arcadia is visited every day by detectives, you know."

"You're right, but it's just a coincidence. Can't you see that?"

"If you say so, Honey. I guess you're right."

Seth turned to Jack and Nellie and said, "She's not convinced, kids. I'm going on over to the courthouse and have a little talk with Margaret Stevens. She and Blanche know everything going on at the courthouse and the Southern. Hey, lady mine, give a fellow a smile. What's with this long face?"

"I guess it's that I've been on the run for so long, it's hard to let go, Seth."

"Now's the time, Honey. Now's the time. Hey, let me help you with this burden. I've got broad shoulders and can take a lot."

Maggie hugged him hard, buried her tear-stained face in his neck and said so that Jack and Nellie could barely hear, "I love you, Seth. I love you so."

He held her for a minute until she could compose herself and left the hotel whistling.

"You've got yourself a good one, Maggie," Jack said.

"You don't have to tell me that, because I know it. I think I'd die if anything happened to us, all of us. That's why I'm so concerned."

SOUTH SPRING

"Honey, how many times do I have to say it. Now, right now, you're to stop even thinking of going to Arcadia. We're going to abide by Raine's wishes and not go down 'til December for the wedding."

"But we could stay with Callie and Clay. We wouldn't even have to be in town with her. I still can't believe that they didn't let us know that she was there."

"They probably didn't know who she was. After all, they'd never seen her, and Meade was away at school. We'll find out all the particulars when we get there. She sounds so happy that I don't think we should rock the boat."

"I know you're right, and I don't want to interfere, truly I don't. That's not it at all, Honey. It's just that she could wear my wedding dress, just like SuSu did, and she could plan the wedding party and make all the decisions and......"

Layke took her hands in his. "I know it hurts you to not help with the wedding, now I know that. But Raine wants to do the whole thing by herself, even to planning her own wedding dress. It's like Jonah said last night at supper, Honey, Raine wants to just be Raine and doesn't want us to even be a part of this new life...just yet. She's allowed us to re-enter it, and I think we should be thankful for this little bit. She'll come around."

"I can't believe that you're saying that, you and Jonah. I'll admit that I've never understood her, but then she's never understood me either. And why doesn't she want Callie and Clay aware of who she is? That doesn't make any sense either. Is she ashamed of us, is that it?"

"Berta, you know better than that. Yes, it does make sense - at least to her. She has her reasons. She said that her fiance understands her reasoning and approves. What more do we need to hear?"

"I'll not do anything to upset either one of you, Honey. It's just that it is such an important occasion, and I'll miss being in on it. I relive SuSu's wedding day over and over. Memories are important, Layke, at least they are to me and every other woman I know, and she's shutting us out."

"I know that. I understand completely, but we'll abide by her wishes as we promised, even thought we don't understand them, won't we?"

MONTICELLO

Rose was upstairs in her quarters. She had finally packed all of Seth's things and had them ready for Harrison to take to the train station. Seth'll be so busy at the newspaper he probably won't have time to do much else, but I am going to send his bat and glove anyway. Harrison and Easter gave these to him...how long ago? Oh, how proud he was of them. But he has a new home and a new life ahead of him now. I'm so happy for him. I can hardly wait to meet his Maggie."

"Juanita, is that you?" she called down the stairs. "No, Aunt Rose, it's Delia. Mama will come in later. She wanted to get everything ready for Nolan's party."

Rose ran down the stairs. "Is Harrison coming in with her?"

"She didn't say, but I imagine he will. Why?"

Rose hesitated, then continued, "I finished boxing up Seth's things, and Harrison said he'd take them down to the depot for me."

"Oh," is all Delia responded.

How she's changed, Rose thought. Just a few months ago she was the old Delia, demanding, unthinking, spoiled, but look at her now, and all because Tucker Williams didn't visit for the Fourth's activities. One little thing happened and it's thrown her for a loop. I'm glad that Seth's found someone else, I truly am. Oh, she'll turn out all right, but if she'd had to put up with what her mama and I did, she probably couldn't have managed. I'm glad Seth had to work for his, I truly am. She's had too much.

"Aunt Rose," Delia said sweetly, "Mama said that you're going to make Seth's betrothed her gown, is that so?"

"I couldn't believe it when she wrote me and asked me if I would. It was truly a shock. Did Juanita tell you that she drew a picture of what she'd like?"

"I think she mentioned something about it."

"Here, and here's the note she sent. She writes like a child even if she is a school teacher - teaches high school, you know. Seth said that they're going to continue living at the hotel even after they're married, because Aunt Beulah, as he calls her, asked them to. Wasn't that nice of her? And did Juanita tell you that he got a big raise and is now the assistant editor?"

"Yes, she mentioned it. I'm real happy for Seth. You know that he was always more of a brother to me than Nolan. Guess it's because he's closer to my age. I'm sure he'll be happy." She sighed and looked out the window.

Finally Rose asked, "Delia, did you want something in particular?"

"It's just that Mama thought I'd be able to help you in the shop. There's nothing doing at Athea right now, you know, except the party, and Mama's got that all tended to."

"Oh," is all Rose could come up with, too.

"I do need to run this gown over to Janet Dole's for the party tomorrow night. Would you mind watching the shop for me?"

"Oh, not at all. Give me something to do," she sighed again.

Don't know how Juanita will last until October with her around sighing every other breath. I hope she doesn't think she can hang around here every day. Why, I'd lose my mind.

"Delia, if Mrs. Montrose comes for her gown, it's on the second shelf in the back room. I won't be but a minute. Why don't you sit right here and sketch some ideas for Seth's Maggie's wedding dress? I'd appreciate some fresh ideas. She seems to lean toward the apricot or peach color. And she said that she doesn't like real fancy things, more plain, you know. Maybe a little lace or a few ruffles but, not much else."

Delia sat at the drafting table and began to sketch. Rose glanced at her, then at the sketch. She's just like Conner, can turn out a sketch fast as he could. Never saw the likes of it. Heavens, it takes me and Juanita forever to get it right. Maybe she won't be too much of a burden after all. But I doubt that she can use a needle without sticking herself.

"Be back in no time, Delia. If you don't mind, how about sketching several ideas. It certainly will help. Then I can send them to Maggie and she can decide on the one she wants. Thank you, dear."

Delia looked at the first sketch. If this were my wedding dress, I'd like a set-in yoke with high collar covered with that heavy Brussels lace Mama bought in Savannah in that beautiful watered silk fabric of a soft cream, with a fitted long princess bodice. Maybe the skirt would look pretty in tulip panels edged with rich velvet roping, a full skirt with the panels longer in back, making sort of a train. But I guess Seth's Maggie would think it too fancy.

Delia sat back and studied the sketch. Why can't this be my dress? I know Tucker loves me. I just know it, and he didn't seem too upset when I told him about Mum and Da. But why didn't he come to Athea for the few days like he promised? He can't use his sister as an excuse anymore, now that they know she's all right. And it shouldn't be because of the dagblasted bicycle race. I wish he'd never even heard of that wonderful Tallahassee Bicycle Club. It's obvious that he thinks more of that than he does of me. Dullest Fourth I've ever spent. I don't understand why Mum wouldn't let me go to Tallahassee for the festivities and his race. It's not like we would have been all alone at his house. Heavens, they have servants all over the place.

She sighed and turned the sketch to the back of the large pad and began on the next one. When Rose got back from her errand, she was amazed at how many Delia had completed. But more than that, she was amazed at the quality of her work. I bet Juanita doesn't even know she can draw.

"Delia, where did you learn to draw so well? I don't remember that you could draw."

"Oh, we had to study art at St. Joseph's. I mean we HAD to. Also dance, especially ballet, and some musical instrument. I chose piano but am not very good at it. They said every well educated young lady had to be accomplished in the arts. I enjoyed the acting and elocution the best. I like to draw, too, but its not my favorite."

She's talking like I wound her up, without any expression. I simply will not be able to stand this attitude until she leaves. "Delia, you have a beautiful talent, dear. I doubt that your mama even knows about it. Let's surprise her and do a lot of sketches. Then when she gets over Nolan's birthday party, she won't have to do all the work. I bet she has at least ten orders from Tallahassee for the inauguration ball, and you know what a snit she gets in when it's something important."

"I don't mind. There's nothing else to do, anyway."

"I thought that you were going down to Tarpon Springs to visit your roommate. Don't you have to get packed for that?"

"That won't take long. Mama wants me to go, but I'm not too anxious to. Meriam's folks are very nice and I do like them, and I like the idea of going bathing in the Gulf." What she didn't mention was that Tucker had also promised to accompany her there, but because he had seldom written since June she had given up hope of that ever transpiring. All he could talk about was that darned old bicycle race, anyway.

Delia tore off the last sketch and said, "Here, Aunt Rose, this one's for Seth's intended. How do you like it?"

"Why Delia Rose O'Farrell, it's perfect, just perfect. What type fabric do you think?"

"Probably a heavy cotton sateen. I know it's not formal, but if they have a daytime wedding in a small church, I believe it appropriate. I doubt that Arcadia has a large church. From what I've heard it's mostly a cow town, isn't it?"

"Seth loves it no matter what kind of town it is..."

"I didn't mean anything by that, Aunt Rose. I only meant that it was a small town, and I doubt that they have a lot of formal functions like we do here or in Tallahassee, that's all."

"You're probably right, Honey. I'll get these off in the next post. But, Delia, I know she'll select the apricot cotton sateen, I just know it."

ARCADIA

Callie and Clay were on their way to the Arcadia depot to meet the afternoon train, as they had promised Berta and Layke that they would. Raine had asked that they not see her until the actual ceremony, and although Berta thought it ridiculous, Layke had assured her that they would abide by her wishes. They'd spend a few days at Tall Ten with the Willetts before the ceremony. Layke had promised Clay that he'd give him a few pointers for his bid for the mayoral race in Arcadia.

When Berta wrote Callie about Raine and gave her the few particulars that she felt were needed, she received a return letter immediately. Callie had written that the whole town thought the world of Raine, or Maggie as she was called in Arcadia. She also said that Seth Roberts was a fine young man, industrious, talented and well liked by everyone. Her Aunt Beulah had practically adopted the entire family. That rankled Berta. Raine had casually mentioned in one of her letters that she had taken up with two young children in her travels and that they had become like a family. Well, I guess that everyone in that town thinks that they are her own brother and sister.

Berta complained to Layke, "I don't know how we're going to explain this mess Raine's got us in. I really don't."

"We don't have to make a fuss over it. It would appear from Callie's letter that everyone has accepted them and thinks highly of them. What more should be said?"

"I would think that living a lie would mean something to someone, say, like the school board."

"Apparently not, Honey. She said in her last letter that she had met with them to explain what happened and that they brushed off the incident as if it were nothing. She sounded so relieved. I'm glad that Seth chose to accompany her. He sounds like a fine young man, and we're fortunate that Raine found him."

"I know you're right and I am glad that things are going well for her. It's just that I hate to be shut out of her life. Heavens, she even asked his aunt to make her wedding dress. Now, really, Layke."

"What's wrong with that, Berta?"

"What's wrong is that she won't even let us see her before the wedding, meet the man she's marrying or have anything whatsoever to do with her or the wedding. That's what, sir!"

"If it were SuSu, I'd not understand. But it's Raine, so I do."

"And why should someone, simply because they won't play by the rules of common decency, be excused, Layke? Why?"

"I guess I'm feeling guilty, Honey." He got up from his chair, went to her and tiredly said, "We tried to make Raine into someone we would approve. We should have helped her to develop her own qualities. I guess that's why I can excuse her."

Berta sighed, thought a while and responded, "We've had more fights since we heard from Raine than we have in all our married life. Do you realize that? I'm not going to let her come between us again. As a matter of fact I'm going down to Arcadia and have a wonderful time getting reacquainted with the Willetts, such a delightful couple. I'm truly looking forward to spending some time at Tall Ten. You don't have to be concerned about how I'm going to handle myself, kind sir, because I'm going to do just fine. The Raine Williams chapter of my life is over. Don't look at me that way. I mean it. If she wants to be Maggie whatever, then let her. I'm Mrs. Layke Williams and that's enough for me."

Berta rose, reached for him, hugged him and said, "That should be enough for any woman in the world, my husband. I just hope Raine and Seth will be as happy, and I mean that with all my heart."

"This is almost like being with Kate, Callie. Now, I mean it. We saw each other rarely, but when we were together it was like we had just seen each other at church or in town." Berta and Callie were in a separate buggy driven by Sap, and Layke and Clay were in the buckboard with the luggage. "And would you look at those two. They've talked non-stop just like we have."

Sap helped Berta out of the buggy while Callie hopped out the other side. I can't get over how much she looks like Kate. I never thought so when she was younger. And she seems so happy, or maybe I should say content. "Why, Callie, you didn't mention that you'd added a wing to the place. Isn't that nice!"

"We were outgrowing it, Berta. When Meade's home he needs a room to himself to study. At first he used Jay's studio, but that left Clay without a place to write. Just seemed the thing to do. Here, let Sap get those things."

A young girl rounded the corner of the house, and Berta would have sworn it was Callie Meade reborn...until she spoke. This was as self-assured a young girl as she had ever heard. "Thought you'd never get here. Lily was riding herd on Jimmy and me 'til I wanted to bop her one."

"That's quite enough, Annie. Here, I want you to meet Mrs. Williams, your grandmother's good friend from up Old Town and Tallahassee way and Uncle Jay's mother-in-law."

Annie nodded, then proceeded to give Callie an accounting of everything that transpired from the time she and Clay had left that morning. Callie rolled her eyes at Berta, and Berta had great difficulty restraining her amusement. That child will certainly take to the stage. Never have I seen anyone that dramatic. I bet she's a handful, but, oh my, what a delight! She caught herself thinking, I wonder if that is how people thought of Raine. I bet it was. Layke is absolutely right in his evaluation. I wonder if I wanted another little SuSu or a little Berta? Why is it that when we are given children the Lord doesn't give us that extra wisdom that we need? Maybe we're so busy listening to ourselves that we don't hear him. Can I ever make it up to her? I am certainly going to try...

"Are you hard of hearing, Mrs. Williams?"

"I beg your pardon?"

"I asked you three times."

"I'm sorry, Annie, but my mind was elsewhere..."

"It must have been. Daddy Parker was hard of hearing, you know."

"No, I didn't know. What did say, dear?"

"Mama said that I should ask you if you had a good - no, a pleasant trip. Did you?"

"Yes, Annie, it was very comfortable, thank you."

"I like the way you talk. It's sort of like humming your words."

"People say that is a Georgia accent, Annie. I'm glad that you approve it."

"I don't approve or disapprove it. I just like how it sounds. There's a difference, you know."

"No, I don't believe that I do."

"Well, it's like this. If my Mama tells me that I can go somewhere, that means that she approves my going, but that doesn't mean that she's happy that I'm going. My big brother told me that. He's very smart - about some things. But there are ways where he's positively foolish. You wanta hear some of his foolish ideas? I can tell you lots of them."

"I must unpack Mr. Williams's and my things and get them hung up before they get mussed. But later on, perhaps."

"You don't have to be polite to me. I'm used to people shushing me. Doesn't bother me a bit. You're pretty. I like looking at you. If you find me staring, then that's just the way I am. If I see something I like to look at, then look at it I will."

"Annie, don't you be bothering Mrs. Williams. Berta, shoo her out. She'll talk your head off."

"I'm enjoying her, Callie. She reminds me a lot of Raine. Raine's my daughter..."

"Oh, I know, the one who goes by Maggie. Her brother, well, he's not really her brother, but he is going to be my husband when I get grown."

Callie overheard her, "What did you say, Annie?"

"I told Mrs. Williams that I'm going to marry Jack Pope when I get grown. Don't worry, Mama, that won't be for a long time, say, seven or eight years."

"Have you told Jack of your plans?"

"No, of course not. I'm letting him think that I hate him. Do him good, too. Don't want him to think that I'm in love with him just yet. Let him linger..."

"Annie Willett, I think we had better have a little talk about this, young lady."

"Let's wait until after the wedding, please. I need to work on him some more. You see, men don't have an idea how our minds work." Throwing her arms in the air, sighing, she sashayed out the door and flopped in a parlor chair.

Berta and Callie stood with mouths open, not saying a word. Finally, Berta whispered. "How old is that child?"

"Nine going on twenty, I'm thinking. I haven't the vaguest idea where she got all that, but she does have big ears. Probably overheard the girls talking at Maggie's shower. I bet that's it. She and Maggie's sister - I'm sorry, Berta, I mean Nellie - were at Beulah's and were probably in the other parlor taking everything in. Clay said she was going to be either an actress or politician or lawyer. I'm thinking all three." Berta thought, and I'm thinking that you'd better keep an eye on that one. But she found her amusing.

"I think it wonderful that you could be home for the wedding, Meade," Berta said. But the entire time the conversation was taking place she kept remembering Annie's opinion of her older brother, and she had a difficult time keeping the smile off her face. Callie set as good a table as Kate had, she thought, while looking around the long table.

"No thanks, Lily, that was delicious. Berta and I both have to watch our waistlines. Tucker gets in tomorrow on the morning train. I guess Raine's already told you. He had a bicycle race in Tally or he'd have been here before. Beulah said she would save him a room, or he could share with Seth. They met in Monticello when Tucker was seeing a young lady up there. Isn't it a small world, though?"

"I don't think it's such a small world. That's a ridiculous statement, begging your pardon, Mr. Williams."

"Annie Willett, that's quite enough!" Clay said sternly.

"Yes, Annie, you've got a big mouth!"

"Meade, enough from you, too. I do hope all this seems like home to you two and not just two rude children."

Layke laughed, "Frankly, I'd like to hear what Annie thinks about this being a small world or not."

"No, you wouldn't!" Meade chimed in. "She'll drive you crazy with her half-baked ideas. She sure does me!"

Annie rolled her eyes at Berta as if to say, see, I told you he was foolish. Berta had to turn her head.

"Annie," Layke continued, "I really would..."

"It's like this. I keep hearing grown-ups talking all the time about what a small world it is, and I don't for the life of me understand where they get such ideas. Daddy says it's a figure of speech, whatever that means. How can it be a small world when I can't see the Gulf of Mexico or the Atlantic or Europe or..."

"Like I said, she'll drive you crazy. If she can't see it, then it's not there."

"That's not what I said, Meade. I'm well aware that Europe exists as do all the other places. But it is not a small world. It's a very big world, and I intend to see every speck of it. It might take almost forever, but I'll do it. So there!"

"I, for one, hope you have that opportunity, Annie."

"Oh, I intend to create the opportunity, Mrs. Williams. My brother, the one I'm not going to speak to for a very long time, says that I'm upset that God created the world and everything in it and didn't ask me for assistance. He thought that I hadn't heard that stupid remark, but as you'll soon find out, my hearing is very acute. I'm not the least upset with God. Now, that would indeed be stupid."

Clay rose, clicked his finger once, Callie also rose and Jimmy sat laughing his head almost off. He knew that Annie was going to really catch it. Boy howdy, when his daddy clicked his finger, that was the end of Annie and her mouth.

It was a cool December day. Berta was glad she'd thought to take along her coat with the rich velvet collar. She and Layke had decided to ride into town with Callie and Clay and not drive in early. They were both hesitant about seeing Raine. Layke could tell that Berta was nervous, so he talked about everything but the wedding.

"Callie, have you seen any sign of that Texas tick we're reading about? Reuben has been keeping abreast of the situation and believes that we're going to have a mess on our hands."

"And well he should. Sweet is upgrading our stock. He seems to think that the healthier they are, the more resistant."

"We'll end up with a compulsory state-wide law, you can bet on it."

"What do you mean, Layke?" Clay asked.

"It's bound to happen, Clay. Some ranchers will drag their heels like always, and then the state will be the bad guy. I've seen it across the board. And why should another law have to be legislated? After a while one gets tired of being the bad guy. Reuben said that some ranchers up in Paynes Prairie are already building dipping vats to combat the ticks. But more needs to be known. First they thought that they would only breed on cattle, but I just read that the females will feed off any animal, rabbit, fox, you name it. It's going to be a problem, all right."

"Could we please speak of something more pleasant, husband mine?"

"Of course, my sweet. Clay and I were discussing his first run for public office. It's a good beginning, running for mayor. Get your feet wet, then go for bigger and better..."

"Whoa, Layke. I'm ambitious, it's true, but this is more of a feeling of pride. I mean it. We're so behind the times that it's frightening. Do you know that we don't have a public water system? Nor fire fighting equipment? If there was a fire in downtown Arcadia we'd have to resort to a bucket brigade. That's ridiculous!"

"You can see that my husband is going to be the perfect mayor, can't you?"

"Callie, you know as well as I do that Bartow has outdistanced us by a mile! If I am elected the first thing I'm going to do is work with Ed Scott on his idea for that utility company. He wants electric lights, ice plant and telephone company, and, by gum, I'm going to help him realize it. We'll have it operating inside of a year. While Oak Street is dusty and lined with horse troughs, Bartow's streets are paved..."

"Hey, mister, I am well aware that we're way behind a lot of towns in the state, but Clay, you're not going to change things overnight." She laughed and said, "Unless you have Annie on the same ticket with you."

That's how Raine saw them as they drove up, laughing and happy. She couldn't believe how glad she was to see them. She'd made sure that Seth remained in his room with Tucker. After all, it was supposed to be bad luck to see his bride on their day.

Layke said not a word, just jumped down and was at the hotel door even before Clay halted the rig. Berta was not far behind. Clay and Callie looked at each other, took their time to assure the threesome a chance to be alone for a little while, then followed. Beulah was hugging Berta and Layke and carrying on about how glad she was that they let her have their beautiful daughter as a guest at the hotel, and everyone was talking at once.

Beulah pulled her through the crowd and said, "Come on, Berta. I want you to meet Seth's Aunt Rose, who came all the way from Monticello for the wedding."

Berta wiped her tears and asked if it was time to go to the church? She wanted to tell Raine how beautiful she looked, for she did, and how much she loved her gown. It was indeed beautiful, and she thought her hair looked so nice that short, and she could have gone on forever. But there was no time. Is there ever enough time, I wonder? They're born, and before you know it, they're grown and gone, and where did the time go? I must ask Annie, she thought with a smile.

"What's so amusing, my sweet? Is it seeing our beautiful Raine on her wedding day? Is that it?"

"That's only part of it. I'll save the rest for our train ride home."

Beulah rang the dinner triangle and shouted, "It's that time, folks. Rube has got George in the pew, and our bride is anxious to repeat the vows. Let's get to the church."

Berta could see that Layke was taken aback when he saw Jack walking beside Raine down Oak Street. He'd assumed that he'd be giving the bride away. She squeezed his arm and he put on a brave smile, but she hurt all over for him. When they entered the church a young man took her arm and said that she was to sit behind the bridal party. She smiled and with head held high accompanied him. She hoped that the muttering she heard was about how lovely she looked and not about how she was the mother that Maggie abandoned.

I don't really care about myself, but her own father. Surely she knows how he loves her and how hurt he is. I was going to be good and not open my mouth, but, by gum, I'm going to give that one some sound advice before I leave this town, so help! And who are these waifs she's taken up with? Are they more important than her own flesh and blood?

Apparently so. We're going to have it out before I leave here, wedding day or not."

Layke looked down at her and whispered, "What's wrong? You look like you ate a gallberry."

"Nothing's wrong. I'm just..."

The organ began and Seth and Jack came out with the preacher. Berta thought, Seth is a nice looking young man, and from the way the guests are grinning they all like him. I guess she's had the decency to ask Tucker to give her away. Why do I get myself so upset? There's no telling what Raine will do. There never has been.

Everyone stood and turned. Raine had added a large lace bow centered with an apricot rosette with streamers to her hair and carried a nosegay of coral bougainvillea and ivy on a heavy round of ecru lace. Why couldn't she have let us enjoy this with her? Why did she feel that she had to shut us out, especially Layke? That's the only thing that I can't forgive.

Where's Tucker? Maybe he didn't get here after all. I don't believe this. Just when does a dagblasted old bicycle race mean more to him than his sister's wedding? I wish SuSu and Jay could have come, but Jay was right in not trying to make the trip. SuSu needs to rest more than coming for this. I know how angry she'd be at Raine, and that might affect the baby.

She felt rather than saw Layke move over. When she looked up, she saw him with his arm linked inside of Raine's, and then she felt him grab hold of her arm, and like a sheep she followed them. Not knowing what was happening, she saw Tucker approach and felt him take her other arm.

The music stopped, and the preacher in a rich bass voice asked the four of them before him, "Who should I say is giving Maggie Pope Raine Williams to this man in holy matrimony?"

Raine whispered, "You're supposed to say, `We do' ", and she grinned a very Raine Trudy Williams grin.

"We do," they said in unison.

Seth reached for Maggie, taking her arm firmly, and when he did, the look in his eyes told Berta that she didn't have to be concerned about one Raine Trudy Williams Maggie Pope Roberts ever again.

I think I can forget that talk with Raine, she thought, relieved. She felt Layke's warm, moist lips on her cheek and heard him whisper, "I love you." She could feel everyone's smile surround her.

Thanks, Maggie, she wanted to say.

CHAPTER III TARPON SPRINGS

THE YEAR 1904

"If Delia has made up her mind to go to Tarpon Springs when she graduates from Miss Baldwin's, there's no stopping her, Juanita. She's as stubborn as you ever were, not to mention having that O'Farrell blood to compound her stubbornness," Rose said emphatically.

"I find no fault in her going. It's just the timing, that's all. Why can't she wait until the fall, after we've given her more instruction in how to run a shop? It takes more than knowing how to design to be a success."

"Why don't you give her credit? She's practically lived in here for four years - at least when she wasn't in school. What I don't understand is why she hasn't made an effort to find another fellow..."

"You know why just as much as I do. She's afraid of being hurt again. I truly believe that she thought Tucker would eventually resume their relationship. Well, that is, until he was married last summer. You know what a blow that was. And to think that he wrote her practically up until his blasted wedding day! That was despicable! But, fool that she is, she forgave him. I'll never understand that. Why I'd 've - well, I would have done something."

"Hand me that edging, Juanita, the silver and black one. Yes, that's it. Juanita, it's easy for us to sit here and criticize our children, isn't it? When Maggie wrote that she and Seth and the baby were all going up to Tallahassee to the wedding, I almost died on the spot. Why, the little tyke wasn't but three months old, and here they go traipsing all over the countryside..."

"But I didn't hear any complaints when they came by here, Miss Rose Shorter. And she is a precious thing, isn't she? Wouldn't it be wonderful if Joe Bob could look down and see his granddaughter? Have you ever thought about ...?"

"You know full well I have. I asked Seth why they decided on the name Catherine, and he said that it was Maggie's idea, but he didn't seem to know anyone named that. Probably a family name. It is pretty, isn't it? Catherine Lorraine. I'm glad they're calling her Raine, and I know that the Williamses are pleased."

The front door bell tinkled announcing a visitor, and Juanita got up and peeked around the curtain that separated the workroom from the dress shop. She turned back to Rose and said, "It's Richard with the mail. I'll be right back."

"Well, Richard, you're early today. I hope you have something interesting for us."

"Got one from Delia, Mrs. O'Farrell, and it appears to be a long one."

"She's gotten so she does write long and interesting letters, although I don't know when she finds the time. That girl burns the candle at both ends, so to speak. What with all the dances and parties she attends along with her sorority functions I don't ..."

Rose overheard Juanita and sat shaking her head. Why does she continue to say such things? Everyone in town knows that Delia hasn't looked at another boy since Tucker Williams threw her over. Juanita should know better.

"Miss Shorter got one from Arcadia. Must be from Seth - no, it's from his wife."

Rose poked her head out and reached for the letter, then retreated into the alcove to read it. "Good day to you ladies. Oh, Mrs. O'Farrell, Mrs. Bartram asked me to tell you that she's still waiting for the sketches for her gown. Been near two weeks now. That's what she said that I should say." Richard began whistling and out the door and down Jefferson Avenue he went to spread his gossip. The saying around Monticello was if you wanted news to get around, all you had to do was tell Richard.

Juanita whirled around and said loud enough for him to hear, "Not so, Mrs. Bartram. It's been only eight days!"

To Rose she said, "The old bat! It'll take ten yards to cover her two hundred pounds. We lose money on her every time we make one."

"What did you say, Juanita? Oh, listen to this. Maggie writes that they've decided to look for a place of their own. Maybe not this year but next year for sure. You know, ever since Uncle George died Seth and Jack have almost more than they can handle. Beulah's really going down hill, and Maggie doesn't want to leave her, but her girls want her to sell the hotel and move in with one of them. It's a problem."

"What's happening with Delia? Is she coming back with you after the graduation, or is she going straight to Tarpon Springs?"

"She says that Meriam wants her to go straight down there and stay with her folks and look at the various shops that her father has listed. I truly think that I should go with her. Why is she being so obstinate? Nolan will be out of school and could accompany me, and we could make it a nice vacation. I'd like to go on to Tampa and stay at the elegant Tampa Bay Hotel. I read you the brochure, didn't I? Everyone who has been there says it's more beautiful than the Ponce in St. Augustine. That's hard to believe. Elda Shifrar and Louie stayed there two weeks and said it was like a palace."

"Yes, but that was a few years ago. Since the big freeze in '97, you know the one where they even had snow, well, I've heard that it's not doing nearly as well as the Detroit Hotel in St. Petersburg. Heavens, you and Nolan can stay a week at each. That would be a really nice vacation. But you know that I want to be in Arcadia for Raine's birthday. You haven't forgotten that, have you?"

"How could I, since that's just about all you talk about, but that's in April and we wouldn't be going until May. There shouldn't be any problem at all."

"Oh, listen to this, *Mr. and Mrs. Lawrence are coming up for the graduation and mentioned something about stopping off in Monticello to see your shop.* Rose, that would be perfect. I believe that after I've told them about how difficult it is to find accomplished seamstresses that they'll postpone the opening of the girls' shop until I've had a chance to train them. That would be perfect!"

"What you mean, Juanita, is that it will keep Delia home a little longer."

"It also means just what I said. Delia's an excellent designer and has turned into a good buyer, but you know as well as I do that neither of those things is any good if your seamstresses aren't trained. In a way I'm glad that Delia has decided on Tarpon Springs."

"And why is that, pray tell?"

"For one, Conner and Mr. Lawrence have something in common. That's comforting to me. It still amazes me that Meriam's father and Hamilton Disston were such good friends. Conner thought the world of him. Always said that this state could boast of only one visionary, and that was Hamilton Disston. He didn't think too much of Flagler or Plant. Said that all they did was build railroads and hotels, and anyone could do that given enough money and assistance from the state. But he certainly sang the praises of Mr. Disston. Really upset him when he died in '96. He was always good to Conner even when Conner was drinking. But enough of that."

"Mr. Lawrence also told Delia that if Mr. Disston hadn't died so young, the people in Tarpon Springs felt that it would be as big a city as St. Augustine by now. After he laid out the town and built the Tropical Hotel and then spent a fortune in advertising it in Europe, even getting that English Duke to purchase land and build his mansion there, the townspeople just knew that it would prosper."

"What happened? Delia told me that it's not even as big as Monticello. Was it the hurricanes?"

"Yes, I'm sure that had a lot to do with its growth, or lack of it. Mr. Lawrence said that after the Duke brought his wife over from England, apparently they got bored with the small town, so they moved back to England. He was a cousin of Queen Victoria, you know, the Duke of Sutherland. Isn't that romantic? Monticello can't boast of anything like that. The Duke apparently loved to fish - spent most of his time on the Gulf. I don't imagine that his bride took to that very well."

"Here, Rose, how does that look? I hope Delia likes it. Well, if she doesn't, then it's her own fault. She designed it and even selected the fabric. You know, this might be the last gown we make for her? Pretty soon she'll be doing her own."

"Don't count on it, Juanita. She might decide that she doesn't like living down there. After all, she's been there for only short visits."

"I doubt that. She loves the area, and Tampa is just a short train ride south. She's hoping to develop that market just like we did Tallahassee."

"I, for one, hope she can find a nice young man when she gets there. Maggie told me that Tucker's life was planned for him the minute he decided to go into public life. Did I tell you that?"

"You didn't have to. I knew he'd end up marrying someone whose family was in politics, but would Delia believe me? Of course not. She was stupid enough to think he'd marry for love. Did Maggie say whether or not Tucker even loved the girl?"

"No, but she said that the girl had been in love with Tucker since she was in high school. Apparently the families were very close. I believe she said that her father and the girl's father had served in the senate together almost since they'd been in Tallahassee."

"I'd not be surprised. I believe that the girl's father's law firm is the one Tucker joined. I'm sure it is. What chance did Delia have? None, of course. I do wish them well, though. I always liked Tucker, but I never thought he was the right one for Delia. Don't you ever let on to Delia that I felt that way, Rose."

"Good grief, Juanita! You must think I'm daft. Well, I never!"

****

THE YEAR 1905

The Lawrence home, located on the Spring Bayou along with the many other mansions, was pretentious but comfortable. Delia had grown very fond of the Lawrences when she and Meriam roomed together at St. Joseph's, and then when they both went to Miss Baldwin's in Virginia their friendship deepened, and she had spent several weeks with Meriam each summer, loving every minute of her stay.

Meriam was barely five feet tall, and as Delia was nearly six feet tall, they did seem an odd sight together. She had a wonderful sense of humor, and although she was not as pretty as Delia and was aware of it, she did admire Delia's beauty, stature and intelligence and did not feel inferior. She was well aware of her shortcomings. Not having a good figure was one, but she did have a good personality, made friends easily and was very popular. She also had her father's flair for business, having scored very high in the business courses at Miss Baldwin's. Everyone liked Meriam.

She and Delia had been planning their joint venture ever since Delia realized that Tucker was not going to marry her. Meriam had been her rock, her confidante, and in a way her future.

It was Mr. Lawrence who suggested that they start their own dress shop in Tarpon Springs. He promised to finance it and help them select a good location, for he was very involved in real estate. Juanita had approved the venture with the understanding that after a period of time if the venture hadn't been successful, she would repay Mr. Lawrence for Delia's share. He agreed, even though he thought it unnecessary. He was a good business man and knew that Tarpon Springs needed and would support an elegant dress shop, and he also knew that with Meriam's personality and Delia's flair for the dramatic they would succeed.

Delia and Meriam shared a large room overlooking the bayou on the second floor of the three-story home. One of their favorite pastimes was sitting on the balcony off their room and watching the colorful boats in the evening. The homes surrounding the bayou had very ornate boat houses, and boating was also a favorite pastime for the young people of the area. Tarpon Springs had a true mixture of nationalities, so unlike Monticello. Delia loved the international flavor of the small shops and restaurants.

Mr. Lawrence had been as good as his word and found an excellent location for their shop on Tarpon Avenue, the only paved street in town, even though it was paved with clay. That fall Delia and Meriam had traveled to Monticello and, accompanied by Juanita, went to Savannah for their fabrics and notions. Juanita was very pleased by Meriam's business knowledge and Delia's keen eye. She had taken Delia on other buying trips so was comfortable with her skills, but she had been hesitant about Meriam as a business partner. She was no longer. The girl was astute and undaunted. She appeared to have been in business for a long time, and the merchants hadn't taken advantage of her inexperience. Juanita returned to Monticello with a light heart even though she knew she'd miss Delia terribly when they opened their shop the following spring.

Delia and Meriam had spent hours over their shop's name, and when she wrote to Juanita of their dilemma, Juanita and Rose and even Nolan pondered their problem. It was Mr. Lawrence who eventually came up with the name. He suggested that they combine their two names and suggested Del Mer Shoppe. It pleased everyone. So on April 2, 1905 the new shop opened on Tarpon Avenue with a fanfare that the town had never seen before.

The attendees read like the *Who's Who* of a large city. The New York Clemsons, residents on Spring Bayou and whose fortune was made in hacksaws, were there along with Soledad Bonillas de Safford, who married Gov. Safford, former territorial governor of Arizona and friend and business associate of Hamilton Disston. He'd acquired title to huge tracts of land for a dollar an acre. All the local politicians, as well as those from Tampa and St. Petersburg, and their wives were at the champagne reception. Frank Lawrence was well known in that area.

The list was impressive, and Juanita was happy beyond belief for Delia and Meriam. She had been allowed a part in their venture and felt so very special. She, too, was fond of the Lawrences, Roberta and Frank. They both were from the mid-west and had had to struggle for their position in life. They all understood each other. Roberta was a bright, warm, middle-aged woman, who made a good home for her husband and five children and wanted nothing more from life than to be allowed that position. She and Juanita enjoyed having a glass of sherry on the front porch and sharing their experiences regarding their children and husbands.

The guest room - there were three - that Roberta had selected for Juanita was very nicely decorated. Juanita would have done it differently, but she approved of Roberta's taste. Conner would have died, she thought, as she looked at the drapes and bed canopy. He would surely have said, "This most assuredly is the taste of a plebeian." Juanita could see his long arms waving dramatically in the air and began to giggle.

"I do believe you gave me too much sherry, Roberta, or is it because we drank it on top of the champagne." I can't believe that I'm tipsy. Oh, Conner. I wish that I could be assured that you are a witness to all this, to Delia's beautiful opening and... If we could just share this, then I wouldn't feel so lonely. Did you know that Rose told me she talks to Joe Bob all the time? Conner, she knew him for only a few weeks. Imagine! Hmmmm... She was soon sound asleep.

Juanita felt the light streaming through the floor-to-ceiling windows leading to the balcony. When she finally realized where she was, she also realized that she had fallen asleep without drawing the drapes. "My, my, what time is it? I hope I haven't overslept. She found her lapel watch on the ornately carved mahogany dresser and gasped at the time. I don't believe I did this. Delia will already be at the shop, and I promised that I would help. What'll I wear? Why did I do such a thing? She sighed, looked around for her dressing gown, the one she and Rose had finished just before she left for the trip down here, and sat on the edge of the still covered bed.

"Delia, perhaps you should see if Juanita is all right. She was weary last night. You know that she has had a very busy week what with her own business and now Del Mer."

"Certainly, Mrs. Lawrence. I'm sure that she just overslept. Like you said, she was very tired."

Delia rushed up the white, wrought iron stairway, down the long hallway and knocked soundly on Juanita's door. "Mum, it's me Delia."

Juanita opened the door immediately and began apologizing. "I cannot believe that I slept so soundly, Honey. I don't know when I've slept like this."

"It's the water, Mum. I always sleep soundly when I'm near water. We've got to hurry. I don't want to be late the very first day. Can I help you get ready?"

"No, you can't. You go on and I'll follow. It's not important that I be there every minute, you know. Go on, hurry!"

Afterwards, Juanita often said, she wished that she had been there. Maybe if she had, things would have turned out differently.

The morning mist had burned off, and Delia declared it to be a beautiful day as she rushed down Tarpon Avenue. Meriam was already in the back of the store unpacking bolts of fabric, stacking them in order of color and labeling their fabric content and number of yards on each bolt. "Why can't each bolt be the same length? This is ridiculous. Why can't they be uniform? People have no sense of order."

"What are you mumbling about, Meriam? I can't hear you." Delia said when she opened the front door. "I'll start dressing the window right away. Sorry I'm late, but Mum overslept." She stood back and looked at her work, then went outside to see it from the front. "Think I need to drape the scarf differently." Back into the shop unaware of the crowd she was drawing, she called to Meriam, "Come look at this window. I want to have it finished by the time Mum gets here. You know her - she'll want to dress it herself. I'll admit that she's good, but this is Del Mer not Cherie's House of Fashion."

Meriam came from the back and started laughing. "Do you realize that you have an audience?"

"What're you talking about? Oh, my! Who are those men, and why are they laughing?"

"I would imagine it's because they've never seen a mannequin before. They're probably Greek sponge fishermen, probably from Mr. Cheyney's packing house. He's brought a lot of them up from Key West, and Father said last week that Mr. Cocoris has plans to bring hundreds more from Greece this summer. We'll be crawling with them, but it'll be good for business. We'll have to order lots of black. Those people are always in mourning for some deceased relative or other."

Delia smiled at them, and they laughed and smiled back. Finally one of them was coaxed into entering the shop. Meriam and Delia were enjoying their sport, and both hoped that any prospective customers would delay their visit to the shop until after he left.

Delia stepped out of the window, caught her foot on the backdrop and landed in his arms. "Oh, I'm sorry. How clumsy of me!" She wondered if he spoke English and soon found that he did, but with a delightful accent.

"Are you hurt, miss?" he said glancing at the three men who had taken it all in.

"I'm quite all right, thank you." Oh, he is so handsome in a dark, mysterious way. I wonder if he's really Greek? His eyes are the color of the sea. "May I help you? Perhaps you'd like to see something for your mother or wife?"

He smiled conspiratorially knowing that she was trying to find out if he was married. "No, I was dared into coming in. I had to show the men that I was not afraid of one who is so beautiful. They call you Helen, who was the most beautiful woman of Greece - my country."

"I find that very flattering." She turned to them and smiled. "But here in Tarpon Springs I'm just Delia O'Farrell and certainly not the most beautiful woman of my country."

"To me you shall always be Helen." He tipped his cap, turned and over his shoulder said, "I am without a bride, and my mother is still in Greece. But if I have need of something beautiful, I'll know where to come. I'll no longer have to go to New York."

Delia found her heart racing, and when she turned toward Meriam she said, "I think I'm in love."

"Don't be ridiculous, Delia O'Farrell! He's probably just a sponge fisherman." She stopped, went to Delia and looked at her, and said, "You are serious. How can you say such a thing when you've only just met him? How soon you've forgotten about that very same reaction when you first saw Tucker, and look where it's got you."

"Stop, Meriam. It was just this terrific pounding of my heart, that's all. I usually don't react like that. Have I ever reacted that way since you've known me? Have I?"

"Only when Tucker was around, I suppose. Delia, we're just getting started, and I don't want you to get side tracked by some Greek fisherman. I can't believe you!"

"I said that it would pass. See, it's all gone. Now, you'll have my full attention for the rest of the day, and I'll not even think of how handsome he was. Did you ever see such eyes?"

"Delia, that's enough! You can't afford to get interested in him or any other Greek. They marry only their own. His family has already selected his bride for him in the old country."

"I was only teasing you, Meriam, for Heaven's sake. And how do you know he's already betrothed? You could be wrong, you know."

"No, I'm not. That's the way it is with those people."

Juanita was only an hour late but was so put out with Delia for not waiting for her to dress the windows that Delia allowed her to make a few changes and had to admit that they did look better. By noon half the influential people in Tarpon Springs had visited the shop. The three were so glad when one o'clock arrived that they closed the shop and walked down Tarpon Avenue to a small outdoor Greek restaurant.

Juanita was fascinated by everything in the entire town. She asked Meriam to order something that she knew she'd like and told the waiter that she wanted to try lots of different things, that she felt adventurous. Delia and Meriam were trying to hide their amusement, and Juanita was quite put out by their actions. "Mum, he barely speaks English and doesn't understand half of what you're saying."

"Oh," she sighed, "I really don't care. Isn't this delightful! Just think, Rose is sitting in stuffy old Cherie's eating something she's had brought in from the St. Elmo, no doubt, and it's probably cold, and look at me? Here I sit in a delightful sidewalk cafe with a cool breeze blowing off the bayou - or is it the river? - and eating exotic food and looking at carts filled to overflowing with every flower I've ever seen and..."

"Mrs. O'Farrell, I've ordered the stuffed cabbage leaves. I know you'll love them. They're stuffed with ground lamb and, oh, I don't know what all besides rice..."

"Delia, wouldn't your da love this? Conner would find out about every dish they serve, usually end up in the kitchen, and before we left he'd no doubt speak Greek. Well, maybe not real well, but he'd try, wouldn't he Delia?"

"Yes, he certainly would have, Mum."

"Meriam, what's the cabbage leaves dish called in Greek? I want to learn a few words at least to try on Rose and Harrison and Nolan."

"Here, look at the menu. It's lahanodolmades - see, cabbage is lahano, and soup is soupa, and salata is salad, and..."

"That's easy. Why, I'll really surprise them. I'd like to learn to make some of the dishes, too. Does Roberta know how?"

"She has several favorites, and I'm sure she'll teach you. She's really very fond of you, Mrs. O'Farrell."

"Please call me Juanita while we're at the shop. You two make me feel so old.."

"Mum, that Mr. Forrest didn't think so at the reception. Why he..."

"He was just being attentive. And besides, he probably had had too much champagne." She thought a while and added, "Do you really think that he thought that I might be, say, thirty-something?"

"I don't think he cared, Mum. He certainly couldn't keep his eyes off you."

"Probably married with a dozen children..."

"Oh, no, Mr. Forrest is a single man, but I'm not so sure that you'd be interested in him, Mrs....Juanita."

"And why not? He was handsome in a way and certainly polished..."

"He is very nice and, as you say, cultured, but rumor has it that he is..ah, he...ah.."

Juanita looked at her, "Oh! Well, he is very nice anyway and would be a perfect companion for an evening out."

They were finishing their meal when Delia felt Meriam kick her beneath the table. When she questioned her with her eyes, Meriam nodded and rolled her eyes at the table behind Delia. Not wanting to turn around, Delia dropped her napkin and got up to retrieve it, when she saw him out of the corner of her eye.

"Here, let me get a fresh one for you, miss." He clicked his fingers for the waiter, and Delia noticed that he had changed his clothing. He still wore black trousers but had added a white full-sleeved shirt and smelled of evergreen. Delia was flustered and was afraid that her mum would sense her interest in him, so she turned back to Juanita and Meriam without even thanking him.

Juanita said, "Why, Delia Rose, that young man was trying to be polite. I've not known you to be rude." She said it softly, but he overheard. "Aren't you going to at least thank him for his assistance?"

Delia made a face at her but turned to face him. Feeling breathless, she nodded to him, trying unsuccessfully to not look him in the eyes. "Thank you for your kindness," and turned back around. Later in the afternoon when Meriam could get away, she told Delia that she thought that he had followed them there and that they had better be careful on their way home.

"For Heaven's sake, Meriam. The man is not going to do a single thing to us. Can't you tell that he is a gentleman, even if he is a foreign one? I thought that you were a better judge of character than that. He was just being polite and had a perfect right to be eating there."

"Well, you don't have to get angry about it! There are dozens of Greek restaurants he could have eaten in. Why did it have to be the same one where we were?"

"Maybe he owns it? Did it ever occur to you that he could be a restaurateur? Did it? No, all you could think of was a fisherman. I'm sure there are Greek businessmen and doctors as well as ship builders and fishermen."

"He was dressed like the others, and they were definitely fishermen."

"I really don't know why we're having this conversation anyway. I'll probably never see him again. I have to wait on a customer, and I hope that this conversation is finished."

"You don't have to get uppity, Delia. And you're wrong about him. He has his eye on you, and that type doesn't give up easily."

"Who doesn't give up, Meriam?" Juanita questioned as she entered the storage room.

"Oh, just someone Delia and I know. He's not important."

Juanita could feel the tension in the room. She went to Meriam. "Honey, it's your first day, and there's bound to be some nervousness, because everything is so new. It'll work out fine. Let's just relax and enjoy this new venture. I know what! I'll treat you and Delia to a nice cup of coffee in one of those coffee houses I've heard about."

"I'm afraid not, Juanita. They're for men only."

"That's ridiculous! Who says?"

"The Greeks who own them, that's who. It's their custom and even their own women aren't allowed in."

"Well, I never! Conner would have loved that. I wonder why he never thought of that? That's all right. We'll find a nice sidewalk restaurant where we are allowed. It'll be lovely, and we can discuss our eventful day."

"That'll be nice, Juanita. Why don't you tell Delia. She seems tired, too." Under her breath she said, and she's out of sorts, and he'll be there, just you wait and see, Delia O'Farrell. I could tell by the way he looked at you. We're in for trouble. I can feel it.

I simply can't get anxious, Delia thought as the three, after closing the shop for the day, walked north on Pinellas Ave. Juanita was oohing and aahing over every small shop. With the coming of so many sponge fishermen downtown Tarpon Springs had become an array of Greek shops. They were told that by summer John Cocoris would have brought five hundred fishermen from the Dodecanese and Kalymnos Islands. He had already brought his brothers George, Louis and Gus from Leonidion, his home in Sparta, and also a wife.

Always independent, farmers, fishermen or merchants, who didn't care for mass production industries, they set up the little restaurants, food stores, flower shops and shoe-shining parlors. Soon rich smells of roast lamb and coffee, oranges, Greek pastries, Greek brandy and tobacco permeated the air. Juanita and Delia loved it. They could feel the energy of the people and knew that it made for a good business climate. They were musical, laughing and seemingly always happy.

The Greeks had created a home away from home. They bought what they wanted, spoke their own language and could gamble a little. The businessmen had already started arriving. Frank Lawrence was feeling the long awaited growth finally arrive. Hamilton Disston would have been ecstatic, even though it was not the kind of growth he'd envisioned. The wealthy Greek business men, primarily investors, came to finance boat building, boat trips from the old country and diver supplies. Dealers and agents for the big sponge dealers in St. Louis, New York, Philadelphia and Chicago also arrived. The Greeks were already going into banking and real estate and invested heavily in property.

Packing houses were being built, sponge presses installed, and what delighted Frank even more was that Tarpon Springs was being touted as *The Greatest Sponge Port in the United States*. They said that the floor of the Gulf was like a garden of beautiful flowers or a bountiful orchard of fruit, thickly studded with black sponges. They could fill the sponge nets in ten minutes, and the sponge was sheep's wool, an excellent quality for which they were paid a handsome sum.

But all was not well. The hook boat men got wind of the Greek divers with their deep water equipment, rubberized suits, copper helmets and air pumps, and raised a clamor that the metal-shod feet of the divers would destroy the beds. The deep, untouched sponge beds extended for hundreds of miles and these sponges brought a much better price then the shallow water sponges they could get with their long hooks, going only 45 to 48 feet deep.

The Greeks had already set up their own kraals, 8 to 12 feet in length and 6 to 8 feet wide, on one of the Anclote Keys where they deposited their week's catch. The kraals were made by driving poles or trunks of small trees into the ground in the shallow water. The sponges soaked in the water and were ready for cleaning the next Saturday. Baillie's Bluff north of the Anclote River mouth became the center of great activity. Boats from Key West, Apalachicola and Tarpon Springs deposited their sponges there for safe keeping. Tarpon Springs was in the middle of a boom, and Juanita and Delia and the Lawrences knew that the Del Mer Shoppe was bound to prosper.

"I told you he'd follow us," Meriam said in a whisper to Delia.

"He has just as much right to walk this street as we do, Meriam," Delia retorted.

"What are you two mumbling about? Is it about Young Nolan coming next month, for if it is, you can rest your tongues. I've already told your folks that I have found a small house for us to stay in until the summer's over. They protested vehemently, but I prevailed and have already placed a payment on it. Oh, Delia, it's darling! Right on the water. You know how Nolan loves the water."

"Mum, that's not what we were talking about at all. I might as well tell you. Meriam has it in her head that the young man whom you saw in the restaurant this morning and who came into the shop even before you came to work, well, she thinks that he's following us."

"Really? How romantic!"

Meriam looked from one to the other and shook her head in dismay. "If he is, Juanita, what do you think we should do? I mean if he goes to the same cafe?"

"Invite him to join us, of course. You're well chaperoned by me, and besides, he looks interesting. He is also handsome. Have you ever seen such green eyes? Conner's were, as are Delia's, certainly different, but those of that young Greek can run them a second place."

"If anything happens, it'll be your fault," Meriam said, restraining a smile. "But why not? We've had a busy day and some laughter should be in order."

"That's more like it, Meriam. You were getting positively stuffy," Delia said with a smile. She found herself smiling at the young man, who had crossed the street and was walking toward them.

But after nodding and tipping his cap, he continued down Tarpon Avenue. Delia could feel her disappointment mount but decided that she was being silly. Juanita turned to Meriam and said, "I believe that was wishful thinking on your part, Meriam. It would appear that he had other plans."

A month had gone by since the opening of Del Mer, and Delia had seen the young Greek almost every day, but he always just nodded and tipped his hat. It was obvious that he was not a fisherman, probably a merchant. In the meantime she read everything she could find about the Greeks and their customs, telling Meriam that if they expected them to become their customers they should find out more about their likes and dislikes, their saints days, etc. Meriam hoped that was all she was interested in, but, knowing Delia, she doubted it.

It was as Meriam had said. The Greeks did indeed marry their own. Some of the fishermen John Cocoris had brought over, housed, fed, and assigned to boats, had also sent their letters and money drafts back home to bring their intended wives to Tarpon Springs.

They were a close-knit group, living in barracks, cooking and washing their clothes outdoors and singing at night, but they were also homesick. Some men sent for brides chosen by photograph, and their weddings were arranged by their families in Greece. The makeshift sloops and schooners were no longer good enough. They needed authentic sponge boats, so skilled boat builders arrived with their adzes and the immemorial boat designs they carried in their heads. Inside of that first year they had fifty new diving boats on the Gulf, and they had established Greek Town.

Juanita had trained three seamstresses by the fourth week. It was difficult to keep up with business, she wrote Rose. Young Nolan was arriving by train as soon as school was out in a few days, and she was excited. Their small house had at one time been the guest house of one of the mansions, but since a newer and larger one had been built, the Gardners, whom she had met through the Lawrences, had rented it to her and Nolan.

Delia had pieced together her young Greek's habits and found the intrigue stimulating. She needed a release from the day-to-day tension of trying to please the Tarpon Springs and Tampa elite. She knew that he was called Nikki but had not found out his last name. She also knew that he either owned or operated three businesses on Tarpon Avenue and assumed that he lived above one of them, the restaurant where she had seen him, the flower shop next door, or one of the most popular coffee houses, if one could tell by the number of men coming and going and the smoke and music spewing from the doors.

She figured that he was probably in his mid twenties and had probably come to New York via an uncle or older brother and had lived in the States for about ten or so years. He was well known in town, everyone calling cheerily to him, and he was seldom alone. Delia was surprised that he was not married. She was also glad.

She and Meriam had begun having lunch at his restaurant, Olympia, almost every day at one o'clock. They'd put the CLOSED sign on the door and walk the three blocks to the outside cafe. For the past few weeks he'd been there, always sitting at the same table in the back next to the cash register, supervising the employees but rarely getting involved with the actual operation. He always smiled at them, nodded, and resumed sipping his coffee.

It wasn't until the day Nolan arrived that Delia actually met him. Frank Lawrence had met the train, and he and Nolan met the girls and Juanita at the Olympia. After getting Nolan seated he excused himself and walked over to the table where Nikki sat. When they shook hands, Delia realized that Mr. Lawrence knew him. She was elated.

When they approached their table Frank introduced them. "Ladies and Nolan, I want you to meet my good friend, Nikki Kanares. Nikki's now the owner of this fine establishment. His uncle Ernie and I have had a good business relationship since the turn of the century. How long have you been here, Nikki? Four or five years?"

"Here for four years but before that in New York for six. Good afternoon, ladies and Nolan, is it?"

Nolan rose and shook his hand. "I've been studying about Greece this last semester, old Greece, that is."

"It's a beautiful country and I miss it. Tarpon Springs is as close as I've come to being there."

"I thought Ernie said that your mother was coming over, Nikki. Do you expect her soon?"

"I had hoped that she would have been here by now, but it appears that she will be coming with my cousin next year. At least I hope so. We've been saving the flower shop for her."

"Well, if I can be of assistance, finding a house for her or whatever, just let me know."

"She'll be staying with me in the apartment at first, but I'm sure she'll want a house before long. She has to have a garden. Thank you, Frank."

Before he left, he told them to try the melitzanes and that the goggilia was especially enjoyed by southerners, he was told.

"What's that?" Nolan inquired.

Frank replied, "The melitzanes is eggplant and the goggilia are turnip greens cooked in a very un-southern way with olive oil and lemon juice. They steam them until they're tender. Roberta fixes them often that way."

So I was partially right about him. But why isn't he married? I think I'll just worm more information out of Mr. Lawrence.

"He speaks English quite well. Do they teach it in school in Greece?"

"I don't think so. All the ones that I've met can't understand a word when they first get here. But Nikki comes from a very fine family from what I can gather. His Uncle Ernie brought him over when he was a young lad about Nolan's age and trained him in his business ventures in New York. Ernie's a very wealthy man, very shrewd. He thinks the world of

Nikki and has no sons of his own. Believe he has four or five daughters, and I think that Nikki was the one responsible for bringing his other brothers over. They're in New York, I believe."

"I'm surprised that he isn't married. I thought that they married very young and had large families," Delia added and could feel Meriam's eyes boring holes in her, not to mention Juanita's renewed interest.

"How would you know his marital status, Delia?"

"Oh, he came into the shop and mentioned that he didn't have a bride and that his mother was still in Greece."

"Oh," is all Juanita replied.

"Ernie said that they brought a young girl over for Nikki, but that she died of pneumonia before they could get married. That was when he was in New York. But you're right, Delia. It's strange that another match hasn't been made. She'd have to be from a well-to-do family now though. They've accumulated quite a lot of wealth since they've been here these past dozen years. She'd have to have quite a dowry."

"That's archaic! I had no idea that civilized people still did that sort of thing."

"Civilized or not, that's what they do, and it seems to work very well for them. Seldom hear of a bad marriage among them. We could take some lessons from..."

"Yes, as long as their women are subservient, they'll always have good marriages. Treated like sheep. I'd never stand for it."

Delia had not noticed that Nikki had joined the couple at the table next to theirs and had overheard her, but Frank had. He tried to cover up the outburst by laughing and saying, "Guess you and Meriam can't be put in that category, can you, Delia? Not two well educated young ladies who don't need us men around, huh?"

Delia finally realized what he was doing and hoped her face wasn't red with embarrassment. "Not so, Mr. Lawrence. Meriam and I are allowed choice, and I do think that important - at least it is to me. I'd hate to think that I had to be married to someone I didn't love, or even more important, whom I didn't respect."

"It's what makes our country so colorful, isn't it, Juanita? So many different cultures."

"I love the diversity, too. In Conner's Ireland he'd probably not have been able to marry me in the church without me becoming Catholic. I'm so very glad he was a renegade," and they all laughed. Juanita was enjoying the stimulating conversation, the setting and the fact that she could tell that Delia had an interest in the handsome Greek. Oh, I hope

I'm here long enough to nudge this along. But, I'll have to work fast before that mother arrives. Oh, what fun! Conner, are you watching, my sweet? Isn't this exciting?

Delia's next encounter with Nikki was arranged by Juanita and Roberta. One evening as they sat having their sherry on Roberta's front porch Juanita told her of her concern about Delia, about Tucker and about this absolutely gorgeous Greek named Nikki. The two of them, being utterly romantic, decided to do something about Delia's plight.

Roberta decided to have a reception for the O'Farrells to introduce them to the old-timers and the newcomers, and Nikki fell in with the latter. It wasn't unusual for her to have Frank's business friends and acquaintances for dinner or an afternoon affair on the patio. She and Juanita planned the entire thing over several glasses of sherry inside of a few hours. They wanted it to be a light afternoon function with interesting hors d'oeuvres and an international flavor. By the time they'd finished their bottle of sherry, the party had grown into a costume party and quite elaborate.

Delia and Meriam had not caught on to their plan. Actually, they had thought it was to give them more business, which they did not need. They were swamped. Delia was enjoying the challenge, and Juanita was kept so busy that she was almost sorry they had concocted such an elaborate function.

Nolan was unconcerned by the whole affair, because he and Roberta's boys, Ted and Bobby, were usually at the docks, either fishing or swimming, and she hardly recognized him since he'd got so brown with his reddish hair turned almost copper.

The Saturday of the party had been overcast and the heat almost unbearable. Every paddle wheel fan in the Lawrence house was turning full speed when the first guests arrived with no breeze forthcoming. Roberta was so upset that it took Delia, Meriam and Juanita to calm her. The ice soon ran out, and Nolan and Ted had been sent to town to acquire more.

When Nikki arrived, dressed in the traditional Greek costume of his region, he sensed the problem. He approached Frank first and offered his services, and Roberta and Juanita almost hugged him. The next thing they knew he had the kitchen staff organized, more ice on the way and had ordered the band from the coffee house to perform while strolling the grounds and patios. He said people seldom thought of their discomforts when they heard music. He was correct. There was a clarinet, violin, mandolin and zither, and when they played the bouzhouki, the men he had brought began doing leaps and twirling until the guests found them so entertaining that they no longer noticed the heat.

An afternoon shower was seen in the distance, fast approaching the bayou and heralded by thunder and lightning. "What else could possibly happen to this brilliant idea we had, Roberta?" Juanita lamented when she heard it. "All this just because Delia doesn't know how to attract one Greek. I doubt that they've spoken a single word to each other."

"You're wrong, my friend." Roberta said. "Why, she was helping him in the kitchen just like one of those sheep she assured us she'd never be."

"She was? Where was I? I didn't see them."

"I have an idea we don't have to worry about your Delia. The next one on our list is one Meriam Rollins Lawrence."

Roberta had been right about Delia joining in and working beside Nikki. It had surprised her as much as it apparently had Nikki. "I didn't know that southern women worked beside men, Helen."

"Please don't call me that."

"I told you that you'd always be Helen to me, didn't I?"

"Yes, you did," she laughed, handing him the bowl of ice. "But I love my name, and I'd prefer that you call me by it."

"I don't want you to feel like a sheep, Delia."

"I apologize about that, Nikki, truly I do. It's just that I don't believe in forced marriages."

"Perhaps you'd feel better about them if I had the opportunity to tell you some stories of my country. I'd like to do that if I may."

"Yes, I'd like that. I've been reading everything I can find about Greece and ..."

He looked at her, smiled, took her arm and said, "The music of my country is invigorating. Come, Delia, and I'll give you your first lesson in that which is Greek."

Her full ruffled skirt whirled around her, her feet seldom finding the patio as they twirled round and round. Exhausted, they found the seawall surrounding the bayou and sat on it. They talked into the night, seldom catching their breath.

When Nikki left, Delia knew that she'd have him, and he wondered how he'd be able to live without her. If only his mother would...no need to even think of it. She'd never understand. But have her I shall, he declared to the evening star. I wonder if it is an omen, it is so bright. He walked back down Tarpon Avenue and climbed the steep stairs up to his apartment. He should have been happy - normally he would have.

Two weeks passed, and Delia did not see Nikki. She was getting desperate, and it reflected in her work and disposition. Finally Meriam had had enough. "Why don't you call the restaurant to see if he's out of town? It's not like him to not be there. Heavens, we've eaten there at least five times a week."

"Oh, Meriam, you be a dear and call for me. I'd die if he answered and recognized my voice. Please, oh please."

A man with a heavy accent answered and said that Mr. Kanares was not in and that he did not know when he'd return. When Meriam asked if he was out of town, the man replied that he believed so.

"Now, what do I do?" Delia asked.

"I suggest that you be as patient as you were with one Tucker Williams for all those years, Delia."

But she didn't have to be patient past 4:00 o'clock that afternoon when a very excited Nikki rushed in to Del Mer, took a surprised Delia by the arm and almost dragged her into the back room. "I'm sorry that I didn't call or come by, but I've just returned from a hurried trip to New York. I've hardly slept for thinking of you. Do you have any idea how I feel about you?"

"Well, frankly, Nikki, when you didn't call or pass by or..."

His lips pressed hard on hers. When he released her, she was trembling. Their breathing was labored and he clasped her to him.

"Can you get away from here? I mean, right this moment?"

"Mum isn't due in today and that would leave Meriam alone, but, yes, I can get away."

"Thank God!. I have to be with you. I can't work, I can't even think straight..."

"I've been the same. Oh, Nikki." She kissed his cheek and said breathlessly, "I'll get my things." Delia heard him talking to Meriam in the salon, and when she came out of the work room Meriam had her back to her.

"When can I expect you this evening, Delia? I mean are you coming home for dinner? I need to let mother know." It was obvious that she was none too happy with the situation.

"She'll be dining with me, Meriam," Nikki said, not taking his eyes off Delia's. "And thank you for being so understanding."

Delia went to her and hugged her. "This means a lot to me, my friend. I'll return the favor, and I hope very soon. Don't wait up for me, and tell Mum that I'll talk to her tomorrow."

After they left, Meriam went to the shop window, pulled back the curtain and watched them as they rushed down Tarpon Avenue. "She's lost her mind. She's as crazy about him as she was Tucker. Poor Delia, always leads with her heart."

Nikki held her tightly by the hand as they weaved their way toward the back of the restaurant and the stairway that led up to his apartment. He went to the kitchen, put his head inside the door and called, "Louis, I don't want to be disturbed. I'll order dinner later."

Delia didn't know what to expect, he was so spontaneous, but she knew what she hoped would happen. *I don't seem to have any control with this man. With Tucker at least I could plan or dream. But that was so long ago, and I was just an impetuous child.*

He closed the door soundly. "Now, where were we? Was I doing this?" He kissed her warmly, his hands stroking her back, then moved up to her neck pulling her even closer. She opened her eyes and pushed him away, gasping for breath.

"Nikki, I..."

"Don't say a word, my sweet, not a word. Just love me, Delia. Just love me."

"Oh, Nikki, I do. Oh, I do." They kissed passionately, clinging to each other, her nails dug into his muscled back as he loosened her long hair and blouse.

"You are the most beautiful woman on earth, my Delia, my Helen." His kisses caressed her body as she writhed in ecstasy.

"Shhh, you said no more words, Shhh. Oh, God, Nikki! Oh, Nikki!"

****

"I hate so to leave you and Raine, Honey. But I'm sure that between Aunt Beulah and Nellie you'll manage."

"You're on your way, young lady. I know how important teaching is to you, and if you have to attend the normal school workshops at Summerlin, then so be it. It'll only be for a few weeks, and then you'll be home. Now, off with you." Seth hugged her, assisted her up the train steps, stood back and waved.

"It'll be the dullest two weeks of my entire life, sir." Maggie found her seat and settled in for the fifty-mile train trip to Bartow. She knew that she needed to upgrade her teaching skills, and actually it was required

for all the teachers in Florida now. Most had not had the training of the northern school teachers, and the state was aware of it. It's necessary, she thought, and sighed, but, I'm going to miss them so. Every one of them.
It was mid September and school would resume in October. In a way Maggie was looking forward to the training because some of her fellow teacher friends would be attending. It should be exciting, she thought. I'm sure everything will be fine.
I know Aunt Rose would've liked to come down, but with Juanita still in Tarpon Springs, it's impossible. I think it despicable of her to extend her stay just because she feels that Delia needs her. How about Rose, her business partner? I have a feeling that union will be short lived if Juanita doesn't start being more considerate, and so does Seth.
The train pulled up to the depot, and even before Maggie got out she saw Lois Morgan and her sister Ona, who had taught with her the very first year she'd taught in Arcadia and had subsequently moved to West Palm Beach. She hailed them. They turned when they heard her, and the three if them were soon reliving old times all the way to the hotel.
She did not see the old man leaning against the building, who was wrapped up in a heavy coat even though it was September and warm. But he saw her and grinned. The deep red scar was still vivid along his cheek. He hobbled around the corner when he saw the station master coming and followed the women at a distance.
I knew my luck'd change. They think they can fool old Mac. Well, best keep their eye out 'cause I'm thinking they'll be needing to. I'll be keeping a close eye on that one. She'll be leading me right to them.

****

The weeks had flown by, and Maggie had to admit that she hadn't missed Seth and the baby nearly as much as she had feared. Actually, she'd had a wonderful time and learned a lot. She was grateful that she had been able to go.
School began again, and between Aunt Beulah and Nellie, when she got home from school, little Raine did not lack for anything. She was a good baby, was walking and already jabbering. She didn't resemble either Seth or Maggie but did have Maggie's coloring, and they doted on her.
Plans were under way to sell the hotel, and Beulah was going to move in with Maida, because she had more room than Marta, and she would be close to everything downtown. Maggie and Seth had been unable to find

a suitable house and had decided to stay at the hotel until one could be found. Jack and Nellie both wanted to stay close to downtown so they could be near their friends, Jack's work and school.

Juanita had finally returned to Monticello, but Rose had said that she was changed. She couldn't put her finger on it, but her mind was still in Tarpon Springs, and all Nolan would talk about was that as soon as school was out he was going to spend the summer with Delia. Rose had agreed to spend Thanksgiving with Maggie and Seth and to stay on for another week with Juanita's blessing.

Mayor Clay Willett had kept his promise to his constituents, and there were now electric lights in Arcadia. The Arcadia Electric Light, Ice, and Telephone Co. was organized the year after he took office, and streets were paved and sidewalks widened. There was no concern about his being re-elected.

The phosphate industry was practically gone in DeSoto County, but the mines in Polk county were still operating well. Ranching was still the biggest industry in both counties, but citrus groves were being planted by many of the ranchers. The tourist trade was alive and well, but mostly on both coasts with the Miami area booming. Plans were being made to build an opera house above the drug store in Arcadia and excitement was high.

The Everglades Drainage District was created by the legislature, and Gov. Broward saw the first dredge operate west of Ft. Lauderdale. The draining of the Everglades was underway. He was a powerful governor, and being a self educated man he hoped to ease the path for coming generations by consolidating the state educational institutions and promising an improved school system. He favored increased salaries in the hope of attracting able men to political life and demanded additional taxes on corporations and relief for overtaxed farmers. In pool halls, barbershops and wherever there was a gathering of men there were lively discussions about the governor. The lobby of the Young Hotel was one such place.

"Come on, Annie," Nellie called. "Maggie said that we could go to the icecream parlor so's not to have to listen to all this talk about politics." Annie and Nellie had become friends, on Annie's part so she could hang around Jack and on Nellie's part because she liked Annie. It was the day before Thanksgiving and Maggie was feeling especially generous because Rose was visiting, so she allowed them a treat.

On their way back to the hotel Annie saw an old man wrapped up in a coat sitting beside the old Presbyterian Church. "Poor old man. Bet he won't have any Thanksgiving dinner tomorrow. Think we ought to tell Preacher Bascom?"

"Might tell Maggie and Aunt Beulah so they can at least take him a plate of food. Why's he all wrapped up? It's so warm I can hardly stand these long sleeves."

"Maybe he's sick. I'm gonna tell Jack and Seth so they can tend to him. Not right having no family on Thanksgiving."

When the girls got back to the hotel and told Jack and Seth about the old man, they went to Beulah and she suggested that they go to where the girls said they saw him and invite him to the hotel at least for the night and Thanksgiving dinner. "Not right for anyone to be homeless or hungry when we got so much. Not right at all," Beulah said.

When they got to the church there was no sign of him. So they walked around the area for a while and decided that he had probably moved on or jumped a railroad car for a free ride somewhere else.

Mac could not contain himself. Grown up little snots. Think they can try to kill their old man and get away with it. Not on you life, mister. He'd begged enough money from the stupid travelers at the Bartow station so he could get him a bottle of shine and was curled up on the hay in the livery stable at the rear of the Gore and Scott Store. Probably be able to stay here tomorrow, too. Then it'll be good-bye Poke and Catherine Inez. Good-bye you little snots...good-bye you... The cigar butt rolled out of his hand as he passed out.

It was 8:30 in the evening. Callie, Clay and the children had just left for Tall Ten. They wanted Beulah and the Robertses to enjoy their very own Thanksgiving Day without them this year. "Clay, I smell smoke. Have you been sneaking a smoke again?" She turned around to Meade and said, "It'd better not be you, young man!"

When she turned she could see the flames in the distance. "My Lord in the morning, Clay! There's a fire. We've got to turn around!"

"I was afraid of this. Now, maybe they'll listen to me. Would they levy taxes so we could have a public water system? Hell, no! Hell, no! We're in for trouble, Callie. This entire town could go up in a few hours!"

It took only three hours for Clay's fears to be realized. Forty-three buildings went up in smoke, the Young Hotel among them. Six hours later while the townspeople walked around in a daze, Mr. Gore rushed to a worn out Clay and said, "Found a man dead as can be in my stable.

Must have snuck in there to get some shut-eye. Don't know who in Hell he is, but he's got a long scar on his face."

"What'd you say, Mr. Gore, sir?" Jack asked.

"Said I think I know where the fire started. Found a tramp in the..."

"I mean about the scar, sir."

"Oh, he's got a scar on his face...well, what's he in such a hurry about?"

Seth looked at Maggie and they followed. "I don't want Nellie to know about this, Honey. Not until we're sure. Let her stay at Maida's with Beulah."

They found Jack kneeling beside what appeared to be a sack of rags. He was crying. Maggie held Seth's arm and whispered, "Leave him be, Honey. It was his pa even if he wasn't a good one. Well, now we can go forward. Jack and Nellie never stopped looking over their shoulders. Now they can."

****

THE YEAR 1906

Business was booming for the Del Mer Shoppe, and Delia was in love. Meriam, who was normally a happy person, was now almost glum. She and Delia had had more spats in the past few months than they had the entire eight years that they had roomed together. It was all because of Delia's affair with Nikki Kanares. It wasn't that Meriam didn't like him, for she did, and it wasn't that she didn't admire him, for she did that, too. It was simply that she could smell doom.

Delia had moved into the small house that Juanita and Nolan had rented over the summer, and Meriam knew that Nikki was there most of the time. So did everyone else in town. No one ever found out who had got word to Nikki's Uncle Ernie in New York, but someone had, and the day after New Year's he showed up in Tarpon Springs unannounced.

"I told you that it wouldn't work, Delia. I can't believe that you've been here for almost a year and still don't understand the Greeks - especially since you and Nikki are...are.."

"I don't mind if you say it, Meriam. Nikki and I are lovers. See, I had no trouble saying it at all. We love each other, and the time for a marriage is just not clear. We have discussed it though.

"Delia, you know how fond of you Mama and Daddy are. You've got to know that. The other night - by the way, I had not planned to say a word of this to you, but you leave me no choice - well, the other night we had a conference, you might call it. It's all over town that you and Nikki are keeping company, to put it nicely."

"Nikki and I have not tried to hide anything..."

"You should have. Daddy believes that this...ah affair, might affect the business. He didn't ask me to say anything to you, but I'm sure he'd appreciate it if you and Nikki could at least not be so obvious."

"Meriam, what Nikki and I do is our affair. We're not hurting a soul and..."

"Wrong! You are hurting Del Mer, and you're hurting your own reputation, and you are hurting the people who care for you, like me and Mama and Daddy, not to mention your own family."

"What would you have me do, Meriam? Would you have me stop seeing Nikki, is that it? For if that is what you have in mind , you can forget it. I could no more stop seeing him then I could stop breathing. If you had ever felt this way, you would understand."

"That's quite enough, Delia. How I've felt has nothing to do with this conversation. All we are asking of you is that you be more discreet, that's all. End of conversation."

"No, not end of conversation. Since it's obvious that you have some guide lines in mind, I'd like to hear them. If I'm going to be put in the position of following your dictates concerning my private life, I'd like to hear just what you have in mind."

"For one, you can stop hanging all over him in public places. And for another when he visits you in your house have him at least have the decency to leave before daylight, so the neighbors cannot see him. I don't think that's asking too much,"

"Oh, it's all right for the neighbors to see him arrive in daylight and to know that he is spending the night, but Heaven forbid that they should see him leave. Really, Meriam, you sound as two-faced as that stuffy Sister Agnes."

The bell jingled when the front door opened. It was Nikki. Delia didn't like his expression. "What's wrong?"

He asked Meriam to excuse them, that he had to talk to Delia alone. He practically dragged her into the workroom. Delia was glad that Gladys and Rachel weren't there. They did most of their work in their own homes.

"What's wrong?" "You'd better sit. Now, I don't want you to get upset, but Uncle Ernie arrived on the morning train and we've had a talk. It appears that someone wrote him of our arrangement."

"Why does that upset you, Nikki? You're a grown man, twenty-eight years old."

"I want you to listen, Delia. This is very important. Uncle Ernie practically raised me and my brothers and has taken care of our mother for a long time. He is the one who with my mother's family's approval will decide who I marry. And I can tell you that she is Greek and from a very respected family. The arrangement has already been made."

He sat, caught his breath and started to continue, but Delia stopped him.

"What you're saying is that we can never be married because you owe everything to your uncle. Is that it? That this is a business arrangement and nothing more. That he virtually owns you and your family, and he dictates who you marry, what business ventures you can enter, everything…"

He grabbed her and kissed her soundly, then passionately. When he let her go, he rose, and said, "He said that you would not understand the situation because you are different. I knew that he was right. Now, don't say anything else. I love you with my entire being and always shall. There will never be another woman for me, my Helen, but it is as you say. I am Greek and I am owned. And I'm not sorry for our ways, for they are good ways."

By now she was sobbing, not able to answer him. He held her shoulders firmly and said, "My mother and bride will be here by the week's end. But I hope, no, I pray that you and I will be as before."

She could not even answer him. Meriam found her sobbing, uncontrolled. "I was afraid of this. You wouldn't listen, would you? When are you going to learn that using your head is also a part of a relationship? Oh, Delia, my friend, I hurt for you. Here, use this." She handed her a handkerchief.

They were in each others arms when the door bell sounded. Meriam looked through the curtain and saw Nikki's Uncle Ernie. "Delia, he's here. It's Nikki's Uncle Ernie. Get yourself together. Hurry."

Meriam had known Ernie Limiatis for years. He'd had dinner at their home many times and was a good friend of her daddy's. She stalled him for a while and when Delia walked into the showroom, she couldn't believe that she'd pulled herself together so quickly.

"You must be Uncle Ernie. I'm Delia O'Farrell. It's a pleasure to meet you. Nikki's told me so much about you. I'm sure that you know how fond of you he is."

She's going to pull it off. God, she's regal! I think we both learned a lot at St. Joseph's. Sister Agnes would be proud of us.

They arranged to meet at Nikki's restaurant to discuss his and Delia's future. The arrangement was as Nikki had suggested, that he and Delia would continue to be lovers, but discreetly, so as not to embarrass the family. Delia would be given a share of Nikki's wealth just as if she were his legal wife. If either Delia or Nikki decided to end the relationship, then a document would be signed releasing both parties from the arrangement.

Delia signed the document, and as she left them she kissed both on their cheeks and whispered to Nikki loudly enough so Uncle Ernie could hear, "I am now one of your sheep, my love. I have ceased being Delia Rose O'Farrell."

CHAPTER IV TITANIC

THE YEAR 1912

Maggie, Seth and children Raine, Harrison and Norwood were at Tall Ten having Sunday dinner with Callie and Clay. It had become a Sunday ritual that the families get together after church. Jack and Annie usually joined them but didn't have to come far, because since their marriage the previous year they had built a house beside the old pond a quarter of a mile from the main house.

Jack had a good job with the First National Bank, one of the few buildings that had survived the Great Fire of '05, and since he knew that Annie Willett was not going to give up on him, he decided to go ahead and marry her - at least that's what he told everybody. Nellie was attending college in Tallahassee at the Florida State College for Women, previously the West Florida Seminary, with plans of becoming a teacher and got home only during vacation.

"Maggie, when did Berta and Layke say they were going to leave Europe?" Callie asked.

"I was saving that information for dessert, y'all, and I'm going to make you wait. I bet I smell guava pie. Do I?"

Seth looked at her. "You're not, are you Maggie Pope?" Everyone laughed because every time Maggie got pregnant she craved guavas. "No, sir, I am not, but even when I'm not, I love guava pie. Now you know that. I thank the Cubans every time I eat one."

Clay spoke up, "That was one of the things I used to look forward to when I lived in Tampa, that and the guava paste with hard yellow cheese and that wonderful Cuban bread."

"Go ahead and say it, you like their cigars too, don't you?" Callie chimed in.

"Actually, you might say that I do, but I hope you've noticed that I never have one when I'm home anymore. I know how you hate it."

Callie got up from her seat, walked to the end of the table, bent from her still small waist and kissed him on the forehead. "I'm still trying to train this one, but he's coming along right well, as Mattie used to say. I'll be right back with the pie and coffee."

"Oh, Clay, tell them about the trip you made to the opening of Plant's hotel when I couldn't go with you. You know, when I was out to here carrying Annie. I know they'd get a kick out of it."

"If you insist, my sweet. But hurry up the pie. I'm almost as bad as Maggie. It all began when I was contacted by the *Tampa Tribune*, the paper I used to work for, and told that Henry Plant himself had asked that I cover the grand opening of his famous Tampa Bay Hotel, and as Callie said, she was expecting our Annie and couldn't accompany me. But being the darling girl that she is, she insisted on my going, and so I did and wrote the special article and happen to have a few dozen copies if you ever want to read it."

They all laughed and Annie excused herself stating that she had heard the story only a hundred times and coaxed Jack into joining her for a walk. He too had heard it a few times.

"Has either of you ever seen the hotel?" They shook their heads no. He resumed. "Plant was trying to outdo Henry Flagler, and everyone in the state knew that there was a rivalry between the two of them, but also that it was a friendly one. The day the hotel opened Plant got a telegram from Flagler: *Henry, where is Tampa?* Plant sent a reply, *Follow the crowd, Henry.*

"Well, outdo him he did. I covered the opening of the Ponce De Leon in St. Augustine, too, and well, actually, they both are magnificent structures, but the fanfare that Plant presented was unsurpassed. Basically, the architecture was Moorish, with minarets rising to the sky. It is five stories high, the bricks were brought in from Atlanta by Plant's trains, of course, and the building was braced by steel beams, making it fireproof."

Clay began to laugh, then cough, and Callie looked around the corner of the kitchen and said, "See, that's what those Cuban cigars do to a person. Go ahead and finish, I'm just about done in here."

"The hotel was so long that Plant provided rickshaws for the guests to go back and forth - that hotel was 1200 feet long, imagine! Some of the furniture had been the personal property of Marie Antoinette, and there was scarlet carpeting embossed with black lions. Priceless statuary and paintings abounded, and to really outdo Flagler every guest room had a telephone. He did him another good one - he lured the Boston Symphony to perform. And the mirrors! I couldn't believe it when Jerry Gold from Boston's *Saturday Evening Gazette* started counting those mirrors, and when he finished he shouted, right at the very time the orchestra was playing softly, `ONE HUNDRED AND TEN OF THE BLOOMING THINGS!'"

We've never let him forget it. Every year on the anniversary of the opening, he told me the last time I saw him, he gets at least a dozen telegrams repeating *One hundred ten of the blooming things*. I'm glad, because he needs some happiness in his life. In a wheel chair, now. Don't know how much longer he's got."

Callie announced loudly, "Pie's served. You want it here or out on the porch?"

"Let's sit outside. It's such a gorgeous day, isn't it? Have you ever been witness to such a glorious spring? Father wrote that Italy was like this. He said it reminded him of the west coast near Cedar Key and Tarpon Springs. They're having such a wonderful time."

"Are you keeping something from us, young lady?" Callie teased.

"Yes, I am, Callie. Guess what Father is giving Mother for their wedding anniversary? Their thirty fourth, I think. Give up, because I cannot hold it in another moment. He has passage on the *TITANIC*! Can you believe it? He said that they're sailing only second class, but can you imagine how thrilled Mother will be? We were told to not breath a word of it to her. Tucker and Barbara will meet them in New York."

"Seth, where would they be now if they left on Wednesday like they planned?"

"I'm not your advanced navigator, lady mine, nor do I know what the weather conditions are, nor do I..."

"All right, smart drawers, I thought that you might know more than I do about that sort of thing. After all, the route has been in your very own paper, and I've been so swamped with school work that I've hardly had time to see it."

****

Berta and Layke had tried to see every section of the magnificent ship since they left Southhampton the day before. They put in at Queenstown harbour about noon the next day to take on mostly Irish immigrants. A crowd had formed along the deck rail and was watching them board. As she watched, Berta wondered if this was anything like the boarding young Conner, his sister Maeve and their mother made after the famine and the death of their father. How horrible it must have been, but also how exciting! Conner would have found it exciting, she knew. She could feel Layke watching her and knew that he was reading her mind.

Every day was filled with meeting interesting people. The John Jacob Astors were aboard as were Henry Harper of the publishing family and Robert Daniel, the Philadelphia banker. Berta had already filled two pages of her diary with names of famous people. She knew that she'd never remember all of them. She collected the daily menus and the ship's brochures to show their friends in Tallahassee and Old Town.

She had written page after page of descriptions. The Turkish baths on F deck were so garishly interesting that she wrote four entire pages about them. The decorations were not quite Victorian, more Moorish in feel: mosaic floor, blue- green tiled walls, gilded beams in the dull red ceiling, stanchions encased in carved teak, almost indescribable in words, but Berta was having fun trying to express her observations.

It was the fifth night out. She and Layke had finished their dinner. She had been daring and ate the curried chicken and rice, and Layke the spring lamb with mint sauce, one of his favorites. They had decided to have the fresh fruit, cheese and biscuits for dessert. When the biscuits arrived they couldn't contain their laughter. As Layke explained to the Dutch couple who were at their table, the biscuits in Europe were like scones and certainly not the ones most Americans were used to.

After dinner they had danced to Wallace Henry Hartley's Band with its eight fine musicians, as they had since their first night on board, and Layke had been invited to have a nightcap with a senator from Virginia. Berta had insisted that he do so. "I want to fill in my diary, Honey, so you go on and stay as long as you wish. I don't know why I'm so tired. It's the excitement I guess. I'll not wait up for you."

"Are you sure? He's just a bag-o-wind, and really I'd just as soon..."

But Layke had acquiesced and joined Senator Thurmond, who was traveling first class and had invited Layke to join him in the first class smoking room on A deck. The room was filled with men having a highball or hot whiskey and water. Some were playing bridge but most were winding down from a full day's activities.

"Sidney, I'm saying it again, if Florida doesn't start policing these land sharks and their crooked tactics, there will be no future land sales in the state. People will stop even attempting to purchase land, and I wouldn't blame them. They're ruining it for any honest land dealer. I'm worried and I almost wish that I hadn't retired. Did I tell you that our son Tucker is thinking of running for the house, state house, that is? Then, there's no stopping him. I wish that I'd started earlier in life. Oh, well."

He looked at his watch and said, "It's 11:50 and time to turn in."

"What's all the commotion?" Sidney asked. "What're those whippersnappers shouting about? You'd think that with their education and background they'd have learned some manners!"

Layke watched them as they rushed outside through the after door, past the Palm Court and out on to the deck just in time to see the iceberg scraping along the starboard side, a little higher than the boat deck. As it slid by, they watched chunks of ice breaking and tumbling off into the water. It faded into the darkness astern. It was too bitterly cold to stay outside. When they came inside throwing chunks of ice in the air and asking if anyone would like ice for his highballs, he agreed with Sidney that they did indeed need to learn some manners.

"Iceberg, did you say? Don't be ridiculous! Iceberg, indeed," Sir Harvey Rinsley, seated next to them, commented. The men at the tables resumed their bridge game. Layke noticed the silence around him, then realized that the engines had stopped. He excused himself, telling Sidney that Berta had not been feeling well and that he was going to turn in, too. He had not been quite honest. It was true that she had said she was tired, but that was not the reason that he had excused himself. Something was not right. He didn't know what, but he knew that he needed to get to Berta. As he went to their deck he overheard someone say, "We hit an iceberg, and there it is." A shiver went over him. Then he remembered what he'd read in the tabloid, *God himself could not sink this ship*. But he rushed to his Berta anyway.

By the time Layke got to their cabin he knew that there was a problem, but so as not to alarm Berta unnecessarily, he entered their cabin with a smile. "Lady mine, are you still awake?," he asked and kissed her on the cheek. She was not misled by his humor. "What's wrong?" is all she said.

"I heard someone say that we hit an iceberg and..."

"Things don't feel right, Layke. I noticed it a while ago. You don't suppose that we are in ..."

"No, I'm sure that if we were..."

There was a knock on their door, and Layke answered it as Berta got dressed. When he turned around she said, "All I want are the children's pictures and my heavy wool wrap. We must leave."

The deck was now crowded with pushing and shoving crew members and people carrying packages. They didn't need to be told that there was trouble. "Why is she listing?" someone asked. The answer, "She shouldn't be doing that on such a calm night."

It was 12:05 and the captain gave orders to uncover the lifeboats. A crewman came by and said, "As a matter of form the captain has ordered all ladies and children on deck." There were no bells or sirens, no general alarm, but all over the ship the word was passed. They were told to put on their life jackets and heaviest coats to ward off the cold. Berta tied her hair back with a ribbon instead of putting it up, and Layke smiled down at her and whispered, "You are as beautiful as on the first day I saw you, my love."

"Layke, I want to stay with you. Now, I mean it. I do not want us to be separated. No matter what happens, we will be together. That's the way I want it." He squeezed her hand three times. She responded by squeezing his four times.

Most of the people around them seemed unworried but confused. There had been no boat drills nor boat assignments. The crew moved like sleep walkers, barely speaking. They removed the canvas covers from the wooden lifeboats, clearing the masts, putting in lanterns and tins of biscuits, one by one the cranks turned, the davits creaked, the pulleys squealed and the boats slowly swung out free of the ship. Berta and Layke silently watched.

They could hear the band playing, it was playing a lively ragtime tune in the first class lounge, where many of the passengers waited for orders to lower the boats. Later the band moved to the forward deck near the entrance to the grand staircase.

Someone grabbed Berta's arm and said, "Women and children first, come on, lady." She clung to Layke. He looked down at her and whispered, "Are you sure, Berta?" She nodded and smiled, "My life wouldn't be worth living without you. Let someone who needs more time on this earth take my place."

The woman who was next to her overheard and smiled at her. Berta recognized her as Mrs. Isador Straus, whose husband founded Macy's Department store and also served in congress. She overheard her say to her husband, "We have been living together for many years. Where you go, I go."

The sudden rush of steerage passengers, who had sensed the danger and got top side, aimed for the boats. They were strictly on their own, mingling with first and second class passengers, who as soon as the stewards got them in the boats would jump out and go inside where it was warm.

Berta and Layke huddled against the wall watching. The steerage people were like a stream of ants curling their way up a crane in the after well deck, crawling along the boom to the first class quarters, then over the railing and on up to the boat deck. There was no more shouting nor unusual commotion than at any other large gathering. They were like sleep walkers weaving in and out. The brightly lit windows of the first class a la carte restaurant with its tables beautifully set with silver and china for the following day shone on their disbelieving, desperate faces. No one actually believed that the *Titanic* could sink.

Berta hugged Layke closer. She thought, if this is the end I'm glad we're together. I'll miss seeing the grandchildren's lives unfold, but I'm happy that our children have found good mates and that they seem to be happy. Is there anything I'd change? She looked up at Layke and knew emphatically that there was nothing.

Layke felt her looking at him. She's satisfied and so am I. If there is no room for us in the lifeboats then, it is a fitting farewell. He stroked her still blond hair and said, "I'd be mighty pleased Miss if you would give me the pleasure of a dance." Berta smiled and they made their way to the grand staircase and the orchestra. There was not much room, but then they didn't need much. They never had. He squeezed her hand three times and she responded by squeezing his four times. I love you. I love you, too. His lips found the top of her head and they moved to the music saying nothing. Their hearts beat as one. They could feel the boat list more, and finding it difficult to keep their footing held each other harder.

In every boat the passengers' eyes were on the *Titanic*. Could this be happening? How could this happen to the unsinkable *Titanic* with her tall masts, the four big funnels standing out sharp and black in the clear blue night, the bright promenade decks, the long rows of portholes all blazing with lights? How? They could see the hundreds of people leaning against the rails and hear the ragtime in the cold, still night air.

They were told to try for the steamer *Carpathia*, which had come to their aid and whose lights could be seen in the distance. They began to row and to wonder if they would have the strength to travel that indeterminate distance. Some said the rosary, others mumbled prayers, some hummed tunes, some were silent. All were disbelieving.

Suddenly, the ragtime music ended, the air filled with silence, then as the wooden life boats inched farther and farther away they heard the Episcopal hymn "Autumn" - then nothing, no bright lights, no silhouette of the majestic ship, no music, only their own heavy breathing and frightened sobs.

Tucker and Barbara had rushed down to the White Star office early the next morning. The first survivor list was up, and crowds stormed the office. Berta's and Layke's names were not listed. Tuesday turned to

Wednesday, and Wednesday to Thursday, and still no news. Thursday the *Carpathia* steamed by the Statue of Liberty with 10,000 people watching from the Battery. She edged towards pier 54, where 30,000 more stood in the freezing drizzle. As the *Carpathia* steamed up the North River, tugs chugged beside her, full of frustrated reporters shouting questions through megaphones.

By 9:35 the ship was moored, the gangplank lowered, and the first survivors walked off. "Can you see them?" over and over again Barbara asked Tucker. He only shook his head. "You can't give up hope, Honey. They'll be along any minute."

Somehow, she knew better. She said later to SuSu and Maggie that she had a strange feeling inside her from the moment they heard of the disaster. Nine months later she gave birth to a daughter, and they named her Berta Norwood. She and Tucker had been childless for ten years. SuSu said, "Well, like Miss Trudy would have said, 'the Lord giveth and the Lord taketh away.' Mama would have liked that. She was such a romantic, you know. I can't get over how much Little Berta looks like her. Can you believe those blue eyes? Blue as any cornflower in the hills of Tennessee, Layke always said, and they're just like her grandma's."

BOOK FOUR:

NEW BEGINNINGS

CHAPTER I THE BIG LAKE

THE YEAR 1917

"What time does Delia's train get in?" Rose asked Juanita, who was busily sorting out old correspondence and photographs. They were in the dining room at Athea, and the long dining room table was covered with boxes.

"Can you believe that she gets in four hours before Nolan does? That means that Harrison will have to sit at the train station for all that time, then turn around and have to go back to town for Nikki tomorrow."

"I know what you're going to say, but I'm going to put in my two cents anyway. All of Tarpon Springs knows that she's his mistress, Juanita, so why don't they just come together instead of putting on a face?"

"You're right, Rose, you know what I'm going to respond. She's a businesswoman, and you're wrong about all of Tarpon Springs knowing. Actually, only the old-timers know. They've been very discreet as Ernie requested. Heavens, they have so little time together, mainly when she goes on her buying trips to New York and..."

"But since his mother passed away, I'd think that they could at least ride on the same train."

"Well, friend of mine, what we think doesn't matter, does it? After all, he has a wife and children, and it's Delia's and Nikki's business, so if they want it this way, then so be it. I had wished that Nolan could have come on the same train, though, but he needed to be in Tampa for the closing on that land deal. Seems to me that he's investing too much in real estate, but Nikki approved it, and you know Nolan. If Nikki says to jump in the river, he does it."

"I know it's a comfort to Delia having them so close, though. Hand me that box and I'll help you sort."

"What on earth did I keep this for? Look at this. This is the first hat I ever made when I was with Maeve in the shop in Palatka. Grief, it's the ugliest thing I've ever seen. I can't imagine what on ..."

"What's this, Juanita? Looks like a land deed. *Southern States Land and Timber Company, 1899. Section 17, East Beach, Florida.* Where on earth is East Beach? Looks like it says 40 acres, and it's signed Charles Hogrefe. Who is he and what's it doing in here?"

"Here, let me see that. I don't know anything about it. What else is in that box? Oh, Rose, those are Conner's things that Harrison packed away right after he died. Look, it's Conner's watch fob. I'd forgotten all about these."

"Sit down, Juanita. I can't believe how you still act every time someone even mentions Conner, I really can't. It's been eighteen years, for Heaven's sake."

"I'm much better than I was. It's just selling the shop and now Athea. Well, it's making me sad. I'll do better when Delia and Nolan get here. I'm glad Andrea decided not to come. I'd like Nolan all to myself for a change. Don't look at me like that. I like Andrea, really I do. It's just that since they married I am never alone with him. I wish that they could have a child. She seems to feel.. inadequate I guess is the word. It's hard to believe that they've been married almost five years, isn't it?"

Rose handed her the land deed, and Juanita tucked it in her skirt pocket. "Thanks, I'll show Nolan and Nikki this to see if it's any good. I don't remember ever seeing it before, but then I was in shock, I guess."

"How long do you expect to stay in Tarpon Springs? A month, two?"

"That's up to you. All you have to do is to call me from Seth's, and I'll join you in a few days. Then, we can sit down and map out our future. I'm getting excited, in a way, aren't you?"

"It's probably the stupidest thing I've ever done, I declare it is."

"More stupid than coming up to Monticello with me twenty years ago?"

"At least I knew where I was going then. But to just sell out and move and not even to know where, well, I guess I'm a little scared. And at our age? Everyone in town thinks we've lost our minds."

"Rose, how could we have turned down the offer on the shop? You were as tired of it as I've become. Now you know that. Pretty soon everyone in Monticello will be motoring to Tallahassee or Jacksonville for ready-to-wear gowns, and then where would we be?"

"I know you're right, and I know that Simpkins has been after you for years to purchase Athea. But Juanita, to not have any place to go, it frightens me."

"Stop it this instant! You've got Seth, Maggie and their three children, and if you weren't so stubborn you could build a small house near them like they suggested..."

"Yes, and you could do the same with Delia and Nolan in Tarpon Springs, but I haven't heard you say yes to them, have I?"

"No, and you won't. I don't believe in living close to my children. Besides, Delia would have me in the shop, and I'm closing that chapter of my life. I don't care if I ever have to try to fit another two-hundred-pound woman who wants to look like she weighs only one hundred thirty."

Rose started to laugh and soon Juanita joined in. "I know just how you feel. Remember Gladys Palmer? I know she weighed at least that much. I don't know how she could breathe in that gold satin you made for the Christmas Gala at the Opera House. And Betty Jo Barwick in that royal blue. Remember?"

"How could I forget? Delia is doing very well without me and Meriam. Did I tell you that Meriam's husband had some kind of attack? He's not doing well at all. I'd not be surprised if she moved back to Tarpon Springs and needed to go back to work. He'd over extended himself in Miami on those stupid land deals, her father said, and Delia is concerned about her."

"I hope that if she does come back to Del Mer that Delia hires her on just as a sales woman. She owns it outright, now, and she'll need it for her future."

"Nikki takes very good care of Delia, Rose, and you know it."

"Yes, but if something happens to him, then where is Delia? Out in the cold, and his wife and children will get everything."

"And that's as it should be. Delia knew what she was getting herself into. But, I'm not worried. She owns that beautiful home on the Bayou outright and also the shop. I think she's doing very well, but I intend to give her and Nolan part of the money from Athea just in case."

"Juanita, that's ridiculous! What if something happens? I mean you might just need that money to establish yourself. I think you're making a mistake."

"I don't think so. There should be plenty what with the sale of the shop, too, and I intend to invest in some land like Nolan suggested. I've talked it over with Harrison, and he's agreed to stay on with Simpkins until I send for him. Like he said, he has nothing to keep him here since Easter passed on. I think he's as anxious to leave as I am."

"There. That's the last box. Why do we hang on to all this junk? Most of it is just that."

"I think I hear Harrison driving up now. Oh, Simpkins said that he'd buy the Model T Ford, too. I guess with seven children he needs more transportation."

Juanita had insisted on Harrison's joining them for cocktails and dinner, and Melvia had been told in no uncertain terms to keep quiet about it.

"This is our last formal dinner at Athea, and since Harrison is practically a member of the family, Delia, Nolan and I want him to join us. Why is that so hard for you to understand, Melvia? You know how much we think of him. Just because he's colored, it shouldn't make any difference."

"No'am, it shouldn't, but it do."

"I give up, Melvia." Juanita threw her hands up dramatically, and Nolan laughed heartily, just like his da would've. Melvia left the dining room shaking her head and mumbling, "Not right, jes not right."

The evening was as festive as the six of them could make it. Nolan had taken the lead, and he and Delia were trying to outdo each other with tales about Conner and some of the colorful characters in and around Monticello. Nikki fit right in and enjoyed the exchange between them.

They went to the back patio that Juanita had had built after Conner's death. Dicey brought out the coffee, and Nikki and Harrison served the brandy. It was a cool October evening with a soft breeze blowing through the rows of pecan trees that lined the back lawn at the bottom of the knoll. The rolling hills in the distance, topped with the neat rows of the fall crops made a picturesque setting. Juanita was determined that she'd not get maudlin but was having difficulty. Rose noticed it and to get her mind off leaving said, "Juanita, did you think to show that deed to Nolan?"

"You know, I think my mind's going. I forgot all about it. I'll run up and get it."

"I'll get it, Mum, I need to get a handkerchief anyway. Where is it?" Delia asked.

"It's on my dresser, Honey. And, Delia, bring down my lace shawl please, I'm feeling a little chilly. Think we'll have an early fall. Here it is only the end of October and already there's a chill in the air."

They all knew that she was talking out of nervousness. Nikki pulled up the rattan chair beside her's and took her hand, smiling. "It will work out beautifully, Juanita, you'll see. What an adventure! Did I ever tell you what it was like to go to tiny Tarpon Springs from that big bad city of New York in the dead of winter?"

"Only a dozen times, Nikki, sweet. Thank you for being concerned. I'm all right, now. I didn't expect it to be easy, you know."

"My Delia has a wise mother." He raised her hand and kissed it.

He reminds me of my Conner. The same sensitivity. Delia is a fortunate woman, I don't care what anyone else thinks. He's a gem.

Delia saw the piece of paper on the dresser and was bending over looking for Juanita's shawl in the bottom drawer. Suddenly she seemed lightheaded. What on earth, she thought. I shouldn't have bent over after such a heavy meal. She slowly sat on the edge of Juanita's bed and held her head in both hands. Breathing deeply, she began to feel better. "Think I'll have a brandy. Maybe that'll clear my head."

"Here, Mum. Nikki, pour me a small brandy, sweet."

Nikki looked at her with a questioning look. "Aren't you feeling well?"

She shook her head. "It's been a horrendous week with every overweight woman in the entire town wanting a dress and, of course, wanting it at that minute. And it's been a very long day, that's all. I'll be fine, honest I will."

"Harrison, do you ever remember seeing this before? Rose found it in Conner's things."

He began to laugh. "I'll add another tale to your's and Delia's, Young Nolan. This," he held it up for all to see, "is the last transaction that your da made. He won forty acres of land in a town I've never heard of in a hot poker game." Harrison continued to laugh.

"Nikki, since you didn't know Conner, you probably can't appreciate the humor in it. I was told that he had cleaned out a gentleman from some midwestern state who had put up this land deed so he could stay in the game. I have no idea if it has any value, but knowing Conner, I'm sure that he just wanted the gentleman to stay in the game, so he didn't care either. Conner no doubt was having an eventful day and didn't want it to end.. Oh, how he loved the game!" Harrison had a faraway look.

"Here, let me see that," Nikki said. "I've heard of the Southern States Land And Timber Company, and so have you, Nolan. They bought millions of acres from Hamilton Disston at the turn of the century. This probably has some value, Juanita. How much, I don't know, but I can certainly find out."

"Wouldn't that be a hoot, Mum, if Da left us wealthy?" Nolan said with a laugh.

"I doubt that forty acres could be worth much, son, but thank you, Nikki. I'd appreciate what you can find out."

Harrison added, "The gentleman in question, this Charles Hogrefe, did tell me that he intended to have the land officially deeded over to you, Cherie. He was so upset by Conner's sudden death right after the poker game that he said he wanted to take care of Conner's widow and children."

****

Juanita spent Christmas with Delia in Tarpon Springs, and Rose was with Seth and family in Arcadia. She had called Rose and told her that she wanted to stay with Delia for a while longer, because she was concerned about her. She was paler than usual and without much energy. As much as she hated it, Juanita had started going to Del Mer daily for a few hours, and Delia slept later than usual and would join her and Meriam about noon. She was sure glad Meriam had returned.

It was the second week in January, and Juanita had called Rose to tell her that she had decided to go to East Beach on Lake Okeechobee to see the land that Nikki had found did exist and should have some value. She doubted that Rose would want to join her, so she had made arrangements to have Nolan accompany her.

Rose was tiring of staying in Arcadia, even though Seth and Maggie had been showing her a good time attending the plays at the Arcadia Opera House, and said that she'd love to go with her. They made arrangements to meet in Ft. Myers and take a boat on to Alva, the small town Rose was from, then on to LaBelle, where Juanita was from, before going by boat on the Caloosahatchee into Lake Okeechobee to the southeastern side of the lake to East Beach.

When Juanita called Harrison to tell him of their plans, he said that he wanted to join them and that he'd meet her in Tarpon Springs so they could all go together. Juanita could tell by his voice that he was lonely. Nolan was ecstatic at having Harrison with them on their trip.

The night before they were due to leave, Delia had planned a wonderful dinner, and Nikki had managed to join them, something he rarely did in Tarpon Springs. Harrison had arrived two days before and had spent most of the time with Nolan at the Sponge Exchange, where Nolan was a vice president, thanks to Nikki. He had insisted that Nolan learn the business from the ground up, though, accompanying the men on the small boats and the mother schooner that carried the supplies when they were on their long bi-annual trips. Then he worked the packing houses, learning how to grade the sponges. Nikki swore to Delia that Nolan had to have been Greek in one of his lives.

Juanita was in her room changing for dinner when she heard a faint knock on her door. It was Delia. "What's wrong? Now, don't you say nothing again. I know that something is wrong and I want to know - no, I demand to know what it is!"

"I'm pregnant!"

Juanita sat down and sighed and said, "Delia Rose O'Farrell, is that all? You had me and Meriam scared half to death. Why, we had you with every incurable disease you can imagine. Oh, Honey, how wonderful!"

"Aren't you upset, Mum? After all. I'm not a young girl, you know, and am unmarried and..."

"Do you want Nikki's baby, Delia Rose?"

"Of course, I do. I can hardly stand not telling him and had a terrible time not telling you."

"Honey, I just wish your da were here. My, my, how he'd carry on." Juanita hugged her and said, "We have to make plans. I can hardly wait to tell Rose."

"Mum, I haven't even told Nikki!"

"Well, do it tonight. All right, you could go to Europe, but with the unrest over there that wouldn't be such a good idea. How about an extended vacation, say to see friends in California and..."

"What? Come home with a baby who'll look exactly like Nikki? Mum, that won't hold water, and you know it."

"That's not what I was going to say at all. We must be more original than that, mustn't we?" Suddenly she yelled, "I know! Nolan and Andrea can't have children, at least I guess that they can't. We'll say that she's expecting and wants to go to West Palm Beach to be with her parents and her family doctor. Then - oh, Delia, this is a pip - you can join us in East Beach, pretending to be assisting me in my land affairs, and have the baby. Andrea returns to Tarpon Springs with your baby, pretending that it's hers and Nolan's. What do you think?"

"I think that you have a wonderful imagination. That's what I think. Why can't I go to Ireland, or pretend to, but go to some place where I'm not known, return and find that Nolan and Andrea have adopted a baby while I'm gone. What's wrong with that?"

"No one will believe it, that's what's wrong. Let's have Nikki decide which plan is best."

After dinner that night Juanita, Nolan and Andrea, Harrison and the prospective parents put their heads together and decided to go along with Juanita's idea. But first they'd go to East Beach as planned to make sure that there was a doctor, adequate housing, etc. Then they'd send for

Delia, and Andrea would go on to West Palm Beach to be with her parents for the duration as planned.

When Delia raised her glass of sherry to toast the plan, Nikki took it from her and said, "Only a sip, my sweet, this child must be perfect, but how could it not be with such a mother?"

Juanita had to leave the room, she was so touched, and Harrison followed her. They sat on the front porch overlooking Spring Bayou, and Juanita turned to Harrison and asked, "Do you think Conner is with us, Harrison? I don't think I can stand it if he's not. Oh, how he'd love the adventure of this."

"He's here, Cherie. I can feel his presence. *Absence is to love what wind is to fire; it extinguishes the small, it enkindles the great.* And, Cherie, there was a great love between those two. He is here all right."

****

Juanita had forgotten how busy the Caloosahatchee could be with boats everywhere you looked, and since the river had been dredged by Disston it looked almost like a canal. She missed the corkscrew bends that were so sharp that the boats had to be equipped with bells to alert the other boats of their presence. When she was a young girl she'd listen to the bells and dream of going on one of the boats far, far away. She and Rose were both disappointed to find that nothing was the same in Alva and LaBelle. Both towns had grown from hamlets to small towns, especially LaBelle. Juanita was able to learn that her sister Bonnie and family had moved down to Naples on the Gulf and that her mother had died in her sleep ten years before. She knew that she should be saddened, but even her memory of her mother was so faded that she could barely see her face, even when she tried real hard.

Nolan and Harrison were the ones who were excited about the entire adventure. Neither had been to the Everglades and they were entranced by everything they saw. Mr. McCoy, Jack, who owned the *Olivia* that they boarded in Moore Haven for their ride across Lake Okeechobee, was explaining to them about all the little towns that had sprung up around the big lake. When Nolan asked him what he could tell them about East Beach, he chuckled and said that there was not much to tell, not much of a town and not many people living there, but that it did have a beautiful white beach, and the fishing was good. They decided to not tell Juanita and Rose.

Jack said that there was talk of building a hard road connecting West Palm Beach on the east coast to the town of Canal Point only a couple miles north of East Beach, and then all the way north to the town of Okeechobee. What with the Palm Beach Canal having been opened up last year and the trains already to Okeechobee, folks were moving in fast, and everyone expected things to start hopping around the lake.

Nolan was getting a little concerned about how primitive it would be for Delia. He decided that he'd better ask Jack if there were any doctors around. "Funny you should ask that. Well, there ain't ever been a better doctor then Doc Anner, but she lives over in Tantie, or in Okeechobee as they're calling it now. Her real name is Anna Darrow, and she'll get to anybody who's sick whether in that beat up Model T or a push pole canoe or her motor boat. All you got to do is get word to her."

"How far's that from East Beach?"

"Well, now here's where we are, see those little specks, they're all islands almost hugging the shore, first one's Ritta, then we go on to Torry, then on past Kreamer, named for Disston's engineer, you know, then we oughta be pulling into East Beach, and way up there is Okeechobee," he said pointing up ahead.

"That might take a long time for the doctor to come all that way. Don't they have any doctors closer?"

He thought on it, scratched his head and said, "Seems to me that Oscar McClure said that a new doctor come into East Beach back about last month from up Parrish way. Come in a old cut-off Model T Ford and ain't stopped doctoring since he got here." He laughed and said, "Believe his name is Spooner. Yep, that's it, Doster Spooner. That's a handle, ain't it?"

Nolan seemed relieved. Harrison explained, "His sister wants to be with her mama when her baby comes in June, that's why we're concerned."

"Heck, by June we might have another hundred or so folks moved in and another doctor. Word's got out 'bout this black muck growing vegetables so good, and since the freeze of last year where it got down to 27 degrees in Miami... You heard 'bout that?" They shook their heads no. "Well East Beach was the onliest place down here with any green left. A hamper of beans was bringing $24.00, and every fisherman around who'd been farming a little on the side done quit their fishing and took to farming serious like."

By now Nolan and Harrison were very attentive. "Hell, Jim Bacom and Noble Padgett sold a acre of cabbage for $1,000.00, cleared

$7,000.00 over all, and made even more money on beans and then their spring crop of tomatoes. Don't blame them for giving up fishing. Padgett went ahead and bought all of Section 20. That's why we got such a rush on land around here. Hell, Moore Haven gets frozen out, and folks on East Beach are sitting around counting their money and taking sun baths."

Harrison was licking his lips, and Nolan took him by the arm and whispered, "I think that we might have just fallen into a gold mine, Harrison. What do you think?"

He shook his head in disbelief. "Don't know if he's exaggerating or not. We'll soon find out though. Looks like we'll be coming in soon. Better get your mother. For Heaven's sake, Nolan, don't say anything to her. We don't want to get her hopes up, now do we? He might be just blowing steam."

Juanita and Rose came to the bow of the boat, Juanita trying in vain to keep her broad brim hat from flying off. Finally she removed it and explained, "I do hope that I don't make a false impression to the people of East Beach, Captain McCoy, Usually I am very presentable."

"I'm thinking that you'll do just fine, Mrs. O'Farrell. These folks, for the most part, are just working folks, even Dr. Armstrong and his missus."

"A doctor, how nice. I'm hoping that my daughter will come to East Beach to have her baby..."

"Oh, ma'am, he's a dentist."

"Oh! But it's nice to have a dentist available, too, isn't it, Rose? It sounds like a lovely town."

Jack McCoy looked at Nolan and Harrison and rolled his eyes upward. Finally, he walked over to Nolan and said, "I think you best level with your mama 'bout East Beach. There ain't no town to speak of, just a lot of tar paper shacks and not but a few frame houses, and lots of folks still living in tents, and..."

"Once we get settled in at a hotel..." Nolan began.

"What hotel? There ain't no hotel in East Beach. That's what I been tryin' to tell you. Now there is one on up to Canal Point. Matter of fact, there's two. They got the Glades Inn and the Custard Apple Inn. I think you best be thinking about going there for the night."

Nolan and Harrison stood off to the side and discussed their situation. Their discussion did not go undetected by Rose. She soon joined them. "What're you two talking about that you don't want us to know?"

Harrison responded. "Captain McCoy has informed us that there is no hotel in East Beach, but that about two miles north in the town of Canal Point there is one."

"Well, there is nothing more to discuss then, is there?"

When they told Juanita, she said, "Nolan and Harrison, I am surprised at the two of you. Now, Rose, I can understand. She and I have both become used to comforts befitting ladies. But I thought that we were adventurers and that we have to make do with less than we are used to. That is what Conner would wish..."

"What, pray tell, does Conner have to do with this, Juanita? What?" Rose inquired not three inches from Juanita's face.

"Without Conner, Rose, we would not be here. He is responsible for our having this land and..."

"And if he were here, he'd have enough sense to want to stay at a hotel instead of out on the beach being eaten up by mosquitos and maybe alligators nibbling at our toes - that's what, and you know it!"

"Begging your pardon, Mrs. O'Farrell, but the missus is right. You ladies ain't got no business staying around here for the night. They got a real nice hotel in Canal Point named the Custard Apple Inn and..."

"Captain McCoy, I do appreciate your concern, sir, but East Beach was our destination and East Beach is where we're going ashore. Besides, I'm anxious to see our land."

They skimmed over a patch of gar grass, and Captain McCoy ran the *Olivia* right up on the wide sandy beach. Rose asked, "Where is the dock, Captain McCoy?" When she looked at him she realized by his expression that there was none. She thought, no dock and no hotel, so that's what those two were talking about.

The sandy ridge was densely wooded with rubber, cypress, potash and cabbage trees and a tangle of moon vines. Off the beach tucked in among the trees were tents, tar paper shacks and shanties built of anything that the builders could find, and most were protected from the lake's northwesters by sawmill slabs. There seemed to be only a trail that twisted among trees and shacks on the ridge - but no road.

Juanita stood on the bow looking, disbelieving at first, with everyone on the *Olivia* waiting for her to say, let's go on to Canal Point - but she didn't. Instead she hiked up her skirt, pulled off her slippers and called to Nolan, "Son, help me down, please."

She turned to Rose and said, "Rose, Harrison will help you and then we must all go see our new land. Isn't this exciting? I imagine it's like the gold rush in California and Alaska, don't you imagine?"

"Pardon me, sir, but I'm Mrs. O'Farrell and I own forty acres of Section 17. Would you have any idea where that might be?" Juanita asked the very first person she saw. She saw two or three small children - they moved so rapidly that she wasn't sure - barely clothed and running around to the back of their shanty and then peeking around the corner at her. She smiled and they ducked, but not for long. They soon had resumed their position beside the edge of the building and were looking at her in the most curious fashion. I must look a fright even to small children, she thought.

The man, presumably their father, said that he didn't know, that he had been given ten acres of frost free state land to farm, but he didn't know anything about any sections. She could see a woman's head appear for an instant around the only door in the shack. Captain McCoy took it upon himself to intervene. After all, they had paid him handsomely when they could have come on the *Eight Bells* or the fancy *Eagle*. They seemed to be real nice people, but he was sure that they'd be back on the *Olivia* the very next day.

"Mrs. O'Farrell, I'll go on over to Ridenour's packing house, and there'll be someone there who can help you, I'm sure. Why don't you and Miss Rose take these bean hampers and sit up there underneath that rubber tree. Late as it is, it's still mighty hot."

"Captain McCoy, that is a splendid idea. Nolan why don't you accompany the captain?"

He hopped at the idea. He was so curious he could hardly stand it.

"Cherie, you want me to begin taking the trunks off?" Harrison asked.

"Let's wait for a while, Harrison." She was fanning herself very ladylike while the children watched the show. Juanita smiled at Rose and nodded in the direction of the children. "They've probably seldom seen ladies before." Rose didn't comment, just rolled her eyes in dismay.

Juanita smiled at the little towheaded boy of about three and he smiled back. When she crooked her finger beckoning him to her, he shook his head no. Backward little things. I bet I was like that when I was his age. She sighed and continued fanning herself, this time more rapidly.

She turned to Rose. "I can't imagine what's keeping them." By now her dress bodice was soaked through as were the long sleeves. "Why are those children still staring at us?" Rose asked.

"I can assure you that I don't know. Whew! I'm soaked with perspiration!"

Juanita bent over to take her shoes and stockings off and when she looked up all three children had their hands over their mouths. "Grief! Haven't these backward children ever seen..."

When she screamed, they ran out from their hiding place, and before she could even move off the hamper they were fighting over the long yellow snake that had fallen on Juanita's head.

"IT'S MINE...NO, IT'S MINE...I SAW IT FIRST...PA, JOEY GOT THE SNAKE AND I SAW IT FIRST..."

"Cherie, are you all right? Are you hurt?" Harrison questioned.

"No, I am not hurt!"

Juanita marched herself over to the fighting children and said, "No, it's mine, and I demand that you give it to me!" She grabbed the chicken snake behind its neck and marched herself back to her bean hamper and was sitting holding the wiggling four foot snake when Captain McCoy and Nolan came around the tree with a gentleman in riding britches and high polished boots.

"Mum, what on earth are you doing?" is all Nolan could think to say.

"And what does it look like I'm doing? I'm sitting here about to burn up holding a snake that thought that he or she, whichever it might be, could make a fool of me by dropping on my head, causing those uncouth children to think that they could use me for bait and..."

"Hey, Mum, it's all right. I want you to meet Sam Darien. He knows just where our land is."

"Mr. Darien. Oh, excuse me. I need to put this snake out of its misery." She slid her right hand down the side of the unsuspecting snake and with one crack sent its head flying. She turned toward the family that was lined up in front of their shack, curtsied ladylike, tossed them the headless snake and turned back to Mr. Darien.

Smiling, she said, "They deserved that. That should teach them that you can not tell a book by its cover. Who said that, Harrison?"

"I'm sure I don't know, Mrs. O'Farrell."

"And, besides, I grew up in LaBelle and certainly knew how to pop a snake's head off by the time I was their age."

Rose just stood with her mouth still open and shaking her head in disbelief. Aloud she said, "Lord, what have I got myself into?"

"Captain McCoy is correct, Mrs. O'Farrell. At present we have no hotel here, but I'm sure that I can arrange for you to stay at the Lair home or perhaps the Armstrongs'. There are no fancy houses in East Beach yet. I have been here since last summer and haven't completed my cabin as yet."

"How does Mrs. Darien like it here?" Rose asked.

"There is no Mrs. Darien at present, Miss. I've recently come from Moore Haven, and before that, Colorado. You see, I'm a man who follows a dream, and most women do not take to a wandering life." He smiled down at Rose, who instead of looking away returned his smile. Juanita was enjoying the exchange. I think we're here to stay, she thought.

Sam Darien was not what you would call a handsome man, but rather, distinguished looking with a prominent nose, sparkling blue eyes, an abundance of graying hair that at one time had been reddish brown, and an outgoing personality. He was also a church-going man and had in the short time he'd been at East Beach started weekly services at the Ridenour packing house with hopes of building a Methodist church when enough people showed an interest.

"Mr. Darien, I truly appreciate your assistance, but I believe that I'd enjoy staying right here on the beach beneath the stars."

"Begging your pardon, ma'am, but if you do not wish to stay with some of the locals, I'm sure that Mr. Ridenour wouldn't mind if you bedded down at the packing house. That way you would have shelter if a storm occurred..."

"Oh, please, Juanita, please let's do what Mr. Darien suggests," Rose pleaded.

"Rose Shorter, I think that you simply have no adventure in you at all." But she smiled when she said it. "All right, we'll do as you wish. Harrison, now's the time to remove our trunks from the boat."

"I'll get some help, Mrs. O'Farrell," Sam said. "The packing house is two miles from here."

"Two miles!"

"Darth Bliven has a cart and oxen. Don't worry, we'll have you set up in no time."

When Juanita glanced at Rose she was amazed that she was smiling. The heat was oppressive, the path not more than six feet wide with not a house in sight. Maybe I shouldn't have been so insistent, Juanita thought. Nolan and Harrison were engaged in conversation with Sam and Captain McCoy. Sam was telling them about the freeze the year before, and that was why he left Moore Haven for East Beach. He was also talking about the need for better drainage, that the Palm Beach Canal and the

North New River Canal from Ft. Lauderdale had helped drain the farmland but more was needed. He seemed very knowledgeable.

He turned around to address the ladies. "There aren't a great many people here now, ladies, but I can assure you that in a few years this place will be bustling. You're getting in on the ground floor. We already have enough children for a sizable school, and when B.A. Howard gets all the lots of Section 18 sold, that should give us some thirty new families. I like the idea of selling a ridge lot with the ten acres so they'll have a nice high place to build their houses, and the rest they can farm. You can grow a lot of vegetables on ten acres around here.

"Howard and a man from Okeechobee, a Mr. Porse I believe, think that Howard's new real estate company, Pahokee Realty, will be highly successful. Oh, that name Pahokee is Indian for grassy waters. Seems that when Porse came to visit Howard there were some Indians camped along the shore, or so the saying goes, so he suggested that Howard call his town site Pahokee. The Indians pronounced it differently, though."

"Mr. Darien, where is your place?" Rose asked sweetly.

"I got twenty acres of Section 17 too, Miss Shorter, isn't it?"

"Yes, but call me Rose and Mrs. O'Farrell's name is Juanita. Since we're going to be neighbors I don't see any reason to be so formal, do you?"

"No reason at all, Rose. Oh, are you ladies church going folks? 'Cause if you are we're going to be having our Wednesday night prayer meeting right at Ridenour's packing house tomorrow night, and I'd be mighty happy if you'd join us. That way you could meet the folks around here."

"I'd be delighted, Sam. Juanita?"

"Oh, yes, Rose. That'd be fine." Juanita was taken aback by Rose's attitude and lively conversation with Sam. I haven't heard her talk this much with a man in all the time I've known her. She said that she and Joe Bob talked constantly the three weeks that she knew him, and that was one of the reasons she loved him so. Maybe she has at last decided that she can have another life...

"Juanita? Where on earth is your mind? I've called you three times now."

"I was thinking of other things obviously, Rose. What is it?"

"Sam said that Dr. Armstrong's wife Blanche - and did you say the Ingrams, and Morrises and Galloways? - would be at the prayer meeting."

"Never miss a one. We'll have a church before long, I'm sure." He had by now taken Rose's arm and was assisting her over the rough path. I do hope he is the one. She's missed so much and all for Seth. He's settled now and there's no reason...

"I declare, Juanita, I'm going to stop including you in our conversation. Your mind is miles away. Are you remembering Monticello?"

"Heavens no! I'm thinking about how exciting this all is. Rose, do you remember as a child in Alva twisting the moon vines together and using them for a jump rope? That was such fun, I remember. And in LaBelle the vines grew so thick up over the trees that we'd climb up them and jump up and down on them just like they were filled with air. Oh, that was fun and..."

When Juanita looked at Rose for a response she found that she was being ignored. Rose and Sam were looking at each other in that very special way and smiling. He had taken her hand. We might be having a wedding even before Delia has the baby. My, my, my!

Harrison and Nolan had made their bed on a sand mound underneath the packing house, which was built high enough to hold the prayer meetings. The next morning Juanita and Rose decided that they would place their beds there the next night. That wooden floor was hard even with the blankets piled high beneath them. Sam had brought mosquito netting for them to hang from the ceiling, and they could hear them but weren't bitten.

"What a night! Do you ever remember anything like it, Rose? Why does a meal always taste better when it's cooked over an open fire? I don't remember ever tasting better fish, do you?

"And those hushpuppies! Light as a feather. I'd never had them with onion in them before, had you? And grits with tomato gravy. He grew the tomatoes and said that Mrs. Friend canned them for him. He's a nice man, Rose. I'm glad you two have hit it off so well."

Rose let out a long sigh, stretched her plump arms toward the rafters and said, "So am I. Yes, he is a nice man and smart, too, and churchgoing. He said he sings bass and wants to get a choir going when we build the church. Won't that be grand." She was humming as she rolled up the blankets.

"What time did Sam say he'd be over this morning?"

"Should be here any minute. Harrison, Nolan, where are you two? We need a bucket of water." Where did those two get off to, Juanita? Did you hear them leave? They know that we need water. With all this water around you'd think we could drink it, but Sam said not to."

"Maybe we could boil the lake water and use it for coffee. What do you think?"

They heard people coming. Rose smoothed her hair back and Juanita quickly rolled up her bedding. It was Harrison, Nolan and Sam with another man.

"There you are," Juanita said. "We were looking for you. We don't even have water to start the coffee."

"No need to, Mum. Sam brought a big pot already made and corn dodgers to go with it."

"That was very thoughtful of you, Sam," Rose almost purred.

"No bother at all, Rose. I'm an early riser and like to get my breakfast out of the way so I can get to the fields."

"Mum, we went ahead and bought the tools we'll need to clear the land. Sam and Mr. Kaltenbrunner knew just what we needed, so Harrison and I ..."

"I'm glad that you did, son. What did you get? But before we go into that I want to post this letter to Delia. Sam, where is the post office?"

He laughed and replied, "Give it to me, Juanita, and I'll put it in the bean hamper for Harry Loy to pick up when he comes by this way on the *Observation* on his way to Moore Haven."

"My gracious! Not even a post office! How long do you think it'll take to get to Tarpon Springs? A week? Two weeks?" "Probably be reading it inside of a week, don't you think Anton?"

"Not more dan dat." He spoke with a heavy accent, and tipped his large brimmed hat to the ladies as Sam introduced them.

"Anton came over to this side of the lake about the same time I did. We were both frozen out in Moore Haven."

Nolan and Harrison began taking the tools off the cart. "Sam said every one of us needs a machete, hoe and rake. We'll have to order some hand plows from West Palm Beach, and the *Observation* can bring in anything we need, right Sam?"

"That's right, Nolan. Now, I don't expect you ladies to do any of the clearing. Dr. Armstrong had some workers brought in a couple years ago. Had a man from Okeechobee bring them in, and you can do the same. As for the materials to build your house..."

"Sam, I haven't even seen the ridge site yet!" Juanita exclaimed.

"We did even before you and Rose awakened, Mum. Oh, there is a beautiful site with giant cypress and rubber trees..."

"They'll have to be cut down unless you can teach Rose how to pop a chicken snake's head, son. They dearly love a rubber tree."

"Then the rubber trees will have to go, Juanita. I hate snakes."

"You'll have to tolerate them, I'm afraid, Rose," Sam said. "There are always a lot of snakes in the semitropics, and the Everglades are full of them."

"Even on the ridge?"

"Even on the ridge, I'm afraid."

"Well, so be it. The Lord must have put them here for some reason, although I can't imagine what."

"To eat mice and rats for one. Actually they do a lot to keep that population under control."

"If you say so, Sam. I'll try my best."

"Oh, I know you will."

Nolan looked at Harrison, and Harrison looked at Juanita, and Anton Kaltenbrunner smiled at them all. He later told Harrison on their way back to where they'd docked the previous evening that his friend Sam had need of a good wife and that he thought he'd found one in Miss Rose.

"As soon as we've had our breakfast, I want to go to our site. And, Harrison, we'll need a horse for riding - I don't want a nag, either - and a mule to pull the plow..."

"And mule shoes for the mule to wear," Sam interjected. "This is soft muck, Juanita, an early stage of peat, I'm told. But I've read that it was formed by thousands of years of sawgrass decaying. Whatever, it is soft and a mule will sink up to mid way his legs if he doesn't wear the special shoes."

"What on earth do they look like?"

"Oh, they look almost like an animal trap made of metal, and they are slipped around the hooves like this..."

Juanita and Rose were bent over with laughter at Sam trying to show them how the mule was fitted with the shoes and at the expression of the two young girls who had come up behind him.

"I'm sorry Sam but you have an audience and I'm sure they're perplexed by your demonstration."

"Oh, hello, girls. I want you to meet Juanita and Rose. These are the Friend girls, Wilda and Ruth. They arrived from Fellsmere only last year, where their dad did some farming. Frank was from Colorado like Oscar McClure, who I was telling you about. People come from all over to farm this black muck, don't they, girls? Or as some call it, black gold."

The youngest one asked, "Do you have any little girls we can play with?"

"I wish I did, but my little girl is a grown woman and she's going to have a baby of her own soon." Juanita replied.

Rose spoke up, "I have a little granddaughter, or at least I call her that. Actually, she's my nephew's little girl. I'm sure they'll be visiting us when we get settled."

They left, skipping down the trail holding hands and singing, their long blond pigtails swinging in time with the song.

When Juanita and Rose arrived at the ridge site not far from the packing house, they agreed with Nolan about the house site. "It will have to be far enough from the lake's edge to assure that there will be no water problem so I'd say at the highest elevation on the ridge. What do you think Sam?"

"That's a good idea, but you won't get more than a few feet, Juanita. You're in flat country down here, and this ridge took hundreds of years of northwesters to build it this high. Now you take Moore Haven and that west side of the lake, well, they don't have anything like this beautiful beach, and the sawgrass is waist deep all along the lake's edge. Makes for good fishing though."

"Rose, what about between those two largest cypress trees? I hadn't thought of a large place at first, but if we want to later, we can always add on. What do you think?"

"That would be perfect. And look, Juanita, if you did the old Georgia type house, like up in Monticello, you'd get the breezes blowing through and the morning sun could come up over the fields and the afternoon sunsets over the lake should be spectacular of an evening while sitting on the porch."

"You're right. I know! An old fashioned dogtrot style house built up off the ground so as to cool it. I wish Conner were here. He'd know just what kind..." She couldn't go on.

"I'm sorry, Juanita. I didn't know. When did he pass away?"

Rose answered, "Conner's been gone for going on twenty years, Sam, but Juanita hasn't let go yet."

"And I'm not going to ever let go, Rose Shorter!" She looked at them and continued, "I'm sorry, but I'd not be here or anyplace else had it not been for Conner." Rose wanted to correct her but knew that it'd do no good and kept quiet.

Nolan had his arm around Juanita and said, "I think your ideas are sound, Mum. You don't want a fancy house, but a comfortable one.

After supper tonight we'll sit down and figure out how much wood we'll need to order from the sawmill. Sam, do you know anyone around here who does carpentry work?"

"Most folks do their own, but I'm sure that Dr. Armstrong and Dr. Lair will have some names. There are several men out of West palm Beach who're reputed to be good, and I know of at least two in Okeechobee who do good work. You just decide what you want, and we'll go from there. In the meantime, ladies, we're going to have to get you a place to stay."

"We're at your mercy, sir," Juanita said.

"How about the hotels in Canal Point? Now, Juanita, don't look like that. We have to stay somewhere and..."

"And nothing, Rose. I want to be right here overseeing everything. Now, if you want to go to the Custard Apple Inn, then do so. I'm sure that Harrison and Nolan can assist me in building a small shelter for..."

"Mum, I don't think that's such a good idea. I have a feeling that Delia will need to be arriving within the next few weeks..."

"Can you believe that I'd forgotten about Delia! What on earth was I thinking about? Of course, we'll have to get settled in right away. I can't believe that I could be so selfish!"

"Won't take more than a couple of months to get this all cleared, Juanita. The elders, custard apples and moon vines don't take a lot of grubbing. We can get a few strong backed men and have your forty cleared in no time. If you weren't in such a hurry, my men could get to yours after they're through with mine."

"That would be fine, but as you say, I'm in a hurry to start farming."

"Don't count on getting rich, Juanita. Some have already done very well, but you always have the problem with water. There's either too much or not enough, and freezes and, of course, rabbits. A heavy rain can drown a crop in no time and ..."

"I'm not adverse to gambling, Sam. As a matter of fact, I think I'll take to farming this muck just like I did the dress business. That was a gamble, too, but there I was faced with mostly irate customers, not God. I'll take God any day, and of course this black gold." She let the black earth trickle through her fingers as they watched. Rose wondered if she had any idea of what she was talking about, and Sam, as he looked at the petite, blond, middle-aged woman, wondered if the Glades was ready for her as well.

CHAPTER II BIRTH OF A TOWN

"Everyone in Canal Point thinks you're a millionaire, Juanita."

"And why's that, Rose? Just because I decided that we couldn't afford to buy a horse and buggy from one of their shysters and had Sam get them in West Palm Beach instead? You know that Delia's arriving any minute, and that I couldn't postpone buying the lumber for the house. Is that why? Well, that's stupid. After all, I'm fifty-six years old and in a hurry to..."

"Fifty-seven!"

"Fifty-seven years old. What does a year matter anyway? As I was saying, these people seem to think that you have to pussyfoot around forever. That muck is just waiting to be planted. It cannot plant itself, you know."

"Even I know that, Juanita. Oh, hello, Mrs. Erickson. Lovely day, isn't it? And, oh my, it's been a busy one too. Did you or your boys see the barge of lumber come in? That's Juanita's for the new house. Oh, you already heard about it?"

They were sitting on the front porch of the Custard Apple Inn watching the canal traffic pass by on its way into Lake Okeechobee. The saying was that, *You can watch all of south Florida go by in Canal Point*, and Rose believed it. The *Observation* came in daily from West Palm Beach loaded with supplies, passengers and mail, but best of all, new settlers. Juanita had never seen Rose this way. She was so animated that she'd start a conversation with perfect strangers and inside of a few minutes be telling Juanita their life's history. Sam certainly had been good for her, and their weekly prayer meetings had meant so much to them both.

Why am I so out of sorts? Juanita wondered. Is it because of Delia? Or is it because Nolan had to return to Tarpon Springs earlier than expected? Whatever the reason, I am sorry that it happened now. Rose is having such a good time, and all I do is stew about every little thing. Is it because I have no one to share my burden with, and now she does? But I don't want anyone else. I never have and never shall. I guess it's that I feel unsettled. When I was young I loved the uncertainty of that sensation, but now it frightens me. I wonder why that is? I wonder if men ever feel that way?

"Juanita, I want you to meet the Knight girls. This is Onida, Lamorah and Ruth. Their dad bought some lots up at Long Beach about a mile north

233

of here and has cleared it and is already building his own grocery store up on the ridge."

Juanita smiled and got up. "How very nice to meet you. Did Rose tell you that my daughter will be joining us soon? She's expecting her first baby in late June and wants to be near me. I've heard that Dr. Spooner is an excellent doctor. Delia is a little old to be having her first, so I'm concerned, naturally."

"We're not married, Miss Juanita, but it'll be nice to have another girl around," Ruth, the oldest said.

"Miss Rose tells us that you're dress makers and milliners. Our mother and her cousin were dress makers and milliners in West Palm Beach before Daddy decided to move out to the Glades," Onida volunteered.

"And they made dresses and hats for the rich people in Palm Beach, didn't they, Snip?" the shy one, Lamorah, said.

"Snip? What an unusual name. Is it short for some other name?" Rose asked.

"Oh, no, my Daddy said that when I was born, I was a very tiny baby and could fit in a shoe box. Well, he said, 'My, she's a snip of a thing, isn't she?' and ever since I've been called Snip. And Lamorah is called...stop pulling on me, Lamorah, they don't care if Boe couldn't say your name.

"Of course we don't care, do we, Juanita?"

"I'd enjoy meeting your mother, girls, since we have so much in common. Does she plan to open a shop locally? After all, they say that Canal Point is the coming town in the Glades."

Ruth spoke up, "I don't believe so, since her cousin stayed in West Palm Beach. Mama plans to help Daddy in the store, I think."

"Please tell her that we're staying at the Inn and should be here for a few months. I don't want my daughter to leave too soon after the baby arrives, so we'll be here longer than we had expected."

"Oh, she already knows you're here..." Ruth quickly covered her mouth, thinking that she'd said something she shouldn't have. It was obvious that Juanita and Rose were the talk of the sewing circle. Onida spoke up, "We'll tell her, Miss Juanita. She might come to town with us for the dance Saturday night at the Glades Hotel. I'll be playing the piano for the dance, and I'll tell her what you said."

Rose and Juanita watched them walk down the sand road toward the path that bordered the lake. "There go three beautiful young girls," Juanita said.

"That's what Edna Thomas said they're called, the beautiful Knight girls."

****

"I cannot believe that you came alone, Delia. I thought that Andrea would accompany you and then go on up to her folks in West Palm Beach. What on earth possessed you?" They were sitting upstairs in the Custard Apple Inn in Juanita's room, where Juanita and Rose had been staying while waiting for their house to be finished. The iron bedstead had been painted soft green, and the only other furniture in the room, other than the night table with an oil lamp on it, was a three-drawer dresser and a wicker chair.

"Mum, would you quit! Why you're in such a snit, I don't know. I can certainly take a boat trip alone. You know it's amazing to me and Andrea that not a single person in Tarpon Springs said, `Why, Delia, I believe that you've put on a few pounds.' I guess that I'm so tall that they didn't notice. That, plus the fact that I designed different dresses and even made padding for Andrea to wear so as to fool them. I really am sick of all this."

"You have to think of the baby, Honey."

"Why? Now I mean it, why? I don't know who makes up all these rules, and Nikki is getting sick and tired of them, too. He's grown up thinking that the Greek ways are the only ways, and I'll agree that they have a lot of merit, but Mum, we have been denied a beautiful life because of them, and he and I are suffocating. We had our first fight - our first fight! Can you imagine?"

"Yes, I can imagine. How much time have you spent together? How much? If you lived the day to day that your da and I did, then, my little girl, you'd have had more, I can assure you. That is, if you had any backbone in you at all. It seems that the male of the species thinks that they are next to the Almighty. Rose and I have had many conversations about this and have come to no conclusions. All I know is that there are two people in a marriage or in a relationship, not just the male.

Your father and I were drawn to each other like a moth to a light. Why? I'll never understand it! And, you know what? I talk to him every day, and whenever there is a situation that needs solving, I refer to him. I know that it is stupid, but I do it nevertheless, and it is most irritating, but I can't seem to change it. I was hoping that my children would be wiser than I."

Delia rose from the chair and looked out the southern window overlooking the canal. "I've never seen so much activity. Is it because they're building the canal locks, or is it like this every day?"

"Just about, but of course with the building there are more workers here, and they all seem to like to race their speed boats. Rose and I sit out on the front porch most every afternoon after our naps, and the ladies in the town site usually come over and we visit. It's very pleasant. Rose has decided to join their quilting club. They meet at each other's homes. Mrs. Knight is having it next time. Said that her husband rigged up a quilting frame on their front porch overlooking the lake and added a pulley so that when they're finished quilting she just pulls some ropes and the quilt goes right up to the ceiling protecting it from the weather. Then when they want to work on it again, she just lowers it. Isn't that clever?

"Come on and let's get our walk in. I talked to Dr. Spooner last week, and he said that you needed to walk and eat lots of fruits and..."

"I know all that. Let's walk on the lake front. Maybe we'll get a breeze. Is it always this sticky here?"

"We'll start getting the afternoon rains before long. That should cool it off. You'd better wear more comfortable shoes. Can you believe that the beach is hard enough for people to ride their bikes on?"

They walked the narrow path and were soon on the beach. "I still get a thrill every time I look at the lake. It's so large that it's almost like an ocean, and when we get a northwester the white caps make you think that it is indeed one. It's hard for me to realize that we're here. Harrison said just the other night that he was positive this was the right move for us."

"Did Harrison ever finish his cabin? The last time you wrote he had it under roof."

"Didn't take him but a little over a week. It's temporary, though. Just as soon as we get the main house done, we'll build him a more substantial one. The northwesters can be lethal, I'm told. Rose said that they were able to float all the cypress and heart pine that they brought in from the sawmill in to shore and already had the oxen and wagons ready to carry it to the house site when she and Sam looked yesterday."

"He's certainly been a big help to you, hasn't he?"

"Watch out, Delia! For Heaven's sake, that sawgrass will cut you to shreds! Here, walk on this side. Yes, he has been a big help. But the best thing to happen is his relationship with Harrison. They get along just about like Harrison did with your da. They've already planned a hunting trip at Big Cypress for next fall. Of course, Rose is head over heels in love with him, and I know he feels the same about her."

"Are those girls out in the rowboat? Looks like girls."

Juanita waved and called, "Hello, Snip and Lamorah. How many did you catch today?"

"Did real well, Miss Juanita. Must have caught two dozen cats and a lot of bream and saw six big gators this morning."

"Those are the two younger Knight girls I was telling you about. They have a trot line, and every morning and evening you'll find them checking it. They came down from Georgia to West Palm Beach, where their daddy was with his uncle in the hotel business. But he did just what a lot of people did. When he heard about this black gold he moved his entire family here. He had a grocery store in West Palm Beach before they moved and just opened the one up on the ridge. I love the excitement of this growth."

Delia took Juanita's hand in hers and smiled. "What're you smiling about?"

"I think you like everything about the Glades, Mum. I haven't seen you this excited in years. Nolan said the same thing when he returned to Tarpon Springs. It's hard to believe when I think of all you gave up. I mean to give up electricity and indoor bathrooms and running water and your car, and I could go on and on."

"I guess it's because it's so alive. There's not a square inch of space here that isn't alive with something. Look at this blade of sawgrass. Look at all the insects doing their daily work on it. And look at this soil." Juanita kicked a clump of maiden cane with her shoe. "See all the ants and other insects scurry around and the earth worms wiggle by. It's alive, Delia."

Delia hugged Juanita to her and placed her hand on her belly. "He's alive too, Mum. Feel him kick. He's gotten so active lately. Only a little over two months to go."

"Why do you constantly refer to the baby as he? Might be a girl, you know."

"I'm positive it's a boy. Andrea wants to name him John Nicholas. I thought that was a fine name. John for her dad, and they've already asked Nikki to be his godfather, and I'll be his godmother. Andrea was hesitant at first about Nikki, but Nolan convinced her. After all, where would Nolan be without Nikki's help? And if by some fluke it's a girl, Andrea thought that she'd like to name her Maeve after Da's sister and Catherine after her mother."

"They would be pretty together. Let's turn around, Honey. I think we've gone that mile Dr. Spooner suggested. Did you want to go over to Maggie's for an ice cream? That would taste so good, wouldn't it?"

"I'd love it. My appetite has certainly picked up since I've been here."

"It's all those good vegetables. Harrison has already put in beans, peppers and tomatoes. I hope it's not too late in the season, but Sam said that last year some of the farmers got in four plantings. Can you believe that they don't even use fertilizer? Just plow a row and throw in the seeds. It amazes me."

"Do you think that Pahokee will ever be as large as Canal Point?"

"There's no doubt according to the townspeople. It seems that every time I go there another building is going up. Most are just corrugated iron buildings, but people are doing a good business in them."

"You can use my speed boat whenever you need to, Juanita, I've already told you," Sam said to a very nervous Juanita. They were in the parlor of the Inn, and Sam had just brought Rose home from the prayer meeting in his motor boat. "And, besides, Doc Spooner has that Model T that he can use now that they've widened the road to Canal Point. Or better yet, why don't you two come on into Pahokee, since you're so concerned about Delia. I've got most of my place finished."

"You've already done more than your share for us, Sam. I'll ask Delia what she wants to do. But having no phones truly causes a problem."

"Grief, Juanita! We didn't have phones for years and years, and babies kept on being born," Rose interjected.

"Yes, and we didn't have electricity either for years and years, but you were complaining the other night about the lack of it when you were doing your mending, weren't you?"

Rose and Juanita began to laugh, and soon Sam joined in. "We're no better off than we were when we lived in Alva and LaBelle, are we?"

"Not so. At least now we have the money to buy things."

"But we don't have the things to buy. Now, that is peculiar, isn't it? I know one thing I'm going to get when the house is about ready."

"What's that?"

"The biggest bathtub that the Glades has ever seen. That's what!"

"Did Delia say that she wasn't feeling well? It's not like her to go to bed this early." Rose commented.

"I think that she's probably writing Nikki again. She's written him almost every day since she's been here. Meriam wrote that he manages to slip into the shop every day to collect them. Sometimes he'll receive three in one day and then go for days without receiving any. I'll be so glad when we get a post office, won't you?"

"Probably about the same time that we get telephones, trains and every house will have electricity. Dr. Lair said the other day that by 1920 or '22 we should be a full service area, and that some of the men had already started looking into establishing a bank." Sam added.

"That's only two to three years! Rose, I told you that it wouldn't take long to get this area moving once the word got out about the farming, and when the war ends in Europe things should move even faster, huh, Sam?"

"There's no doubt of that, Juanita. But, I'm afraid that the land sharks are getting the state in a mess. The old-timers seem to think that they're overselling the land and pretty soon the value will go down. They've seen that happen other places - boom to bust."

"Nikki was saying the same thing before I left Tarpon Springs. His advisors suggested that he and Nolan taper off on the real estate purchases. He's also concerned about the sponge business. Feels that they're working the beds too often. What was that?"

"What, Juanita?"

"I'll be right back. I would have sworn that I heard Delia."

"The Inn is completely filled with roomers, and she thinks that she can hear Delia. I wish that baby would hurry up and get here. She's going to drive everyone around here crazy!"

"Now, Honey, let her have her fun."

"Fun! Sam Darien, you don't have to listen to her day in and day out like I do!"

Juanita came running down stairs. "I told you, she's in labor. Gotta get Dr. Spooner, and, Rose, did Lilly and Edna Thomas say they'd help?"

"You know that they did. I'll go over to the hotel and get them. They're probably still cleaning up in the restaurant. Sam, wanta come with me?"

"He has to go for the doctor, for Heaven's sake. Can't you go by yourself? It's only across the canal, Rose. It's not like you have to walk to Pahokee, you know."

"You can stop yelling at me right this minute, Juanita O'Farrell. This minute, do you hear? Or you can bring that baby all by yourself!"

"Oh, I'm sorry, honest I am." Juanita sat down hard on the settee, bit her lower lip and began to sob.

"Now look what you've done. Now I'm so upset that I'll not be one bit of good for Delia."

"Stop it this instant and go to her, Juanita. I'll be back with the girls in a minute. And Sam has already gone for the doctor. That boat of his can really move." She went to Juanita, pulled her up by both hands and pushed her toward the narrow stairs.

When she got back to the Inn with the Thomas sisters, Juanita was still upstairs with Delia. Rose ran up but slowed down as she approached Delia's room. She didn't want to appear nervous in front of Juanita. Edna had said that since it was her first, they were in for a long night. She agreed. She had been in labor with Seth for a day and a half. How well she remembered. Heavens, that was thirty-nine years ago. It was hard to believe that he was a year away from forty.

Rose knocked lightly on the door, and Juanita opened it immediately. "Her water just broke. Is the doctor here yet?"

"Juanita, Sam hasn't been gone but half an hour. There's plenty of time. It's her first, and it always takes a long..."

"I don't think so, Aunt Rose. You'd better get Lilly and Edna up here. I think little Nikki is anxious."

"Oh, my, are you sure, Delia?"

"I'm sure as can be."

Juanita sat down and said over and over "Dear Lord... dear Lord, what'll we do, what'll we do?"

There was quite a gathering in the hotel lobby when Rose got there. Seemed like the men from the back room of the Glades Inn decided that placing bets on the time and weight of the baby was more exciting then their poker game. They had promised the Thomas girls that they'd not cause any commotion and had managed to be quiet. Most had congregated out in the narrow front yard, where they could smoke and take a nip if the need arose.

Edna looked at Lilly, and they put their heads together and decided that Delia was well into her labor, as she had said. Lilly rushed down to the kitchen to stoke the wood burning stove and sent one of the men to the quarters out in the custard apples on the east side of the hotel to fetch Aunt Thelma, the black woman who often assisted Dr. Spooner or Doc Anner.

Juanita was wringing wet by the time Aunt Thelma got to her. She had been holding one of Delia's hands, and Rose the other. They had wrapped rags around their hands so Delia's fingernails wouldn't gouge them. Rose had placed a heavy towel in Delia's mouth so she could bite down on it when the pain became severe. All she could think was, that doctor won't ever get here in time. Why didn't we listen to Sam and go on into Pahokee? Why?

"Juanita, take this damp cloth and wipe her forehead. That would help, wouldn't it, Aunt Thelma?"

"Sho won' cause no trouble. Hmmmm!"

"What do you mean by that?" Juanita questioned loudly.

"We's 'bout to have us a baby born here on dis day o' June. Yessum, we's 'bout to have us a baby..."

"Go ahead and yell, Honey, if you feel like it." Juanita said to Delia, who by now was wringing wet with perspiration.

"No...no..."

"Yes...yes...go on if it makes you feel better. No one cares if you do."

"Gotta push some more, little mama, push a good grunt. Dat's de way. Now give Aunt Thelma one more good grunt and Ah tink we gonna have us a baby."

I think if she says that one more time, I'm gonna bop her one, Juanita thought.

"Gonna have us a baby right now inna minute, we is. An' it's a gonna be a big one, too. Now it's a comin'..it's a comin'...yessir, we gonna have us a baby inna minute.."

Rose got to Juanita and told her to sit down or to go down to the kitchen to help the girls with the cloths. She could see that Juanita wouldn't hold up much longer, and she wasn't sure that she would either.

Juanita had just closed the door and was almost to the stairs when she heard "MUM....MUM...."

"Dat's it. We got us a baby sho 'nuff, an it's a boy baby. Look at dat, little mama, you done yoreself proud wid dis one." Juanita burst inside in time to see Aunt Thelma hold John Nicholas up so Delia could see him. Rose caught Juanita just before she collapsed into the chair.

Sam and Dr. Spooner didn't have to go upstairs to find out about Johnny. The men on the porch were hooting and hollering for the entire town to hear about him. It so happened that Dr. Spooner had been attending a man who, it turned out, had appendicitis and was helping get him ready to go to the hospital in West Palm Beach by boat. By the time Sam found the doc out in the muck in not much more than a shack and the doc rode in his buggy back to town, it was three hours into Delia's labor.

As he told Sam on their way back to Pahokee, it could have been disastrous for her. She was almost past childbearing age, and the baby weighed in at nine and a half pounds. "The Lord wanted that one to be born. There's no doubt about it. Funny, but I've seen babies just as healthy looking as that one, and they were stillborn. No rhyme nor reason. Yep, the Lord wanted that one to be born."

THE YEAR 1922

As Juanita and Sam predicted the town of Pahokee had taken off. It was incorporated in March of '22 and was one of three incorporated towns around the lake, Moore Haven and Okeechobee being the others. In May a bank was established. That same year a telephone line was built from West Palm Beach, which connected Pahokee with Belle Glade, South Bay and Okeelanta. A large dock had been built at the foot of Lake Avenue by Anton Kaltenbrunner, who also built and operated the first gasoline station in town, even though there were only a half dozen cars around.

The eight-room school house had been completed in the fall of '18 with Charles Mack Todd as principal, five teachers and 86 pupils. One of the teachers was Nellie Pope, who had fallen in love with the area when Rose and Sam got married that summer, and she had accompanied Seth and Maggie, their children and her brother Jack, his wife Annie and their two small children to the wedding. She never left and made her home with the Dariens the first few years.

The following fall Canal Point's school opened with 28 pupils. There had been another school established in 1913 one mile north in the Long Beach Colony and several small schools in the settlements of Torry, Kreamer and Ritta Islands as well. Churches were springing up in both towns, and the new hard road from West Palm Beach to Okeechobee being built by Fingey Conner was under way, Canal Point being the midway point for men and materials.

The Pahokee Drainage District had been established and none too soon. Poor Moore Haven had gone from being burned almost to the ground in '21 to being flooded in '22, and that closed the sugar mill, and the vegetables rotted in the ground, because they couldn't be hauled from the fields with tractors and wagons.

There was some concern that sugar cane would replace a lot of truck farms. In 1920 the U.S. Department of Agriculture had started a Cane Breeding Station in Canal Point. The area's freedom from heavy frosts made it one of the few places in the United States where the growing season was long enough for sugar cane to produce seed with regularity. The breeding had to be done from seed, and it took about twelve months to mature.

When Frank E. Bryant, an English engineer, began working with his brother Harold selling Everglades lands, he became interested in growing cane. So he and G.T. Anderson organized the Florida Sugar and Food Products Company two miles down the Palm Beach Canal from the lake and built buildings, installed a four-hundred-ton mill and began their operation, expecting to produce their first sugar in a year's time. There were only 900 acres of cane in the entire Everglades, and most of that in Canal Point.

But Juanita was not concerned about sugar cane production. She and Harrison formed Shamrock Farms, Inc., and had bumper crops of bush beans and green peppers every year since he planted that first row of beans. People around the Glades said that Juanita O'Farrell had the Midas touch. Whenever everyone else was flooded out, Shamrock Farms was high and dry. It wasn't quite true, but she was the talk of the area.

They had brought in twenty-five workers from Georgia, all colored, and had built rows of wooden houses for them to live in. Juanita insisted that they have a better education than the local colored school provided and persuaded Harrison to supplement their schooling three evenings a week. He was a natural teacher and loved this work. Shamrock was so good to them that they no longer went from farm to farm seeking work and stayed in Pahokee year around. She knew them all by name, and when she put on her riding britches, her wide brimmed straw hat and gloves, straddled Jiggs and made her daily rounds, all the children would run out to greet Miss Juanita.

The summer months were lazy ones. Juanita had planned to take off for a few months the summer of '24 and spend the time in Tarpon Springs with Delia, Nolan and family. Andrea had become pregnant the year after Johnny was born, and she and Nolan now had two beautiful children of their own.

Juanita knew the minute she got off the train that all was not well with Delia. She looked drawn and was terribly thin. She was furious that neither Nolan nor Andrea had had the good sense to write her to tell her of Delia's condition.

They were driving down Tarpon Avenue when Juanita decided to tackle the problem head on. "All right, what's wrong? I've never seen you like this."

"I'm just tired but now that you're here, I'm sure that we will be able to take some little trips, and I can get some rest."

"There's more to it than that, isn't there?"

"I was never able to keep anything from you for very long, was I?"

"And why should you? Confession time."

Delia bit her lip, shrugged and said, "It's about Johnny..."

"What about Johnny? He's not sick is he..."

"No, he's beautifully healthy. That's not it. After I returned from the Glades I'd go over to Nolan's house every morning before work to nurse him. That was what Andrea and I had agreed on. Then after I closed the shop I'd do the same. That went on for two months. But even after I stopped nursing him, I felt welcome and would go over every day. Andrea seemed to like having me there so she could get some rest. But Mum, since Maeve and Robbie arrived, it's as if she didn't even want me around."

"That's ridiculous! Why not? You're his mother, for Heaven's sake!"

"I know that and you know that, but it's as if she didn't want my influence. I don't know. I've spoken to Nolan about it, but he's so concerned about the business that it seems to be all he can think of."

"Have you said anything to Nikki about it?"

"That's the other thing. We aren't as close as we were. Now, don't get upset. We still love each other, but since his other children are older, it's harder for him to get time to be with me. And he almost never sees Johnny."

"I'm sorry to hear all this, Delia. Truly I am. My life is so full what with Shamrock Farms, and now that we've got the vote and I've become involved in local and county politics, I haven't read between the lines as I should have."

"We'll work it out, Mum. I just want us to have a carefree vacation. Let's forget all about it for at least tonight. I've had Sophia prepare a Greek feast for us."

"I'll allow it for tonight, but tomorrow, young lady, we are going to have a talk with Andrea and Nolan, and the first thing I'm going to do when I get to your place is give them a call. We did not have to let them have Johnny, you know. You could have stayed in Pahokee with me and raised him by yourself. I know what you're thinking. When would I have seen Nikki? Well, when do you see him now? Just on those buying trips in new York? And how often is that?"

"I know you're right, Mum. If it weren't too late, I'd insist on taking him to Pahokee and raising him myself."

"I don't think that would be wise, Honey. It would be too upsetting for him and for you, too."

"That was a feast I'll long remember, Delia. Here, lets go sit on the seawall and dangle our feet in the Bayou."

"You'd have to have very long legs, I'm thinking. Look how low the water is."

"Did I write you that Rose and Sam are spending two weeks in Arcadia with Seth and Maggie? Then they'll stay with the children while Maggie and Seth are in Tallahassee attending Tucker's big senatorial to-do. I'm glad that they've patched up their differences, aren't you?"

"Yes, of course, but the last you wrote you said that Rose and Sam were going to Colorado for a month, something about him wanting Rose to see the Rockies."

"Well, they're going to Arcadia first. She called right after they got there, but the connection was terrible. Said something about going out to Tall Ten for a barbecue with Jack and Annie. They won't get to see Callie and Clay though. They're doing so much traveling now that they've gone into citrus so heavily. Annie has taken over that division, so they now have time on their hands."

"Did they get out of the cattle business altogether?"

"Heavens no! Callie has a foreman who has been with them for years handling that, but with the understanding that Annie keep her nose out of it. Callie almost lost him, Rose said. Things are all right now but for that new dipping law. But what do they expect the government to do? They have to enforce the tick eradication program with the state-built vats or it will get completely out of hand. Always something, isn't there?"

"Is Nikki going to get over while I'm here?"

"He called the other night and said that he wanted to, but that he had to be in Tampa on business all week. Don't worry, you'll get to see him."

"He's a nice man, Delia. What's this about Nolan's work? If Nolan is in trouble, why didn't someone tell me?"

"The sponge business has fallen off terribly, but he still has his real estate holdings. But, Mum, you know how he loves the Exchange. Nikki said recently that he thought Nolan should start looking for some other line of work to protect himself."

"I wish he'd consider coming in with us at Shamrock. It's more than Harrison and I can do just to keep up, honest it is. Do you think that I should mention it?"

Delia stared out toward the sea, and Juanita realized what she'd said. "Honey, I was just talking. I know how much Johnny means to you, honest I do."

"It would be very difficult for me not to see him often, Mum. But the way things are now, I don't feel welcome when I do visit."

"Nolan said that tomorrow afternoon would be fine, Honey. Then we'll go out to dinner. It seems that another of Andrea's cooks has left. I'm worried about Nolan. He didn't sound good. We're going to get things straightened out, and soon."

They walked back to the front porch and sat outside for a while longer. "Oh, I forgot to ask. How did Maggie take the news about her half-brother being killed in France? Was his name Wesley?"

"Seth said that she hadn't been around him often. He was Berta's baby by Reuben, you know. Think that he had taught at the Citadel. That was such a shame. I hope that our boys never have to fight another war. They say that it was the war to end all wars, the last big one."

"Let's hope so. The idea of Johnny going to war is enough to make me..."

"Delia, is there something you're not telling me?"

"Actually, there is. I need an operation. Now, it's not serious, but Dr. Dimitri wants me to tend to it very soon."

"What kind of operation?"

"Oh, the usual female problem. He's sure that it's just a fibroid tumor..."

"Then you're going to have it done in West Palm Beach. That way you can come to Pahokee to recuperate, and I can take care of you. Now it's settled. I don't want any more discussion about it."

"Oh, Mum, it's so good to have you here. I've really been down."

"I'm here now - everything will be fine."

But when Juanita went to bed that night, she was so worried that she couldn't fall asleep right away. Her mind hopscotched from Delia to Johnny to Nolan to the sponge business to...She sighed and thought, the worst thing about being considered strong is that you have to prove to everyone that you are. I have no one to share my burdens with. I guess that's how Delia feels. Rose is the fortunate one. You know, we almost never have a good old girl talk since she married Sam. I miss them. We got a lot of things out in the open that way. She yawned, sighed, and fell asleep just before dawn.

"Such a lovely evening!" Juanita said. Andrea and Nolan had just joined her and Delia on the front porch where it was cooler. "Delia and I were just talking about her trip to Pahokee with me."

"Mum, do you think that wise? I mean Dr. Dimitri suggested the hospital in Tampa and..." "Delia knows that the hospital in West Palm Beach is just as good, Nolan, and that'll give her a chance to recuperate at home. Meriam has already said that she'll be happy to handle Del Mer for her, and besides I think they can use the money."

Juanita decided to plunge headlong into what she and Delia had decided was the best course of action.

"I'd like for Johnny to be able to spend a few weeks with me this summer, and Delia's recuperation seems like the ideal time. What do you think of the idea?"

Andrea looked at Nolan, but before she could reply he spoke. "I'm not so sure that is such a good idea, Mum. Well, I'll go ahead and say it. Every time you come over, Delia, we have an awful time calming Johnny down when you leave. It's got so that Andrea can't handle him, he gets so belligerent."

"I always make a special effort to pay attention to Maeve and Robbie, too, Nolan. But since Johnny is older there's so much more I can talk to him about."

"Andrea and I understand that, really we do, but you have to understand our position, too. He's come to be quite a handful."

"All the more reason for him to come to Pahokee, Honey. That'll give you and Andrea a chance to be around your own children and..."

"Mum, Johnny is our own. At least that's the way we think of him."

"He is in your keep, Nolan and Andrea, but he is not yours and never will be. You've got to understand that and accept it. Actually, I'd like for you to come to Pahokee for a while too, Nolan. I'd planned to discuss this at another time, but now seems like as good time as there'll be."

Juanita caught her breath and continued. "Delia tells me that things aren't going too well at the Exchange and that Nikki has suggested that you look into something else for your own protection. Is that so? If it is, why haven't you said something to me about it?"

"I didn't want to worry you, Mum. It's not all that bad, anyway."

"Harrison and I could certainly use your marketing know-how, son. Shamrock Farms is now almost more than we can handle since I bought that hundred acres. We're getting in almost over our heads with work, and I just can't put in those long hours like I used to."

"Do you mean for us to move down there?" Andrea asked horrified.

"There are worse places, Andrea. You haven't been there since it has become a town, and your folks would be only forty-five miles away. The schools are really very good. Now, I know that there is no Catholic church around, but that should be remedied in a few years when more Catholics move in."

"I can't believe that you'd even suggest such a thing, Mama Juanita. I truly can't."

"Now don't start crying, Honey. Now, look at what you've done, Mum."

"What have I done, Nolan? All I did was to offer you a job that'll take care of you and your family. Is that so awful? Well, is it?"

"You know as well as I do that there is no way that Andrea would ever be happy in such a place..."

"And what kind of a place is it, pray tell?"

"You know exactly what I mean. There are no cultural advantages or opportunities or ..."

"And what kind of culture do you have here? Answer me that."

"We can drive into Tampa whenever there's something going on, and the restaurants are..."

"Well, I'll grant that our restaurants cannot hold a candle to the ones here or in Tampa, but now that Conner's Highway is completed we can get to West Palm Beach inside of an hour and a half. So if and when you feel the need of some culture, you can drive to town and absorb it until you're steeped in it."

"Don't get angry, Mum. I enjoyed the area when I was there, but then I knew that I'd be coming back here. If I had thought that I had to live down there..."

"You do not have to live down there, Nolan. It's obvious to me that you'd rather stay here in this wonderfully cultural atmosphere and starve to death. Come Delia. I'm sure that your brother and his wife wish to read a little Shakespeare before retiring.

"But, Andrea and Nolan, I expect Johnny in Pahokee for a minimum of two weeks during Delia's recuperation. And if you cannot afford to send him to that uncivilized place, then his uncultured grandmother will pay his way! Good evening."

****

"How fast the time has flown by," Delia said to Juanita. "I'll never forget this summer, at least these past few weeks, and I'm eternally grateful that you insisted that Nolan bring Johnny down to Pahokee. Why is it that when Nolan isn't around Andrea that he becomes a different person? I mean that he becomes himself again."

"Hand me that glass of tea, Honey. My, my, look, the ice is already melted. I've noticed it, too. Maybe it's because when he's around her he feels that he has to be the big man, you know, knowing all the answers and doing everything right. Men can't stand to fail.

"Sam said that Nolan is really interested in the newly formed Southern Sugar Company and that Dahlberg offered him a good job. If he does accept it, I know that Andrea will have a fit, because Clewiston is not even a town yet, not as big as Belle Glade or South Bay even. They'd have to live in either Moore Haven or Pahokee."

"When did Rose say that she was bringing Johnny home? I hate it when he comes home covered with muck. I've never seen him so happy. I just wish that he didn't have to start school this year and that we could stay longer, really I do. Can you believe that I've not missed Nikki as much this trip? Why is that do you suppose?"

"Perhaps it's because he's never been down here with you, and you can't see him in this place. Maybe he's like our cultured Andrea..."

"Mum, you really put those two in their places. Do you ever remember laughing so hard? I didn't think I'd make it to the bathroom, you had me laughing so."

"Here come Rose and Harrison, and would you look at Johnny. I'll have to wash him under the pump before he's allowed inside. Look at you! Out to the back porch, young man. What on earth were you doing?"

"Show your grandmother, Johnny. Show her," Harrison encouraged him.

Johnny held up the tin can proudly and declared that he'd sold three cans of worms to the fishermen down at the dock and that he brought that one to her.

"Well, thank you, sir. I'll put them in the shade and cover them with more muck, and tomorrow morning early we'll go to the lake and catch our dinner, won't we?"

"We sure will, Mamam, a whole string of 'em."

Juanita got a catch in her throat when she looked at him. He had Nikki's olive complexion, like Andrea's, and his mama's and Conner's pale blue eyes and the O'Farrells' curly auburn hair. Actually, he looked a lot like Nolan did at that age. He was handsome and sturdy and she loved every inch of him, and he knew it. There had been no sign of belligerence since his arrival, and Juanita wondered if he'd shown it previously because he sensed that Andrea didn't care for him as she did her own. Juanita had told Andrea and Nolan both that if she sensed any discrimination on their part, she would take him and raise him herself, and she meant it. They knew that she did.

The original arrangement had been that they would raise Johnny as their own, Delia visiting him whenever she chose, and that she and Nikki would share in his financial support. But as Juanita had said many times, that was all well and good until Andrea found that she could have children of her own.

Delia and Johnny arrived back in Tarpon Springs to a tearful Andrea and a distressed Nolan. Andrea had told him in no uncertain terms that she would not move to that muck town, that she'd rather starve to death and that she was going home to West Palm Beach and live with her folks, if he insisted on taking that job in Clewiston. When Nolan told her of their financial situation and that they were probably going to lose the house and most of their possessions, that they had been living over their heads for years and that they really had no choice, she took to her room, and it took Nikki to get her out.

It was Nikki who called Juanita and apprised her of the situation. She talked to Nolan and invited him and his family to Pahokee to stay with her, enroll Johnny in the first grade and to try to work their problems out, but Andrea was adamant about not living out there in the sticks.

Juanita advised Nolan that he was to bring Johnny to Pahokee, that she would raise him, and that Andrea could take Maeve and Robbie to West Palm Beach. "You can either accept the position with the sugar company or come to work for Shamrock Farms. You simply have no choice, Nolan."

The bank foreclosed on their beautiful home on the bayou. Nolan was unable to sell off any of his real estate holdings, and they had long ago gone through the money he had inherited from the sale of Athea. Juanita did not offer to bail them out to the surprise of Andrea.

"It's going to be a long winter, Harrison," Juanita said that morning. She was sitting in the kitchen at the large, round oak table finishing her morning coffee. Dicey, who had come down to Pahokee from Monticello and was now the house woman for Juanita, had been up since first light and added her two cents. "Yessum, Miss Juanita, dat little boy gonna sho 'nuff miss his mama."

"I doubt that, Dicey. It's just not pleasant to be separated. I remember when we first got to Monticello and Conner was still in Kissimmee, I thought I'd die, I missed him so. But the move had to be made. Just like Nolan had to get himself a secure position so that he could take care of his family. It's too bad that Andrea can't see that. But just as Rose said the other night, she's spoiled rotten, and Nolan never did show a strong hand to her. Can you imagine Conner letting me get by with that behavior?"

"No, I can't, Cherie, but then Nolan isn't Conner. Not that he's weak, for he isn't. It's just that he hates controversy, whereas you and his da loved it, and face it, Cherie, you still do."

"Harrison, you were always able to read me." They both laughed, and Dicey hummed as she went about her kitchen chores, happy to be with them again. Juanita was in her riding britches and getting ready for her morning rounds of the farm. It was her habit to get Johnny up and ready for school, and Harrison took him in the car while Juanita had her breakfast and dressed and, astride Jiggs, made her rounds.

Nolan had settled in in Moore Haven and was glad that Andrea hadn't decided on living there. Most of his time was spent in working with the engineering firm that the company had hired out of Indiana and contracting local companies to dig the ditches and install the pumps for draining the land. He loved his work and managed to get to Pahokee to see Juanita and Johnny and on to West Palm Beach to be with Andrea and the children most every weekend. He had managed to sell most of his land holdings on the Gulf coast, and he and Andrea had plans to build a house in West Palm Beach when he got more established.

Delia continued to operate Del Mer, see Nikki when she could and visit Pahokee on at least two occasions each year for a month at a time. Nikki managed to get to Pahokee once a year and tried to time it while Delia was visiting. When he was around Johnny, he seemed to dote on him, but he seldom called or wrote. It was hard for Juanita to understand her children's acceptance of their life styles. She and Delia had discussed it as had she and Rose.

"I cannot imagine being away from Conner for such long periods. I wonder if our children got any of our fire, especially Nolan? How he allows Andrea to yank him around by his ear, I don't know. She needs a good spanking, then I bet she'd straighten up."

"Yes, Juanita, I can just see you allowing Conner to spank you," Rose laughed.

"If he had, then I'm sure that I would have deserved it."

"You deserved a lot of spankings, dear, but he was wise enough to not give them. He took care of you verbally, just like Harrison said."

"He certainly did, didn't he? But Nolan doesn't even do that. Do you realize that they've been separated for two years? There's simply no reason for her not to move to Clewiston. I know that there's not much there yet, but it is growing, and with the new Clewiston Inn that the *Palm Beach Post* said was lovely, well... She tells Nolan that it's because of the church, and that she wants Maeve to start school in the parochial school over there, and he's fool enough to believe her."

"Is that Sam riding up here? I told him that I'd walk home." She smiled because she dearly loved all that attention. He certainly enjoyed fussing over his Rose. I miss that part of my life, Juanita thought. Not that Conner actually fussed over me. It wasn't his nature. But he did enjoy giving me presents and flowers and a special bottle of brandy and perfume - I guess that's fussing.

Juanita went inside and called to Johnny. "Lights out, young man. You've got school tomorrow, and Harrison said that if you did well on your arithmetic paper he'd take you fishing." She heard him say, "Oh, boy!" and saw the darkness replace the light from under his door. I wonder what an eight-year-old boy finds to do in his room with the door closed for hours on end? He seems happy enough, but I know that he misses Delia. I can't believe it's already the middle of September.

She went into the living room and turned on the radio. "Grief!" she said aloud. Another hurricane scare. I wonder if Nolan left Moore Haven for West Palm Beach? If Andrea has her way he'll be there protecting her from the big, bad wind. Do her good to have to take care of herself once in a while. She sighed and decided that she'd be true to her promise and not meddle in their affairs. It was hard.

Sam knocked and called. Juanita said, "Come on in. I guess you've heard the weather report."

"Actually, no. I was in Denton's store, and Boss Wilson said that he heard it on his radio. Said that it was coming in from the Caribbean and should hit in the Miami area by tomorrow. I guess Nolan hasn't gone to West Palm Beach yet since it's Friday, but with this rain, he might have left early. Boss said that the lake's up to twenty feet in the Moore Haven area, and that some sections of the muck levee are low and weak and that they're really concerned."

"I read earlier in the week that the Caloosahatchee is full. Where in the world are they going to put all that water? The canal locks at Citrus

Center and Lake Flirt are open, but the river can't handle it," Juanita added.

"I imagine Nolan will stay there to help them sandbag the levee, don't you?"

"Knowing Andrea, she'll probably be on the phone to the company begging him to go to her and the children. But I hope he's in Moore Haven doing what he can to help. She has her folks, who'll calm her fears."

She felt better for having said it and asked Sam if he'd like a brandy. He declined and said that he'd better get back to Rose, but that they'd better make arrangements to leave if things got worse.

Juanita poured herself a brandy while listening to the hurricane warnings. "I wish that they'd stop trying to scare people to death with all these warnings. They're going to keep people from settling down here. Talk, talk, talk!"

She went in to check Johnny and thought, I wish Nolan were here with us. I'm worried about the lake being so high. I can't believe that they think that the levee will keep the lake from breaking through. Heck, they only built it to help the poor farmers, certainly not to withstand a hurricane. She bent down and kissed Johnny's forehead. He didn't even stir. He surely looks like his Uncle Nolan. Even has his smile. I've got myself two handsome boys.

Juanita had trouble falling asleep. The wind had picked up and the rain was coming in sheets. I should have put Jiggs in with the roadster. That new garage is sturdier than his shed. I'll do it the first thing in the morning.

CHAPTER III SURVIVAL

When Nolan awakened Friday morning the sky was dark and stormy. "Just what we need, more rain." He decided that he'd better postpone calling Andrea until he found out if he'd have to stay on top of the pumps. She'd be angry, but it couldn't be helped.

Nolan drove his Ford to Dowd's Drug Store on Main Street, and there was quite a gathering already there. They talked about the hurricane, but no one seemed especially concerned. They were sure that the muck levee wouldn't hold if they had any wind to speak of and talked about getting volunteers to sand bag the various pumping stations, but there seemed to be no special alarm. Nolan figured that he was overreacting.

Throughout the day they went about their business and talked very little about the hurricane, mostly about the party put on by the Woman's Club for the school faculty at the home of the Westergaards that night. Nolan decided to not attend, but by midnight could not fall asleep. He got up, dressed, and drove into town to the State House on the canal bank near the locks, where he was sure he'd find Fred Flanders, the state engineer.

Fred said that when he showed folks the telegram that he'd received from the Miami Weather Bureau that morning about the impending hurricane, most of them didn't seem too concerned, and even at the party he showed it to a number of people, and they just kept on talking and laughing. He and Nolan stood outside the State House, the wind increasing as they spoke.

"I'm going to inspect the docks and the power plant. Wanta come with me?"

"You bet I do. I don't know why, but I don't like this, and I'm usually not one to overreact."

"I don't like it either, especially with the lake this high. Can you imagine what would happen to Moore Haven if we did get hurricane force wind with only this dike to protect us? I hate to even think of it. I doubt if there'd be a building left standing, and the loss of life would be tremendous."

"Yeh, it sure would."

They saw the water lapping dangerously close to the dike's top at both the fish docks and power plant. Fred looked at Nolan and they both said, "It's time to sound the alarm!" In no time every able bodied man around came to help reinforce the levee with the sand bags. They worked until

254

daylight, but it appeared that their efforts were futile, and they and the townspeople resigned themselves to another flood.

By now the hurricane winds were blowing in full force, and the lake water was pounding furiously against the already weakened dike. Shielding his eyes from the rain and wind, Nolan saw the water break through and rush down Main Street like a raging river and realized that there wasn't a building in the entire town that was built to withstand a force this great. Before he and the other men could get to their cars, houses began floating by, tearing to pieces as they drifted.

With the wind-driven rain, visibility was less than a hundred yards. Nolan thought he saw a boat bouncing off the Altamont Hotel in front of him. He swam for it, but with the current so strong he wasn't sure he'd make it. Finally he reached it and climbed in, but before he knew what was happening the swift current had taken him sailing down Main Street. The wind was howling and there was no controlling the boat. He saw a mattress with a baby on it churn by. He reached for it, but the water was so swift that he couldn't grab it. He thought, that could be Maeve or Robbie. Suddenly, without warning, his boat pounded into a partially submerged building. Water rushed in, then nothing...just blackness...

****

"But, Harrison, you have to find out if he's alive! You have to! Go for Sam! He'll know what to do!" Juanita lamented.

"He's already trying to call the American Legion 'cause someone said that they're going in there to help with the rescue and cleanup. Now I don't know what more we can do. They've already got a train coming down from Haines City with two freight car loads of boats and engines and the men for the rescue. They're on their way. The talk in front of the bank was that they'll launch them from the closest point to Moore Haven."

"When are they going to send in the National Guard? Have you heard?"

Harrison just shook his head. "They're doing all they can, Cherie. You've got to calm down."

What Harrison didn't know was that Juanita was not just frightened about Nolan but was feeling guilty that she had wanted him to stay in Moore Haven instead of joining Andrea and the children. She had been in contact with Andrea's parents, and they were fine, although their house had received some damage, but they said that Andrea was a wreck.

It was Wednesday and they still had not heard from anyone concerning Nolan. The *Tampa Tribune* and the *Estero Eagle* were filled with horror stories beyond belief. The water was still so high that everyone had been taken out of Moore Haven and moved to higher ground. They were given typhoid shots, and the National Guard was not allowing anyone to return to homes or businesses. But no word about Nolan. Delia had been sent for and arrived on Thursday. She found Juanita totally out of control, and even Rose could not reason with her. She had even tried to call the governor and had managed to reach her influential friends in Pahokee and West Palm Beach and lambasted them for their complete inefficiency. She spared no one.

The first thing Delia did was to contact Dr. Spooner, and he gave a protesting Juanita a sedative. The next day, Saturday, one week after the hurricane, they heard about Nolan.

The call came in the morning about ten o'clock. It was from a Red Cross worker in Sebring who had volunteered to assist with the refugees. "Mrs. O'Farrell, I am Martha Scruggs of the American Red Cross." Juanita sat down, and Delia took her hand and stood next to her, patting her shoulder. "I was told to inform you that your son, Nolan O'Farrell, is in the hospital in Sebring and should be able to travel within the week."

Juanita dropped the phone, and Delia grabbed it before it hit the floor. "Yes, this is his sister. Could you repeat that, please. He's all right and..." She could say no more. Harrison, Dicey, Rose and Sam all stood beside Juanita, and they were all crying.

The following Friday Nolan arrived at the depot in Canal Point. Andrea had been sent for, and there was a big family celebration awaiting him in Pahokee. As he told them his tale, not a word was spoken. He told one horror story after the other. No one had realized the enormity of it. Over 200 people had been killed in the Miami and Ft. Lauderdale areas. Moore Haven alone had over a hundred deaths. Some reports said two hundred. Fortunately, the areas were sparsely populated, or the death toll would have been much higher.

A very sober-faced Nolan said, "The water was swirling around me, and I knew I was drowning. I felt a hand grab me and that's the last thing I remember until I awoke and found that I was inside a tiny boat cabin with six adults, four children and a dog. There we stayed until a rescue party found us, tied a rope to the boat, and we inched along the rope into the Gram building. The water was up to my chin. I and the others were so exhausted that we ignored the gators that swam by. Thank goodness they were as tired as we were and ignored us, too."

He later told Juanita that when he blacked out he thought he saw his da's face, and he knew that he heard his voice. She just smiled and shook her head, yes. "I'm sure that it wasn't a dream, son. Your da dearly loved his children. That was my Conner all right."

****

Shamrock Farms had had mostly good years up until right after the 1926 hurricane. Lack of proper irrigation was still the main problem, and intermittent frost the other, but still they prospered. Juanita had become a voice at the town meetings, although she did not seek an office and had refused every nomination. Sam Darien did run for councilman and won, and Rose became very active socially. Juanita saw her less and less, although they usually talked by phone several times a week.

Nellie Pope had married Roscoe Bruner, a farmer, the year before and moved to a small house in Belle Glade and taught school there. Rose and Sam truly missed her. She was a sweet girl and everyone liked her, especially her school children.

Even though the Miami area was devastated and the paper land owners had turned tail and run after the hurricane, the Everglades area continued to grow rapidly, Clewiston and Belle Glade in particular. Nolan continued to encourage Andrea to move to Clewiston, where he had moved after the hurricane, but she would not even discuss it. It had turned into a lovely town by 1928.

Nolan's involvement with the Southern Sugar Company and Mr. Dahlberg was intense these past two years. Nolan assisted in the company's getting control of almost 100,000 acres of top farm land. It consisted of most of a four mile belt from Canal Point to Moore Haven, about 52 miles in length. It was reputed to be the best cane land in the world, and Nolan was especially proud of his part in the deal. There was still the battle with state officials about lake levels, and getting money for planting cane and building the mill was a struggle, too.

No one ever saw a horse, ox-drawn cart or mule and plow in one of Dahlberg's cane fields. He ordered machinery, crawler tractors, and they ran day and night, turning 100 acres a day, following each other like a circus parade. Then there were cane diseases, rats, and high water constantly plaguing them. Labor was always a problem, because the cane had to be cut by hand. Little towns sprang up on each plantation with their individual problems, but the biggest concern of all was the chance of an over supply on the world market. That was Nolan's expertise, learned while he was with the Sponge Exchange in Tarpon Springs.

It was the summer of '28. Juanita and Rose were bemoaning the fact that they were approaching old age, but neither had slowed down noticeably. Juanita still rode Jiggs out in the fields almost every day and spent part of the summer with Delia in Tarpon Springs with Johnny in tow. Rose and Sam usually went to Arcadia to take care of Seth's and Maggie's three children, so they could get away to the Georgia mountains for a while. But this year Maggie and Seth had promised U.S. Senator Tucker Williams and his wife that they'd be in Tallahassee for Tucker's speech before the state senate. It was to be a big affair, and Rose and Sam thought that the least they could do was to support them. All the McRae and Williams children would be in attendance, and a large family reunion was planned for afterwards. The only sad note was that Berta, Layke and Wes did not live to be a part of it.

Maggie would miss the first week of school but had acquired a substitute teacher, and Rose and Sam had settled in. They had many friends in the Arcadia area now and had become very popular with the townspeople. Callie and Clay were in town. They had just returned from an assignment to Mexico for the National Geographic Society. Clay was acquiring quite a name for himself, and Callie had learned to love traveling with him.

Rose and Sam would visit Tall Ten often to see Annie and Jack, who had taken over the bookkeeping for the ranch, left the bank and opened his own business in town as a CPA and was doing very well. Meade and Jimmy had both become doctors, Meade practicing in Apalachicola and Jimmy in Ocala. They were proud to be graduated from the University of Florida in Gainesville and had attended medical school in Georgia at Emory.

Rose and Sam planned to return to Pahokee on Monday, the 17th of September. They never made it.

"I never saw a child as smart as you are, Johnny O'Farrell, who disliked school the way you do. Why is that, do you suppose?" Juanita asked while trying to slick down his rambunctious auburn curls.

Johnny, with lips tightly closed, decided to not answer. It wasn't that he hated school. It was that he'd rather be with Harrison on the tractor or fishing or gigging frogs or swimming with his friends, all the things a ten-year-old boy had rather be doing.

"Turn around. There, now, I believe Mrs. Cunningham will think that you're presentable. Why the sad face? Why, Johnny? Tell Mamam."

"The other kids don't like me. They call me names and..."

"Don't you try to pull that one on your Mamam, Johnny O'Farrell. You're just like your granddad. You can charm the birds right out of the trees. I'm wise to you. I know you'd rather be with Harrison on the tractor. You think I don't know that? Huh?"

She hugged him to her and watched him go out the front door, where Harrison was waiting. What would I do without him, I wonder? I just wish that Delia would sell out and move down, but she can't leave Nikki. I'd like to go to my grave without worrying about my children, I declare I would."

"Dicey, you going to be in there all day? Gotta get to that ironing. That child goes through more clothes when he's in school! Dicey? Where are you?"

"Ah'm rat heah, Miss Juanita. He ain't a gonna be widout clean clothes, not while Ah'm heah, nosiree."

"Do you know whether Harrison saddled Jiggs yet?"

"Miss Juanita, ya knows he always does. Now, why'd ya ast dat?"

"I think it's because I didn't have a very good night last night. Kept dreaming about Conner. You know, he looked so handsome, just like he did when we first met. He was calling to me, and I startled myself by answering him aloud." She laughed. "Have you ever done that, Dicey? I mean call out in your sleep?"

"Course Ah have. Everybody does dat, Miss Juanita. Next ting Ah knows you gonna be sayin' dat de Indians is predictin' a hurricane 'caus de cane done turn de wrong color, or de chicken snakes is a droppin' outa de trees more, or sometin' crazy lak dat. Ah heared on de radio all de tings de Indians say 'bout de big storm a comin'. Ya heah dat?"

"They say that every year. I quit listening to that stuff right after we moved down here. Now, Miss Rose believes everything they say. If they knew what they were talking about, then we'd have a devastating hurricane every blasted year. She's an alarmist, she is."

"Maght be, but she yo bes' friend. When her and Mistah Sam comin' home?"

"I don't know what day, but I think she said by the end of the week. I know that Maggie has to be back teaching by the 17th, so they'll probably come on back around Friday."

Thursday and Friday were gorgeous, cloud-free, balmy days, the kind Floridians and the travel brochures loved to talk about. Juanita was a little disturbed when Harrison told her that Rose and Sam had not returned from Arcadia that Saturday afternoon. That wasn't like those two. They were always on hand for Sunday services. Well, Juanita thought, they probably had some car trouble. They'll get in by tomorrow afternoon, I'm sure.

Saturday was cooler than usual and the wind from the northeast brisk and welcome. "I love this weather, don't you Dicey?"

"Yessum, Ah sho do. Makes me wanta eben put on my stockin's fer services. Dey's so hot down heah, dat Ah hates to weah dem."

Juanita was sitting at the kitchen table when Harrison came rushing in and said, "Just got word that a terrible hurricane hit Puerto Rico and is headed toward the Florida coast."

"Harrison, Puerto Rico is a very long way away, isn't it?"

"Yes, but the report said that hundreds of people have been killed, Cherie. Now, I know that you don't like for me to get..."

"That's not it at all. I know that we have to be cautious, especially since we saw what can happen. But, I do not want us to get hysterical. Where's Johnny?"

"He was out playing with the Ramey boys on their tire swing the last I saw."

"I'm going to call Nolan. I want Johnny home in case Nolan decides to come here. You know how concerned he's become every time we have a storm."

The phone rang and Juanita jumped up to answer it. Harrison and Dicey looked at each other. They could tell that Juanita was nervous.

"But Nolan, I don't see any reason for you to...No, emphatically not! I'm not going to rush off to Sebring every time a storm is predicted...all right, hurricane, if you insist. And if you insist, I'll have Johnny ready, but I'm not going with you!"

"I guess you could tell that was Nolan. He's in West Palm Beach, and Andrea's having her annual hurricane fit, and he wants Johnny to be ready. They're going up to the hill country, probably Sebring. Won't cause any harm. Johnny'll enjoy getting out of school." She laughed and so did Harrison and Dicey, but with reservations.

"All that rain in August raised the lake three feet, Cherie. I think we have reason to be concerned if it heads this way..."

"Concerned, yes, but not ridiculously hysterical like a lot of people have become since the '26 one. I'm staying right here. This house is as sturdy as any building in town and is three feet off the ground. We'll do just as well here as any place on this lake."

"You might be right, but we need to get in some drinking water, and like Nolan said, we'd better get in candles and make sure the lamps are full and get some extra canned goods, blankets and..."

"Why we be needin' blankets, Harrison?"

"Nolan said that as warm as it was in the '26 hurricane, you felt chilled. Nerves, I guess."

"Well, if it does hit here, I just hope that the weather bureau does a better job than it did in '26. Poor people had no warning whatsoever."

"It's difficult to do an accurate job, Cherie. Do you remember that after the '26 storm the *Post* had a long article about how they track hurricanes?"

"Yes, I read it, but that was two years ago almost to the day, and I don't remember much of what it said. I don't imagine that my memory will be anywhere as good as your's when I'm in my eighties, Harrison."

"It said that they have to rely on ships that are in the area and you can imagine how difficult that is. And, of course, the ships have to have a good radio system in order to relay the hurricane's position. Besides, my memory isn't nearly as good as it was when I was eighty. These past five years have taken their toll, Cherie."

Johnny came rushing in out of breath as usual. "He's here, and he wants me to get my things."

"Well, for Heaven's sake, Johnny, he'll come in for a little while, I'm sure. You don't have to rush so!"

"Hi, Mum, Harrison and Dicey. Is he ready?"

"Can't you at least stay for a little while?"

"Want to get started, Mum. I'll call Andrea and the kids, and we can at least go to the bathroom and get something to drink."

"I should think so. You'll get there before dark if the weather doesn't get any worse. You are going to Sebring, aren't you?"

"That's the plan right now. But it could change. It all depends on the direction the hurricane takes, you know."

"Well, we've decided to stay right here..."

"Mum, that lake is high, now you know it. Why anyone in his right mind would stay near the lake when a hurricane is coming, I don't know."

"Did it ever occur to you that you might be right in the middle of it up in Sebring?"

"Yes, it has, but at least we won't be drowned, and the water, not the wind, is what killed all those people in Key West, Miami and Moore Haven. You weren't there, so you don't understand. You should at least consider going to the new high school."

"I know you're right, but I've lived a wonderful life, so if my time is now, then so be it, and I want to go to my maker while in my own house."

"Harrison, tell her that is crazy! She won't listen to me or anyone else, but she will sometimes listen to you."

"Not on this one, she won't. We've already been over that one. She's a fatalist just like your da was." He laughed.

"What's funny?"

"He always said that he was going to live the good life right up until the Devil came calling. And he did. He'd just won at poker and was at a ship's rail with the cool wind blowing on his face and a brandy in one hand and a cigar in the other. I can't imagine a better way to be called home, can you?"

Andrea stood to the side and shook her head at him. She couldn't fathom anyone's wanting to die like that.

Nolan just smiled. "I've always wished that I could have known him longer and better."

"If you had ever met him, you didn't forget him. Your mum had telegram after telegram from people who had met him only once but who had been touched by him in some way. He was quite a man."

"And I'm ready to go to him, if it's to be," Juanita added. "Goodbye, son. Good-bye, Maeve and Robbie. Come give Mamam a hug. My, how big you're getting, Robbie. Andrea, let Nolan handle Johnny. He knows that he needs a firm hand. Bye, bye, my Johnny. Remember that your Mamam loves you. When you get back maybe you and Harrison can make a sack swing and hang it from the big rubber tree out back. Would you like that?"

He hugged her around her waist. He was up to her chin already. "I declare you're going to be as tall as your grandaddy, Johnny. Look at how high he is on me, Harrison? We're going to have to stop feeding you all those good Shamrock Farm vegetables, aren't we?"

They stood beneath the towering cypress out in front of the house and waved good-bye. "I don't know how they're going to ride in that all that time without those kids' killing each other. Why, they're crammed in that Maxwell like sardines."

"What would you have him buy, Cherie? A Pierce Arrow? Maybe when he becomes the president of the company, huh?"

"Well, you'll have to admit that he doesn't have his da's style, does he?"

"No, but Delia does."

"I'm glad one of them got it. We'll have to work on Johnny."

"Miss Juanita, look what Ah done fin' unnerneath Johnny's bed!"

"Why, they're just books, Dicey. Here, let me see them."

Harrison began to laugh. "What's going on here, Harrison? Do you and Johnny have secrets that you're not telling me about?"

"You might call it that, Cherie. Johnny thought you might think him a sissy if you saw him reading books. He certainly doesn't want his buddies to know about them."

Juanita laughed and said, "When he comes home we'll teach him how to tell the tales like his grandaddy did. He'll have his buddies gathered around just like Conner did at the St. Elmo. I imagine that you're the one who gave him these, aren't you?"

"*Robinson Crusoe* and *The Call Of The Wild* never hurt any ten-year-old boy, Cherie. Now, you know that."

"Is that Sam's Jacob walking toward town, Harrison?"

"Think it is. You want me to find out if he's heard from them?"

"I can't imagine why they haven't called. I know that Rose won't step one foot near this lake if there's a storm brewing."

Harrison caught up with Jacob and was soon back with the news. "Sam called Felix this morning and said that they were going to stay in Arcadia until the storm passed. Jacob thought that we knew. Said that Lawtey was supposed to tell us, but that she had been so busy mopping up 'cause the back roof was leaking, so he guessed she couldn't get over here."

"She could have picked up that phone just like Dicey does now. I declare, if Rose knew that she didn't use it when she wasn't here, she'd have a fit. I bet that she got word to Rose's Sunday School class, though. I'm going to give her a piece of my mind before the day's out, I am!"

263

Saturday's *Post* had reported that the storm was headed for the lower east coast, but when Juanita and Dicey got the news that evening on the radio, it said that wasn't likely. Nobody really knew what to believe. Juanita did have Harrison get the extra canned goods in, some extra candles, and they always kept the oil lamps full because it seemed that the electricity went off almost every night. He had also filled the gas tank in the Reo and had the battery charged and tires checked, but he didn't tell Juanita.

Sunday morning, the 16th, was cloudy but cool. The wind and intermittent rain seemed no more than any other stormy September day. When Juanita went to town to church that morning at 10:00 o'clock, everyone had a different opinion of where the storm was and what should be done if it did hit. Some said that they'd go to the high school, but others said that they'd ride it out at home. She also heard a number of families had already headed for Okeechobee with plans to go on north to higher ground, mostly to escape the lake.

Juanita had Dicey fix a bountiful Sunday dinner and Harrison joined her. It had become a ritual, but they missed Johnny. He dearly loved fried chicken. There was the fried chicken with rice and rich brown gravy, some of last year's cut corn that she'd canned, fresh young mustard greens, avocados with dill sauce and lots of fresh lime juice, her favorite way of eating it, radishes fresh from the garden and Dicey's pickled beets with allspice. No one could pickle a beet like Dicey, Conner always said. Dicey always kept a big bowl of fresh ambrosia sweetened with orange wine for dessert in the ice box. Juanita and Harrison had that beneath the large avocado trees in the back yard, and both commented about the nice cool weather, but they were soon chased in by another shower.

Juanita had been up from her afternoon nap about an hour when she heard a knock on the front door. She looked at the mantle clock. It was 4:45 p.m. It was Fred Simmons, who worked at the lumber yard and was staying at Elliott's rooming house on Main Street.

"Why, Fred, what can I do for you? Come on in. You're getting drenched."

"Mrs. O'Farrell, I can't. We just got word over the radio that the hurricane is coming over Palm Beach with winds of 175 miles per hour and that it's headed this way at 10 miles an hour. It'll be here inside of three to four hours. The high school is open, and I'm to tell everybody to head that way. Now, Mrs. O'Farrell! I gotta go!" And he left on his rounds.

Juanita rushed to the back and called Harrison but he couldn't hear her. So Dicey trudged through the ankle deep water to his small house and got him. When he heard the news, he said that he thought they should take Fred's advice and head for the school. Juanita said that she'd already made up her mind to stay there but for him and Dicey to go on. He knew that she knew they wouldn't leave her.

"You've got to go to the quarters to warn the people, Harrison. Tell them that they can come up here, and I'm sure that if Rose and Sam were here that they would allow them to stay at their place, too."

He got in the little Ford and did what Juanita requested, but he knew that they wouldn't go to the main house. They'd not want to be that close to the lake, and he didn't blame them. They'd be better off where they were, or so he thought.

They turned on the radio and huddled around it, but there was so much static that they could hardly make out a word. They had closed and secured the outside shutters on the front windows. When the electricity went out it was dark in the living and dining rooms. Harrison and Dicey both got up and lit two lamps and took them back to the living room. By now the wind had picked up and was howling through the trees. Juanita was having trouble keeping up a lively dialogue to quell their fears. Harrison knew that she was nervous. She always talked about Conner when she was.

The chiming mantle clock rang 7:00 o'clock. Harrison had already checked Jiggs's stall and secured the heavy door. Juanita and Dicey had moved her potted ferns out of the screened porch on the north side of the house, because the wind had shifted and was coming from the northwest now. The cabbage palms seemed to be bending almost double. Harrison wondered why they didn't snap in two. The dead fronds sailed past the kitchen windows along with the rain, that was now horizontal and slashing against the windows, and he wondered if he should have nailed some boards over them. It was too late now.

"Cherie, we can still get to the school. I'm sure of it!"

"It's probably too late, dear friend. We'll be fine here, I'm sure. The worst is probably over."

How wrong she was. By 8:30 the full force visited them and all along the south and east of the lake. All the islands, Ritta, Kreamer, Torry and the tiny towns of Chosen, South Bay and Belle Glade were feeling a wrathful God rush across their land as if the gates of Hell had been opened. Houses were snatched from their foundations with entire families inside, ands they were tossed, tumbling over and over across that sea of muck and sawgrass that had just the day before been their means to a better life.

Endless torrents of water smashed against their businesses, homes, churches and schools indiscriminately taking their occupants with them. Uprooted trees sailed as if straws in the wind with no destination. The O'Farrell home, built out of heart pine and cypress just ten years previously was as sturdy as any house in the area, but the walls seemed to be breathing in and out. Juanita sat in her favorite chair with her feet on her needlepoint footstool and watched them and heard them groan loudly above the hollow sound of the ferocious wind.

When Dicey began singing *Just As I Am, Lord* Juanita and Harrison joined in. When they were in the middle of the third stanza Harrison heard a large crack above the wind's anger and said, "I'll check it, Cherie!"

He got to the back door, looked out the window but everything was so black that he couldn't make out what had happened. He held up the lantern and saw that there was no porch. "I'll not tell her," he said to himself.

"What was it?"

"I couldn't see, it's so black."

Dicey resumed singing *The Old Rugged Cross*, and finally Juanita began humming along with her, but Harrison remained quiet. They were in trouble and he knew it. But what can I do? If the lake comes in, then we're all gone.

He had no sooner thought it than he saw the water begin to creep in on the north side of the room and rise quickly. He knew that either a tree trunk or log had pierced the wooden house. Juanita saw it at the same time. All they could say was, "Oh, my God...Oh, my God!" In only a few minutes it was up to their waists, and they could feel the house begin to move off its brick and concrete foundation. They knew they'd not escape. Suddenly the wind ceased, as if by the hand of God, but the silence was more frightening than the wind.

"What's happening?" Juanita screamed. Dicey began to yell and shout, and Harrison called to them, "It's the lull, like Nolan described, Cherie. I don't know how long we have, but we have to get out of here!"

He waded to the kitchen past floating furniture. When he looked out the kitchen window he couldn't tell where they were. He opened the window, held the lamp up and saw that the house was covered by debris. Trees were down all over, but it was so dark that he couldn't make out their position. Are we out by the road or in the fields? He heard Juanita behind him asking if he could see Jiggs. He held up the lamp again but could not see anything past the fallen trees, but when he saw the water moccasins slither by he quickly closed the window. "We can't go out there," is all he said. He took a now sobbing Juanita by the elbow, and they pushed through the water to the other room and a hysterical Dicey. Juanita went to her and held her.

Harrison could hear the wind's roar and knew that the lull was over. Its growl swiftly erupted. He put his hands tightly over his ears, but it was as Nolan had described it, the most horrifying sound he'd ever heard. By the time he gulped to prepare himself for the next onslaught, the unleashed fury had arrived, and the breath went out of him as the house, once the pride of Pahokee, broke into a flying, swirling, tangled mass, as if a giant sledge hammer had wreaked vengeance upon it. He called to Juanita but did not hear a response. He was conscious enough to know that his leg was smashed and to know that he was holding on to a tree that was apparently wedged, for it was going nowhere. He knew nothing else until the next day.

He could feel the light, but did not have the energy to open his eyes. Harrison could feel someone pulling him. He grunted, cleared his throat and could hear himself moan.

"This old nigger's alive. Come here, Buck, give me a hand. It's all right, old man," he heard the voice say. He wanted to laugh because he didn't think of himself as an old man even though he was approaching eighty-five. "What's he smiling about, you suppose?" he heard the young one ask. "He sure ain't got nothing to smile about. You see that leg?" That's the last thing he heard.

****

"Who was on the phone, Meriam?" Delia asked. She was in the work room doing their weekly inventory like she did every Monday morning. "Rose? What did she want? Is anything wrong with Mum? Johnny?"

"It isn't good news, Delia. You know the hurricane that hit Puerto Rico last week? You know the one that killed all those people..." When she realized what she had said she apologized. "I don't mean that Juanita or Johnny are..."

"Are what? for heavens sake? What are you trying to say?"

"Rose couldn't believe that we hadn't heard.."

"Meriam Jefferies, if you don't get to the point, I'm going...I'm going to..."

"Nikki Kanares, please. Mrs. Kanares, this is Meriam Jefferies. I'd like to leave a message with you for Mr. Kanares if I may? Tell him that his friend Nolan O'Farrell and family have apparently been in that terrible hurricane down in the Everglades. Perhaps you haven't heard about it, either. We just got word, but no one can get through to them. It appears that a great number of lives have been lost, and since he is a friend of Nolan's, I thought that he should know."

"Well what did she say? Where's Nikki? Is he in town?"

"I'll answer one at a time, Delia. Nikki is not at home. He is in town, and she thinks he is probably at the restaurant."

"I've got to get to him. Meriam, have Gladys go to the train station and get a ticket for me for West Palm Beach. I'll go to the restaurant, then home to pack. And, oh, please call Rose back and tell her that Maggie should call Tucker to see if he can assist us in getting in there to see about everyone. On the radio they don't seem to think that we'll be allowed in because of disease, but the Red Cross and Legionnaires are already getting volunteers to go in by boat. I know Maggie is worried sick about Nellie Pope. She lives in Belle Glade, and it appears that it was demolished."

"Louie, is Mr. Kanares in? It's urgent or I wouldn't bother him."

"Delia, what is it?" Nikki knew that she wouldn't have come to the restaurant if it hadn't been necessary. "Here, let's go in to the back office." He turned to Louie and said that they didn't want to be disturbed. Louie could tell by Miss O'Farrell's expression that she was worried about something. He smiled. All Nikki's old friends knew of their relationship but thought nothing of it.

"Sit down. What's wrong? Is it Johnny?"

When Delia caught her breath and told him he said, "I'm going with you."

"No, Nikki, I don't think that's wise."

"It might not be wise, but I'm going nevertheless. It might be days or weeks before we have any news, and I'll not be able to stay here and not do anything. I'll go home, pack and meet you at the depot."

He thought a minute and continued, "Delia, Nolan and I are very close, as you know. He and his family mean a great deal to me, and of course there's Juanita and Johnny. I never told you, but Nolan told me a great deal about the hurricane of '26. I need to be there, my sweet."

Delia cried all the way down Tarpon Avenue and while Sophia helped her pack. When the phone rang and Sophia said that it was from Nolan, she shouted with joy!

"Nolan, where are you? Are Mum and Johnny with you? Where's Mum?" Delia sat down on the side chair and said aloud, "Mum wouldn't get out, Sophia. We don't know where she is. Johnny is with Nolan up in Sebring."

"Oh, Miss O'Farrell, I'm so sorry. Are you still going down there?"

"You bet I am. There is no way that I could stay here. Nolan and Andrea and the children are on their way back to West Palm Beach and I'm to meet them there. We're going to get to Pahokee. I don't know how, and I don't care what the authorities say."

When she got to the depot, Nikki was already there. She thought he'd change his mind about going when she told him that Nolan, Johnny and everyone had escaped to Sebring, but he said that he'd like to be with her at least for a short time, that it had been a while since he'd seen Johnny, and he had already packed and bought his ticket.

Andrea's parents met them at the train station and told them that Nolan and Andrea had arrived about an hour before. They still could not get any information about Juanita. They did not tell them that the death toll had already reached over a thousand, and their chances of getting into the area were next to nothing. The only way anyone was getting in at that point was by boat.

It was now Tuesday, and Delia, Nolan and Nikki had tried every avenue to find out about Juanita and Harrison. Rose and Sam, Maggie and Seth and Jack Pope had all arrived in West Palm Beach, and the men volunteered to help with the rescue. They had been warned that they'd have to have a strong stomach because dead fish, wild animals as well as domestic animals were bloated and already rotting everywhere. They had already been told about the bodies, debris, mud two to three feet deep and standing water with no chance of receding.

"Rose, did you read this? They're already burning the bodies. And this picture! Why'd they have to show all the caskets lined up at the Belle Glade bridge? I don't know if I can stand much more of this waiting. Andrea said that she'd watch the children if we wanted to help at the shelters. Rose, Mum could be in one of them and not be well enough to say who she is, couldn't she?"

"Of course she could, Honey. I think that you have a very good idea. We'll borrow Nolan's car and go to the hospital. I'm sure that they will know where the shelters have been set up, and we can go there, too. *The Everglades News* sent the story to the *Post* and reported that some victims had been taken there, and we can check with them. If anyone knows what's going on in the Glades, it's Howard Sharp. I told Seth that Howard was the best editor that this state has, and Seth seemed interested in hearing about him. Imagine having a paper of that reputation in little Canal Point? Wouldn't that be something if he and Maggie and the kids moved down here? The paper also said that a lot of Red Cross volunteers have been bringing the victims in by car after the National Guardsmen and Legionnaires got them out by boat."

When Delia and Rose left Nolan's house, Maggie met them in the driveway. She had been to the depot to pick up Tucker. Delia got a catch in her throat when she saw him. He was a very distinguished looking man and used his politician's smile on her. He got out of the car and she slid out from under the steering wheel. They were soon embracing. His arms were comforting to her. When she explained where they were going, he insisted on accompanying her - so did Maggie.

"Scoot over Delia, I'll drive. I know how worried you are, and why shouldn't you be? I felt just this helpless when I heard about the *Titanic*, and Mother and Father were on it. So I know first hand how you feel." He patted her hand and smiled down at her.

"You're as beautiful as ever. I've thought of you so often." Rose looked at Maggie, and they tried to not eavesdrop from the back seat. "Have you ever wondered what kind of life we'd have had if things had been different? Now, you don't have to answer if you don't want to."

"Tucker, I'm sure that Aunt Rose and Maggie don't want to hear about our personal affairs, especially at a time like this."

"Actually, I have wondered about it myself, Delia," Maggie interjected.

"So have I and your mama, Delia Rose," Rose added.

"It does no good to dwell on the past. We're supposed to learn from the past, I'm told. But, I'll answer anyway. Yes, I've wondered. You were my first love and therefore very special. Of course, I've wondered. But, I like my life the way it is," she lied.

"I've kept up with your success, you know."

"No, I didn't know. It was easy for me to read about you, your marriage and the birth of your daughter. But, how did you keep up with my life, pray tell?"

"We senators are great talkers, you know, and I'm very close to the senator from your district. We try to keep up with our constituents."

Delia knew by the way he was talking that he knew about Nikki. Well, so what! It was none of his blasted business. If he'd not wanted her to find someone else, he could have done something about it. He probably even knows that I had an illegitimate son. Like mother, like daughter, is probably what the old stuffed shirt is thinking. Well, Mister Senator, sir, I don't care if you know or not. She started to cry then and couldn't seem to stop.

"Delia, here, let's stop and take a walk around this little park. Maggie, be a dear and wait for us. We'll be right back. She just needs to get it all out."

Rose called after them, "Delia, do you want me to come with you?"

Delia shook her head no and continued to sob with Tucker holding her close, his arm around her shoulders and they could see that he was talking nonstop.

"I guess the senator knows how to soothe distraught ladies, Rose. It's probably one of the things he does best. He's not a bad sort, though. Actually, he's turned out better than I thought he would. He is sensitive, even though he doesn't always show it, and he does seem content in his marriage."

They sat in the shade. From the ocean there blew a soft breeze that had been a raging hurricane just two days before. The only signs of the blow were a few palm fronds and small limbs scattered on the lawn. "Go on and get it all out. I'm a good listener, you know."

She gasped for breath. "I'd forgotten how we used to talk. Why, we'd talk about everything under the sun, wouldn't we? I guess that's why I had difficulty dealing with your sudden silence, Tucker."

"If I had had my way, Delia, I would have written to explain. It never was that I didn't love you. You've got to believe that. I've never stopped loving you. Now, don't look at me like that. I mean it. It doesn't mean that I don't love Barbara, because I do, and I appreciate her and I admire her. But, Delia, I have never loved her the way I love you. Do you realize that there's not a day that goes by that I don't think of you?"

"That's ridiculous, Tucker. After all this time?"

"After all this time. I'm serious. Do you remember when we snuck down stairs and hid in your father's study?"

"Yes, I remember very well."

"If Seth hadn't passed out in there and seen us, have you ever wondered what would have happened between us?"

"I'll have to admit that I have."

"Oh, Delia, I've wondered about that so often. I've never been unfaithful to Barbara, except in dreaming about that night and in my fantasies..."

"Tucker, I don't think that this is the time or place to be discussing this sort of thing, really I don't."

"You're quite right, my darling, but I had to say it. If things had been different, we would have made quite a team. With your beauty and class there would have been no stopping us."

"Always the consummate politician, huh, Tucker? Well, perhaps we would have made quite a team, as you say, but I have a very full life and a happy one. I'd like for parts of it to be different, but I'm not unhappy that things turned out this way. I think you have the kind of wife who is right for you, and Nikki is perfect for me. He's my lover, you know?"

He actually blushed. "I didn't know his name. I'd heard it but had forgotten. He's Greek, isn't he?"

"He certainly is, and he's here, by the way. He, Nolan, Jack and Sam have gone into the Glades to search for Mum, Harrison and Nellie. I'm anxious for you to meet him. He's quite a man - not just handsome, wealthy and intelligent, but sensitive and caring and takes beautiful care of me...in every way, Tucker. And I mean in every way. Thank you for being so understanding. Let's go. I'll be fine now. Rose and Maggie are waiting."

When Delia and the others got to the hospital they were given a list of names of the victims, those who were alive and those who had died since arrival. Neither Juanita's nor Harrison's name was on it. "Delia, perhaps Harrison's name would not be listed with these." Tucker said.

"Why not, because he's colored?"

"Oh, miss, I didn't know. Here, we have another list. Wait right here and I'll get it." She was reading it as she came toward them. Did you say Harrison? We have one that's a T. Harrison."

"That's him! Where is he?"

"Oh, he's in the colored ward. Just follow me and we'll be there in a minute. According to this, he was brought in by a Red Cross worker yesterday about noon. I have to warn you that he's not doing very well though."

Tucker held her arm securely as they approached the bed. There were at least fifty cots in the ward: men, women and children. She hadn't realized that he had turned so gray. My God! Is he dead? Then she looked down at his chest and the sheet was moving slightly.

Delia bent down and whispered, "Harrison, it's Delia. We're here to take you home."

He didn't stir. Her hand went to her mouth, the tears started streaming, and Tucker took Harrison's frail hand in his and said, "Harrison, this is Tucker Williams. We're here to find out about Miss Juanita."

His eyes fluttered, his dry mouth began to move and all they could make out was that she was gone.

"Do you mean that she's gone away or that she's dead, Harrison? Miss Delia needs to know."

He managed to mumble that the lake took her.

The nurse had gone for one of the volunteer doctors, and they were approaching them. After shaking hands with the senator, he explained that Harrison's leg had become infected and that they were going to have to remove it, but that his fever had been so high that they were trying to bring it down before operating.

Delia explained that he had been with her family since he was a young man and that he was like family to them. He said that he understood and that if she wanted to, she could sign the papers for him so they could go ahead and operate, thereby removing the hospital from any responsibility should anything untoward occur.

"I'll be happy to sign for the O'Farrell family, Dr. Hatton." Tucker said.

"That won't be necessary, Tucker. I'll sign for my family, thank you just the same." Delia said sternly.

"Delia, I didn't mean to offend you..."

"You didn't offend me, it's just that I'm very capable of signing for Harrison. He is a member of the O'Farrell clan, you know. He and my Da took a blood oath when they were young men." She lied, but enjoyed doing it. He's become so pompous. He can't hold a candle to my Nikki. Dreams of me, indeed! Probably has a cutie in every town. She didn't really think that, but it bolstered her determination.

Wednesday dawned with still no word on Juanita. The men had returned with the good news that Nellie and her husband had managed to get off Kreamer Island, where they had been having Sunday dinner with her in-laws before the hurricane struck and found room at the Tedder Hotel in Belle Glade. What they didn't tell them was that Nellie said that they were lucky enough to get there in time to get upstairs to safety. The people who had to stay downstairs because there was no room for them upstairs perished, and so did her in-laws on the island.

They would not even talk about the conditions except to say that it was unbelievable what had happened to the entire region. Belle Glade, South Bay and the islands had been hardest hit. It was true that the unidentified bodies had been set afire, but it had been necessary. They all wondered if Juanita and Dicey had been among them, but no one mentioned it.

Delia and a very tired Nolan went to the hospital to see Harrison and Delia allowed Johnny to accompany them. Nikki had remained at the hotel to rest. They'd none had any sleep since the day before. Nikki not only needed rest, he needed to clear his mind of what he'd seen. He'd never seen anything like it and hoped he'd never be a witness to it again. His gut feeling was that they'd never find Juanita. Even if they had, they wouldn't have been able to identify her. He'd given up hope, but he wouldn't let Delia know it. He had the hotel maid take his clothes and suggested that she burn them. He knew he'd never get the stench of rotting flesh out of them.

Harrison had been operated on early that morning, and the doctor said that he was doing as well as could be expected for a man of his age. They had been allowed to see him immediately since they'd taken him right back to the same ward. Delia was horrified. "We'll be happy to pay for a private room, Dr. Hatton. As I tried to explain, he is a member of the family."

"We understand that, it's just that we don't have a room. Every ward is filled beyond capacity."

"Can one of us stay with him? I mean we have several relatives who can take turns."

"I see no reason that you can't, so I'll go ahead and approve it. This is not the usual procedure, you know, but under the circumstances..." His voice trailed off. They could see that he was exhausted.

Nolan went home, took Johnny with him and told Delia that he'd have someone spell her as soon as he could. He needed to get some sleep and go back out to Pahokee.

Delia sat beside Harrison. She, too, was exhausted. She lay her head down, resting her chin on her arm, that was on the side of the bed and finally dozed off. She stirred when she heard Harrison call her.

"About time you awakened. You gave us quite a scare, you did."

He smiled when she took his hot dry hand in hers.

"Johnny came by to see you but you were still asleep. He's so worried that you won't get to take him fishing or build that sack swing Mum said you could or..." She began to sob then. "Oh, Harrison, we can't fine Mum anywhere. They've been out for two days looking and they can't find her. What're we going to do if we can't find her? What?"

His voice was so weak that she had trouble understanding him. "Delia, your mum was right where she wanted to be. She wouldn't leave..."

"I know. Nolan told me, but..."

"But nothing. If you don't find her then you've got to know that she's with your da, and that's where she's wanted to be for over twenty years."

"I know that, too, but what're we going to do if we can't find her...her body?"

"Just what all those other people are going to do. You'll have a memorial service. Is that what you wanted to know?"

"I guess. I'm not sure what I wanted to know. But we'll miss her so, and there's the land and..."

"You let Nolan worry about that." His voice trailed off, and Delia could see that he'd gone back to sleep.

She felt someone staring at her. When she turned around it was Nikki.

"I didn't want you to come over, Nikki. You need to rest. Why can't Rose come sit with him? What's happened? Did they find Mum?"

He took her in his arms and he was crying. "They found Dicey, and she told them where to look for Juanita, Honey."

"Did they find her?"

"No," he shook his head. "Delia, they found the dress she had been wearing, but they didn't find Juanita. I'm sorry."

Later she was to say that a voice came to her, and she couldn't tell whether it was her mum or her da, but it was a voice. She felt so calm. She knew what she was to do.

"It's all right. It's as Harrison said, Honey, she's where she wants to be. She's with Da now. Nikki, we need to talk."

"Delia, are you all right? You seem so strange."

"I'm fine, really I am. Let's go out to the lobby. There's something that I need to tell you."

He wasn't suspicious, just curious. "Have I done something terrible, my sweet?"

"You could never do anything terrible, Nikki. Not you. You are the most wonderful thing that ever happened to me, except for Johnny. But, I now realize that...I don't know quite how to say this."

"Try being honest and direct as you always are. That's one of the things I love about you."

"All right. I'm going to leave Tarpon Springs and move to Pahokee. Now, I know that you think that I'm under a lot of stress and that when everything settles down I'll change my mind. But, Nikki, I'll not. Meriam needs to work, so I'll sell her the shop. I know that she can't afford to pay me all at once, but she can a little at a time. I'll sell the house and that should give me enough to rebuild. Why're you looking at me like that?"

"Delia, do you hear what you're saying? You'll be giving up Del Mer and all you've worked for..."

"I am giving up nothing, Nikki, don't you understand? I told you once - it was when I met with you and Ernie - that I would become a sheep if I became your mistress, and there would no longer be a Delia Rose O'Farrell. Do you remember that?"

"Yes, I remember your saying something like that."

"I want to be Delia Rose O'Farrell again, Nikki. I want to be in charge of my life once more. I want to be a mother to Johnny and build a life for us in Pahokee. I know that I know absolutely nothing about farming, but I can learn just as Mum did. I want to be a part of something, Nikki, something that has stayed with me ever since Mum said it when she first moved to the Glades."

"What was that, my Delia?"

"She said that there was a vitality, a constant change, a newness in the Glades. Nikki, she was so alive down here. She loved it so, and just because she...she is gone, it doesn't mean that this vitality can't be realized again through Johnny and me. I know that Nolan will never leave. He told me this morning that as soon as the water recedes, he'll be right back out there rebuilding it. And he also said that Andrea and the children will be moving to Clewiston."

"Oh, and has he told her that?"

"By now, he has. When I left him he said he was going to tell her as soon as he awakened. Nikki, he meant it. I've never seen him so adamant. He said that he was no longer going to be a part-time husband and father."

"I'll be anxious to hear her response, won't you?"

Rose and Sam came up to them. "We're here to relieve you, Delia. Did Nikki tell you about..."

"Yes, Aunt Rose, he did. It's as Harrison said, she's where she's wanted to be for over twenty years. She's beside Da."

"Delia," Rose added, "That doesn't mean that they'll not find Juanita. I mean just because they found her dress doesn't mean that they'll not find Juanita alive and well. It just means that..."

Delia turned and said almost happily, "Coming, Nikki? Let's get an ice cream on the way. I'm starved."

"You'll not be needing that right away, Andrea. Here, pack this and then get the linens," Nolan reminded her. They were packing for their move to Clewiston. They had found a rental house in one of Captain Duff's developments and would live there until their house could be built. Andrea reached up on her tiptoes and kissed Nolan's cheek.

A month had gone by since the hurricane. The banks of Pahokee, Canal Point and Clewiston had withstood the wind and water, and Nolan and Delia found that Shamrock Farms had indeed prospered. Bodies were still being found. Juanita's was not among them. Delia had sold Del Mer to Meriam, as she had planned, and put her house up for sale. Her furniture, and other household items had already been shipped to Pahokee. She decided to motor down in her Reo and supervise the building of her and Johnny's home on the same house site, using the Custard Apple Inn as a base just as Juanita had ten years before.

She had never been happier. Her last night with Nikki had not been sad. Instead, it had been festive. He, too, knew that it was over. They had not even made love, but had talked into the night. She told him that she hoped that she could find someone to love who felt about the Glades as she and her mum had so that Johnny could have a father. He understood. They held each other until dawn, and when they said goodbye, they both cried. It was not a sad cry but a cry of resignation, of acceptance.

"Johnny O'Farrell, how on earth did you get so dirty? You're covered with muck! Harrison won't help you build that swing, will he Dicey? I declare you are..."

She held him close to her. They stood looking out over the lake. It was calm with an occasional fish surfacing to grab a minnow, but Delia knew that a northwester could arrive unannounced, and the lake would churn white and with enough force spread over the black land again.

She thought, Mum, it is indeed as you once said, "Delia, look around you - everything is busily creating this paradise. We are in a sea of constant change. And look, Delia," she picked up a handful of muck and let it trickle through her fingers, "THIS IS BLACK GOLD - THIS EARTH - THIS PAY-HAY-O-KEE!

AFTERWARD

The 1928 hurricane was the nation's third largest peacetime calamity, and yet so isolated was the location, that not until three days later did Florida's governor Martin learn of its enormity. Over 2000 people lost their lives within one hour. Only the 1900 hurricane in Galveston and the Johnstown flood surpass it in loss of life.

As a result of public outcry came the fantastic proposal that a wall be built around Lake Okeechobee, which has an area of over 700 square miles. That wall was built and compares in size, not length, to the Great Wall of China. The Herbert Hoover Dike was dedicated January 12, 1961, and the former president was in attendance.

As I said in the dedication, through the vision and adventurous spirit of these Florida settlers we who have come afterwards and have come to love and cherish this state's uniqueness have been given a monumental task. Florida will remain unique only if we continue to revere it, as these pioneers did, and its natural beauty will remain only if we protect it.

My sister and I still own that house that our grandparents built on the sand ridge in the Long Beach Colony north of Canal Point. We visit it often, and can still feel the spirit of the beautiful Knight girls. We can picture them as they rowed their boat on Lake Okeechobee, rode their bikes on the hard, white sand beach into the little town to visit friends at the Custard Apple Inn. We can almost hear Onida playing the piano for the Saturday night dances and envision her flirting with the handsome newcomer, Frank O'Connell, whom she later married and who is our father. Yes, their spirit lives on in that Pay-hay-o-kee, that land of grassy water.

If through this series I have reached your heart and your appreciation of what was, I have succeeded in my task, for my grandparents and my parents felt as Juanita did about this land. They, too, were enveloped by its newness, its constant change, its energy, and loved it - as do I.

The Author

About the author:

Ann O'Connell Rust is a native Floridian, a "cracker". Her parents were pioneers in the Everglades in the early part of the century. Her father, Frank O'Connell, moved to Canal Point on Lake Okeechobee to work on Conner's Highway—the first hard road into the Glades. Conner was a friend of the West Palm Beach O'Connells, and young Frank wanted to be a part of Conner's thrust into the mysterious Glades. There he met Onida Knight, one of the beautiful Knight girls, whose father had homesteaded their land the previous year, and opened his own Knight's Grocery and Dry Goods Store in Canal Point. Luther Knight ultimately became a farmer/rancher and her father, a farmer, deputy sheriff and chief of police in Pahokee.

After schooling in Palm Beach County schools, Ann embarked on a very successful career in modeling—in Miami and New York City, where she met and married Allen, an FBI agent, and followed him to Puerto Rico, New Mexico, Washington, D.C., Mexico City and finally back to her love — Florida. She has had an on-going love affair with romantic old Florida all of her adult life .

She is the owner of a modeling and talent agency in Orange Park and since her retirement has devoted all her energies to writing and sharing her love of this magnificent state. She and Allen spend their time between their home on the St. John's River and their ranch in Wyoming.

Are you unable to find *"The Floridians"* in your book stores?

Volume I Punta Rassa: Fiction, 1988, 275 pp., soft cover and hard cover

Volume II Palatka: Fiction, 1989, 231 pp., soft cover and hard cover

Volume III Kissimmee: Fiction, 1990, 208 pp, soft cover and hard cover

Volume IV Monticello: Fiction, 1991, 232 pp, soft cover and hard cover

Volume V Pahokee: Fiction, 1992, 276 pp, soft cover and hard cover

Mail to: AMARO BOOKS
5673 Pine Avenue
Orange Park, Florida 32073

Please send check or money order (No cash or C.O.D.s)

I enclose $ ——————————— for books indicated.

Book Title: ———————————————————

Book Title: ———————————————————

Book Title: ———————————————————

Number of books: ————————————————

Name: ——————————————————————

Address: ————————————————————

City: ———————————————————————

State: ———————————————— Zip ——————

Please enclose $12.95 per book plus $1.50 for postage and handling of first book and .50 for each additional book. For hard cover please enclose $17.50 per book plus $2.00 postage of first book and $1.00 for each additional book. Florida residents add 7% sales tax. Please allow 2 - 4 weeks for delivery.